THE FIRE AND THE SERPENT

THE FIRE AND THE SERPENT

Book One: Sojourners

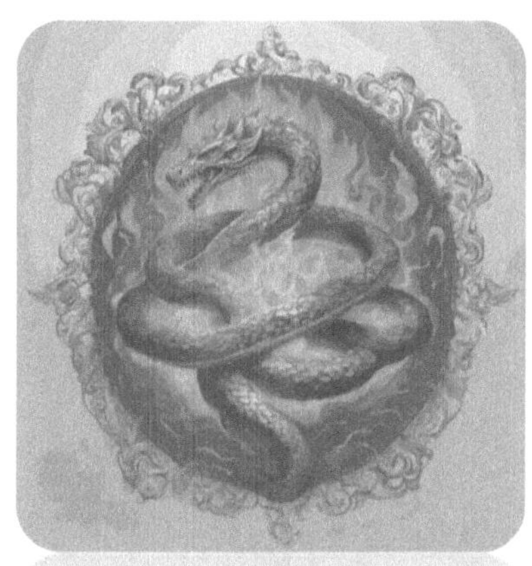

Dieta Scheidecker

This is a work of fiction. Any resemblance to actual persons, living or dead, events, or locations is entirely coincidental.

ISBN: 979-8-9931833-0-5

Cover Design by Dieta Scheidecker
Published by Spoken Flame Company

Chapter 1

It's the stillness that hits me first. It's not just quiet—it's an overwhelming, absolute silence that drowns out even the sound of my own breath. How can something so silent be so deafening? I strain to open my eyes, trying to see something, anything, only to realize they're already wide open. The darkness is that complete.

It stretches endlessly, this void of sight and sound, carrying a sense of eternity that I can't explain, but seems right in the moment. The vastness envelops me like a womb, yet suspends me on the edge of time. A strange anticipation pulses around me, rippling along arms I can feel, but not see.

A flicker catches my eye and disappears before I can pinpoint it. Then another, and another. Small fragments of light burst through the blackness, filling in the spaces until a twinkling canopy surrounds me. Stars. Millions of sparkling stars. And at the center, the soft glow of the moon—pale, almost dull in comparison.

There's a subtle shift, and a different light appears in the distance, stronger than the moon and stars, its radiance pushing against the night. Shadows and shapes emerge, tugging at me, pulling me down, grounding me in their dull, gray world. A golden hue explodes over the horizon, driving back the darkness, erasing its power. A rainbow of light ripples across the sky, expanding until it reveals a wilderness before me.

Tall grass surrounds me, interspersed with an array of wildflowers—pinks, purples, whites, yellows and oranges—all vying for attention. A cool mist hovers low, stretching across the field as a narrow dirt path disappears into its whiteness. In the distance, enormous trees stand thick and heavy like a wall, blocking the field's advance.

Spinning around in amazement, I try to take it all in. The smell of the dew, the chirping of birds, a light breeze tickling the back of my neck. Everything is so… alive. Taking a hesitant step forward, I wonder where I am. What is this place? Is it real or am I dreaming?

I run my hand over the damp grass, wiping the water between my fingers. My shoe catches my eye, then my clothing. That's weird—I'm dressed in hiking gear. My boots, my water-resistant pants, even my favorite sweatshirt. A wide cloth headband covers my forehead, holding back the stray blonde hairs falling out of my usual messy bun. My backpack pulls on my shoulders, its weight heavier than I'm used to. Reaching back, I can feel my water bottles tucked in place. I even have my utility knife clipped on my waist strap within easy reach.

"Huh."

I take another look at the wild terrain stretching out before me. This is serious hiking territory, definitely not the kind I would ever choose to do alone. Why would I end up here of all places? I'm surprised I don't feel panicked. I'm not exactly calm either, but the sense of wonder outweighs everything else, sparking a desire to discover what's ahead.

Okay, well, I have two options: follow the path cutting through the field or stand here, hoping someone comes along to explain things. A quick glance around reaffirms how unlikely that is.

"It's not a yellow brick road, but it's something, I guess." I smirk to myself, thinking it's too bad no one's here to appreciate my humor.

Heavy dew collects on my pants and boots as I walk the dirt path, heading in the only direction I see it going. The sun rises higher, warming the air and burning off the mist. The sky is cloudless overhead and a large bird soars in lazy circles off in the distance. Buzzing insects fly from flower to flower, searching for nectar, while a gentle breeze sways the tall grasses, bending them in a soft wave that ripples along to the tree line. Now and then, the raucous call of a crow rises in the woods, carrying across the plain. Others join in, their discordant voices escalating before cutting off only to start again.

I scan my unchanging surroundings, searching for familiar landmarks or signs that might tell me where I am, but there's nothing. I push up my sleeve to check the time and do a double take, halting in the middle of the trail. My mind struggles to catch up with what I'm seeing.

My wrist is bare. There is no watch.

Frantic, I pat my pockets and check for my cell phone, feeling the same areas over and over with the same result.

"You've gotta be kidding me! There's no way! This can't be real."

My heartbeat pounds in my chest, and panic tingles through my body, making it hard to catch my breath. Clutching my head, I try to comprehend what this means. What if something happens out here? How will I call for help? And how could I have not checked earlier? I can't believe it didn't even cross my mind.

I should go back. Maybe I dropped it, but it's already been a good hour since I set out. And I couldn't have lost my watch too. Pacing back and forth, I'm unsure of what to do. If there's no cell service, it won't matter anyway, right? But if there is service and I need help, then what? Does anyone even know where I am? Have they noticed I'm missing? Who was the last person I spoke to?

I don't know.

What was I doing before I ended up here?

Again, I don't know.

How can I not remember? Why can't I recall anything?

I look at my hands and feel my face. Everything's the same. I'm still me. Forcing out a breath, I close my eyes. Okay, what *do* I know? I know I like coffee and donuts, but am seriously afraid of snakes and spiders. My favorite color is green, though sometimes red depending on my mood, and Fall is *always* my favorite season.

I open my eyes and frown. How can I remember these things, but not the others? I can't picture any friends, a job, or even a family. Am I married? A quick glance at my left hand confirms no ring. This is really weird and unnerving—like amnesia, but not.

Rubbing my hands down my face, I look around, searching for someone—anyone—who might help, but nothing's changed. There's only a path in the wilderness and me standing right in the middle of it.

What the heck? What do I do? The novelty of this experience has worn off, giving way to fear. Yet, my options are still the same: stay or go. I stare at my feet, blinking away tears. This choice now feels overwhelming, more real, more… serious. I know I should keep going; that's the logical decision. But part of me wants to sit down and cry, to pretend this isn't happening, to sit here and hope it all goes away, that I'll wake up somewhere else. But deep down, I realize I can't do that. So, I force myself to continue in the direction I was heading, my steps slower and less enthusiastic than before.

I trudge along for what feels like hours, the scenery not changing much—wide open fields, the dense forest along the edges. The monotony continues until my body moves on autopilot and my mind disengages. It isn't until my foot slips and my knee almost buckles that I realize the trail has changed. Snapping to attention, I notice the path is veering down a steep hill. Struggling to keep my footing, I slide down the loose gravel, grabbing at the few small saplings growing along the trail.

"Hallo!"

I jerk my head up at the sound and almost land on my butt. A female hiker waves from down below. Though she looks excited to see me, I have no idea who she is. Nervous flutters fill my stomach as I approach, trying to appear casual as I sneak glances at her. Her backpack rests beside a couple of large rocks, and she's drinking from a dark green canteen. Her smile widens and she beckons me closer, her thick red braids falling over her shoulders.

"Come, come! Have a seat and rest a bit!"

My body aches with relief as I slip off my backpack, the lack of weight making me lightheaded for a moment. I sway to the side before steadying myself and aim for the closest rock to sit on. Landing harder than intended, I wince, embarrassed by my awkwardness, but the woman doesn't seem to notice. She's busy rummaging through her pack, searching for something. When she finds what she's looking for, she tucks it into her pants pocket, then straightens up and offers me an apple.

"Thank you," I say, wondering if I should be taking food from a stranger.

"You're so welcome," the woman replies, settling on the other rock. "It's wonderful to have someone to share with. This trail is usually pretty quiet."

"Oh, so you hike here often then? On this… trail?" I ask, trying not to blurt out that I don't know where I am.

The woman waves a hand in the air and says, "Oh, I've been out here hiking every day for many years now."

"Wow, you must know this place really well. Do you live around here?"

"I guess you could say that," she says with a cryptic smile.

I don't know what to make of her non-answer. Is she evading my question, or am I reading her wrong? I bite into my apple, brushing aside a fleeting thought of poison, and stare off into the distance, observing the woman out of the corner of my eye. She's shorter than I am, and older, with a solid, athletic build. Dark freckles dot her weathered, sunburned cheeks. Her clothes are clean but well-worn, and not the latest fashion. And while she's full of energy—upbeat and confident—there's a vibe I can't quite lay my finger on. It nags at me, and just when I think I've got it, she jumps up and dusts off her pants, sending whatever thoughts I had into orbit.

"Well now," she says, cleaning off her hands. "Are you ready for your directions?"

"Um, I-I'm not sure what you mean."

"Your directions for walking the path," she replies, moving in front of me. "There are some things you should know before you continue on."

"Oh." She's assuming I'm supposed to be here. Do I tell her—

"Alright then!" she exclaims, smacking her hands together. "It is vitally important you continue on with the utmost seriousness." She wags a finger at me. "You must stay on the correct trail. No wandering off and no shortcuts. Ever."

She tilts her head towards me, raising an eyebrow. I lean back, nearly losing my seat, and give her a hesitant nod.

Her eyes narrow as she continues. "There will be other trails along the way, so you must pay attention. You are to stay on this path. Got it?"

"Okay… but how do I know which path to take? I haven't seen any signs or markings at all."

Reaching into her pocket, the woman pulls out a faded leather pouch. She rubs her thumb across it, a smile tugging at her mouth and her eyes sparkle as she hands it to me.

"What is it?" I ask, unsure if I should be accepting gifts from this woman. Though I've already accepted the apple, so clearly, I've opened the door for more.

"Look inside."

I untie the thin cord holding it closed and peer inside, but I have no idea what I'm looking at.

"Go ahead, take it out."

Reaching in, I pull out an old, round metal case. It's tarnished and worn, but I can still make out an engraving of a royal crown surrounded by flames.

"This will guide you on your journey. Keep it on you at all times and do not give it to anyone else. It is only for you to use. Trust this over your own instincts or another's instructions. I promise, it will not fail you."

Looking from the woman back to the object in my hand, I lift the lid with care. It's a compass—an unusual one. A thick golden arrow glows under the glass encasement, even in the bright sunlight. Beneath the arrow lay multiple layers of different sized silver stars, and below them, a vibrant shade of blue creates the illusion of rippling waves.

The instrument fits perfectly in my hand, radiating warmth and a palpable sense of power. It's the most amazing thing I've ever seen, and I have no idea how to use it.

"There are no letters or words," I say, tilting it as if that will help me figure it out. "How do I know which way is which?"

Leaning over, the woman taps the glass top. "The golden arrow will always show you which direction to go. You must only go the way it points."

I stand up and turn in a slow circle, watching the arrow shift into place. It points to a grouping of trees a short distance away, where I see a thin trail disappearing into their midst. That must be where the woman came from.

"If you ignore the compass's direction and choose another way, you will have to deal with the consequences. Some could be deadly, so please, be careful."

Dread washes over me, bottoming out my stomach. Deadly? Is she serious? What kind of journey am I on that I need such a thing to avoid danger?

"I'm sorry, I can't do this," I say, holding out the compass to the woman, but she's already shouldering her pack and tightening her straps.

Her hands freeze at my words; she looks at me with fierce determination. "You *must* follow the path."

I withdraw my hand at her tone and she takes a few steps up the hill before looking back at me.

"One more thing. When you get to the clearing with the stumps, you will find a shack for travelers. You should stay there tonight."

With a nod, she turns on her heels and continues climbing the rocky path, disappearing over the top. I'm left holding the compass, staring at the hill as if she'll return and things will somehow end differently. This is all wrong. She must have me mixed up with someone else. She didn't even ask my name or where I was going. There's no way she could have known I'd be here at this time and place, right? Except... she seemed so sure.

With a sense of detachment, I turn to face the woods. What I thought was a simple day hike has turned into a whole different ball game. Throughout the day, I've tried to convince myself that I'd soon wake up and laugh off this bizarre wandering dream. Or that maybe I'd run into a group of friends who would confess to drugging me and leaving me in the middle of nowhere as a joke.

A heavy lump forms in my throat. This is not a dream or a harmless prank. It feels real—very real. I'm thirsty, hungry, tired, and confused. The compass pulses in my hand as I face the path before me, with no idea where I am or where I'm headed. All I have is a firm directive to follow where the golden arrow leads. I've never camped overnight on a trail or relied entirely on myself for survival. I have no weapon other than a pocket knife, and no hunting or foraging skills whatsoever.

Letting out a long, slow breath, I try to pull myself together. Staying here isn't an option, that's for sure. I want to be inside that shelter before the sun goes down. There's no way I'm sleeping outside in the dark if I can avoid it. I tuck the compass back in the pouch and secure it to my belt loop. My pack feels heavier than before as I slip it on and tighten the waist strap.

Anticipation revives inside me despite the circumstances. This is all way outside my comfort zone, or any zone for that matter, but I feel like I'm headed towards something significant. Whatever my life was before doesn't seem as important as what's happening here and now. I'm not sure why or how that's possible, or how hiking along a trail in the middle of nowhere could change anything. But it is an adventure. I'll give it that.

***

All-day hiking is not my thing. Why did I ever think it was something I wanted to do? Sure, it's peaceful and beautiful, and I love nature, but diving in like this? Not a good idea. Don't get me wrong; I've hiked long distances before, even climbed a mountain once. Granted, it was a small one, but it still counts.

My experience level is more along the lines of casual hiking—just a couple of hours here and there, with weeks or months in between—not really enough to keep in shape or call myself an avid hiker. Nothing like what I'm doing now. Not for this many hours.

I stop at the next stream to fill up my bottles, hoping like crazy the water doesn't make me sick. Apparently, I don't have a water filter, or a cook stove, or even a pot to cook in. I did find some snacks and a large box of matches in my pack, so at least I won't starve—yet—and can build a fire if needed. But seriously, who packed this bag? How am I supposed to survive on my own without more gear? At least I have a tent and a sleeping mat, and a change of clothes. Thank you for small favors.

The path continues to wind deeper into the woods with no end in sight, and my anxiety grows with each step. I'm exhausted. My neck and shoulders ache under the weight of my pack, and my feet are killing me. What if I don't make it to the cabin? Will I really have to camp out here alone?

The path soon curves around a narrow bend and opens into a small clearing scattered with old stumps. To the left is a rugged log cabin with a large front window and a good-sized woodpile stacked under a low-hanging eave. Nearby, a small corral holds piles of manure and leftover hay, but no animals.

"Oh, thank goodness," I breathe, heading for the door.

I hesitate on the narrow porch, unsure if I should just go in. It doesn't look like anyone's around, but I knock anyway. No one answers, so I push hard on the warped door and peek inside. The room is well-lit and larger than I expected. Two bunk beds are in the back corner, arranged in an L-shape, each hugging a wall. In the opposite corner, next to a small window, stands an old bookcase stacked with dishes and supplies, and a battered metal wash tub atop a barrel serves as a sink.

In the front corner sits a black cast-iron stove with a pile of kindling on the floor next to it and an oversized rocking chair nearby. There's also a solid looking wooden chest pushed up against the wall under the front window. The only other furniture is a scarred wooden table in the center of the room, surrounded by three homemade chairs and a stool. On the table, a tin coffee cup holds some dead flowers—someone's idea of a centerpiece, I suppose.

I slip off my backpack and drop it on the bottom bunk nearest me. It feels so good to get it off. I check out the beds, finding thin mattresses on each one. Anything's better than the hard ground and I can double up for a decent cushion to sleep on tonight.

Grabbing a metal bucket from the floor beside the sink, I head back outside to get water. There's a creek right behind the cabin, just down a short bank. It's clear, like the ones I crossed earlier, winding its way over rocks and fallen branches. I fill the bucket and make my way back to the cabin, trying not to spill all the water before I get there. Without my heavy pack, I feel off balance and keep overemphasizing my movements. It would be comical if I weren't so tired and sore.

Inside, I set the bucket in front of the rocking chair and unlace my boots. I sigh with relief as I slide onto the rocker and ease my bare feet into the cold water. What I wouldn't give for some painkillers and a hot bath right now. I rest my head back against the chair and close my eyes while the water soothes my swollen feet. I can't believe I made it.

Lulled into a sense of security by finding shelter, I'm drifting into that pleasant in-between state just before sleep, when a noise outside startles me. I jerk my feet out of the bucket, sending water flying everywhere, and scramble for my socks. They cling to my wet feet, refusing to go on straight, so I give up and shove my shoes on over the twisted folds.

I'm tying my shoelaces when I hear heavy footsteps thudding on the porch. The door bursts open, banging against the wall, and a giant of a man strides into the room. My breath catches in my throat as every horrifying scenario I can imagine races through my mind all at once. I'm frozen, bent over my shoes, while the man slams the door shut and crosses the room, tossing his saddle bags down by the table. He yanks out a chair and heaves himself into it, the wood groaning beneath his weight.

"Ya makin' any grub?" he growls with a deep drawl.

A flash of anger cuts through my fear. Oh my gosh, did this man really just barge in and ask me to cook for him? Am I about to be kidnapped and made into his woman, forced to live in this cabin, cooking and cleaning and meeting his needs whenever he wants? Oh no, that is so not happening! But what do I do? Make a run for it or stay and beg for my life? I think both usually end up with the girl dying, right? Maybe I should try to charm him with my winsome ways and then stab him in his sleep. Not to kill him, of course. I don't think I could murder someone, but it would be self-defense, wouldn't it?

My brain is not taking me to a good place right now. I don't know if I'm in real trouble or not. Unable to speak while all these crazy thoughts run through my mind, I just stare at the man. My body, on the other hand, has taken these ideas to heart and reacts as though attacked when the man grunts and reaches into his bags. I fly backwards, landing hard against the rocking chair, and knock the bucket of water all over the floor.

The man doesn't even spare me a glance. Instead, he pulls out a couple of large tin cans and a brown burlap bag. He unties the bag and slides out a loaf of homemade bread.

"Ya knows how to start a fire?" he says, nodding at the stove. "I got some stew here, enough to share if yous hungry."

"Y-yeah," I reply, finding my voice.

My answer seems to satisfy him; he gets up, grabs a cooking pot from the shelf, and starts prying open the cans. Halting mid-pour, he turns and locks his gaze on me, sending me scrambling to my feet. The stove door creaks as I pull it open, revealing paper and small sticks already set inside. I lay kindling on top, light the fire, and watch the flames consume the paper and wood. Then I close the door, secure the latch, and sit back on my heels.

"Sorry, I ain't got no butter," the man says, pulling off chunks of bread with his huge hands. He tilts his head towards the cabin door. "We's gonna need logs from that there pile outside."

"For the fire," he says when I just stare at him, which seems to be my default reaction to everything right now.

My thigh muscles protest as I stand up and sidestep across the cabin. I keep my eyes fixed on the man while aiming for the door and tug it open. The sun is hanging low, with a few rays still filtering through the trees, lighting up the front of the cabin. It won't be long before daylight is completely gone. I could run, but I'd be heading into the woods in the dark without my pack. Not the wisest move.

Okay, I reason to myself, I've totally overreacted. If he's a homicidal maniac, he probably would've killed me by now and, as for other things, well, he doesn't seem interested. In fact, he hasn't done anything except offer food. So, maybe he's just a bit rough around the edges, you know, like he doesn't get out much.

I take a deep breath, hold it for a few seconds, then let it out with a sigh. Alright, here goes nothing. I grab an armful of wood and head back inside.

Closing the door behind me, I see the man has moved to the stove and is stirring the stew, his back to me. I bring the wood over and stand a few feet away, unsure where he wants me to put it. The man turns, reaches across the space between us, and grabs a few logs all before I can react. He feeds them into the stove, then gestures at the kindling, implying that I should put the rest there. I dump the wood on the pile and ease my way over to my bunk. Nonchalantly, I unsnap my utility knife from the side of my pack and shove it into my pocket, still unsure if there's an actual threat or not. Like before, the man doesn't seem to be paying attention to me, but now, at least, I feel like I have the element of surprise. With his size, I'll need it.

I take a seat on the stool at the far end of the table and watch the man. He's taken off his long coat—a duster, I think it's called—and it hangs off the chair he sat in earlier; the bottom bunched up on the floor. His wide-brimmed hat rests on the table by the bread bag. The man stands well over six feet, with broad shoulders and muscles that strain against the fabric of his shirt. He exudes power and strength, but he's made no move to use either to his advantage. There's a gracefulness to his movements I wouldn't expect from someone his size. He's tied back a portion of his thick brown hair with a piece of leather to keep it out of his eyes, and his mustache and beard are long and scruffy, as if it's been a while since he's had them trimmed. I suppose he's good-looking in a rugged, outdoorsy sort of way. You have to look for it, though, because everything else about him detracts from it. Especially the way he talks. His words are slow and drawn out, his grammar atrocious, but there's intelligence in those brown eyes. He might sound like a redneck, but I don't think he's dumb. I'm hoping he's also the honorable type.

The man brings the pot over, pours stew into a couple of bowls, and pushes one towards me. He grabs a chunk of bread and dips it into his bowl, eating like it's his first meal of the day. I continue to watch him as I take small bites, my anxious stomach making me nauseous. I'm only halfway through my bowl when he refills his, and just finishing as he fills his third.

"Thanks for sharing with me," I say in a soft voice.

"Yous welcome," he says, wiping his bowl clean with the last of the bread. "Ya git enough?"

"Yeah. I'm good, thanks."

The man stares at the empty pot, seeming unsure of my answer, then pushes his chair back with a loud scrape. "I'll be gitttin' some water. Fer the dishes." Swooping up the tipped over bucket, he heads outside.

Once he closes the door, I release a squeaky breath and lay my head on the table, my arms crossed underneath. The adrenaline rush is wearing off, leaving me drained and shaky, while the stew sits like a rock in my stomach. Despite the man's gruff manner and intimidating size, I haven't sensed any hostility or actual danger from him. The perceived tension might be all on my part, imagined or not, but realistically, given where we are, I can't head out on my own.

So. For better or worse, it looks like I'm going to spend the night with this strange guy.

I lift my head and stare out the window, resignation settling in my gut. Eventually, I notice the darkening shadows and search for a lamp to light up the room. Finding a pair of lanterns on the supply shelf, I bring them to the table, wondering if there is a trick to getting them going. I don't see a bulb or a switch to turn them on. While I'm still trying to figure things out, the man returns, his entrance far less dramatic than before.

Grabbing a kettle off the shelf, he fills it with water and sets it on the stove. After adding a few more logs to the fire, he glances at the lanterns on the table. His brows furrow briefly, and he stands up, reaching for the top of the bookshelf. He takes down a long, thin stick, and lights it from the fire, guarding the flame as he returns. Catching my gaze to make sure I'm watching, he flips up the glass on the first lantern and sticks the fire under it, lighting the wick. He lowers the glass and adjusts the flame, blowing out the fire on the stick at the same time.

"Easy enough, huh?"

I nod, surprised. He's just shown me how to light a lantern and done it without condemnation or ridicule. A curious trait for such an intimidating person. There may be more to this guy than I first thought.

"There be towels in that there trunk," he says, taking the hot water from the stove and pouring it into the tub to wash the dishes.

Funny how he makes a statement sound like a command.

Opening the trunk, I find an assortment of towels and blankets stacked inside. I grab a towel off the pile and shut the trunk. The man holds a bowl out for me and soon enough we have everything washed, dried, and put away.

Nodding in the lantern's direction, he says, "Ya better take that and git yer business done 'fore dark sets in good. Privy's just past the corral."

As I take the lantern and head towards the door, he adds, "Don't dawdle now. There be things out there yous don't be wantin' to mess with."

Chapter 2

Outside, it's just dark enough to need the lantern, but not yet the pitch black that will soon come. A few faint stars appear in the night sky, only visible if you don't look straight at them. It seems so long since I watched the stars burst into being and found myself in this place. I can't believe it was just this morning.

Forcing myself to be brave—and hoping like crazy the big man inside will save me if something happens out here—I step off the porch into the shadows and follow the handmade fence of the corral. A shuffling noise sets my heart racing until I notice a dark gray mule watching me. His nose twitches, and his big eyes give a slow blink before he lowers his head and continues munching on his hay.

As my heart slows back to normal, I mumble a "well, hello to you too" and continue on towards the outhouse. Assuming that's what a privy is. I hadn't noticed it earlier when I arrived, most likely because it blends in so well with its surroundings. And surprise, surprise—it looks handmade, just like everything else around here. But I'm not complaining, a bathroom is a bathroom.

Inside, there's a hook for the lantern, a worn wooden toilet seat, and an old tin coffee can with real toilet paper.

Ah, luxuries.

I keep a close eye out for spiders and don't waste any more time admiring my surroundings. I finish in record time, crack open the door, and peek outside, scanning the area for wild animals, monsters, or a mixture of the two. Anything is a serious possibility in this place. Seeing no imminent threat, I make a dash for the cabin, trying not to appear spooked while the mule's mocking eyes follow me.

The cabin door slams shut behind me, and I cringe, bracing for a condescending comment. To my surprise, the man says nothing and I relax a notch. He's seated on a stool by the stove writing in a small notebook with a whittled pencil, the second lantern casting a soft glow nearby.

"Do you want a turn?" I ask, holding out my lantern. He glances up, and an odd expression crosses his face. Worried that something might have followed me into the cabin, I dare to check behind me, but nothing's there.

"Naw, I's good," he says when I give him a puzzled look.

I return the lantern to the table and take a seat in the vacant rocking chair, debating if I should try to engage the man in conversation or wait for him to say something. He continues to write and I try to be patient, not wanting to interrupt.

"Ya trying to git somewheres with that there rocker?" He says into the quiet.

It takes me a moment to catch on and notice how hard I'm rocking. I plant my feet, stopping the chair, but then notice my leg bouncing, so try for a more casual, non-aggressive rocking.

"I don't think we introduced ourselves earlier," I say when the man doesn't continue the conversation. "I'm Kenna."

He says nothing.

"Do you have a name?" I ask.

"Yep."

Okaaay. He's not much of a talker, or he's being evasive. "Would you care to share it with me?"

"If that would put yer mind at ease, I s'pose I could."

I think he's trying to hide a smile, but with his head turned away, I'm not sure.

"It would," I reply, my tone cautious.

After a dramatic pause, he responds, "My given name is Kohnrad, but most know me as Keeper."

"Why?"

With exaggerated patience, he sets his pencil down and looks directly at me. "Cuz I be Keeper of the Path."

"What does that mean? Are you a forest ranger or something?"

"I provide for those that be walkin' the path," he says, his eyes unwavering.

That doesn't really answer my question. "Is this your cabin?" I ask, fidgeting under the weight of his gaze.

"I built 'er and most of what ya see here, but she ain't mine. I don't own 'er.

"Oh. So… does she… it… I mean the cabin, does the *cabin* belong to… um… an organization that supports the trail?"

"The cabin is for any that be needin' it," he replies, returning to his notebook.

I'm not sure what else to say. This entire conversation is frustrating and didn't go where I thought it would. Kohnrad's words carry a deeper context that I don't understand. It feels like he's humoring me, but I can't pinpoint what I've done wrong. I don't want to let on that I don't know where I am or what trail I'm following, and he's avoided all my attempts to get that information. It reminds me of my encounter with the woman earlier today. What is it with the people around here?

Trying again to engage him, I ask, "What are you writing?"

"Notes."

At this point, I can't help but roll my eyes and a snort escapes before I think to stop it.

Kohnrad finishes up whatever "notes" he's writing and places the notebook on top of the wooden chest. Leaning forward, he rests his elbows on his knees. His posture is casual, but he meets my gaze without blinking.

"Is there somethin' yous be needin' to know?"

Now that I have his full attention, I can't seem to answer. My thoughts are racing in circles. If I voice my concerns, I risk exposing myself, and I have no idea if this man is trustworthy or not. He could use my inexperience against me and take advantage of the situation. How do I ask questions without putting myself in danger? What can I say that won't make me look weak or… afraid?

"Yous can trust me, ya know," he says, his voice low and calm. "I ain't some crazy murderer or rapist or anything like that."

The dam breaks, and I laugh and cry at the same time. Of all the things he could have said, this guy has either read my mind or he's one crafty dude.

He stays quiet, letting me work through my emotions. That in itself gives me the courage to admit I need help.

"I-I don't know where I am or what I'm doing here."

"Well, now," he says, clasping his hands together. "S'pose we get that cleared up."

I smile with gratitude and wipe at my nose, relieved I'm finally going to get the answers I need. Or so I think.

"See, this here be a place of decision. Ever'one who comes this way is given a choice. To stay and make the journey, or not."

"So, I have a choice in being here? I don't have to follow the path? I can go home?" This information makes me sit up straighter in my chair. Could I be done with this, whatever it is, and get back to… to…?

"Some make that choice. Many actually," Kohnrad replies. "It ain't easy here. There be challenges and dangers, but also great reward. All are given an invite, but few'r found worthy enough to continue."

Worthy? What in the world? You have to be worthy to walk this trail? Oh boy, this guy might not be all there. Is he messing with me? His vague answers and odd phrases are really starting to irritate me. I don't understand what's going on, and he isn't being helpful at all. Does anyone actually choose to stay here after talking to him? I mean, if he's the selling point for this place, then he's failing miserably. If you want people to stay, there should be someone here who's not quite so… offensive.

Someone more personable, who can actually answer questions. Seriously, what kind of place is this?

"Wait," I say, my mind latching onto an idea. "You mentioned something about a reward. Is there a prize at the end of this thing? Is this one of those wilderness challenges where the last man standing wins a hundred thousand dollars or something?"

"Nope." He just stares at me, his expression neutral.

"Look, I don't know what your angle is or what you're alluding to. You're not making any sense, so just tell me, as plain as you can, how to get back home. Please."

Unfolding from the stool, Kohnrad looks down at me. Something like sorrow flickers in his eyes, and he shakes his head in disappointment. "Yous know what all them that leave here be hav'n in common?"

I shrug, trying to appear casual. Of course I don't, but I'm sure every single one of them had a good reason after talking to *him*, so he can stop looking at me like that.

"They's were offended," he replies, then turns out his lantern and heads to the back bunk. "Best tuck in fer the night. I'll show ya the path back in the mornin'."

I swear it's only moments before he's asleep, his snores rising and falling in a slow, steady rhythm. I turn the other lantern down to barely a flicker, not wanting the room to be completely dark, before heading to bed myself.

The thin mattress is anything but comfortable and I'm upset that I didn't throw another one on earlier. I did have a legitimate distraction, but still. I shift around, trying to ease the pressure on my shoulders, but every time I move, the mattress wrinkles, making it more uncomfortable. With a groan of frustration, I give up and lay still.

My body is so tired and sore, but my mind won't shut down. I watch the shadows in the room, mulling over my conversations with Kohnrad. I still don't know where I am or where this darn path goes, and every question I ask gets some obscure answer that only leads to more questions and more nonanswers.

Why did he say that odd thing about being worthy? Something like, "All are invited, but only a few are worthy." Who gives an invitation and then decides if someone's worthy or not?

Kohnrad also said people leave here because they're offended. I can see that I let my feelings and insecurity lead me in the same direction. I totally judged Kohnrad and made a rash decision based on that judgment. I've chosen to leave without understanding why I'm here, just because I felt put out with the way things were going.

If the journey doesn't matter, then why go through the effort of offering me a choice? And why is Kohnrad disappointed I want to leave? Why does he care? There has to be something I'm missing, some important piece that I haven't caught on to.

Around and around these thoughts circle in my mind until exhaustion finally takes over, and I fall into a fitful sleep.

***

I wake the next morning to the clanking of metal and the smell of freshly brewed coffee. Snippets of dreams float through my mind, but I can't grasp any long enough to remember details—just a vague sense of darkness and someone following me. I sit up with a loud moan, wishing I'd never stepped foot on this trail.

"Coffee's hot if yous be wantin' some," Kohnrad says. "Porridge will be but a minute."

I hobble over to the table, and Kohnrad slides a cup of hot coffee my way. It's strong and bitter, but the caffeine is much welcomed. Placing a steaming bowl of porridge before me, he sits down to eat his own. My appetite is back today and I scarf down the entire bowl, surprised at how good it tastes.

Gulping down the rest of my coffee, I figure I should get the conversation started. "You think I should stay, don't you?" I blurt out.

"It be yer choice to make," Kohnrad replies, focused on his bowl.

"But you have to have an opinion. I mean, you know the trail, right? So you know if it's too difficult. You can tell me if you think I can do it or not."

Kohnrad takes a moment to finish his food, then gives me his full attention. "It ain't a matter of being able, it be a matter of choice. I ain't gonna lie, the Path ain't easy. But it be yer decision to walk it that's in question right now. The choice's been given. It be yer decision to make, not mine."

"But why? Why have I been given this choice?"

"This here be a place of inbetween. Of what is and what will be."

"You need to elaborate on that, please," I say, trying very hard not to be irritated.

"Yous been called to make a decision between two kingdoms. One way will take ya back to where yous came from and yous won't be rememberin' yer time here."

"And the other?"

"The other's a path to a king and his city beyond the Great Mountains."

"Is one way good and the other bad?" I ask, feeling it's very important to understand the difference between the paths and their kingdoms.

"Yeah, one's good and one ain't."

"Okay, so just tell me which one's good and I'll choose that one."

"I can't be doing that. That's what yous be needin' to figure out."

"But I don't know anything about either one of them. How can I make a decision without any information?" Now I am irritated and unable to hold back. "I can't believe people are brought here and then just told to choose without being told anything about either place."

"I aint never said yous couldn't ask questions to figure it out, just that I can't be tellin' ya which one's right fer ya. Yer the one that needs to be figurin' that out. It can't just be told."

"Oh. Sorry. I should've thought of that," I say, fiddling with my spoon.

"Yer forgiven. Now, whatcha ya be needin' to know?"

"Okay, well, you said everyone comes here, and it's a place of decision. So, I guess the first thing I need to know is if this decision is final once it's made?"

"Usually."

"So I could change my mind later and go the other way?"

"Depends on which way yous be goin' first." Kohnrad says, leaning back in his chair.

I glare at this infuriating man, wishing I could shake him. I've never had anyone agitate me so.

Alright, I can do this. Focus Kenna.

"Okay… so the decision's important, and final for one way, but not the other. One way is also chosen more than the others. Do the people who chose to go back ever return here?"

"Nope."

"So… those who leave here do so because they're offended, which means something, or *someone*," I raise my brows at Kohnrad, "does something to turn them away. Is this done on purpose?"

"Yep."

"See, that's a problem!" I say, throwing my hands up. "Why would you purposely offend people and keep them from going a certain way unless it was bad? You say everyone's invited, but then you also say not everyone's worthy. So, who are the worthy ones? Those few who aren't offended?"

"Uh huh."

"Oh," I reply, easing back into my chair.

Kohnrad's watching me, like he can see the gears turning in my mind. Like he's waiting for me to figure this out and get it right.

"Okay, so… those who aren't offended stay and walk the path to the king and his city."

Kohnrad's quiet and I realize I didn't ask, but made a statement. One I'm confident is true.

"So the path that's least taken—the one you say is hard, but rewarding—that's the one that leads to the king?"

"It does."

"That path is good, then?"

"It leads to good, yes."

"Then the other way—the one that goes back to… to where I was before here—it's not good?"

"It be a place of great darkness."

"But if that's true, then why do so many go back there?"

"'Cuz their hearts be shadowed and theys don't be seeing the light of the other kingdom. Theys can't be seeing past their offense or fear or anger. It blinds 'em."

"Are there others on the trail now? To see this king?" I ask, wondering if I'll have to walk alone.

"A few."

"Only a few?"

"Not many's willin' to join the king and serve him. Theys be thinkin' they's choosin' freedom by going back, but they's just enterin' another kingdom and becomin' slaves to its master."

"Slaves? So he's not a good master?"

"No. Not at all."

"But this king, he's good?"

"He be."

"So then, the best choice is to stay and walk the path to the king and his city."

"This be yer choice, then?" Kohnrad asks, leaning forward.

"Just one more thing. You said I would go back to where I came from. Do you mean the darkness? I-I came from the darkness?"

"Yous did."

"So, I was a slave."

"Yous were."

"So then, my choice is really about staying a slave, or going to this king and… and becoming his servant."

Kohnrad nods. "Yer choice be service to one or the other."

"And everyone makes this choice? Every single person?"

"Ever' single one."

"Then that's why I'm here? Because it's time for me to make a choice?"

Kohnrad nods again.

"What if I get there and the king doesn't like me?"

Kohnrad smiles, his eyes crinkling around the edges. "The king's pretty good at helpin' people. Anything he don't be wantin' in his kingdom has a way of workin' its way out of those he chooses. If ya be makin' it all the ways there, most likely yous won't be the same as when ya started."

"Wait," I say, laying my hands flat on the table. "You just said *if* I make it there. There's a chance I won't?"

"There be those who turn back or choose another path along the way. Like I said, it be hard. There ain't no shortcuts or easy way to get where yer needin' to go."

"This is the path you say you're the keeper of, right? You don't keep the other way?"

"I can't help those who go back. Their decision be made and that path can only be walked one way. Those on the King's Path are my responsibility."

"What of those who take a wrong turn or get lost? What happens to them?"

"I find 'em and help 'em, if they let me."

"And if they don't?"

"Then theys be settin' themselves on the paths that lead to the other kingdom."

"Paths. As in plural. There's more than one path?"

"Only in that direction."

"Wow. I had no idea this was such a big decision." I slouch back in my chair, overwhelmed by the seriousness of it all. If I'd stayed with last night's decision, I would've chosen to head back to a place I don't want to be. I'm not a hundred percent sure about this king, but I know I don't want to be a slave to darkness.

"Hey, I just thought of something," I say, lifting my head. "If the way, or *ways*, back lead to a kingdom of darkness, then this king's path should be the opposite, right? It should lead to a kingdom of light."

Kohnrad smiles wide. "I knew you'd be one to figure it out. Yer going to the king ain't ya?"

"Yeah," I say, grinning back at him. "I guess I am."

***

The sun's breaking through the clearing when we step outside. My shoulders ache with the weight of my pack and it's going to take a bit for my leg muscles to warm up. Kohnrad steps off the porch and strides past the stumps, expecting me to follow. Shaking my head, I make my way after him.

Somehow, I've come to like this guy.

I'm surprised to see trails leading out of the clearing in all different directions, except on the eastern side where Kohnrad is headed. He stands by the tree line, waiting for me to catch up.

Trying to see around him, I ask, "Where's the trail? Is this the right spot?"

Kohnrad points to my leather pouch. "Yer gonna be needin' that."

I look down, wondering how he knows what's inside? I untie the pouch and pull out the compass, feeling its warmth in my hand. As soon as I open the lid, the arrow eases into position, pointing straight into the woods in front of me.

"This be where yous start." Kohnrad indicates the same direction as the compass.

"But I don't see a path." I look around at the other trails. "Why are there so many other trails if this is the one to take?" I ask, gesturing around me.

"Most of 'em be return trails, but a few choose to start out on 'em. There be those that stay but don't want to walk this path. Theys don't get the revelation you got. Theys be thinkin' they can choose their own path to the king. It don't work that way though, sos don't be trying that. Follow the compass and yous'll be where yer s'pposed to be."

"Why aren't there any signs saying this?" I ask with a shiver. His words are eerily similar to those of the woman who gave me the compass. "You just let people go on those trails without telling them where they lead?"

"They's warned. No one's forced to walk this path. The way's shown, and theys be given a choice, same as yous."

I take an uncertain step forward, peering into the shadows of the forest. It's dense with brush, and I can't see very far. There are still so many things I don't know, yet the journey beckons me in a way I can't explain. A small ember of light awakens inside me, glowing, ready to burst into flame.

I shake my head to clear the vision that just flashed before me and am relieved when it fades away.

"How long do you think it'll take for me to get to the king?" I ask, stepping back from the unseen path.

"It'll take as long as it takes."

Of course that's his answer.

Kohnrad reaches for my shoulder and gives it a squeeze. "There be places to stay along the way, so rest when yous can. It be easy ta get turned 'round out there, so check yer compass often. There be others on the trails. Don't be listening to them if yer compass says to go another way."

"Will I see you again?" I ask.

"Most likely. I tend to get 'round," he says with a wink. "Nows, journey well, my friend."

I take a couple of breaths, trying to settle my nerves. Alright, I've made my decision. I can do this. Moving forward before I can change my mind, I step into the forest.

"Master, I have news of the woman."

"Excellent, indeed. This one has fled almost as swiftly as the previous. I must say, this is proving to be no challenge at all."

"Um… no Master, the woman has… um… she has… she has… ahh…entered the King's Path."

"How, my little Messenger, was this allowed to happen? I was guaranteed she would not last the night. Was she not terrified and offended by the brute?"

"She was Master, yes she was, she was. He was as gruff as ever. Not eloquent at all, no, not at all."

"Then tell me, how is it she is still here and has found her way to the Path?"

"Well, Master, apparently she was able to… um.. set aside her offense. The Keeper, er… the brute… seems to have worked some charm on her and…"

"And?"

"The woman, she has, well, she…"

"Spit it out, fool, or I will have your tongue!"

"Yes, Master, yes, well, she… she has something. I-I don't know how she got it. Maybe it's nothing, but it seems to… a… um… well—"

"What is it she seems to have gotten?"

"A compass. She has a compass."

"Really? A compass, you say. Interesting. How has one shown up after all this time? No matter. She will be unable to use it, she is no one of consequence."

"Right Master, of course, of course. You're always right, Master."

"That I am. Now, my overly eager Messenger, you had better listen like your soul depends on it, for I assure you, it does. Tell those incompetent imbeciles to get that woman off the path and back to her pathetic little existence of a life. Is this message one you think you may be capable of conveying?"

"Yes, yes, Master. I will tell them, I will tell them, Master. Right away, Master, right away."

"Good. And remember, my faithful little Messenger, I do not tolerate failure."

Chapter 3

"How in the world…?"

I've pushed my way through the thick brush—maybe ten feet or so—with the branches poking and scraping me the whole way. Looking back, the trail is open, and I can see Kohnrad standing on the edge of the clearing. He gives a short wave and nods before walking away. I turn back around and stare at the mess before me.

"How is this even possible?"

The trail is narrow and overgrown with ferns and a variety of plants I don't recognize. Tree branches hang low and heavy, their leaves and needles wet with dew. In fact, the whole place is damp, like it just rained. My sleeves are soaked and I can't even see my boots.

I'm only two minutes into this adventure and already doubting whether this is the right path. Except the compass pointed this way, and unfortunately, it still does. If this is what I'm in for, I might as well sit down and cry—get it done with, because I know it's coming.

Instead, I continue to claw through the bramble, stumbling over roots and rocks, relying solely on the compass for guidance. It's slow and grueling. To my frustration, every time I look back, the trail remains wide open. It's the craziest thing. How can it be so difficult going forward, but so easy leading back? Shouldn't it be the other way around?

I press on, and to my relief, the trail widens out enough to reveal the ground before me. After a while, it widens further and the dense underbrush thins out, allowing me to see the path winding through the forest ahead. Relaxing, I begin to enjoy my surroundings. The air is no longer damp; instead, it smells fresh and sweet. Birds flit about and an occasional bee buzzes across the path. I tuck the compass away, figuring I'll only need it if another trail appears. It should be easy enough to tell where to go if the path stays like this.

Sunshine filters through the trees with streaks of yellow beaming down like floodlights. I'm so absorbed in this stunning display, I'm almost run over by a man charging down the trail towards me. He's clutching a briefcase, his expensive-looking suit a wrinkled mess and his tie hanging off to the side. I jump out of the way as he passes by, his free hand running through his disheveled hair.

"I can't believe it," he says, his voice high and squeaky. "I just can't believe it. How could I be so stupid? I can't believe it, I just can't believe it."

I check the trail for anyone following him, but no one else comes along.

"Excuse me, sir," I call out before my brain fully processes what I'm doing.

The man stops dead in his tracks and spins around, his eyes wild. He seems as surprised by my presence as I am by his.

"Hey, hi," I say. "Is something wrong? I think you're headed in the wrong direction."

"Wrong? Is something wrong? It's all wrong!" the man replies. "I was told there would be riches and prosperity along this path. That all my problems would disappear. All I had to do was make a sizable donation, and I was guaranteed, *guaranteed*, he said, an easy walk right to the king's doorstep. Hah! It's all lies!"

The man takes an aggressive step towards me, waving his free arm in the air. "Look at me! Just look at me! I'm a mess, completely exhausted, and starving. I had to sleep in the woods last night. The woods! Can you believe it?" He throws a leg in the air, wobbling to keep his balance. "And look at my shoes! They're ruined! Do you have an idea how much these shoes are worth? Do you?"

"Um, no, sorry, I don't," I say, leaning away from the man's flailing leg.

"I've seen nothing resembling civilization since I stepped foot on this wretched path," the man continues, as if not hearing me. His muddy foot lands with a thud back on the ground. "I am going back to that deceiver right now and demanding my money back. All his fancy talk and smooth words. All those promises. All lies, I tell you, it's all lies! I can't believe it. I just can't believe it. How could I be so stupid?"

The man spins around in confusion, his eyes searching but not finding what he's looking for. He moans and clutches his hair, stumbling his way towards the clearing. His whiny voice fades as he disappears from my sight.

What just happened?

I stand looking down the empty path. That guy couldn't have been out here for very long. He only spent one night. Not a happy one either. Did he start from the same place I did? It doesn't sound like it, but if not, how did he get on this path? And Kohnrad can't be the deceiver with fancy language, so who sent that man out here with those promises? He wasn't prepared for a long journey or even to spend a night in the woods. How could someone send him into the wilderness without the proper gear and instructions?

"Kohnrad, I must say, I'm very grateful to have met you. Rough edges and all." I shake my head and start back up the trail with renewed caution.

The encounter with the businessman cycles through my mind throughout the morning. Where was he headed? Was he going back to the other path? Is that what Kohnrad meant when he said some chose to turn back? But how did the man get on this trail if he didn't even know what it was about? How could he think it was about getting rich when Kohnrad said we were going to serve? So many things don't make sense right now, and I have to stop thinking about them before I go crazy.

The sun is high in the sky when I stop by a wide stream for lunch. I wonder how far I'll travel today. I'm nervous about camping in the woods alone, but Kohnrad checked my pack before I left and assured me I have everything I need. He added a few more items and told me to keep moving as much as I could. At least he didn't make any more remarks about there being things out to get me. I don't know if I would have come if he had.

Forcing myself up before I get stiff, I cross the stream using a row of flat rocks that happen to be placed just right. The path angles uphill for a mile or so before veering off in opposite directions. There are no signs indicating where either path leads, although one looks more traveled than the other. I figure I'm safe choosing the more traveled one, but take out the compass to double check.

To my surprise, it directs me to the less worn trail on my left. Shaking the compass, I turn around, but it continues to point in the same direction. I've been told to trust the compass, but why would it choose a less traveled trail? Could the compass be broken? I haven't used it all morning since there were no other trails. Maybe I should've checked a few times. I scrunch up my face, recalling I was instructed to do just that. Instead, I'd forgotten and followed what was before me, not questioning anything. So much for staying alert on the trail.

"Hello!" a cheery voice calls out behind me. "Come now, move aside and let a fellow through. Trail's straight ahead, no need wondering where to go. Straight ahead is the way I say! Just follow the path with the most wear, everyone knows that. The trail's already laid; just follow along now—no time to waste guessing. Sure's the way ahead! That's the way alright!"

With a gasp, I spin around just as a small, wiry man marches past me onto the well-worn trail. He has a crooked walking stick in his hand, a canteen strapped over his shoulder, and a small pack on his back. A colorful, long, pointy stocking cap with a pompom at the end sways side to side as he walks. Without looking back, he continues striding down his chosen path.

Astounded, I watch as three other hikers, dressed similar to the man—including the hat—follow close behind. Not one of them stops to look at the other path or check a compass. Soon, they all disappear around a bend, leaving me alone once again, staring at the fork in the trail.

Did I really just see that? Every instinct is screaming at me to follow those people down the trail. There's safety in numbers, and it would be nice to have others to talk to. That little man seemed very sure of the way to go, and I could just follow along, though I doubt I'd be able to keep up. My stomach knots with indecision. All the advice—commands, really—I've been given has been to trust the compass, not myself or others going in different directions.

So…

I examine the trail to my left. Others have walked it; there is a visible path, though it's not as obvious. It heads straight up, while the other, what I can see of it, is flat. Biting my lip, I falter between the two choices. Kohnrad and the woman were very clear about trusting the compass and so far, I haven't followed their directions as closely as I should have. I've been lulled into a false sense of security by not having to make any choices until now. Lucky for me, there haven't been any consequences—at least, none that I know of.

"Onward and upwards I go," I say, rallying the troops. My legs are reluctant to obey but, with no alternative, fall into line.

***

A few hours later, I'm deeply regretting my decision to follow this path. I've been climbing up and down never-ending ravines and navigating around large piles of boulders. Each creek I cross is just wide enough to soak my boots *every single time.* I'm grumpy and exhausted. My legs are shaking, and I'm drenched in sweat. This is way more exercise than I'm used to and my body is rebelling.

I bet the other path isn't like this. Those guys are probably enjoying a nice leisurely walk on soft, even ground, sharing funny stories and laughing with each other. Although, when they marched past, none of them looked happy or carefree. Still, it's gotta be better than this.

"I can't do any more. I'm done," I say, dragging myself out of what I hope is the last ravine. Collapsing onto the ground, I lean back against my pack and close my eyes. I just need a short rest.

Barking jolts me awake and I have no idea how long I've been out. Confused and disoriented, I sit up with a loud groan. As I struggle to remember where I am, an enormous German Shepherd bounds up to me and attacks my face with its tongue. A young woman with heavily tattooed arms and vibrant pink hair scrambles out of the ravine, bending over her knees, trying to catch her breath.

"Charlie!" she commands. "Down!"

The furry beast, now identified as Charlie, reluctantly backs off and sits down next to me. He stares at me with a lopsided grin, looking rather pleased with himself.

"I'm so sorry," the young woman pants. "He took off so fast up that hill… I just couldn't keep up. Are you alright? Are you hurt?"

"No, I'm alright," I reply. "He scared me pretty good, though!"

"Charlie's a former rescue dog," she says, plopping down beside me. "He just doesn't understand that he doesn't need to save people anymore."

"Aww, thanks, Charlie, you found me. Good job!" I reach out and give his ears a playful rub. Charlie scoots closer, laying his head on my lap, and I laugh at his antics. "Well, he sure is friendly. He seems like a great dog."

"Oh yes, he's the best! I'm so glad you're not offended by him. He really is the most lovable guy!"

I fall silent, still shaking off the haze of my interrupted nap, while the young woman slips off her backpack and stretches out her long legs.

"Have you been on the trail for very long?" I ask, wondering if she just started out like me.

"Charlie and I've been busting the trail for a few months now," she replies with a big grin.

"Oh, wow. Today's only my first day."

"Your first day? That's… exciting."

"Yeah, I don't know if I'd use that word, but it has been an adventure so far. Until I hit those ravines. They sure did me in. Makes me wish I'd chosen a different way."

"Oh no," the young woman says, shaking her head. "You can't go a different way. You have to stay on this path. Those other ways will lead you in endless circles. They never actually go anywhere."

"Well, I sure don't want to go through those ravines again…"

"Seriously, those were killer! I think Charlie's a little worn out too!"

Worn-out Charlie is sprawled out on the ground beside us, legs in the air, sound asleep. He really is the most adorable thing.

"My name's Nola, by the way," the young woman says, extending a slender hand. She's a beautiful girl, younger than me—early twenties, I'd say—with a wide smile and fair features. Her short hair sticks out in a messy array that somehow looks striking on her. A dainty nose ring glistens in the sunlight, as do several studs in her ears. This girl embodies everything I've never been brave enough to be, and it's hard not to feel self-conscious in her presence. And, if I'm being honest, a little jealous.

I reach for her hand, cringing at my dirty nails. "I'm Kenna."

"Well Kenna, Charlie and I would love to have you join us. I mean, if you want to. We can help each other out and stuff, you know?"

As kind as she's been, I hesitate to accept Nola's offer. She's beautiful and confident, not to mention way more fit, but I know nothing about her. What happens if I can't keep up? Will she resent me and leave me behind? I really could use a friend—especially one who's been on the trail a while. When it comes down to it, I'm taking the chance of getting ditched halfway down the trail versus dying alone in the dark. So yeah, that settles the matter.

"I'd like that," I say, trying to sound more enthusiastic than I feel. "Honestly, I was a little nervous about camping alone tonight. Turns out, I'm not exactly the 'solo wilderness adventurer' type I thought I was."

"Oh, I totally get that! My first night was so not fun. Seriously, I don't think I slept a wink! But now you don't have to worry because we'll be together. I'm so excited to finally have someone other than Charlie to talk to! He's not exactly the best conversationalist." She laughs, giving Charlie's belly a playful rub. He moans and rolls to his side, but doesn't wake up.

"So, you said you've been out here a few months. What got you on the trail?"

"Honestly," Nola says. "If you had told me a year ago this is where I'd be, I would've laughed and probably called you some pretty awful names. Everything about this trail made me mad. My whole life I'd heard about this king and his path, but like, there were alway so many requirements and rules to walk it. Seriously? Who has the right to make it so exclusive, you know? I mean, really, I figured there had to be other options, and I wanted to get to the end my own way, on whatever paths I chose. No one was going to make that decision for me. I was pretty ticked off at anyone who said this was the only *true* path."

Shrugging an art covered shoulder, Nola gives me a sheepish look. "I kind of went out of my way to insult whoever I could."

"What changed your mind?"

"Well, I walked a lot of different paths, and let me tell you, I was miserable. Seriously. Not one of those trails got me anywhere near the king. They all went in circles, but you didn't know it at first. Like, you'd think you were on this great journey going to some amazing place, only to find yourself walking the same sections over and over and over again. Every choice I made just led me back to the same stupid circle. It was like the definition of insanity."

Nola rubs her hand over Charlie's ear, collecting her thoughts. With a snort and a shake of her head, she continues. "One day, I just decided I'd had enough. All my life, all I'd heard was how amazing it was to walk the King's Path—that this is the only true path to his kingdom, that the king is so wonderful and kind, and once you start the walk, everything just works out, you know? It sounded too good to be true, but I figured after all those other paths, I really had nothing left to lose."

"So, you just started walking?"

"Yeah, I figured it was now or never, you know? And now that I'm here, that other place seems so far away. Like, I almost can't believe that was me, right? It's like I'm becoming a new person. I mean, for the first time, I really… I really have hope again."

"Do you think that happens here?" I ask, a lump catching in my throat. "Becoming a new person, I mean. Do you think it's possible?"

"It's supposed to be one of the 'mysteries' of the path," Nola says, making air quotes. "Like the journey itself is supposed to transform you into someone better, and then you have this amazing encounter with the king, and he welcomes you into his kingdom, and then you live happily ever after."

"Oh, that sounds more like a fairytale," I say, my shoulders drooping.

"Yeah, but maybe the fairytales are made from this, you know?" Nola replies, gesturing around us. "Like, it's been great so far. Other than being a little lonely, I really have no complaints. I can't quite explain it, but being here is more real than anything else I've ever experienced."

I understand what she means about the realness—I've felt it since the beginning of this journey. But I don't know what to think of Nola's version of the path or the king. It doesn't match with what Kohnrad said. He never mentioned any rules other than staying on the Path. Then again, I don't know much, so she could be right.

"Do you think we'll make it all the way to the king's kingdom?" I ask. "I mean, it's supposed to be hard, but do you think it's too hard for us?"

"Oh, people just say it's hard because you have to give up a lot of things you don't want to. I don't think it's meant literally. Like, those ravines were the hardest thing I've seen yet, and that's only because I was running after Charlie. I'm sure we'll be fine. I mean, it's not like the king would put us in danger, right? He's a good king."

I sit for a moment, mulling over Nola's words. Something feels off, but I can't pinpoint what it is. Could Kohnrad have meant what she's saying—that the journey is only difficult because of the sacrifices you have to make? That's not how I understood it, but maybe the trail only seems challenging to me because I'm not used to it. I haven't walked it as long as Nola. Maybe this really is the hardest part.

But then, why all the warnings? Surely more people would choose to come if all they had to do was give up a few things along the way, right? Is that really what's keeping them away?

"Did you meet someone who showed you the way to the trail?" I ask, trying to make sense of it all.

"No, I didn't need anyone to show me. I already knew the way."

"Oh. So… you started in the clearing? By the cabin?"

"What cabin? No, I started where everyone I know has started. It's been the same place for, like, a hundred years."

"You didn't talk to some strange guy and have him show you the way?"

"No. Why? Did you?"

I feel weird saying yes. My experience is so different from hers—maybe I did it wrong and missed something by not starting where she did. Or am I right and she's wrong? Should she have gone to the cabin? Or… maybe we're both right, and there's more than one way onto the path. It's so confusing. How are we supposed to know what's right?

Thinking back to this morning, I remember how grueling it was pushing forward through the brush, but the way back was always wide open. At the time, I thought it was backwards and listening to Nola, it seems I was right. But then I remember the business man. He was told the path would be easy and was devastated to find out it wasn't. So the trail *is* hard—harder than some think, anyway.

"Well, your strange guy must've had a special entrance for you because that's not the way I was taught," Nola says, interrupting my thoughts.

I don't know what to say; I didn't choose how I came—it was set before me.

"So, um, have you encountered any wild animals or anything dangerous on the path?" I ask, opting for a change of subject.

"Nope, nothing's bothered me. Maybe Charlie's a good guardian or there just isn't anything out here."

There have to be creatures out here; it would be odd if there weren't. I'm thinking Nola might be a little naïve in her expectations of the trail. Realistically, there should be animals, and people get hurt all the time over the smallest things.

"Well, if something tries to attack me, I'm in trouble," I say. "I've only got a pocket knife for protection. There's not much harm I can do with that."

Nola laughs at me. "I don't think you have to worry. Seriously, we'll be fine. We have Charlie. He'll protect us for sure."

"That's only if he does more than lick faces."

"It'll be a surprise attack!" Nola says, springing to her feet. "He'll be our secret weapon!"

Charlie flips over and jumps up beside her, wagging his tail at her excitement.

"He might be a bit too big for stealth mode, but he'll be entertaining anyway, right?"

"Poor Charlie, you're so underestimated," Nola croons, tousling his fur.

"I suppose we should get going," I say, struggling to my feet. "There's only a couple more hours before the sun goes down." I stretch my lower back and flex my toes; everything is stiff and sore. How long before my body adjusts and this becomes just a memory? Not soon enough, that's for sure.

"Let's go, Charlie!" Nola says, swinging her arms forward. He takes off, and she follows after him, setting a pace I know I won't be able to keep up with.

I stagger after her, wondering what I've committed myself to.

"Master, I have come as you requested."

"I do believe you have been evading my summons, Messenger. Tell me, what is the result of my latest orders? Has the woman returned home, distraught and weeping in her bed?"

"Master, I'm afraid there have been some… um… setbacks."

"That does not sound promising. I expect your report to convey the details of the woman's confusion and dissatisfaction with the Path. This is the news you have for me, is it not?"

"Not exactly, Master. She hasn't left yet and um… the, a… um, the woman has joined another and…"

"This had better be your idea of an ill-conceived jest, Messenger. Thousands are kept from walking the enemy's path each and every day, yet this one insignificant female continues to plague me."

"I know, Master, I know. It is most unfortunate. But I have been assured, Master, that a plan is in place and—"

"The *plan* has always been to send her back by any means necessary. You do realize that when those on the Path unite, they forge a bond that enables them to endure incomprehensible hardships. How does this align with my orders to keep her isolated and afraid? Explain to me how she is to sink into utter despair if another is present to encourage her?"

"My Lord, I—"

"Enough! Have I not made myself clear? Guards! Remove this fool from my sight! I do not wish to lay eyes on this pathetic wretch again unless it is to bring me the results I seek."

"But Master! I am just the Messenger! It's not my fault—"

"Silence! I do not tolerate excuses! This woman should never have slipped through. I have spent decades refining countless techniques that even an imbecile like you could carry out."

"Y-yes, Master."

"Fail me again, Messenger, and I shall have your head."

"Your Majesty, I have come as you requested."

"Have you word of the woman?"

"Yes, Your Majesty. She has made it through the Never Ending Ravines and should come upon the others and the Long Valley within a day or two."

"You have posted Watchers as I requested?"

"Yes, Your Majesty, all your commands have been followed. Everyone is in place."

"Good, thank you, Messenger. You may go."

Chapter 4

Charlie runs ahead, zigzagging all over as the day turns to early evening and the temperature drops. Shadows emerge in the forest, creating pockets of imagined threats, making me jump at the slightest sounds. We haven't seen any shelters or spots to make camp, though I suppose, technically, we could stop whenever we want. Nola slows her pace once she realizes I can't keep up, but now my feet are burning so bad I don't know if I'll be able to make it much further, no matter how slow we go.

All of a sudden, Charlie stops, his ears perked forward. I assume it's just a rabbit or squirrel until he takes off, his deep bark echoing through the forest. The sound of cursing sends Nola sprinting after Charlie, and I hobble after her, stumbling into a standoff.

"Call off yer mutt before someone gets hurt!" snarls a hunched old man, standing in front of a campfire.

Charlie is planted in front of him, teeth bared, and hackles raised. He looks terrifying.

"Charlie, come," Nola says, her voice firm and commanding.

Charlie pauses a moment, then dashes back to stand in front of her, his eyes locked on the angry man.

Bending down to reassure her dog, Nola apologizes for his behavior. "I've never seen him react like this before; he's usually friendly. I'm sorry if he's upset you."

"If you can't control yer dog, you got no business havin' him out here," the old man replies, his wrinkles set in a permanent frown. He is not a happy soul.

"Come on now, Harold, no harm's been done," a woman says, emerging from a line of tents just off the trail.

"Name's Ronnie," she says, sticking out a hand to shake ours. Her grip is firm, her hand strong and calloused. Piercing blue eyes assess the situation, and she makes a quick decision. "There's plenty of room for others to join us. You girls can set up over there next to me." Ronnie points us in the direction of her tent and winks. "We women need to stick together."

With relief, we unhook our packs and head over to set up our small tents and bedrolls. It takes a bit of figuring out, but it's not too difficult, and I manage okay with Nola's help. By the time we finish, everyone's gathering around the fire to eat.

"You're welcome to grab a bite," Ronnie says. "There's plenty to go around."

"Well, there was until they came along," Harold mumbles just loud enough for us to hear.

"Don't mind him," a round little man says between sloppy mouthfuls. "His bark is worse than his bite. Ha ha ha, get it? Bark, like your dog?"

Nola and I exchange a look and share an awkward laugh.

Harold grunts, but says no more.

We help ourselves to delicious-smelling soup and find a spot to sit with Charlie lying between us, keeping a careful eye on Harold. I'm beginning to understand his dislike for the man. As the last of the daylight disappears, a chilly night sets in. I scoot closer to the fire, grateful for the unexpected gift of these people who've offered to share their camp and food with us.

The short fat man continues talking, "I'm Bert, by the way. You already met that bundle of joy over there." Bert snorts with laughter and nods at Harold, who just glares at us. "And our fearless leader, Ronnie."

Bert scoops up several bites, then flings his spoon out at the rest of the group. "Zeke's our path finder. He gets us where we're going."

Zeke raises a single finger, his expression unreadable.

"And that tall, quiet one over there is our mighty hunter, Ethan." Bert peers over at a young man slouched against a log, further away from the group. "He don't look like much, but that kid's got a talent for finding supper, let me tell ya." Bert smacks his lips and helps himself to more soup.

Nola and I introduce ourselves and I thank the group for their generosity.

"You look about done in. It's the least we could do," Ronnie says.

"Yeah, I'm not exactly experienced at this, so the trail's kind of kicking my butt," I say.

"Don't worry none, we've all been there," Ronnie replies, and I take an instant liking to her.

"Have all of you been traveling together for long?" I ask, curious about the group.

"Harold and I started together," Bert jumps right in to answer, food still in his mouth. "We've known each other our whole lives, haven't we, Harry?"

"Not by choice," Harold grumbles. "Can't choose yer family."

Bert laughs his obnoxious laugh, unaffected by Harold's attitude. "Harryboy and I are cousins, but we're as close as brothers!"

Harold's eye roll is apparent even in the dim light.

"We were in a bit of a pickle a while back," Bert continues. "It seemed in our best interest to join forces with Ronnie and the others."

"That is because you were starving and lost," Zeke interjects, a slight accent clipping his words. "You are here because your stomach appreciates staying full."

"Well, there's some truth to that," Bert says, rubbing his round belly. "I do have a penchant for a fine meal, and that kid keeps us well fed."

"We don't turn away anyone in need," Ronnie says with an indulgent smile.

"You're all on the path then, to the king and his city?" I ask.

"We are," Ronnie says. "I assume you two are as well?"

Nola and I both say yes, and Ronnie nods her approval. The others seem to defer to her as their leader, like Bert said. She's not tall, but her demeanor carries an authority that makes her seem more than she is. She appears older than everyone by a decade or two, with the exception of Harold. He looks ancient. Even Bert looks young compared to him, and I'd say they're close in age.

Ronnie's attentive eyes travel over her group before coming to rest on Zeke. She holds his gaze for a moment, then gives a slight nod.

"Okay everyone, listen up. Zeke has information for us from his scouting trip."

Zeke leans forward, his dark features sharpening in the firelight. He's a very good-looking man, with long black dreads tied back in a ponytail and a trim goatee. His amber eyes reflect the flames as he speaks, a calm intensity in his voice drawing everyone in without the need to raise it.

"Tomorrow we will head down into a long valley," he says. "There is a river that winds through the center providing fresh water. It should be good for drinking and bathing."

Murmurs of approval ripple through the group.

"There is a spot along the shore for us to set up camp and evaluate our route forward. There are a number of paths leading to and from the water. It will take time to determine which ones should be avoided."

"Did you see the mountains?" Berts asks, his eyes lit with excitement.

Mountains? I nearly choke on the last of my soup.

"I did."

"Yippee! You hear that Harry? We're almost there!"

"They are but a speck on the horizon. We still have a long way before us." Zeke dips his head to Ronnie and sits back from the fire.

"Alright everyone," Ronnie says, taking his cue. "That's all for tonight. Tomorrow we head to the valley. We'll set up base camp, then send groups out to scout and hunt. You'll need a good night's rest, so best be turning in now. We leave at sunrise."

Harold rises to his feet, the lines of his face deepened by the shadows, his scowl almost cartoonish in contrast. Without a word, he turns and strides towards his tent.

"Ladies." Bert performs a wobbly half bow before stumbling after his cousin.

Zeke and Ronnie make no move to leave as Nola and I stand.

Ronnie looks up, the fire softening her tough features. "You're welcome to join us for as long as you like, or go your own way. We break camp early, so be sure you're ready if you want to come along."

I thank her again for her hospitality, and we head to our tents. Nola's been quiet the whole evening. She was so upbeat and talkative earlier that I thought she would enjoy having others around to talk to.

"Are you alright staying here tonight?" I ask, realizing it's too late to do anything now.

"Yeah, I guess," she replies, not making eye contact.

"Is something wrong?"

"No. Not really."

"Are you sure? You seem… not happy about something."

"I'm just not sure about staying with the group past tonight, that's all."

"Oh. Why? I think they're a good group of people. Is it because of that Harold guy?"

"Naw, he's just a grumpy old man. It's Ronnie that worries me. I don't know, she just seems so… bossy."

"Oh," I say again, my posture deflating. "Well, she did say we could go our own way if we want. We don't have to stay, but I think we should consider the benefits of traveling with a group."

"I suppose," she says, looking back over her shoulder.

"With the guys around, we'll be safer if there's danger on the trail. And we wouldn't have to hunt for food."

"Right, but I don't want someone telling me what to do all the time. I had enough of that growing up. I can make my own decisions."

Nola's bitter tone catches me off guard.

"Okay… but we're all going to the same place, so it can't hurt to travel with them for a bit and see how things go. Right?"

"Yeah, I suppose we could," she replies, her arms wrapped around her middle and her shoulders hunched in. "It's just, I like to keep my options open, you know?"

Her demeanor is so opposite of how she presented herself this afternoon that I struggle to reconcile the two sides of her. I don't know which one is more accurate.

"Let's just see how tomorrow goes and we can decide later what we think will work best for us. We'll keep our options open, okay?"

"Sure, whatever."

"Alright, well, goodnight then. I'll see you in the morning," I give Charlie a quick pat. "Take care, boy."

Nola turns away, taking her dog with her into her small tent. I stand outside a moment longer, searching for stars through the tree branches, but there's nothing except darkness. The fire snaps, and Ronnie's low voice murmurs words I can't quite make out. Nor Zeke's response.

A yawn breaks free, reminding me how tired I am. With a last glance upwards, I climb inside my tent and wrap myself in my thermal blanket, moaning at my sore muscles.

What a crazy day. I could never in a million years have guessed where I would be tonight. I thought for sure I'd be camping alone on the trail, too afraid to sleep. Instead, here I am, surrounded by a whole group of people. I chuckle to myself as I recall Bert's exuberant personality. He tempers Harold's crabbiness in a way no one else could. I already admire Ronnie — her confidence and the respect she commands from the group amaze me. I want to get to know her better, maybe learn how to be more assertive myself.

Zeke seems like a natural leader too, and I wonder why he defers to Ronnie instead of taking the lead. A lesser man would, so I guess that says a lot about the kind of person he is. There's an unspoken communication between the two of them that makes for a good team, so maybe that's how they work.

Oh yeah, there's that Ethan kid too. I don't think he said one word the entire night, and he disappeared without anyone noticing. I couldn't even tell what he really looked like, other than having lots of hair hanging in his face.

I wonder how I'll fit in. *If* I'll fit in. I'm not sure I have much to offer as far as experience or skill. I'm worried I'll be more of a burden and hold the group back. If that's the case, then maybe Nola's right about going our own way, though I don't like the tension I'm already feeling with this friendship. She's put me in an awkward position, making me choose between her and the group. I don't know if it's intentional, but it makes me uncomfortable. She seemed so easygoing when we first met. Now I'm not sure what to think.

Another yawn takes over and I close my eyes, the pull of sleep only moments away. I'm hovering in that sweet spot of relaxing limbo when a thought jolts me wide awake. With all that has gone on today, not one person—Nola included—ever mentioned a compass.

***

Morning arrives sooner than I'm used to, yet I've slept better than I thought I would. And though I'm sore, a couple of good stretches help ease the stiffness.

Nola helps me fold down my tent and arrange everything on my backpack. She's quick and capable, and has her own gear ready in no time. Still, we're the last ones to finish and have to rush to catch up with the group as they gather on the trail. I'd hoped for hot coffee this morning, but settle for water and dried fruit from my pack.

Up ahead, Ethan hands chunks of something to Charlie, who scarfs them down before running back to us, tail wagging. Nola reaches down to pat his head, shooting daggers at Ethan. I glance between the two, but Ethan has his back to us and doesn't see Nola's reaction. I tilt my head in confusion, taken aback when she shrugs me off and moves away.

As the group moves out, Zeke takes the lead, with Ronnie close behind. Ethan slips into line, followed by Harold, who marches along like a soldier. Nola and I step in behind Bert, who's having major equipment issues. His short legs force him into a funny skip-walk in order to keep up, causing his backpack to slip off his shoulders with every bounce. Gear hangs helter-skelter from his pack, in serious jeopardy of coming loose. He sways under the shifting weight, tugging at his straps while things clank and bang together. I cringe, wondering how he manages to hike all day like that. It has to be exhausting.

Up ahead, Harold grumbles about the dew on his shoes, the weight of his pack, the direction we're heading, the lack of sympathy from the others. On and on, the old man complains without interruption. How do these people stand listening to this? Doesn't anyone ever tell him to shut up?

Before we go too far, I slow my stride, allowing Nola and Charlie to get a few paces ahead. Pulling the compass from its pouch, I open it, verifying the golden arrow points in the same direction as the path we're on. With a sigh of relief, I close the lid and put the compass away. I'm not sure what I'll do if the arrow ever points away from where the group is going. How will I explain my decision to go another way without revealing why?

We hike a good portion of the morning through the woods before the path begins a gradual descent. It weaves back and forth, taking us lower and lower. Occasional gaps in the trees reveal a valley nestled amidst tree-covered mountains. A river winds its way through the middle, with a bright blue sky above. It looks welcoming and I can't wait to be in wide open spaces again.

Nola's back to her cheery self, talking about anything that comes to mind, and I enjoy walking with her. Charlie stays close, attentive and serious—such a difference from yesterday.

"Nola, can I ask you something personal?" I say, noticing we've dropped back aways from the group.

"Of course. What's on your mind?"

"How have you been deciding which path to take?" I ask. "I mean, how do you know which way is the right way?"

Nola glances ahead before replying. "Promise you won't laugh or call me crazy."

"I promise."

"Well, when I come to another trail, I stop to listen and watch. Sometimes it takes a bit, other times I know right away. But if I wait long enough, I usually know where that path leads."

"What do you mean? How do you know where it leads?"

"Some of the paths are familiar. Like, I remember them from before, you know? There's a darkness to them, a feeling of oppression, sometimes violence. I... I see things too. Scary things. I can't explain how, I just do. Charlie feels it as well. He won't go near those trails."

Nola looks back at me, waiting for a reaction. I don't laugh, but I can't help wondering if she's a bit off. How can someone see and know what she's describing?

"So, how do you know which way to go?" Nola asks, breaking the silence.

I hesitate, wanting to say something, but I'm unsure how to respond. I really do want to trust her since she's just opened up to me.

"Promise you won't tell anyone."

"Of course."

"Say you promise,"

"I swear I won't breathe a word to anyone. Pinkie promise."

"Okay, well, I have a compass that points which direction to go."

"Whoa! That's—"

"Shhhh!"

"Sorry!"

"I've been checking when I can to make sure we're still on the right path. So far, everything lines up."

"This is so cool! You totally need to tell everyone so you and I can lead the group and then we won't have to rely on anyone else."

"Um, no… I don't think that's what I want to do."

"Well, that's what I would do, but whatever. I guess it's your choice. So then what happens if your compass says to go a different way?"

"I don't know yet," I say, pausing to gather my thoughts. "I don't know how the others are deciding which way to go, but if they don't need my help, I'm okay with that."

"Well, I'm not letting anyone make decisions for me," Nola says. "If the group decides on a path I don't agree with, Charlie and I will go our separate ways. There's no question about that for me. If your compass says to go another way, you have to choose that too, Kenna."

"I know," I say, but I don't really. What if Nola chooses a way the compass doesn't point? What if everyone goes another way? A knot tightens in my stomach. Am I brave enough to venture out on my own? Do I trust the compass enough to follow it, no matter the cost?

"I didn't expect decisions like this. I thought everyone would have a compass or something to guide them, but that doesn't seem to be the case. How do we know what's right?"

Nola turns around and stops, facing me head-on.

"I think we use what we're given. You have a compass and I have my knowing thing. We have to do what's right for us. Our way might be better than others, so we need to be careful, especially if they're just guessing."

"I suppose you're right," I say. "But I still don't want to tell anyone about the compass right now. We don't know them very well, and if no one else has one, I don't want them taking mine."

"Seriously, we need to stick together, right? We'll keep each other's secrets and watch out for each other. No matter who else we're with. Deal?"

"I..."

I never intended for the conversation to reach this point. I hate making promises; they always have a way of turning on me somehow. I'd rather wait until I have a better grasp of what's going on, but Nola keeps pressing the issue.

"I'll keep your secrets if you keep mine," she says, staring at me until I have to look away.

"Okay," I reply. I want to like this girl. I really do. She's sweet and funny and wants to be friends, but there's something just below the surface that keeps rearing its ugly head, throwing me off balance. Once again, I feel pressured to side with her, and it's dredging up some serious irritation.

I keep to myself from then on. As the day progresses, we fall further behind and lose sight of the others on the trail. Charlie relaxes and goes back to exploring, content to just be a dog. The trail zigzags downhill, steeper than before, and my toes ache from pressing against the ends of my boots.

At last, we reach the final stretch that opens into the valley, where everyone gathers at the bottom, looking up at us.

As we near the group Ronnie calls out, "Thought we lost you two back there. We were just wondering if we should send someone up to check on you."

"I told them we don't have time for babysitting," Harold says. "Can't keep running back to hold yer hand and guide you along."

"We're sorry to have caused any trouble," I reply, eyeing Harold with caution. "We don't want to be a burden to you."

"But that's exactly what you've become now, isn't it?" Harold says, waving his hands in the air. "I always said women don't belong on this trail, being the weaker sex and all. What kind of woman wanders all over with no man to look after her? A rebellious one, I say. No king I know would have such—"

"Harold, that's enough! Your opinions have been heard and taken into consideration." Ronnie's jaw clenches as she glares at him, her voice steady but edged with tension.

Zeke steps forward, ready to intercede if Harold continues his tirade. He didn't appear intimidating last night, but now, standing tall and glaring down at Harold, he appears dangerous. *Very* dangerous. Harold shrinks back but keeps muttering under his breath, his need to voice his opinion overriding his sense of caution.

"I would've volunteered," Bert says, eager to make up for his cousin's behavior. He shoots a wary glance at Harold but continues to nod, insisting that he'd be happy to help us whenever we're in need.

"Thanks Bert," I say, forcing a smile. "That's very kind of you. I really am sorry. I didn't realize we had fallen so far back."

"Didn't realize, didn't realize. See, just goes to show I was right. You don't belong on this trail," Harold chips in again.

Zeke takes a step towards him, his muscles flexing under his shirt. This time, Harold shuts his mouth and scurries a few yards away. Beside me, Nola tightens her grip in Charlie's fur, keeping him from lunging after Harold. Her breaths come in ragged gasps, as if each inhale is a struggle.

"Easy, boy," I whisper to Charlie, holding my hand in front of his face. He whines, glancing between Nola and me before settling down.

Nola lets out a strangled laugh, her voice shaky as she says, "Well, isn't he a pleasant one?"

"He does not speak for the group," Zeke replies, making eye contact with each of us.

"No, he doesn't," Ronnie agrees. "I'm very sorry that happened. He's usually harmless in his grumbling, but he seems to have taken offense at you two. I should've addressed his attitude from the start, before it got out of hand."

Ronnie glances over at Harold, who stands with his back to everyone. She looks back at Zeke, and something passes between them.

Zeke dips his head. "I will talk to him. I will remind him that respect for others is required."

Ronnie nods in return, satisfied Harold will be dealt with, and shifts her attention back to Nola and me. "You're still welcome here," she says. "I hope you'll stay with us."

Nola's tense posture has not relaxed despite Ronnie's assurances. Her cheeks are flushed bright red, and her hand remains clenched in Charlie's fur.

"I'm okay if you are," I say, hoping she'll just let it go. I don't want to cause a scene and risk having to leave—or worse, watch Nola walk off and be forced to choose who I stay with.

"Just keep that guy away from me," she says, eyeing Harold. "If he starts in again, I'm gonna let Charlie have him."

I think Charlie would relish a go at Harold. He's proving to be an excellent judge of character.

"Duly noted," says Ronnie. "Zeke will handle it."

Zeke gives Nola a nod and smiles at me before walking away. Nola wrinkles her nose in agitation and shoots me a sideways glare. I step back, uncertain of her response, but she ignores me and focuses on Zeke instead.

"Alright, everyone," Ronnie says, clapping her hands to get our attention. "We have a lot to accomplish in a short amount of time. Zeke says we can set up camp just ahead along the river. Harold, Bert, we'll take your packs while you gather firewood."

"You bet Ronnie, we'll get the firewood, won't we, Harry?"

Harold mumbles something about bossy women and doing all the heavy lifting, but he leaves his pack and follows Bert over to the tree line.

"Ethan," Ronnie continues, "any game you can find will be much appreciated."

With a quick nod, he disappears into the tall grass without a sound.

Zeke states he'll scout out the trails he saw yesterday and Nola volunteers to go with him. After exchanging a look with Ronnie, he agrees.

Ronnie turns to me. "Alrighty then, that leaves us to set up camp. Grab those packs and let's head down to the river."

Ronnie and I find a sandy shoreline along a wide curve in the river, where it appears others have camped before. There's a fire pit surrounded by stumps and logs, and a small pile of wood nearby. Harold will be happy to see someone has already done half his work for him.

"I often think someone goes ahead of us and gets a spot ready for the night," Ronnie says, assessing our site.

Her comment makes me think of Kohnrad. "Have you heard of the Keeper of the Path?" I ask as she begins removing tents from the packs.

"I've heard talk of the Keeper, yes."

"But you've never met him?" I ask, pulling out Nola's tent, and then mine.

"Nope. Not sure he's real. More than likely, he's just a story created to explain coincidences on the trail."

Ronnie moves efficiently from task to task. She's very adept at setting up camp; she knows just where to place the tents and how far away from the fire we need to be. I try to follow it all so I can do this on my own someday. I need a serious upgrade in my skill set compared to everyone else here.

"I've met him," I say as we finish up. "The Keeper. He's real."

"Really." Ronnie faces me with her hands on her hips, her expression curious.

"My first night on this path, well, the night before but, anyway, I stayed in a cabin and he was there."

Ronnie raises an eyebrow.

"It wasn't anything weird. Well, actually, it was more than weird, but he was… kind. He shared his food and helped me understand the choice I was making to walk this path." I smile to myself, remembering Kohnrad's gruff manner that had both terrified and offended me. "He said it's his job to make sure people are taken care of on the trail, so, I think maybe this spot could've been prepared for us."

Ronnie doesn't respond, and I can't tell what she's thinking. She stares at me for a long moment, looking lost in thought, then walks over to the fire pit. She picks up some nearby sticks and kindling, and throws them in a haphazard pile, her movements jerky and unlike her.

"Ronnie, are you okay?" I ask. I'm not sure what I've said that's upset her.

"This Keeper. He helped you?"

"Yeah, he did."

Ronnie rubs her eyes and I realize she's crying, or close to it.

"Hey, what's wrong?" Now I'm worried. This isn't at all like her. She's always so strong and in control of her emotions.

"I was lost," she says with a sniffle. "So long ago. I was drowning in darkness. I'd lost all hope and was so close to death."

She lowers herself onto a stump and wipes her nose. She runs a hand through her short curly hair, causing it to stick out in all directions. Sitting on a log across from her, I give her space to talk while she stares at the firepit, her body stiff.

"One day I heard something. A soft voice was speaking to me, encouraging me, guiding me away from the darkness. I never saw who it was, just heard his voice and followed where he said to go. He never blamed me. Never condemned me. I don't know who he was, but I'll never forget that voice. Your story reminded me of that. I haven't thought about him in years. Maybe he's been watching me over me this whole time, and I didn't realize it. Do you think it's him, this Keeper? Do you think that's possible?"

"I don't know. I hope so. He said it's his job to help those who get lost and off the path. Maybe that's what happened to you."

"Well," she says, bracing her hands on her thighs. "Here come Harold and Bert with the firewood. Why don't you head down to the river and freshen up. Take your time. I'll get the fire going."

"You're okay?"

"You bet. I'm good." She stands up, her emotions once again under control.

Appreciating a reason to avoid Harold, I grab my pack and head downstream for a bit of privacy. While our campsite area is sandy, the ground turns rocky around the bend, with large boulders embedded in the bank. The water is clearer than any I've ever seen before; I can see rocks on the river bottom and minnows darting around. Shadows of bigger fish swim by, but I can't tell what kind they are. If Ethan doesn't have any luck hunting, we can always try our hand at fishing.

I shimmy down the rocks into a naturally carved-out pool and take off my shoes. The cool water feels refreshing on my feet and I lift my face to the sun. It's wonderful to be out of the woods and out in the open.

Pretty sure no one can see me down here, I grab my bar of soap (courtesy of Kohnrad) and take advantage of the moment. Scrubbing fast and hard, I worry someone will come upon me, but fortunately, no one does, and I even have time to wash my hair. Afterwards, I grab a fresh shirt from my pack and rinse out the offensive-smelling one, laying it out on the rocks to dry. The sun soon warms me back up, and I let my long hair air dry before twisting it into a braid.

Looking back at the hill we came down earlier, I'm surprised at how large it looms now. We'll lose direct sunlight early on this side of the valley. To the east, the river winds back and forth before disappearing at the bottom of a jagged set of mountains. There's snow visible on the peaks and I wonder how we'll get around them. Unless… snippets of conversations float through my mind. From what I can gather, to get to the King's city, we have to go through the Great Mountains. I was hoping for more of a rolling hill kind of mountain, not the imposing range ahead. They don't look so great to me—unforgiving is more like it.

I turn away, refusing to let the path ahead get me down. It feels good to relax and enjoy the beauty around me without any expectations. The far bank is lower than this side, with tall grass growing along its edge. A doe and her small fawn appear, walking down to the water just across from me. I hold still so I don't scare them. The fawn is so little and wobbly and full of spots. It stands close to its mama while she drinks, and I grin in delight. The doe lifts her head and twitches her ears, looking downriver. Something spooks her and she takes off, the little fawn jolting after her. I look around but don't see anything, though I have the odd sense of being watched. It doesn't feel ominous, but it unnerves me enough that I decide to head back, just in case.

As I walk along the river, I realize I'm adapting to trail life faster than I anticipated. I expected to miss my phone and some other things, but I don't. I haven't even thought about them until now, which is hilarious considering the meltdown I had when I first discovered them missing. The lack of conveniences hasn't seemed like a sacrifice at all. Granted, it's only been a short while, but I'm loving the adventure of exploring and discovering new things, even though my body is protesting. There's so much to see, and while the unknown can be unsettling, it's also exciting. The journey itself is becoming a reward in its own way.

I've come to the conclusion that Nola's wrong about the trail. It has to be hard, otherwise there's no pleasure in overcoming it. If the path has the ability to transform us, then we need trials and tribulations so our character can grow and mature. An easy path doesn't challenge or require change. Only the difficult path does.

I don't want to be the person I was before I came here, and this place—this wild, beautiful place—is doing something to me. There's a heaviness that's breaking off. A peace taking its place. My mind is becoming clearer, more focused. I feel like who I am, who I really am, is finally going to get a chance to come out. I don't have to let my past dictate who I am here. There's still a cloudiness when I try too hard to remember, but snippets of things pop up once in a while. I don't know why I can't just get it all at once, but I think it'll come given enough time. Then again, maybe it doesn't matter here, and I can just let it go. Let the past be the past. Wouldn't that be a relief?

I wander back into camp and find Ethan's returned. He's got a small deer already dressed out and cooking on a spit over the fire. He really is as quick and efficient as Bert said. Thankfully, he couldn't have gotten the doe I saw along the river. Hungry as I am, I'd have a hard time enjoying that meal.

Bert and Harold are over by their tent, messing with their packs. Harold's grumbles are incoherent, but Bert's loud voice carries over. Not wanting to get caught up in their arguing, I make a wide track around them to put my pack in my tent before checking in with Ronnie.

"Is there anything you need help with?"

"We're good for now," she says over her shoulder. "Just waiting on the food."

Nola and Zeke aren't back yet, so I sit on a log near Ethan, who's crafting arrowheads out of deer bone. It's fascinating to watch him work. I never realized the skill and precision that goes into making arrows. His wavy brown hair falls over his eyes as he concentrates on his work, and I'm surprised to see he's older than I first thought — closer to my age, in fact. He's also way more fit than he appeared last night. I don't think there's an ounce of fat on him. A quiet strength surrounds him, like a vibration—felt more than seen.

He tilts his head, revealing a scar over his right eyebrow that travels partway down the side of his face. There's another smaller one along his chin. As he reaches forward to adjust the meat over the fire, more scars become visible around his wrist.

Noticing my stares, he pulls his long sleeve down. Not wanting to embarrass him, I pretend I didn't see anything.

"I saw fish in the river today," I say, hoping to engage him in conversation. "Maybe we could catch some for supper tomorrow."

He doesn't reply, just gives me a nod of acknowledgement.

"I can help if you want."

Again, he nods but doesn't speak. I wonder if he's unable.

Before I can say anything else, Charlie comes bounding into camp and jumps on me, licking my face as if I've been gone forever.

"Oh, Charlie, you found me again!" I laugh, giving him a hearty rub. He turns his head into my hand, reveling in the attention.

Nola enters the campsite in front of Zeke and skips over to me with a huge grin on her face. I watch Zeke head over to Ronnie and lean down to speak with her.

"I need to talk to you!" Nola whispers, drawing my attention back to her. "Away from here."

"We can head down by the water," I say, standing up. I tell Ethan we'll be back soon if anyone asks.

Nola practically dances down to the river, with Charlie bounding along next to her. We turn downstream but don't go far. The sun is now behind the hill, casting long shadows across the valley. Charlie races along the riverbank, sniffing all the unfamiliar scents.

"Kenna, you won't believe this," Nola says, her eyes shining with excitement. "You know how we talked earlier about knowing which paths to take? Like, how I know which ones I've been on before and sometimes see or hear things? Well, Zeke does something similar! He calls it discerning."

"What does that mean?"

"It's so cool! Like, he looks down the paths and sees if they're light or dark. That's how he decides where to go. And get this, he can do it with people too! Isn't he amazing?"

"What do you mean, he does it with people?" I ask, taking a step back.

"He just looks at someone and can tell if they have a darkness in them or not. He says there are different types, like depression and deep hurts come across as dark, but in a different way. More gray, I think he said."

"So you're saying he just looks at people and knows if they have… darkness inside them?"

"Yes. Well, not always. He said some people are hard to read. They have like a protection up that keeps people from seeing what's inside. But, oh, get this! He sees light in people too."

"Wow. That's amazing—"

"I know! Isn't he great? He's so smart, I can't believe how lucky I am. He has to see my light, right? I mean, of course he does. Wow, this is all so much!"

"I don't think—"

"If I can lead with him, that would be the best thing ever! He wouldn't need Ronnie anymore and—"

"Nola!"

"What?"

"Don't you think you're jumping the gun here? I mean, you just met the guy and I don't think, uh…"

"You don't like him, do you?" Nola asks, biting her lip.

"What? No, that's not what I'm saying. I'm sure he's a nice guy."

Nola crosses her arms and stands back from me. "So, what *are* you saying?"

Goodness, how did this conversation derail so fast?

"Okay, let's start over. We were talking about Zeke being able to see things in people. Let's get back to that. You said he sees light in people?"

"Yeah, he said there are different lights too. Some are brighter than others. I think it's the coolest thing, don't you?"

"It is, but it's also very unsettling," I say. "I don't know that I'm comfortable with someone seeing things inside me."

"Yeah, well, I think it's wonderful to be seen like that." Nola drags a foot along the sand, reminding me of a schoolgirl with a crush. "Anyway, he said you're one of the bright ones. Like a Burning One or something."

"Burning One. What does that even mean?"

"I don't know," she says with an edge to her voice. "He says you're different. Like, your light comes from fire."

Chapter 5

That night, the dreams start. They're wild and fragmented, continuing night after night. I toss and turn, feeling like I'm on fire, dying of thirst, wandering in circles, running from something I can't see. Flames surround me. I hear voices but can't make out words. There's always laughter, but not the good kind. The dreams make no sense, and I wake up disoriented and exhausted, my mind distracted and unable to focus.

Nola no longer talks about leaving the group. She spends the days with Zeke, scouting the path and the evenings telling funny stories by the fire. If I weren't so tired and haunted, I'd be more upset. As it is, I'm thankful I don't have to do anything other than follow along. I get a few worried questions about the circles under my eyes, but mostly I'm left to myself.

Our third or fourth morning following the river, the air turns warm and sticky. Bugs swarm our eyes and ears, biting every piece of exposed skin they can. An unnatural haze covers the sun, and an electric charge hangs in the air. It's not hard to figure out a storm is coming.

The valley has narrowed considerably as we've traveled, and the mountains appear closer. Zeke and Nola are struggling with the amount of trails zigzagging around us, and it's taking more and more time for them to decide where to go. Everyone's irritable when we stop for lunch, sniping and snarking at each other, adding to the mounting tension.

By late afternoon, I'm beyond tired and struggling to maintain my footing. I keep tripping on the smallest things and have to remind myself to lift my feet. The more it happens, the more I slow down. I'm on the verge of collapsing if I don't get some rest soon.

Loud shouting breaks through my daze, and I notice the group has halted up ahead. I struggle to catch up, troubled by their rigid postures.

"This is unacceptable, absolutely unacceptable," Harold says, pacing back and forth, his thin arms waving all around.

"We need to proceed with caution," Zeke says, sterner than usual. "A wrong turn could cost us a lot more time."

"Poppycock!" Harold replies. "Those of us capable should go ahead. The others can follow behind at their slower pace." He glares at me with such contempt that I take a step back, stumbling over myself.

"We're taking the needs of all our members into consideration," Ronnie says, her jaw clenching and unclenching.

"Bah, just a waste of time. At this pace, we'll never get anywhere. This is just asinine. I've never been a part of such foolish leadership."

"No one's forcing you to stay," Nola mutters.

"You sassin' your elders, young lady?" Harold says, getting in Nola's face, startling her. "I think someone needs to teach you some respect."

Harold jerks his arm up, and Nola flinches just as Zeke's hand shoots in front of her, halting Harold's arm in midair.

"I strongly suggest you step away right now, old man."

"Unbelievable! The amount of disrespect! If I was thirty years younger, I'd whip your butt, boy, and show you a thing or two," Harold says, spittle flying from his mouth. "That harlot there too."

A blur of fur lunges at Harold, knocking him sideways out of Zeke's grip.

"Get that damn thing away from me!" Harold kicks his legs out, trying to connect with Charlie.

Nola screams and lunges forward. "Don't you dare touch my dog! I'll rip your—"

Zeke grabs Nola around the waist and pulls her back against him, pinning her to his chest.

"You think you can take me, you little—"

"Harry! Stop! Please." Bert's sweating hands pull at Harold, trying to move him away from Nola, but Harold's arm swings out, smacking Bert across the face.

"Ouch! Harry, please!" Bert wipes at his bloody lip and backs away.

Charlie continues to bark and jump around, making things worse. Zeke looks ready to beat Harold senseless; restraining Nola may be all that's holding him back. Ronnie's face is so red I'm worried she's having a stroke. Her mouth keeps moving, but no sound comes out. Things have escalated to the breaking point. Something has to give.

Charlie's barking cuts off abruptly and he whips around, his focus aimed at a trail to our right. A low growl rumbles in his throat, and the hair on his back stands on end. Shouts cut off as everyone turns to see what's going on.

There's the light jingling of bells, then a familiar voice calls out, "Hello!"

The wiry little man from my first day on the trail marches down the path towards us with his crooked walking stick. Tiny silver bells pinned to his shirt bounce and tinkle with each step, and his long, colorful hat sways side to side behind him. Five men follow in a line, all with their own crooked sticks and silver bells. Each one is an exact replica of their leader, right down to the pompom on their goofy hats.

"Well now, make way, make way! Surefooted men coming through. Mustn't waste time standing around, I say. Gotta keep moving. Keep moving now."

Surprised, we move aside as the man leads his followers right through our group. Their synchronized steps never falter, and not one of them looks our way or acknowledges us.

"I say," Harold says, his crooked back straightening a little. "Now there's a leader. No indecision there. Orderly and respectful too."

Harold studies the wiry man and his group with awe. I've never seen his features so lit up. He's fidgeting with anticipation.

"That's where I belong," he says. "Right there. That's where I belong. That group's going somewhere. No weak women holding them back."

Harold sprints after the group and jumps in line behind the last man, adapting his stride to match their quick pace. The man in front of him hands back a colorful hat, and Harold arranges it on his head as if it were a crown.

Bert grunts and stumbles after Harold, yelling for him to come back. His pack slides sideways, pulling him off balance, and he soon falls behind as the group disappears up a different trail away from the river.

Bert stands wailing in disbelief. "I can't believe he left me. He just left me! He didn't even look back. I've stuck with him my whole life, even when things were hard and nobody liked him. How could he leave me like that? He never even looked back. He just left me!"

Ronnie walks over and puts an arm around Bert's shoulders, drawing him back to our group. I feel sorry for him. Harold's a jerk and I'm not sad to see him go, but what he just did is awful. Bert's sobbing and so confused. I don't know if he's ever been on his own without Harold. The way he talks, it seems like they've always been together. I'm not sure how he's going to handle things without him.

As we take turns comforting Bert, a rumble of thunder echoes in the distance. A quick scan of the sky reveals dark clouds rolling in. The wind picks up, whipping around us, carrying the earthy smell of rain.

"Zeke, Nola, we need to move," Ronnie says. "I'm sorry, but you've got to make some quick decisions. We need to get out of here. Now."

Ronnie and I help Bert reposition his pack so it stays in place better, and get him moving ahead of her so she can keep an eye on him. Ethan slips in behind me, a large rabbit hanging from his belt. It's uncanny how he moves in and out of our group without a sound. Most of the time, I don't realize he's been gone until I see him rejoin us.

Soon, the number of intersecting paths decreases, allowing us to navigate faster through the still-narrowing valley. The river accelerates beside us, rushing and tumbling in increased chaos as it heads towards a sheer drop-off. A tremendous roar echoes off the canyon walls as the water plummets over the edge into an even narrower valley below.

I stand at the precipice, gawking at the view before me. I underestimated those mountains I saw earlier—they're massive. They have to be the Great Mountains. And that means we'll need to cross them to get to the king's city.

Our trail disappears over the steep edge near the waterfall and we're forced to descend single file, hugging the side to keep from falling. Spray from the water soaks everything, making the trail slippery and dangerous. I keep my focus on the rock wall in front of me, shuffling my feet along one at a time. Only Ethan is behind me, and only because he wouldn't let me go last.

My boots slip and slide in the mud with every step, and my fingers scrape against the hard surface of the wall, trying to find a better hold. The others disappear around a corner, leaving me alone on the narrow ledge. Panic threatens to take over when Ethan moves closer, a gentle hand on my elbow to steady me.

My legs feel like rubber, and I'm not sure how I'm going to make it down the rest of the trail. I make myself take several deep breaths. Nice and slow. No looking down. Just focus on each section as it comes. I can do this. I *can* do this.

A fat raindrop lands on my cheek, then another splats on my arm. Thunder rumbles again, closer this time. Ethan nudges me forward, and I take a small step, testing the ground before me. Wet strands of hair pull loose from my braid, whipping around my face, stinging my eyes, and catching in my mouth.

"Shelter ahead… hurry… before the storm…" Zeke's voice carries up the trail, but his words are snatched away by the howling wind.

Terror of the impending storm outweighs every other fear at the moment, and I force myself to move. I slip again but lurch forward, using the momentum to rush down the trail. I know I'm being reckless, but I've reached the point of not caring. I just want to be done.

Random raindrops continue to pelt my body, a prelude to the coming downpour. The moment I step into the cave, Ethan close on my heels, the storm unleashes all its pent-up fury. Thunder booms overhead and echoes throughout the cave. A flash of light exposes everything for a moment, and I flinch, throwing my hands over my ears as a loud crack erupts. I swear I feel electricity snapping around me.

"It looks like someone's been here. There's wood for a fire," Ronnie yells over the storm.

She starts pulling things out of her pack while Ethan unhooks the rabbit from his belt and unsheathes his knife. I have no desire to watch him skin the thing, so I move further into the cave and collapse against the back wall without taking off my pack. Nola sets her gear down next to me and raises a single eyebrow.

"You okay?" she mouths.

I nod, trying not to react to the constant onslaught of the storm, but some of the louder cracks still make me jump, and every flash has me reaching for my ears. Nola watches me for a moment, then shakes her head and returns to the others. I shouldn't have expected anything different.

The cave we're in isn't that big, but it has room for everyone. It's more wide than deep, and the ceiling slants steeply into the walls. Still, it's dry and there are no wild animals, so that's a plus.

Eventually, I slip off my pack but stay back from the others as they gather around the fire, waiting for the rabbit to cook. It's too loud to talk, and I have nothing to say anyway. Ronnie warms up some beans, and we share everything once the meat is done. It's not much, so I take just enough to ease my hunger pangs. I can't justify eating more when I know I'm not contributing anything to the group. The others need it more than I do. I scoot back to my pack when I'm done and pull out my mat and blanket. If we're going to be here for a while, I want to rest. Maybe I can nap without dreaming.

***

Hot, burning, a deafening roar, destroying everything in its path. The darkness behind it. Massive and alive. Pushing the fire ahead of it. Surrounding me. Cutting off all escape. It increases in intensity. The fire violent. The heat more unbearable. The sound more deafening. Flames dance in a frenzy of ecstasy. It's building, anticipating, laughing, ready to consume me. Pressing, suffocating, overwhelming. The darkness pierces the flames, deflecting it, slipping through it. Large reptilian eyes, unblinking, calculating, reflecting the dancing flames. Staring right at me. Into me. Knowing me. It moves closer. Its large scaled body impervious to the fire, to the heat. Shock ripples through my body. It can't be. A wicked smile, a split tongue, smoke curling from its nostrils. Blackness envelops me. I'm falling. A scream stuck in my throat, blocking my breath. I can't breathe. I can't breathe!

I wake gasping for breath, the echo of terror reverberating throughout my body. Screaming fills my ears. With shock I realize it's me, but the thought is fleeting, overtaken by the need to escape. My arms flail, wild with fear, tearing at everything around me, fighting an enemy only I can see.

"I've got you, it's okay." Ronnie presses against me, whispering comfort.

Zeke reaches over, his arms covering Ronnie's so I can't throw her off again. My eyes dart around, searching for fire. Searching for danger. I spot Ethan from a distance, pain etched across his face, but I can't process it. I can't speak. Can't get enough air into my lungs. The shaking won't stop. The terror isn't going away. Images flash through my mind, relentless and overwhelming.

What's happening to me? What's happening? *What is happening?*

I have no concept of time—only the faint sense of movement now and then. Someone is always beside me, but I ignore them. I can't, *won't,* fall back asleep. I lay on my side, staring at nothing. Numb. Whimpering. The images won't stop. The terror so close, ready to jump at me the moment I give in.

Morning comes, marked only by the faint shifting of light. The storm has passed, but the rain continues. We spend the day in the cave. It would be foolish to climb down in this weather. I'm unable anyway, so it doesn't matter.

I lie on my mat, tears blurring my eyes. I can't stop them. Can't stop anything except the sleep. My body wants to give in to the exhaustion, but my mind is desperate to fight it. I know everyone's worried. I am too. My mind hovers on the brink of madness, so close to the edge. I can't explain it, can't understand it. But I can feel it, and it terrifies me just as much as my dream.

Nightmares. They're just nightmares. They are *not* real. They cannot hurt me. But my mind doesn't believe me, leaving me suspended in this twilight zone, hanging between what I should know and what I can't accept.

"Kenna." Ronnie is hovering again. "Please, drink something. I made you tea. It will help, I promise. You need to sleep."

I won't. Even if it kills me.

"Kenna, you won't dream. Come on. This will help. Trust me. Please."

Ronnie presses the tin cup into my hands, cupping hers over mine to keep it steady. She guides my hands up, bringing the cup to my mouth. Instinct has my tongue licking the warm tea, wetting my lips despite my resistance. It tastes like bark and dirt with a hint of flower. I try to push it away, but Ronnie coaxes more down until the cup is empty. If nothing else, I've humored her, and now she can leave me alone.

Peace envelopes me, soft and gentle, wrapping around me like a warm blanket. My muscles relax one by one until I feel like melted wax. My eyelids grow too heavy to hold open, and my last memory is watching the shade fall and darkness descend. Then, nothing.

***

"Hey," Nola says when I blink open my eyes.

I try to smile, but I'm sure it's more of a grimace.

"You've been asleep a long time."

I roll over and see a clear, bright sky outside. A light breeze blows through the cave, cool and refreshing. The others are up and moving around, getting things packed and ready to go.

"Is it morning?" I ask, my tongue heavy and dry in my mouth.

"Yeah, you slept like a whole day. The rain stopped yesterday afternoon."

How did I sleep a whole day? Why didn't someone wake me? I'm just about to ask when my brain kicks in, and memories resurface. Oh no. No, no, no! Not going there! I clamp my mind shut, refusing to let the thoughts and images go any further. I force myself to go numb. To lock down every emotion and throw away the key. It's the only way I can cope.

"Kenna?" Nola says, touching my arm. I jump, and she jerks back. "Sorry, geez."

"I… I just need some space," I say, hugging my arms around myself.

"Okay, well, just let someone know if you need anything. They want to move out as soon as you're able."

She moves away to join the others while I put my things away, avoiding eye contact with everyone. Shame and embarrassment surge within me, but I clamp them down along with all my other emotions. It's the only thing I can control right now, so I hold on tight.

The sun is bright and blinding when I step outside. Squinting against the glare, I watch the steam rise from a shallow puddle. The wall along the path is already warm under my hands, a few wet cracks the only evidence of the pounding it recently took.

Ethan and I are once again the last ones on the trail, he and Ronnie exchanging a silent message before she ushers Bert along. It takes longer than I thought it would to reach the bottom. We come out right next to the river, which flows fast and wild from all the rain. The only sign of the rocks beneath are the sprays of water shooting up here and there, creating little eddies below. We're far enough downstream for the river to fan out, its banks almost level with the water.

"We have to cross? You're sure?" Ronnie asks, eyeing the water rushing by her boots.

"Yes, we must cross," Zeke says, sizing up Bert and then me, his concern obvious.

"You gotta plan?"

Zeke takes off his pack and unhooks a long coil of rope clipped to the side. After a careful inspection of both riverbanks, he ties one end around a large rock and straightens up.

"I will cross the river and anchor the rope on the other side. This will provide a safety line to guide everyone across. Ethan, you will come last. Bring Charlie and the rope with you."

Ethan nods as Zeke secures the rope around his waist and grabs his pack. He steps into the water, testing his steps as he goes. It's nerve-racking to watch him make his way across. The current is strong, swirling around his knees and even higher at one point. That's not good. He's taller than all of us, except for Ethan.

Zeke continues across with little trouble and ties the rope around another sturdy boulder. He gives a good tug to make sure it holds, then motions for the next person to cross.

Nola grabs the rope and steps into the water, her legs swaying under the pressure. She finds her balance and slowly makes her way along. My breath hitches in my throat when she stumbles, almost losing her grip on the rope. Next to me, Charlie whines and prances along the shore, searching for a way to reach Nola.

"It's okay, buddy. She's gonna be fine," I say, putting my arms around him to hold him back. He gives me a quick lick, then stands still, watching Nola.

Zeke's in the water, making his way to her from the other side. She's frozen, shaking in the middle of the river.

"Nola! Look at me!" Zeke yells as he gets closer.

She lifts her head.

"Just take it slow. Come on. You can do this." Zeke reaches out a hand, beckoning her towards him.

Nola takes a wobbly step, then a few more until she reaches Zeke, who wraps an arm around her, steadying her as they cross the rest of the river together. Nola collapses on the opposite bank, and Zeke wades back out to help the next person.

"Bert, you go next," Ronnie says. "I'll be right behind you." Ronnie glances back at Ethan and me. "You might have to help her."

Ethan nods and Ronnie steps into the water behind Bert, who's already stumbling and tugging hard on the rope. She tries to help by grabbing his pack, but the water's too deep for him and he ends up bobbing around instead of walking.

"Bert, get your feet under you!" Ronnie yells, trying to steady him and push him along at the same time.

Bert screams and falls face-first into the river. He lets go of the rope and the current sweeps him away, dragging him downstream. Ronnie lunges after him, catching a corner of his shirt. She tries to hang on, but Bert's flailing has him twisting in circles, pulling her down with him. The only thing saving them is Ronnie's unrelenting grip on the rope.

Water splashes up as Ethan sprints past me into the river. He's closer than Zeke and more agile, cutting swiftly through the water to rescue Bert. Sputtering and coughing, Bert slumps against Ethan, his dead weight throwing them off balance. Zeke reaches Ronnie and, after making sure she's okay, plucks Bert from Ethan's grasp, tucking him under his arm like a football. Bert's feet dangle behind him as Zeke marches his way to shore.

"Get Kenna into the water now!" Zeke hollers over his shoulder to Ethan.

I'm already knee-deep when Ethan reaches me, the cold water tugging at my pants. My feet slip along the rocky bottom, searching for solid ground. I turn to face the current, gripping the rope with both hands. This way, I'm better balanced as I advance sideways, one step at a time. Ronnie waits until I get closer, then moves ahead of me in a similar fashion.

"I hope this is the only time we have to do this," I say as we wade into shallower water and my anxiety lessens.

"If we do, I'm tying a rope around Bert and floating him to the other side," Ronnie replies.

I laugh, but silently think that's probably the best option.

"You doing okay?" I ask Nola, stepping out of the water. She's standing with her arms crossed, looking across the river.

"What's he doing with Charlie?" she asks, her voice sharp.

I follow her gaze and see Ethan crouched next to the dog. As he stands up, he points a finger at the water, and Charlie takes off, the rope dragging behind him. He leaps into the water and begins swimming towards us.

"Oh, no!" Nola exclaims, uncrossing her arms as she steps forward.

Zeke pulls the rope in as quickly as he can, working to keep Charlie from being swept downstream.

"What is he thinking? He should have used the rope for himself!" Zeke says, huffing with exertion.

Nola runs along the shore, clapping her hands. "Come on, Charlie! Come on, boy!"

Ronnie and I join her, shouting for Charlie to swim. He's giving it his all, and with Zeke keeping the tension on the rope steady, he gets his footing after a couple of false starts. Water flies everywhere as he stops to give a good shake, and laughing, Nola splashes through the shallows to give him a hug. Charlie bounds to shore, where he shakes again, getting the rest of us wet.

Nola's untying the rope when I remember Ethan. I scan the river and spot him walking to shore, where Zeke is waiting for him. Their one-sided conversation has Zeke gesturing towards the water while Ethan shrugs and nods our way. Zeke looks at the group of us surrounding Charlie, and his expression softens. He shakes his head and says something to Ethan before giving him a slap on the shoulder. The two of them wind up the rope, and Zeke lets everyone have a brief rest before pushing us on.

On this side of the river, the trail is uneven and rocky, making it hard to know if we're actually on the path. The valley continues to narrow, forcing us into a slot canyon with steep, rippled walls. We trudge through ankle-deep water along a slim sandbar while the river rages past on our right. The effect is disconcerting, like we're being squeezed in from all sides, and a vague sense of unease gnaws at my gut.

Zeke waits up ahead, his expression grim. As we gather around him, he points to where the canyon takes a sharp turn and the river vanishes into the rock with no way for us to follow. Our only way out is up.

"Seriously, can this day get any harder?" Nola says, her shoulders sagging. "I can't believe this. How are we supposed to get Charlie up *that*?"

I follow her gaze and spy narrow steps cut directly into the rock wall. There are small handholds carved out on either side, but they don't appear to offer much of a hold.

"You've got to be kidding me," I say, a cold sweat breaking out across my skin.

"Maybe it's not as bad as it looks," Ronnie says, looking up, her brow furrowed.

Right.

Zeke climbs a few feet, testing the handholds and foot placement.

"They are solid," he says, jumping back down. "Nola, if Charlie will allow us, we can pull him up in a sling. You will need to climb alongside him to keep him calm. Can you do that?"

Nola assesses the steps. "I think so. I'm pretty good at climbing."

"Ronnie, I want you up next. I will need extra hands and a lookout. Ethan, you will be my backup down here. We will use the rope as a safety measure. Is everyone satisfied with this plan?"

No, I think, as everyone else agrees.

They strategize together and come up with a contraption for Charlie while I stand to the side, trying not to hyperventilate. Zeke climbs the steps, making it appear effortless, and disappears over the top. His head soon appears over the edge, and the rope uncoils, falling to the ground by Ethan's feet. He ties it around Ronnie, and she climbs the stone steps, taking her time to feel each spot—not as confident as Zeke, but she still makes it look easy.

Once she's untied, Zeke coils the rope up and throws it down again. Nola calls Charlie over, and Ethan ties a series of knots, securing Charlie and his homemade sling to the rope. Charlie's not happy, and it takes a lot of coaxing from Nola before he lets Zeke pull him up. Nola climbs the rock ladder beside him, murmuring reassurances the whole way. She climbs over the edge and helps Zeke and Ronnie lift Charlie over the top.

Bert's next, and I think he's determined to prove himself after the river incident. His technique isn't as coordinated as the others, though, and he gropes around, slipping here and there, yanking the rope enough to make Zeke swear.

"Slow down, Bert," Ronnie calls from above. "Just take your time."

He grunts and tries to speed up, making the situation worse. Somehow, Zeke manages to keep the rope tight, saving Bert from disaster more than once. When he's close enough,

Ronnie and Nola reach down and drag him up over the edge, his short legs kicking out behind him.

Ethan grabs the rope as it comes down again and motions me over. I take a shaky step forward, my heart pounding so hard it's making me nauseous. I should've told them I can't do this. Ethan waits, letting me work it out.

"Okay," I whisper, taking another step forward.

He wraps the rope under my arms and ties a knot, giving me an encouraging smile. He steps back so Zeke can see him and raises a thumbs-up. I stare at Ethan, my eyes wide. He takes a step towards me, making a motion with his hands. I don't understand what it means at first, so he does it again, and I realize he's telling me he has my back.

"Oh. Thank you," I say, fingering the rope. Zeke gives a slight pull, and I glance upward. Nola's waving me up.

"Come on! It's not that bad."

"Right," I mutter, inspecting the wall.

I reach out and run my hand along the smooth stone, then place a wet boot in the first groove and push myself up. Okay. I dig my fingers into a hole above and climb a few more steps. It's not as hard as I thought it would be. With everything spaced out just right and enough slack in the line so I don't feel pressured to hurry, I make my way, one step at a time, working higher and higher.

Wow, I can't believe I was freaking out over this. I peer down to see how far up I am, and the world slides sideways, taking me with it. I squeeze my eyes shut and gulp in huge breaths of air, trying to staunch the panic seizing my body. A tingling sensation creeps along my limbs, paralyzing me as tears roll down my cheeks.

"Kenna, what's wrong?" Nola calls down.

My lungs burn, my breath coming in ragged gasps. Dizziness swirls around me. My hands slip from the holds, and I feel myself falling backwards. The rope tightens, and shouts echo above. Swaying side to side, my toes barely touch the steps. I can't catch my breath, can't focus my eyes.

A hand grabs my leg, steadying me. Another pushes me back towards the wall. Reaching for a handhold, I miss the first two tries. Ethan guides my foot up and uses his shoulder to leverage me while Zeke pulls with the rope. I try to help, but my legs are like jello, and everything is spinning.

The guys keep me moving a couple of inches at a time until I'm close enough for Nola and Ronnie to grab my wrists and pull me up while Ethan pushes from below. Sliding over the edge, I collapse on the ground while Ronnie and Nola hurry to untie the rope and get my pack off.

"Are you okay?" Nola asks over and over.

I'm so embarrassed; I wish the ground would open up and swallow me whole. My body refuses to relax and I turn away to rub tears from my eyes, my heart still pounding in my chest.

"Just let her be a moment," Ronnie says, drawing Nola away.

Zeke gives orders to set up camp while Ethan takes off his pack and sits down next to me. I scoot over, turning away from him. I don't know if I'm going to make it to the end of this journey. It's way harder than I imagined. I don't see how anyone could ever make it alone—I'm barely making it with a group. Tears threaten to break through once more, and I blink them away, mad at myself. I can't break down again. I have to be stronger than that.

"Harold left me with nothing," Bert whines, drawing my attention away from my self-pity. "How am I supposed to sleep without a tent? He just left me here to die!"

"You are not dying," Zeke says, popping up a tent. "You may use my tent tonight. I will rest by the fire."

"We should double up," Ronnie says. "There's not much room here."

She lights the fire and surveys the thick forest butting up to the edge of the cliff. It's dark and foreboding, and I'm glad we're not heading into it tonight.

"Come and get out your wet shoes," Ronnie says, beckoning me over.

I cast a quick look over my shoulder to check on Ethan, but he's nowhere to be found. A little unnerved, I grab my pack and shuffle over to the fire, finding a spot next to Charlie and Nola. My feet are burning, and I examine my white wrinkled toes for blisters. Nola winces beside me as she rubs her own aching feet.

"Put this on any open areas," Ronnie says, handing Nola a jar of salve. "It'll take the sting out and keep them from getting infected. Pass it around. I'm sure we'll all need it."

Ethan approaches, carrying a couple of skinned… creatures. He hands them off to Ronnie, who thanks him and sets to work skewering them on sticks for roasting. Ethan removes his boots and socks and inspects his feet. I hold out the container of salve and he offers a smile of gratitude, before taking it..

"Zeke," Ronnie says, watching him pace in front of the trees. "Come take care of your feet."

Zeke ignores her and continues to pace, rubbing his forehead while muttering under his breath.

"What's wrong?" she asks, confronting him.

He halts next to her and stares at the forest, his body rigid.

I look at Nola, curious if she knows what's going on. She has a puzzled expression on her face, and her eyes dart between Zeke and the dark forest. I want to ask her what's wrong, but hesitate, not wanting to miss any of Zeke and Ronnie's conversation.

"What do you mean you can't see?" Ronnie asks, taking a step back. She looks up at Zeke, then back at the looming woods.

"There are two trails. There and there. I cannot tell you which one is correct."

"Do you mean they're both dark?"

"No. I am telling you I see nothing. Dark or light."

"How is that possible?"

"I do not know. This has never happened to me before. Never." Zeke looks around, appearing disoriented. His gaze lingers on me for an uncomfortable moment, then on Nola, and finally Ronnie. "Your lights, they are growing dim," he says, his tone so low I almost miss it.

Wait, he can't discern the trail? Our lights are growing dim? What is he saying? Confusion churns in my gut as I try to piece together his words. I've never seen him so unsure and it scares me.

"Kenna," Nola whispers, leaning over Charlie.

"What?"

"You have to tell them."

"Tell them what?"

"About the compass," Nola says, rolling her eyes in the direction of my pouch.

"Why? Can't you see either?"

She shakes her head. "No."

Wow. Okay. I haven't looked at the compass for… days. Since… since the dreams. A shudder runs through me and I quickly redirect my thoughts, pushing away the unwanted images that threaten to surface.

"You need to go check it," Nola says, her voice sharper than usual.

"Alright, I will."

I get up and rummage through my pack for a pair of dry socks, then slip the compass out of its pouch and open it up. The arrow points to my right, where I can just make out a faint trail leading into the woods. I study the second trail further to the left that Zeke pointed out earlier, but it looks no different. There's really no way to distinguish between the two to know which one is better. Nola's right. I'm going to have to tell everyone about my compass, and I don't think they're going to be happy with me.

"So?" Nola asks when I return.

"I know which way to go," I whisper. "I'll say something after we eat."

"No. You have to do it now."

"Why are you pushing this so hard?"

"Because," Nola says, ducking her head. "Look what it's doing to Zeke. You have to help him."

I fidget with the compass pouch, then untie it from my belt.

"Hey," I say to the group, my voice catching. "Sorry to interrupt, but, um, if we're having trouble finding the path, I um… I-I might have something that could help."

Five pairs of eyes fix on me, and a large ball of sweat trickles down my back. With a shaky hand, I slide the compass from the pouch and hold it out so everyone can see.

I clear my throat, hoping like crazy this is the right thing to do. "I-I was given a compass at the beginning of my journey," I say. "It's supposed to tell me which way to go."

"You have had this compass the entire time?" Zeke asks, drawing near.

I nod, my throat suddenly very dry.

"Why didn't you tell us?" Ronnie asks.

"Well, at first, I was afraid someone would try to take it from me. No one else seemed to have one, and the woman who gave it to me said not to lose it or let anyone else use it, and I… I didn't say anything later because it didn't seem like we needed it. Zeke and Nola have been able to guide us fine without it — until now, anyway."

Zeke shoots a skeptical look at Nola. "You knew about this?"

"Ahh, yeah…" she says, bright red blotches creeping up her neck.

"Don't be mad at her, please. I made her promise not to tell anyone. She was just keeping her word."

"You still should have—"

"Stop," Ronnie says, putting up a hand.

We all stare at her, waiting for her to speak.

"Kenna, I'm disappointed you didn't share this with us earlier, but I can understand your reluctance. No harm's been done." She puts her hand on Zeke's arm when he leans forward to argue. "We've been relying on the only way we know and what's been working for us up to this point. We never thought to ask if anyone had a different way, so that's on us. Now, let's see what this compass is all about."

I open the lid and the golden arrow points over to the same trail as earlier.

Bert hobbles over and studies the compass. "I used to hear stories about these when I was younger. Harold said they didn't exist anymore—that they're obsolete."

"Well, it's definitely old, but it works just fine. Or it has so far." I don't mention that I haven't used it much, so I can't actually verify its accuracy.

"What do you think, Zeke?" Ronnie asks.

Zeke looks between the trails and then at the compass. "We cannot stay here nor go back. I also cannot advise splitting the group to investigate both paths. Our best option is to follow the compass and have Kenna lead us."

"What? No, wait. I'm not... I can't..."

"Zeke is right. You said no one else can use it, so if that's true, then you need to be out in front."

I turn the compass around in my hand, watching the arrow right itself. Alrighty then, this darn thing better be right. Otherwise...

"Master, I have come with news."

"Oh, you have, have you? Are you reporting the whereabouts of my little missing Messenger, or do you possess something more fruitful to impart?"

"I have an update from the Valley, Master."

"And would this be good news, or must I brace myself for yet more incompetence?"

"It is good news in a way, Master. The Bitter One has chosen another path."

"Hmmmm. It might have been better to retain him and allow the bitterness to infect the others."

"Of course you are right, Master. He was the only one unprotected at the time though, so advantage was taken."

"Yes, it is intriguing that the Watchers have been dispatched. Why, after all this time, have they chosen to intercede for this particular little group of rejects?"

"Master, if I may make a suggestion?"

"You would dare to counsel your Master?"

"No, Master. I would never presume to possess your wisdom. I can only offer a humble opinion."

"Very well. You may present your most *humble* opinion."

"It has been reported that the group has reached the edge of the Dark Forest. The Watchers will be unable to follow once they enter. It seems an opportune time to plan an ambush."

"Yessss. I do believe it is indeed an opportune time, and I have just the circumstance to bring about their downfall."

"Master, I also have been informed that the Messenger has been found and will be brought in shortly."

"Excellent. I am in need of some agonizing screams to soothe my frustrations. When I am finished, I shall require your service to ensure my orders are executed precisely as I request."

"It will be done just as you command, Master."

"Ohhhh, make no mistake, my Dark One. I expect nothing less."

Chapter 6

"It's so dark," Nola whispers, her voice trembling.

"I can't see anything back here," Bert lets us know. "Can anyone else see anything?"

The atmosphere is oppressive, the dense forest blocking all the daylight and swallowing most of the sound. The damp air clings to our skin as tree roots, rocks, and fallen branches threaten to trip us with nearly every step.

"Are you sure it's wise to trust that thing?" Bert pipes up again. "I mean, it's so old. How do we know it even works? Shouldn't we at least check out that other trail? Hey, we didn't even vote. Shouldn't we have taken a vote?"

The glow of the golden arrow gives just enough light for my next step, leaving the rest to fumble around in near darkness. A cold sweat breaks across my skin as anxiety twists in my gut, a heavy weight that threatens to pull me down. What if I'm wrong about the compass and this trail? What if Bert's right? Am I leading us all into danger?

"Kenna, are you sure you trust that thing?" Zeke asks.

Great, now he's doubting me too. Shouldn't we have asked these questions before we got ourselves this far? Wasn't this his idea in the first place?

"We'll give it some time," Ronnie replies before I can respond. "The other trail didn't look any different."

I wish I felt as sure as Ronnie. I don't know how she does it—leading others with such confidence.

The trail continues deeper into the forest, winding between twisted trees and misshapen boulders. If there are any side trails, we don't see them in the dim light. Hours pass by, the silence punctuated only by the occasional snap of a twig or huff of breath when someone stumbles. I don't know how much longer we can go on like this. What if we're here for days, forced to spend the night and expected to sleep in this place? That thought opens up a whole new avenue of anxiety.

"Whoa." I come to an abrupt halt, creating a chain reaction of cursing and scuffling behind me.

"What's going on?" Bert whines from the back. "Are we turning around?"

"Hold on a second," I say. "Zeke, look at this."

On the path in front of me is a large white arrow, looking suspiciously like wet paint. It points left, but all I can see is dense woods—no visible trail. I hold the compass out for Zeke, who verifies the direction before turning his attention back to the conundrum before us.

"This is getting stranger and stranger," he says, shaking his head. "We have decided to put our trust in the compass. That is what we will continue to do. We are too far in to turn back."

I blow out a breath and glance at Ronnie for confirmation. She's pressed up against Zeke, clutching his arm, her wide eyes fixed on the ground.

"We stick to the plan for now," she says, less confident than before.

So, we keep following the compass, but the further we go, the more white arrows we come across—each one pointing left.

"Isn't someone going to check out any of these arrows?" Bert asks, his voice cutting through the heavy atmosphere. "I mean, there's so many of them. Maybe they're warnings we're going the wrong way. What if they mean we should've taken that other trail? How far are we going to go like this?"

"Hold up!" I say, once again stopping the group. "There's something ahead."

We've come to a wooden sign staked right in the middle of the path. Someone has scrawled the words "Last Chance" in the same white paint, with an arrow underneath. Pointing left, of course. A chill runs down my spine as everyone pushes ahead, jostling each other as they try to get a better look.

"What is it?" Bert asks. "Come on guys, I can't see. What's going on up there?"

No one answers as they contemplate the sign.

"What does the compass say?" Ronnie asks, her voice lower than usual.

"It doesn't point that way," I reply, looking into the darkness.

"Zeke, do you see anything yet?"

"I do not. I am sorry, Ronnie. It is as if I am blind." Zeke shakes his head in frustration, his eyes scanning the shadows.

Bert pushes his way to the front, hands on his hips as he stares at the sign. "Harold would tell us to follow the signs," he says.

"Then we definitely shouldn't go that way," Nola retorts.

"That's not fair!" Bert whips around, pointing an accusing finger at everyone. "You guys didn't give him a chance. No wonder he left! He's probably already with the king and here we are, wandering around like idiots in the dark."

Bert deflates as quickly as he blew up, a sob breaking free. "Oh Harold, why did you have to leave me?"

"Shhhh!" I hiss, waving a hand at Bert. "Do you guys see that?"

A light bobs in the darkness, weaving through the trees as it moves towards us. Without a word, we cluster together, the tension around us thick enough to cut. Charlie cowers next to Nola, ears pinned back, tail tucked. I've never seen him scared before and it's unsettling.

The light draws nearer, revealing a lantern held by a shadowy figure. As he steps forward, the features of a striking older gentleman come into view. His glossy black hair is full and wavy, streaked with gray around his temples, and despite his smile, something about him makes the hair on my arms stand on end.

"Greetings travelers! How are you all this fine day?" the man says with a thick accent. "I was just saying to myself, it is a pity I do not have anyone to join me for lunch. But now look, you are here! It is destiny that we should meet at this time and place. Come, come, I have a table all ready. You must sit and enjoy yourselves. Come, please. It is just this way."

The sleeve of his dark, silky shirt flutters as he motions into the shadows. A soft glow emanates, revealing a candlelit table adorned with silver and crystal dining ware, platters heaped with food, and goblets brimming with a deep red wine. The aroma swirls around us, rich and intoxicating. My stomach rumbles and my mouth waters in anticipation.

How did we not see this before?

Bert squeezes past us, rushing to shake the gentleman's hand while stumbling over his thank-yous. The man's smile widens as he steps back, drawing Bert along.

"Please, call me Raoul. It is my pleasure to provide for you. You must all be so hungry. So tired from your journey. Come now, it is not far. See?"

The woods are aglow with a thousand tiny lights hanging from the trees surrounding the table, which is now only a few feet away. Are we moving? No, we're still by the sign. It must be moving, but how is that possible?

Raoul approaches the head of the table. "Please, let me honor such a noble man," he says, ushering Bert into an elegant chair. "I can see you are a gentleman of very fine taste — very fine indeed."

"Oh, I am, I am!" Berts replies, his eyes gleaming with anticipation. He slides into the seat, snatching an embroidered napkin before him, and tucks it under his chin.

Raoul waves for the rest of us to come forward. "Come, friends, please, be my guests. It is a very fine meal, is it not, Bert?"

Bert devours everything within his reach, cramming food into his mouth faster than he can chew. He grabs a goblet of wine, red liquid sloshing all over the white tablecloth, and gulps greedily before slamming it down.

"Ronnie, I have a spot here at the other end just for you. A grand spot for such a fine leader. Come now, you will be honored like a queen, for that is what you are. No man is over you. It is just you, my dear. Come now, your throne awaits you."

Ronnie hesitates, a look of confusion crossing her face as Raoul glides back and forth like a dancer, hand outstretched, teasing and enticing.

"Ah, and Nola, my enchanting maiden, your beauty has me completely captivated. My heart beats wildly inside my chest. You must sit right here next to me. We are like star-crossed lovers who have found each other at last, are we not? We shall never be apart again."

Nola steps forward, her gaze locked on Raoul. Emboldened, Ronnie goes to follow, but Zeke throws out his arm, stopping her.

"Come now, Zeke," Raoul says, a mischievous grin lighting up his face. "You will not be left out. There is a place for you right here next to Ronnie. Come, faithful servant, you must be honored as well. One so trustworthy, never turning your back on another. Come, come."

Raoul's words are seeping in, working past what caution still remains. Ronnie strains against Zeke's arm, telling him we'll just stop and rest for a moment. The group needs food and there is plenty to go around. I can see Zeke wavering, battling the urge to give in. I reach out, intending to tell him to stay strong, when Raoul locks eyes with me and winks.

"You would not deny your friends this pleasure now, would you, Kenna? After all, it's not like you have any power to do anything. Come now, you do not actually think you can stop me?" Raoul raises a hand in mock surrender, laughter rumbling in his chest, his eyes sparkling with amusement.

A shimmering radiates through the air around me and heat surges within my chest—a deep burning sensation, as if someone has just set me on fire. This man knows us, knows all our names. His words flow like honey, smooth and sweet, whispering to our insecurities and inviting us in, but something is wrong with his eyes. Behind his smile lies an unrestrained malice. He is not the friend he claims to be.

Nola reaches Raoul, while Ronnie and Zeke make their way forward. Raoul smirks, beckoning them closer while a horrible choking sound erupts from the far end of the table. Bert slouches down in his chair, his face turning from deep purple to blue and finally gray. His head falls back, and a thin stream of foam trickles down his chin to his neck, his eyes wide and unseeing.

Raoul slides an arm around Nola, pulling her into his side. Her back arches as he lowers his head, brushing his lips against hers. Nola shivers, and Raoul lets her body crumple at his feet, triumph gleaming in his dark eyes. He steps forward, once again reaching for Ronnie just as the shadows shift and Ethan steps in front of her.

"No," he mouths, pointing back towards me.

"Oh my," Raoul drawls, lowering his arms. "I was wondering where the Shadow Walker had gotten to. Trying to save the day, are you now? I am afraid you are too late."

With casual ease, Raoul picks up a carving knife from the table, twirling it between his fingers like a magician performing a trick. A predatory smile flickers across his face as he considers Ethan. He flicks the knife high into the air, catching it with a flourish.

His expression hardens as he addresses Ethan's back. "It is such a pity, is it not? To savor the taste of freedom, only to lose it like a wisp of smoke?"

Ethan's eyes lock with mine over Ronnie's shoulder, clear and steady despite the surrounding mayhem, as if he's already braced for whatever comes next.

Raoul's voice drops to a menacing growl. "I will take great pleasure in snuffing out that freedom and watching the light fade from your traitorous eyes." With a howl of rage, he raises the knife and lunges at Ethan.

"No!" I scream, my hands shooting out to stop him.

A massive explosion of light rockets through the forest, and flames erupt all around us. Raoul falls to his knees, shrieking, his hands clawing at his eyes. Ethan bursts forward, shoving Ronnie backwards into Zeke, who stumbles in a daze before recovering. Quick on his feet, he grabs Ronnie and pushes her towards me, shouting for us to get out of there. Nola lies collapsed on the ground, cradling her head and wailing. Ethan scoops her up and carries her past Raoul.

The fire expands faster than seems possible, consuming the entire table and its extravagant contents. I watch in horror as it engulfs Bert's body and the surrounding trees go up like torches. Raoul continues to scream over and over that his eyes are burning. I've burned his eyes and he can't see. He rocks back and forth as the fire roars out of control around him.

A putrid, sulfuric odor fills the air, searing my throat and my eyes water. Charlie runs in frantic circles, barking and baring his teeth at the fire. There's no time to wonder where he's been or why he didn't go after Raoul. Ethan passes Nola to Zeke and reaches for Charlie as we stumble past the wooden sign, just ahead of the flames.

"Kenna! Which way do we go?" Zeke's shout breaks through the uproar, his tone rough with urgency.

I glance at the compass still clutched in my hand, the arrow revealing a narrow opening right in front of us. "Through there!" I shout, pointing the way, and everyone rushes ahead, disappearing into the darkness one by one.

The fire roars and snaps behind me, the intense heat searing my back as I sprint after them. I push my way through the opening, branches scraping against my hands and face. Glancing back at the last moment, I see the fire devouring the wooden sign.

A sudden darkness pierces the flames, pushing them aside. Large reptilian eyes stare back at me—I know those eyes.

It slides closer, its scaled body impervious to the fire and heat. Shock ripples through my body. It can't be. A wicked grin spreads across its face, its split tongue flicking in and out. Panic grips my chest. I'm seeing my dream.

"Ahhh, my dear girl," the creature croons. "I have been waiting for one such as you. How fascinating that my adversary has chosen someone so... *insignificant*. Who would have thought..."

Its long neck stretches across the space between us, bringing it far too close to my face. Flames dance in its unblinking eyes and I'm frozen in place, invisible coils tightening around me, squeezing the breath from my lungs.

"I know who you are now."

A hand seizes my wrist and yanks me into the dark forest. Laughter echoes behind me as I stumble along, overtaken by shock and horror. I'm dragged down a steep bank, sliding and falling, only to be hauled to my feet time and again. I have no idea where we're going. All I can see is fire and those eyes—those awful, evil eyes.

It knows who I am. How does it know who I am?

Icy water hits my face, jolting me back to my present surroundings. Squinting against the blinding sunlight, I'm stunned to find myself in the middle of a river; water swirling around my knees while everyone regroups downriver. Ethan's hand remains clamped around my wrist, pulling me along as we try to catch up. I struggle to twist free, but his grip is too strong, and I have no choice but to follow.

Without warning, the water deepens and Ethan stumbles ahead of me. The sudden shift sends me barreling forward, now free from his grasp. The strong current wastes no time dragging me down, and I gasp for air, sucking in a mouthful of water instead. Somehow, Ethan has hold of my backpack and yanks the straps off my shoulders while fumbling with the front clasp. With just enough presence of mind, I search for my waist buckle and roll free when it unclips. I break the surface, coughing and spitting, trying to get my feet under me, but the water's too deep and too fast, and I'm forced to swim instead.

Up ahead, the roar of rapids fills the air. Ronnie stands on a sandy section of beach, waving her arms at me while Zeke wades out into the water, preparing to catch me when I get closer.

"Swim!" Ronnie yells, her hands cupped around her mouth.

I kick my feet as hard as I can, aiming towards Zeke. I feel the bottom the same instant he reaches for me, and push up with all of my strength, launching myself towards the beach. Strong arms wrap around me and lift me out of the water, placing me on dry, warm sand. My legs buckle beneath me, and I collapse onto my knees as Ronnie races over to help.

"Ethan," I say, gasping for breath.

"Zeke's got him," she replies, supporting me as I try to stand.

"Kenna, get out of those wet clothes," Zeke says, dumping my soaked backpack at my feet. "Ronnie, Nola is in need of help."

I'm left to fumble around, trying to get my things off, but my numb fingers refuse to cooperate and the process takes a lot longer than it should. When I attempt to pull my shirt over my head, it clings to my skin, refusing to budge past my shoulders. A quick upward tug peels the stuck shirt from my arms, and I'm surprised to find Zeke holding out a blanket for me, his eyes averted.

"Come, you need to warm up," he says once I'm covered, and leads me towards the fire someone has had the courage to start.

I sink into the soft sand next to a shivering Nola and a very wet Charlie. Logs snap as they burn and my heart races, pounding hard against my chest. I can't believe we're sitting before a fire after everything that's just happened,

"We... left... him... behind," Nola stammers, her lips dark blue against her pale skin. "We all... ran... and just left him... there."

"Nola, he was already gone," I say, shivering despite the warmth around me.

"He got out?" she asks, her eyes searching the area.

"No," I say, shaking my head. "I meant at the table... the food... whatever he ate, or drank... I think it... killed him."

"I don't... understand. W-w-what are you talking... about? Raoul wasn't... eating anything."

"What? You're talking about Raoul?"

"Of course... I'm talking about Raoul. Who else? Oh... how could I have left him? He was so beautiful. His words were so... he called me..." Nola's fingers trace her discolored lips, then curl into a fist. Her head drops to her chest and she weeps into her blanket.

I stare at her stunned. Is she serious? How can she be concerned about Raoul after what he just did? Didn't she see what happened to Bert? Or how he tried to kill Ethan? What is going on with her?

"It was so odd," Ronnie says, watching Nola, but making no move to console her. "His words were so compelling. He spoke as if he knew us." Ronnie looks up, her expression shifting as shock registers on her face. "He knew my name. How did he know my name?"

"He knew all our names," I reply, meeting her gaze.

"But how could he have known who we were?" Ronnie asks, fear clear in her eyes.

"I don't know, but he knew what to say to each of you to draw you in." I glance at Nola. "He was very specific and intentional with his words."

"Bert?" Ronnie hurries to her feet and looks upriver, then over at Zeke.

Zeke takes a large breath, his chest expanding as if to protect himself, then shakes his head.

Ronnie stares at him in shock. "Oh," she whispers, sinking back down.

No one says anything for a long moment. The magnitude of what has happened steals any idle chit chat we might have normally engaged in.

Zeke once again takes an audible breath before shifting his attention my way. "You were not invited to the table," he states. His eyes hold mine only for a second before moving on to Ethan. "Or you."

Ethan holds Zeke's questioning look without blinking, his posture relaxed, but with an underlying alertness. Raoul called him something…

"Why would he do that?" Ronnie asks me. "Why would he call us, but not you?"

"I don't know," I say, shaking my head. I pull the blanket tighter, feeling its protection as well as its warmth. "It was all so weird. He didn't even try. It was like he knew his words didn't work on me. He knew I saw what was happening and he… he mocked me."

"But how did you know?"

"It was his eyes. They didn't match what he was saying. His words were sweet and inviting, but his eyes… they were filled with hatred."

"Enchanter," says a raspy, strained voice.

I turn in surprise. Ethan. He can talk.

Zeke shakes his head as if to clear his mind and rubs his forehead. "When I was a young boy, I heard stories of creatures who took on human form and used enticing words to draw people into their traps. Those who fell for their charms would disappear, never to be seen or heard from again. The few that did return were never the same; their minds were broken, their bodies just shells. I thought they were only tales told to scare children into behaving well. I have never thought they were real."

"So, you think that's what he was, an Enchanter?" Ronnie asks, looking between Zeke and Ethan.

Ethan nods, his expression somber.

"So, he wasn't really a man?" I ask, my mind tangled in confusion while trying not to stare at Ethan.

"Man… ruled by darkness," he rasps.

"So he was real?"

"Yes."

"I don't understand what happened. How did we get away?" Ronnie asks.

"It was her," Nola says, her voice dripping with accusation. "It's all Kenna's fault. She did this. She hurt him and took my beloved away. How could you!"

I rear back in surprise. There's so much hatred in her eyes and her accusation stings, even though my intentions were never to do anything other than help.

"What does she mean, Kenna?" Zeke asks, staring down at me.

I scan the faces around me, a lump forming in my throat. Ethan watches, waiting to see what I will say, and I get the feeling he knows. He wasn't under the Enchanter's spell, so he would've seen what happened. I wrap my arms around my knees, trying to gather my thoughts.

"I… I think I…" I pause, taking a deep breath before continuing. How do I explain something I don't yet understand? "I-I started the fire," I finally say, the weight of my confession hanging in the air.

"I do not understand. How did this happen?"

"It was an accident. Really, it was. There was this burning inside my chest, and it just... it just kept growing. I didn't mean to do anything. I was... I wanted to stop Raoul. It just... came out." I look at Nola with pleading eyes, willing her to listen. "I was just trying to stop him. I didn't know... Raoul wasn't what he seemed, Nola. You have to believe me. He killed Bert! And he went after Ethan. He was going to hurt him. Hurt you. All of you. I was just trying to—"

"No!" Nola screams, putting her hands over her ears. "He would never hurt me. Never!"

"But that's not—"

"You destroyed him because you're jealous. He didn't choose you; he chose me. He loved *me*, not you. I can never forgive you Kenna! I hate you! I hate you! You've taken everything from me!"

"No! That's not true! I wouldn't do that to you. I wouldn't do that to anyone," I say, clutching my chest. How can she think this? Why can't she see the truth?

Nola curls into a fetal position in the sand with Charlie next to her, his eyes huge and worried. Ronnie kneels beside her, placing a hand on her back, trying to offer comfort, but Nola's inconsolable. What has that Enchanter done to her? Anger swells in my chest and I hate myself for not realizing sooner what was happening. I wish I had been brave. I wish I had...

Despair washes over the anger and I hang my head. It's all my fault. My uncertainty and fear cost Bert his life. And now Nola—I don't know what to do. I look at Zeke, desperate for him to understand, but he avoids my gaze, staring instead at the fire.

Ethan draws my attention with a shake of his head and whispers one heart wrenching word. "Broken."

***

Everything is different; I can feel it. The encounter in the Dark Forest has changed us all, marking us forever. It revealed insecurities we each kept hidden, forcing a confrontation none of us were ready for.

All my life, I have felt unworthy, left out, unwanted—and it all adds up to what that horrid creature said: *insignificant*. How it could know this, I can't even begin to guess, but being called out like that in front of everyone has sent me into a tailspin. After everything I've faced in this place, the friendships I thought I was making… I'm no longer sure if anyone still wants me in the group. They all know what I am now, and that always leaves me on the outside looking in.

I sense his presence just before Ethan sits down on the sand near me. I've been sitting by the river, away from the group, for most of the afternoon. I know I should be helping dry things out, but I need this time alone. My mind is running in circles, trying to work things out, but nothing makes sense. I keep trying to rationalize what happened, to explain away the impossible, but it's not working. I can't explain any of it. It's too far out of my realm of experience or understanding.

Ethan reaches across the space between us and lays the compass by my hand. I brush my fingers over the tarnished case, taken aback. I hadn't even realized it was gone. Bits of sand fall away as I pick it up and flip the lid open, watching the arrow move into place. It's the only constant in all this craziness.

"I can't believe it isn't broken. How did you…?"

Ethan shrugs a shoulder, not making eye contact.

I snap the cover closed and stare back out over the water. We sit in silence for a long time, but it doesn't seem weird or strained; it's comforting, actually. It feels like I've been given space to be, with no expectation in return. I've never experienced anything like it.

"Thank you for everything you did today," I say after a while, daring to take a peek at Ethan. "I don't know if I would have made it out of there without you."

Ethan sits with his knees bent, his arms draped across them. He looks over, the corner of his mouth turning up, and points at me before tapping his chest. I saved him too.

I look around to make sure the others are out of earshot, not wanting anyone overhearing our conversation. "Can I ask you something?"

Ethan's deep blue eyes lock with mine. His posture appears casual, but I sense a tension in him—not so much nervous, but more like he's always on alert. I think he sees and knows more than the rest of us combined. His quietness makes him easy to overlook, and that may be his goal: to blend in and avoid drawing attention to himself. There's a depth to him that's well hidden, but I've seen glimpses of it—especially today. He isn't all he appears to be.

"Raoul," I say, keeping my voice low. "He knew you."

Ethan gives a slow, single nod, not breaking eye contact.

"You've met him before?"

Another nod.

"What happened?"

His gaze shifts away and he stares hard at the sand, nostrils flaring. With only a slight hesitation, he pushes up the sleeve of his shirt, revealing his arm. Pale scars crisscross his olive skin—lots of scars. This is why he never removes his long sleeves, not even earlier when he was soaking wet.

"He did that to you?" I ask, my heart pounding, unable to imagine the depth of suffering he's endured. I search his face for answers, but he continues to look away.

"Learned to walk… in shadows," he says, his voice straining to be heard. "He couldn't get… my mind… made him mad."

"So he… he tortured you?"

"Disciplined."

"That's not discipline," I say, clenching my fists. "What he did is wrong."

Ethan says nothing, his stare fixed somewhere far away.

"But you got away?" I prompt, wanting to draw him back.

He nods, the effort of talking having taken a visible toll on him. No wonder he keeps quiet.

"Your voice, did he do that too?"

He finally looks at me, a flicker of pain reflected in his eyes before he shuts it down. Anxiety rolls in my stomach as I wait for his answer. What more could possibly have been done to him?

"Fire," he whispers.

"Oh, Ethan," I choke out. "I am so sorry." I try to hold back my tears, but they roll down my cheeks anyway. All his scars, the burns, and then his voice—how was he able to overcome all that? What was he thinking when the fire erupted in the woods?

"You hurt him," Ethan replies, a gleam in his eyes. "You took... his sight." He says this like he's proud of me, which is the complete opposite of how I've been feeling. "That's good," he adds with satisfaction and the hint of a smile.

I don't know what I've done to Raoul or if he even survived the fire. I've been beating myself up over it, thinking I should've done more. But taking his eyes might have been a good thing. Without them, maybe he can't see into people and know their weaknesses. It's just a guess, though—a hope, really. I don't know for sure.

I fidget with the compass, flipping it around in my hand before tightening my grip. There's one more thing I need to know, and it's the hardest thing to ask because the answer could upend everything.

"Ethan," I say before I can change my mind. "Did you... see... anything in the fire? I mean, when you grabbed me... was there...?"

Ethan meets my questioning gaze, his eyes dark with anger. An energy emanates from him, wild and fierce, that both draws and terrifies me at the same time. I know what he's going to say, and I don't want it to be real, but his words will make it so. The creature I saw today is no longer just a dream. It's real—very real—and it has a name.

"Fire Serpent."

Chapter 7

"It's leading us away from the river," I say, peering up at Zeke. "Is that what you see too?"

"It is. The path has led us away before, but it has always returned. This time, it looks different."

Zeke and I stand along the bank of the river, working together to determine which trail to follow. It's been an intriguing experience for both of us. Zeke's "sight" returned after our encounter in the Dark Forest, and I learned it's something he's had since he was a young boy. His ability set him apart from others as he grew up; he didn't understand why they couldn't see what he did, and they feared what they didn't understand.

Although seeing the light and dark in people is like second nature for him, determining which path to follow has been a challenge. Zeke talks about the layers within the trails that the rest of us don't see. Many appear to be light but lead to darkness, and some seem dark at first, but turn to light as you walk them. It's been a steep learning curve for him over the years, marked by many trials and errors.

I can't explain why no one else has a compass, but it's helping Zeke discern the real light from the false, making it much easier to distinguish the right path. It feels good to work together, being useful without all the responsibility on my shoulders. We're building confidence—not only in the compass, but also in ourselves and each other. We've come a long way since the fire.

Right now, we're at a major decision point in the trail. There are sections when the path is well worn by many footsteps before us, making it easy to follow. Other times, like now, it's no more than a faint impression and we have to put all of our trust in the compass.

I stare out over the vast plain before us; the wind catching the tall grass and bending it to its will. If the arrow is true, our path will no longer follow the river, and that means our water supply, along with the fish we've been catching, will no longer be available. The mountain range, which has continued to grow as the days have passed, stretches out as far as I can see in either direction. We're heading right into those mountains, no matter which way we go.

"Let us fill up every container we have, just to be safe," Zeke says.

Ronnie hovers over Nola, helping her fill bottles and encouraging her to keep moving. Charlie sticks close too, not running around to explore like he has in the past. I've tried approaching Nola a few times to talk, but she refuses to acknowledge me. She does what she's told by Ronnie or Zeke, but only that. Nothing more.

We hike through the waist-high grass for the rest of the day and well into the following afternoon. Although the land appears flat from a distance, it's just an illusion. In reality, it mimics the gentle rise and fall of ocean waves, with just enough height to hide what's beyond the next crest. The snow-tipped peaks on the horizon are the only things grounding us, all hints of a trail long gone.

The monotony of the meadow is broken at last when we come over a rise and discover a city nestled at the base of the towering mountain range. This city is unlike any I've ever seen before, shaped in a perfect circle and surrounded by a high stone wall. Water, channeled from the river, flows between planted fields of fresh crops and blossoming orchards. It then curves around the city, leaving the northern section open for a variety of grazing animals and a scattering of domed windmills, their giant blades turning in slow motion.

A faint path winds down the hill before us to a wide wooden bridge straddling the almost moat, disappearing through a giant stone archway set within the wall. Another arch and pathway, complete with its own bridge, are visible to the south. Two more raised arches are visible on the outer wall, one to the north and the other to the east, where the mountains loom close. Tiny figures move along a section of walkway on the northeastern wall, but there's no way to determine what they're doing from this distance. We stop at the top of the rise and contemplate what to do.

"Does the compass take us down there?" Ronnie asks, her expression troubled.

"Yes, it points us right to it," I reply, showing her.

"I don't think that's a good idea," she says, glancing at Nola.

Nola hasn't spoken all day, and even now, just stares at the ground, uninterested in anything around her. Whatever was keeping her going before is gone. I don't know if she's going to make it much further.

"Maybe Nola and I should stay here while you guys check it out. See if there's a way we can go around."

Zeke looks down at the city, giving it a quick assessment. "I think we will have to go through."

Ethan's quiet presence moves between us. "Stay together," he rasps.

Zeke nods. "I agree. We are in need of supplies, and we may find a place to stay the night. We will stay together."

Zeke glances at Ronnie, but she doesn't argue. They've switched roles since the Dark Forest—Zeke has stepped up while Ronnie has pulled back. Nothing's been said, and I know she's been taking care of Nola, but it seems to be more than that.

A small group of travelers has just left the city and is heading uphill towards us. I nudge Zeke to get his attention. "Maybe we should wait, and see what they have to say."

We watch as the group makes its way up the hill, their steps steady, but slow. As they draw nearer, we can make out the rugged features of six men, each looking worn and tired, as if they've endured a very hard journey.

"It's not worth it! Go back now and save yourself the grief," hollers the man leading the way. His voice contains a bitterness that's hard to miss.

Zeke and I share a look. This is not what we want to hear.

As the men reach the top of the rise, their expressions show a mixture of anger and frustration. "That place will put you through the ringer for sure," says a shorter, stockier guy, shaking his head. "We couldn't take one more day. Take our advice and turn around now."

Before we can ask any questions, a commotion breaks out at the back of the group, and grumbles erupt as two men, more haggard and dirtier than the others, shove past their companions. Curses stream from their mouths as they throw furtive glances at Zeke, hurrying by with no explanation for their rude behavior.

Zeke has gone stone still, his eyes locked on the two men. A palpable undercurrent of violence radiates in the air, and it's coming from him. Ethan makes a subtle move, placing himself as a barrier in front of Zeke while keeping a cautious eye on the travelers. The leader and other men in the group shuffle in agitation, sensing the tension. With a mumble of incoherent excuses, they hurry after their friends, looking back several times to see if we're following.

Once they're out of sight, Ethan turns to Zeke, a question on his face. Zeke's posture is tense, his eyes hard and unblinking.

"Zeke?" I say.

He doesn't respond.

Ronnie approaches him, her movements slow and cautious. She puts a hand on his arm and squeezes, saying his name. He looks down at her, but I don't think he sees her.

Something has a hold of him, something deep and dangerous. Ronnie squeezes his arm again, giving it a hard shake.

"Listen to me, Zeke. You are *not* going back to that darkness. You are not that person anymore. That life is gone. It no longer exists."

Zeke doesn't acknowledge her words.

"Come on, I know you can hear me. Zeke. Oh no, don't you dare look away. You keep your focus right here. Right here. That's it. There you are."

Zeke's eyes clear, and his shoulders drop, the fury inside him easing.

"You're a good man, Zeke. I don't say that lightly. You know that. You know how hard it is, but I'll say it again. You. Are. Good." Ronnie taps his chest right above his heart. "In there. Where it counts."

Zeke closes his eyes and hangs his head. He stands like that for a long time, his chest heaving with each breath. Finally, he lifts his head and turns to look at the city.

I wait a minute or two, then ask, "What do you see?"

Taking another minute to respond, he says, "It is very dark down there. There is some light, but not much."

"Do we go?"

"If the compass says that is the way, then we will follow. It has never led us wrong."

Ethan steps beside Zeke, his posture exuding strength and confidence. There's an assurance to him that wasn't there before—an offering of loyalty and determination. This is not a man who hides in the shadows. He places a firm hand on Zeke's shoulder. "We go. Together."

Zeke nods, an understanding passing between the two. An odd feeling rises in my chest as I watch them, a blend of discomfort and something exhilarating. My respect for each of them deepens as they turn in unison to Ronnie, waiting for her response. She considers their unity, aware that a change has taken place.

"Okay," she says, turning to look down at the circular city before meeting their eyes again. "We go."

His expression remaining serious, Zeke gives us strict instructions. "We stay close together. No one wanders off alone. Our goal will be to find supplies and see about lodging for the night. If I say we leave, we leave. No arguments." He ensures each of us agrees before continuing. "Kenna, I think you should keep the compass put away for now. I do not want to draw more attention than is necessary."

Tucking the compass away in its pouch, I look at those I'm beginning to call friends. We're each as different as can be, and it's obvious we've been traveling for some time. I think we're going to draw attention, no matter where we go.

It takes some time to make our way down the trail to the bridge, which, upon closer inspection, doesn't appear as solid as it should. The thud of our boots echoes across the wood as we pass over, announcing our arrival—no quiet entry here.

The wall looms over us as we approach, at least twenty feet high, its stone smooth and bleached white from the sun. A worn flagstone path begins beneath the wide, deteriorating archway which is built from a multitude of colored rocks. The clay meant to hold it all together is crumbling, making the entire structure look unstable and ready to collapse at any moment. I hurry through, watching for falling pieces and notice the thickness of the wall. It must be at least three feet deep. This place took some time to build.

There are no guards or people to be seen anywhere along the way. We walk the wide path in eerie stillness. Stone buildings of varying sizes form rows on either side with overgrown, broken walkways leading down each section. The areas resemble little neighborhoods, now uninhabited and rundown. We pass row after row of similar-looking structures, all with the same abandoned look.

Up ahead, another crumbling archway leads into the city's center. As we step through, noise, smells, and color assault our senses with overwhelming force. A high stone wall marked with numerous deep-set archways similar to ours, encircles a large open area that reminds me of an arena. Small, grassy areas designed like miniature parks are staggered between the openings, each one filled with flowers and trees and beautifully carved benches. Red brick walkways lead from each arch, weaving together to form a wide street that circles a lively marketplace packed with colorful stalls and booths.

"Wow," I say.

There are people everywhere—and I mean everywhere. They sit in the parks, walk the paths, ride through the street, gather in groups, and wander through the marketplace. My senses are on maximum overload after being in the wilderness for a couple of weeks. My eyes jump from scene to scene and person to person, trying to take it all in.

These people are either very wealthy, or there's some sort of festival going on. There are women in colorful sarongs with scarves draped around their heads, some in slim-fitting cocktail gowns, and still others in fashionable dresses with outrageous bustles. They have braided hair, curled hair, hats, beads, tiaras, purses, parasols, and even small animals tucked under their arms or on long, thin leashes.

The men wear fancy suits of silk, suede, cashmere, and velvet. They have long coats, short coats, vests, bow ties, long ties, or no ties. Their hair is slicked back with oil, pulled into ponytails, crew cuts, shaved, and a few even pull off a gelled, spiked look.

The handful of children present are miniature replicas of their parents, marching behind the adults while mimicking their gestures and facial expressions. It's all so surreal, and I can't help but laugh at the absurdity of all this in the middle of nowhere.

"I don't think we're going to blend in," I say.

"You think?" Ronnie says, hands on her hips.

Zeke scans the throng of people, assessing the situation in that matter-of-fact way he has. "Stay close," he says as we make our way through the park area and weave across the road to the marketplace.

We pass stalls filled with beautiful clothing and every kind of accessory, expensive jewelry and fancy hats, housewares and antiques, and so many more items I can't identify. Exotic animals cry and squawk from cages and crates, while vendors bargain with the crowd passing by.

People gawk at us like we're some kind of freak show, covering their noses and turning away in disgust. A few are bold enough to call us names, and all of them avoid us like the plague. There's no one here dressed like us; even the delivery workers are better outfitted than we are, though not as fancy as the others.

We turn down aisle after aisle, searching for food vendors until we find them at the far end of the marketplace. Every type of food imaginable is available, making my mouth water at the smell of fresh bread and roasted nuts. What I wouldn't give for a piece of chocolate right now!

Zeke's attempts to buy a few items here and there are met with hostility and mockery. The vendors either ask outrageous prices or refuse to deal with him, yelling for us to move on and quit wasting their time.

With frustration, we leave the marketplace and gather in front of a burnt section of wall where there is no grass. It's an odd spot, the opposite of the rest of the pristine market area. Ronnie fusses over Nola, settling her on the ground to rest for a bit while Charlie sits at attention in front of them, watching the commotion go by. He's been subdued since the Dark Forest, refusing to leave Nola's side. I think he feels guilty for what happened to her—if a dog has feelings, that is.

"What are you thinking?" I ask Zeke, unsure what our next move is.

He's planted in front of us, arms crossed, glaring at the people as they go by. It's kind of funny to see them going out of their way to stay clear of us. It's so obvious we're not welcome here; there hasn't been one kind face in this entire market area.

"Kenna, can you verify our direction without being seen?" Zeke asks, not turning around.

Squatting beside Charlie, I give him a few comforting strokes while maneuvering the compass until it slides into my hand, warm and welcoming. After flipping it open, I take careful note of the arrow's direction, then tuck it back away. Trying to appear casual, I stretch my back as I rise and move closer to Zeke.

Interspersed between the four large archways on the inner wall are smaller arches, some bright and others dark. It's hard to tell where any of them lead, but I suspect it's into communities where all these people live.

"The third small opening to our right," I say, feigning disinterest while gazing in the opposite direction.

Zeke scowls and blows out his breath in frustration. "This place is like the Dark Forest. There are shadows everywhere."

"And the people?" I ask, scrutinizing the crowd.

"The fancy ones, they are consumed in darkness. The others, the workers, not so much."

"It's definitely the most unfriendly place I've ever been. What do you want to do?"

Zeke looks back over his shoulder at Ronnie and Nola.

"It's getting late," Ronnie says, her face creased with worry. "We're going to need shelter soon."

"We could go back to those abandoned buildings we saw on the way in," I suggest.

Ethan steps forward, entering our line of vision, and nods across the way. Someone is standing in the shadows of the archway we need, watching us. The figure turns away before I can make out any distinguishing features, but glances back at us before moving on.

"Friend or foe?" I ask Zeke.

"I do not know," he replies, his hands clenching and unclenching.

"Are you worried about something?" I ask, though I know he is. This whole place has him on edge.

"I do not think it is safe to stay here tonight," he says. "We should follow the compass and get out of the city before dark."

"You think it's any safer outside?"

"I do not know, but this place is not good."

"What about food and supplies?"

"We will make our way through and figure something out later. We need to go. Now."

The people are more vocal now, having regained their composure after our rude intrusion. They holler at us to go home, to return to where we came from. We're insulted and called filthy names—though I have no idea what most of them mean, their derogatory tone is unmistakable. It doesn't help that Charlie has begun baring his teeth at everyone, clearly not happy, whether from all the noise or because he senses their hostility. It's most likely both.

We move through the crowd, doing our best to ignore them, and make our way to the arch where the figure disappeared. This area is significantly different from where we entered the city. Once through the archway, the road is lined on either side with elegant torchlights and flowering trees. The buildings are stunning, each one unique in design and covered with ornate carvings. Sophisticated people sit on verandas or patios, overlooking gardens, ponds and landscaped yards, staring at us as we pass by. Those on the street make an exaggerated show of stepping aside, their not-so-quiet murmurs echoing after us.

The road doesn't lead us straight out of the city like we expect. Instead, it winds left and right like a maze, taking us up one way then back down another, parading us past home after beautiful home.

The closer we get to the outer wall, the more I notice the change in building structure and design. There is no longer the intricate architecture or lavish decor, just plain stone. The lights grow farther apart and the colorful brick road transforms into flat gray rock. The people we encounter are different too; their clothes are practical instead of fashionable, showing signs of wear and repair. Half-dressed children run about, playing and getting into trouble, while dogs bark and chickens squawk and flutter about. There are cows, goats, pigs and other animals confined to small walled-off areas, each one butting up against their neighbor. There are no pretty flower gardens or elegant verandas here; this is where the working class live.

The people stare at us with open curiosity, not the disdain we experienced earlier. The children laugh and point at Charlie, calling him beautiful and handsome. I swear he understands what they're saying because he's grinning like a fool. I can't believe the marked difference between here and the marketplace.

"You folks just passing through?" asks an old man, stepping out to confront us. He's thin and bent over from years of hard work, but his voice is strong and clear. He's the first person to engage with us and not hurl insults.

"Yes, sir, we are," Zeke replies, stopping in front of him.

"Well now, I can't imagine you got much of a welcome," the man says, taking in our appearance.

"No, I cannot say we did."

"You in need of anything?"

"To be honest, sir, we are in need of a few things—food, mostly. We can pay or trade. We are not looking for handouts."

The old man seems pleased with Zeke's answer and beckons us down a narrow alley between buildings. Zeke disappears into the shadows, and I look at Ethan, questioning if we should follow. He lifts his chin, indicating I should, so I turn into the alley and hurry along, not wanting to lose sight of Zeke.

Despite the obvious lack of wealth, everything here is clean and well taken care of. We follow behind the old man, weaving between more buildings until he stops at the door of a small, flat-roofed structure and knocks. The door opens a crack, and the man leans in to whisper to someone. He straightens as the door closes for a moment before swinging wide open. The old man tips his head, checking the narrow street behind us, then gestures for us to enter the building. Zeke ducks his head and steps through the low doorway. I motion for Ronnie to take Nola in, then follow behind with Ethan. The old man pulls the door shut behind us and fastens the latch.

A tiny woman with deep creases etched around her eyes and mouth greets us, her smile eager and inviting as we enter the warm stone cottage. Inside, the sizable single room is well lit by several lamps and a large stone fireplace. The woman gestures to a long wooden table to our left, its surface marked with years of use, with equally worn benches on either side. The wonderful aroma of food fills the room and I spy a cast-iron kettle simmering over the hearth.

After unloading our gear along the front wall, we slide onto the wooden benches, our bellies rumbling in anticipation. The couple works in unison, like those who have spent many years together, filling clay bowls with a thick, savory stew. They pass them down the table and we barely get our thanks out before digging in.

The man pours out water for each of us from a large pitcher and the woman approaches with a plate stacked with fresh biscuits, all lathered in homemade butter. It's all I can do not to moan with pleasure as they melt in my mouth, and I hold back a smirk when Zeke does just that. The little woman beams at him, fussing to get us anything else before she and the man take their seats at opposite ends of the table.

"I'm Marcus," the man says while we eat. "And this beautiful lady here is my wife, Hannah."

Hannah blushes and waves off her husband's flattery, though it's obvious she's pleased with his affection.

We go around the table introducing ourselves, Ronnie speaking up for Nola and Charlie. Ethan is the last one to say his name and as he does, Marcus puts down his spoon. He stares at Ethan, as if searching for something, while Ethan remains still, offering nothing in return. After a few nods, Marcus returns to his meal without a word.

A second helping of stew is passed around and we finish off all the biscuits, our stomachs full for the first time in over a week. When we're done, Ronnie and I jump up to help Hannah clear the table, refusing to let her do all the work herself. The kitchen area is small and we make quick work of washing the dishes and putting everything away. I feel guilty that we have eaten all the stew and apologize, but Hannah assures me it was meant to be shared.

When we've finished, we join the rest of the group on the other side of the fireplace, where Marcus sits in a wooden rocking chair, puffing on a pipe. Zeke and Ethan occupy a bench they pulled over, while Nola huddles on a blanket close to the fire, her knees tucked up under her chin. Charlie has made himself at home, sprawling out on the floor beside her. Hannah eases into the other rocking chair, picking up a basket of knitting, while Ronnie positions herself next to Nola, and I join the guys on the bench.

"I was just telling your friends that you're welcome to lodge here for the night," Marcus says, the pipe between his teeth. "It's not much I know, but you're welcome just the same."

"We appreciate your kindness," Zeke says, tipping his head.

"Not many Sojourners pass through here anymore," Marcus says. "It's been years since one has made it this far, and now look—there's a whole group of you." Marcus shakes his head in wonder and grins at us.

"I told you, husband," Hannah says without looking up. "They're the ones spoken of."

"I'll get to that, wife," Marcus replies.

"He'll talk you in circles if you don't keep on him." Hannah's eyes crinkle deep in their creases and she smiles at Marcus while continuing with her knitting.

"Why do you call us *Sojourners?*" I ask, wondering at the odd word.

"Well now, there's been many a name for those who walk the Path of Light to the king's city: Pilgrims, Wayfarers, Sojourners—those are the good ones. You probably heard a few of the not-so-nice ones if you came by way of the marketplace."

"That's putting it mildly," Ronnie replies.

"No doubt," Marcus says. "Used to be a day when all were welcomed here and given provision for the journey. It's a shame what's become of this place." Marcus clamps his lips around his pipe and falls silent.

"What has happened to change things?" Zeke asks, bringing Marcus back around.

"Oh, we got ourselves a new self-appointed king, is what happened. Sent his regent in with his fancy clothes and elegant talk to persuade us to change allegiance. Told everyone how much better off they'd be if they stayed here instead of trekkin' across the mountains to some place that most likely didn't exist anymore. He promised those who stayed, riches and status in this other king's kingdom. Said maybe the king would make us his capital city one day. He fooled near everyone."

"And did he fool you?"

Pulling the pipe from his mouth, Marcus lets out a long sigh. "Fooled? No. But I gotta admit, I was tempted. I had Hannah and our boys to take care of. The responsibility wears on a man, if you know what I mean."

"Yes, it does," Zeke replies.

I glance at him, surprised at his honesty. I have to admit, I've taken his strength for granted and haven't considered how this journey must weigh on him, even more now with Ronnie and Nola pulling back. My own insecurities have blinded me to the needs of those in my group, and I cringe at my lack of awareness.

"We'd already stayed here longer than we should've," Marcus says, his gnarled hand gripping the chair. "I justified it by helping others and telling myself it was good for Hannah and the boys to have stability. I convinced myself I was doing a good thing, helping people and all."

"It seemed good at the time," Hannah says, her knitting needles clicking as she rocks.

"Well," Marcus continues, "weeks turned to months and then years. By the time that fancy fool came, I'd made quite a name for myself. I was your go-to man. There wasn't a job I couldn't do or a problem I couldn't fix. I was thinking pretty highly of myself, I was."

"Yep, your britches were getting pretty tight," Hannah replies.

Marcus's eyes cut her way and Hannah lifts a brow without looking up. He chews on the end of his pipe a moment before setting it on the arm of his chair.

"As I was saying, things were going pretty well when in walks that enchanter with his enticing words and turns everyone against me—just like that—even my own sons."

My heart thuds in my chest so hard I wonder how no one else hears it. Did he just say *enchanter?* That was just a figure of speech, right? A coincidence.

Something in our expressions catches Hannah's eye, and she tells Marcus to hush a moment. "I don't believe it's my cooking causing you all distress, so it must be something Marcus said." Lowering her knitting in her lap, she scans the room.

I look away, my eyes resting on Nola. She hasn't spoken a word in days, barely eats, and stares at nothing for hours. Could the man Marcus mentioned be responsible?

"Oh no, you've met him, haven't you?" Hannah says, making the connection.

I choke back a whimper as a burning sensation ignites in my chest, the embers of anger stirring back to life. Panic surges through me. What if it grows and then explodes like before? I don't want to hurt these people. Ethan touches my arm—a soft brush, really—but the effect is enough to make the fire settle.

With relief, I duck my head, heat now flooding my face instead of my chest.

"That man has caused more harm than…" Hannah's voice trails off as she chokes back tears.

Zeke clears his throat, steering the conversation back to Marcus. "You said the regent turned the people against you, even your sons. How is that possible?"

Marcus stares at Nola, sadness written all over his face. His shoulders slump for a moment before he gives himself a shake and continues his story.

"He didn't like me from the start. I don't know how the others didn't see through his charade. They hung on his every word. I tried reminding everyone we weren't meant to stay here indefinitely. This was supposed to be a place of refuge and respite, a sanctuary to take stock, repair, and mend. Our goal was always to help the travelers and then get them on their way again.

"But my words had no effect. I was accused of wanting all the glory for myself. Of being jealous and not wanting to see others prosper. After all I'd done, it was unbelievable how hostile people became. The regent offered me a top position if I would be his *mayor*. All I had to do was encourage every traveler to give up their journey and stay here instead. When I refused, that creature went after my sons."

"What happened to them?" I ask, not sure I want to hear the answer.

"Oh, our oldest was more than happy to take over and become the town mayor. Got himself some expensive outfits and a big house. He prances around town like someone important, trying to mimic the regent. I swear he's got a different woman on his arm every week. He wasn't raised that way, that's for sure." Marcus shakes his head in disgust and fiddles with his pipe, packing in more tobacco.

With another shake of his head, his expression darkens. "Cole, our middle boy, he's not in a good place. He went with the regent for a season, against all our pleading for him not to. When he came back, he had a hardness and cruelty to him beyond anything I've ever seen. He has scars, but won't talk about them." Marcus turns to Ethan with a measured look. "And his voice, it's strained like yours, like something damaged it."

Ethan doesn't say a word, but there's a tension radiating off him that's felt by the whole room.

Marcus clears his throat and continues in a softer voice. "Our youngest boy has been gone for years now." It's Hannah's turn to shake her head, but neither of them adds anything else, and the room falls silent.

"Why didn't you leave?" Ronnie asks, her tone more curious than accusatory.

"We did actually. We crossed the Great Mountains to Neriah, the king's city, when it became clear the people here weren't going to listen to us."

Neriah. The king's city. I didn't know it had an actual name.

"Your sons did not go with you?" Zeke asks.

"No. Hardest thing I've ever had to do was leave them behind."

"But you came back?"

"Hannah and I stayed there for a season before asking if we could return. I couldn't get over all those travelers who would be waylaid and distracted into quitting. It just wasn't right. We were given permission, and a few others joined us. Our little community here is dedicated to helping those who choose to follow through and continue the journey."

"So, the city is real?" Ronnie asks, leaning toward Marcus. "And the king?"

Marcus rocks back in his chair and laughs. "Oh yes, yes, it all still exists. The king is alive and well, despite that charlatan's claims otherwise. Some things may not be what you expect, though."

At that moment, my body decides it's had enough and I stifle a yawn despite my engrossment in our conversation. Hannah catches me and sets aside her knitting, exaggerating a yawn of her own.

"Oh my, you'll have to excuse an old lady. It's getting past my bedtime, you know," she says while giving Marcus a particular look.

"Ah, well, it appears we've talked long enough. I'm sure you're all tired from your travels today, so you won't mind us turning in for the night. We can talk some more tomorrow."

Marcus stokes the fire and offers us blankets if needed, while Hannah promises a hearty breakfast in the morning. Nola's already fallen asleep, her face buried in Charlie's fur, so we cover her up and leave her where she is. The rest of us unroll our mats nearby, offering more thanks and gratitude to the couple for taking us in.

As soon as the first snore rises from the back room, I prop myself up on an elbow and whisper, "Did you guys hear Marcus say enchanter? What are the odds of that being a coincidence?"

No one answers.

"And what about their son, Cole?" I press, glancing over at Ethan, who's lying on his back, not looking at me.

Zeke takes in a deep breath and exhales with a long sigh. "I think it is best we rest now while we can. Tomorrow, we will talk and form a plan."

"Seriously?"

"Kenna, just let it go for now," Ronnie responds.

I flop onto my back in a huff. I'm tired too, but there's so much information running through my head at the moment that sleep seems impossible. Doesn't anyone care that Raoul may be this regent Marcus talked about? And who is the king he represents? Are there more kings round here than just the one we're going to? What if Raoul recovers and comes back here while we're still here? And Marcus has seen the king! He's real, or at least he was. How do we know if he's still alive and well?

I'm about to pop up and ask another question when Zeke speaks. "Kenna, we can hear you thinking. Please stop. We will work it all out. Tomorrow."

I sigh loud enough for everyone to hear and stare at the ceiling. "Fine," I mutter before another yawn takes over.

Chapter 8

I wake the next morning to a door clicking shut and the smell of fresh bread. Nola and Ronnie are still asleep, but the guys and Charlie are missing.

"Your men went with Marcus to get the sheep out to the fields," Hannah says in a soft voice from the table. "Don't worry, they won't be seen by anyone except those we trust."

I get up and join her, eyeing the fresh bread and jam on the table.

"Help yourself, hon," Hannah says, pushing the bread my way.

I cut off a thick chunk and slather it with jam.

"Are you a coffee person?" Hannah asks, reaching for a pot on the stove.

"Oh yes, please," I say, covering my mouth to prevent crumbs from spilling out all over.

Chuckling, she pours me a cup of steaming black coffee. "There's sugar and cream in front of you. Marcus still loads his up every morning, despite my protests that it ruins the flavor."

"I'm afraid that's me too. The sweeter, the better." I pour in a bunch of sugar and cream and moan with contentment after the first sip.

"Doesn't it bother you not to have any windows?" I blurt out, then slap my hand over my mouth. "I'm sorry, that was so rude."

"It's okay," Hannah says, sliding back into her chair. "It took me a while to get used to it. When we first lived here, we had a wonderful home in the western division. That's where you would've come into the city. It has a beautiful rock archway and flagstone path."

"Yeah, we went through there yesterday, but the whole area looks deserted."

Hannah sighs and shakes her head. "We built such a beautiful city; it breaks my heart seeing it come to ruin. Marcus designed that archway and the community around it. He also designed the town center. There used to be a large fountain in the middle, but it was torn down years ago to make room for the marketplace. It's all so far from what we imagined."

"Why did you build the town in a circle? I've never seen anything like it before."

"Oh, that was another grand idea of Marcus's. The city is called Kirkos, although there's been a petition recently to change it. Its simplest meaning is circle, but it also stands for unity and perfection. Kirkos was built to represent a compass used by Sojourners back in the day. Marcus had this idea that all who entered the town, no matter which way they came from, would find the true path and walk the way of the king. We lined the pathway with fruit trees and flowers, creating a beautiful lane for all to see. Its beauty drew so many and opened a door to those who were lost."

I'm blown away by her words. I try to remember what the city looked like from the hill. Four arches in the four directions. The large open center. It is the shape of a compass.

"What happened to the path? I don't remember seeing anything like that when we were in the marketplace."

"I'm afraid that's my son Cole's doing. He charged anyone entering the King's Pathway to be whipped and put on display to deter others from walking it." Hannah shudders, her grip tightening around her coffee cup. "Then, the inner arch was torched and torn down, and the hole got walled in. After all these years, I don't think anyone even remembers it was ever there."

"Except you do," I say.

"Except I do."

"Hannah, can you help me understand something? What did Marcus mean when he said you stayed too long? I don't understand why it was wrong to stay and help the people. You did so much good. Doesn't that justify your decision?"

"Oh, my dear," Hannah says, reaching across the table for my hand. "Good things aren't good if they're done in disobedience."

"What do you mean? How can good not be good?"

"We justified our goodness by our own measure, but it was never ours to decide. We were called by the king to walk the Path to his city. Taking time to rest is one thing, but to stop and decide something else is more important, and delay coming to the king, well, that's just plain disobedience."

"But you walked the Path, eventually. Doesn't that count?"

"We walked the Path in our timing, not the king's. Had we gone ahead like we were supposed to, we would've been commissioned to return and build a stronghold to aid future Sojourners. Instead, we tried to build it on our own, and lost it."

"So, does that mean there's no longer a path to the king's kingdom? It's just gone?"

"Oh, there's still a path. There's just a lot more obstacles in finding it. That's why we came back. It's our fault the way is hidden, so we're trying our best to help those who still make the journey."

A soft rapping at the door interrupts our conversation.

"Oh!" Hannah says, clapping her hands. "That'll be Keeper!"

I sit back in surprise as Hannah hurries to the door and pulls it wide open. A huge man steps forward, wrapping her in a bear-like embrace. I can't believe it. Standing in the doorway is Kohnrad. I stare at him, my jaw dropping.

Laughing, Hannah tugs Kohnrad towards the table, telling him to sit and make himself comfortable. She fusses over him, taking his coat and hat, and rushes to pour him a large cup of hot coffee.

Kohnrad maneuvers his tall frame onto a bench and reaches for his cup. He takes a sip and says with a wink, "Ahh, ain't nothin' like a good cup of black coffee."

"At least someone appreciates it the right way," Hannah replies, beaming like a proud mother.

Kohnrad's boisterous entrance, along with our loud voices, wakes Ronnie and Nola. Ronnie makes a show of folding up her things before bringing Nola to the table. Guiding her to the end of my bench, Ronnie slides in next to me while giving Kohnrad a suspicious glare.

"Girls, this is Kohnrad. He's Keeper of the Path," Hannah says while pouring coffee for Ronnie and Nola. "And this is Kenna, Ronnie and Nola. They're Sojourners. Oh, but you probably already know that. I say, this is all so exciting!" Hannah giggles. She actually giggles, then swivels around to her small kitchen, humming and dancing around while starting breakfast.

"It be good seein' ya again, Kenna," Kohnrad greets me with a grin. "Ya might wanna close yer mouth though—flies and all, ya know.

I snap my mouth shut, heat creeping up my neck. Every clever comeback seems to have fled my mind at this exact moment.

"And it be my pleasure to finally meet ya face-to-face, Veronica."

Ronnie gasps, staring wide-eyed at Kohnrad. "You?" she whispers, her voice trembling in disbelief.

Kohnrad winks and takes a long swig of his coffee. I glance between the two of them, trying to piece together what seems to be a connection.

"I be glad to see yer travelin' the right path now."

"Thank you," Ronnie replies, tears glistening in her eyes.

The low murmur of voices drifts through the door only moments before it opens and Marcus walks in with the guys close behind.

"Ah, Keeper! It's good to see you again," Marcus exclaims, taking in the visitor at our table. "Zeke, Ethan, may I introduce you to Keeper. He's a… a long-standing friend of the family."

The guys exchange nods while an excited Charlie introduces himself by jumping all over Kohnrad. He laughs at the dog's antics and gives him an affectionate pat.

"Come on, everyone, have a seat. Breakfast is ready," Hannah says, placing a dish on the floor. Charlie bolts towards it, nearly knocking it over in his enthusiasm to get at every last morsel.

Marcus sits in his chair as the guys crowd together across from us and everyone helps themselves to the spread on the table. Hannah peppers Kohnrad with questions that he tries to answer between mouthfuls of food. His affection for her is touching, and it's a bit comical watching him try to keep his gruff manners in line. It makes him more real, more relatable. Almost.

"Yer still the best cook in my books, miz Hannah," Kohnrad says, patting his stomach.

"Come now," Hannah says, blushing.

"That she is," Marcus replies, gulping down the last of his coffee. "Well, we've got some errands to run, so we'll just pop out for a bit and leave you all to your business."

"Don't worry about cleaning up. We'll get to everything later," Hannah says, sharing a secret smile with her husband.

They leave the small cottage, closing the door behind them, while we sit in silence, staring at each other.

"Would anyone care to tell me what is going on?" Zeke demands, eyeing Ronnie and me as if we have the answers.

I look to Kohnrad for help, thinking this is all his fault, only to find his eyes twinkling with amusement. Beside him, Ethan rises from the bench, creating a noticeable gap between Kohnrad and Zeke. Moving to Hannah's vacated spot at the end of the table, he pulls her chair back a space, and sits down. The shift feels intentional and doesn't go unnoticed.

Kohnrad continues to smile and shifts his posture to lean sideways against the table. "Zeke Karmichael, I's been lookin' forward to our conversin'."

"How do you know who I am?"

"I's been watchin' ya, of course."

Zeke's hands close into tight fists, and his eyes harden as he keeps direct eye contact with Kohnrad. Everything about him has gone still, just like on the hill yesterday.

"He doesn't mean that in a bad way," I say before things get any further out of hand. "He's just, um…"

"You know this man, that you can say that?" Zeke asks without looking away.

"Kind of," I say, glancing at Kohnrad. "I mean, we've met before."

Kohnrad makes no effort to put Zeke at ease; he just sits there and smiles.

"Kohnrad, you're not helping!" I say through clenched teeth, making my own fists.

"I be here as a friend," Kohnrad says, raising a brow at me.

Seriously? That's his way of diffusing the situation?

"Zeke," I say, trying to draw his attention over to me. "I met Kohnrad, I mean Keeper, at a cabin when I first got on the trail. He's the one who told me about the king and the Path and everything. I know he's… different… but he's a good person. He's called Keeper because he keeps the King's Path and… helps people."

"This is correct? You are this Keeper then?" Zeke asks, his gaze narrowed on Kohnrad.

"I be."

Zeke tears his gaze away to glance first at Ronnie, then Ethan, gauging their reaction to this story. Ethan offers a quick nod, but says nothing.

"He saved me, Zeke," Ronnie says, just above a whisper.

Zeke stares hard at her for a moment, searching for something. I don't know if he knows her story or not, but I'm now positive Kohnrad is the voice that saved Ronnie from the darkness.

Kohnrad continues to wait, his focus fixed on Zeke, who rubs a hand over his face and lets out a grunt of frustration.

"It be hard takin' on all the responsibility, I know, but yous gotta a good team here, Zeke. Trust 'em and yous'll be fine," Kohnrad says, his eyes shining with an intensity I haven't seen before. They bore right into Zeke. "These ones won't be betraying ya."

Zeke's features soften, and he blinks fast, trying to clear away tears forming in his eyes.

Kohnrad leans forward and puts a hand on Zeke's shoulder. "Yous trusted Marcus and Hannah cuz ya saw their lights," he says in a low voice. "And ya know these here be good too. But yer wonderin' why ya can't see mine. Take another look. I ain't hidin' it no more."

Zeke jerks back, his whole body quivering, and stares at Kohnrad in shock. I don't know what he sees, but it shakes him to his core and it takes a noticeable effort to pull himself together. He raises a shaky hand to his heart, then bows his head and murmurs something I don't catch.

Kohnrad gives Zeke's shoulder a brief, but firm squeeze. "We's got much to discuss, brother, but fer now, I be wantin' to help with yer broke one." He dips his head sideways, giving a discrete nod towards Nola.

"Can you help her?" I dare to ask.

"I's believin' so. She just be needin' a little help gettin' out of the darkness." He leans forward, resting his arms on the table, and fixes his gaze. "Nola… Nola… Nola… Nola," he says, his voice gentle and inviting.

I lean around Ronnie, trying to get a better view of Nola who sits motionless, her eyes vacant. Kohnrad continues calling her name like he has all the patience in the world. I wonder how long he'll continue without a response. Then, I catch the subtlest shift.

"That's it, my dear… see that light? Keep yer gaze there Nola, don't be turnin' away. Good job… that's right… take hold of 'er now. Yep, that's a girl, take hold and don't be lettin' go."

It's slow and the smallest of movements at first, but then Nola's left hand raises from her lap.

"Now lift it up and look 'round. Sees where yer at? Yous been here before, remember?"

Nola's lips tremble and release a faint whimper.

"It be okay, Nola, yer not stayin'. Yer gonna walk right outta there. See that door? Yep, that be the one. Head on over to it. That's the way, keep a goin'. Now all ya gotta do is open the door. I know yer scared, but it's gonna be alright. Yer friends are on the other side, waitin' for ya. Good… good, that's it. Okay, now step on through. Ya gotta go through it, Nola. Come on…come on through to us. I know ya can do it. Yer stronger than the darkness. Come on, Nola… that's it."

Nola gasps, her breath quick and uneven. She blinks several times, raising a hand to cover her eyes as if the light's too strong. She soon lowers her arm and looks around the room in confusion.

"You're here. You didn't leave me."

"Oh Nola, we never left you," I reply, blown away by what has just happened.

Looking around again, the remnants of fear dissipate from her eyes.

Ronnie hesitates, then reaches forward. "Are you alright?"

Nola lifts a shoulder in a semi shrug, turning just enough to miss Ronnie's outstretched hand. "Yeah, I think so," she replies, avoiding Ronnie's questioning look. "I… I don't really understand how… where…"

"Do ya remember what happened?" Kohnrad asks, drawing Nola's eyes to his.

She looks at him with a puzzled expression, then frowns in concentration. "We were in the woods. A dark woods. There was this light, and then… a voice. It was… it was the most beautiful voice I've ever heard, and it… reached inside me, and wrapped itself around my heart. It was pulling me, drawing me into a bright light. But… it didn't feel right. There was something… off. I tried to pull back, but I couldn't. I… I had no strength to fight it. Then there was this awful pain. It hurt so bad, like a burning. It felt like I was on fire. I wanted it to stop, but it wouldn't. It wouldn't stop!" Nola rubs a hand over her heart and rocks back and forth, crying.

"It's okay. You're okay now," Ronnie says, rubbing her back. "You're here with us. We won't let anything hurt you again."

Nola stiffens at Ronnie's touch, but doesn't pull away.

"The darkness ain't just in the woods or on a wrong path. It be in yer mind too," Kohnrad says, looking around at all of us. "If yous allow it in, it'll infect yer heart."

"That is the difference," Zeke says, interrupting the silence that had settled. "What I see in people, that is the difference. Those who are swallowed in darkness, their entire being is black. But in others, there is still a light, however dim, surrounding their hearts. It is their minds that are darkened."

Kohnrad grins at Zeke, nodding his head in agreement. "Yer gift of sight's correct. Yer gonna find most people be livin' in the Shadowlands. The light in 'em ain't able to shine fully 'cause of the shadows in their minds."

He shifts on the bench and tilts his head to include the group in his meaning. "Each of ya has areas of shadow that needs be overcome—hurts and unforgiveness that cloud yer thinking. If yous continue to hold on to 'em, yer heart will harden and become shadowed."

"Huh. So what are we supposed to do? Just forget? Pretend nothing happened to us?" Ronnie asks, pushing away from the table.

Her reaction surprises me with its intensity.

"What does it do fer ya to hold on to it, Veronica?" Kohnrad asks. "Unforgiveness always leads to bitterness, and bitterness be a deep darkness that envelopes yer heart and eats away at it."

"Oh!" Nola cries, her head bobbing up and down. "That's what happened to me! I remember! The voice... it was so beautiful, but its words were... toxic. It burned my heart. I-I could feel it eating away the goodness. Then... it became dark. So dark. I couldn't see or hear. There was just... nothing."

"Yous walked many a path in the Shadowlands, Nola. Yer able ta recognize most of 'em and have chosen to stay on the Path of Light. That be good, but ya started out on an old path— one that got distorted over the years, and it be influencing yer way of thinkin'. There be no easy way to the king's kingdom. Yer hurts and yer misconceptions are needin' to be set aside, or yer always gonna be susceptible to the darkness."

There's an uncomfortable feeling squirming in my chest, one I can't quite put my finger on. Kohnrad's words are having a strange effect. It's like he's digging at something and doing it on purpose.

Tears stream down Nola's cheeks as she breaks into earnest sobs. Ronnie doesn't move to comfort her this time. Instead, she sits with her arms crossed over her chest, her whole body shaking. She narrows her eyes at Kohnrad, anger blotching her cheeks a deep crimson.

At the edge of the bench, Zeke holds his head in his hands. His muscles ripple under his shirt every few seconds, his shoulders curling forward as if in pain. Or maybe it's deep sorrow. Maybe both.

Ethan sits apart from the group, watching everything unfold in his usual quiet way. His face remains neutral, yet his eyes are sharp and observant. It's odd, but he seems untouched by the heavy weight of the moment.

Kohnrad also watches and waits, giving us time to collect ourselves, then continues to prod. "Each of ya must face the darkness in yer mind and choose to let it go."

"What if we can't?" Ronnie asks, her tone downright hostile.

"There be a difference 'tween can't and won't. One just needs a bit of help. The other be a decision. One that chooses to embrace darkness over light."

Ronnie reacts as if she's just been punched in the gut. She bends in half, guarding her stomach, the color draining from her cheeks.

Kohnrad motions to me. "Kenna, there be a burnin' inside ya. Yous felt this?

Panic surges as the burning in my chest bursts into a flame and my throat goes dry, making it nearly impossible to swallow. What is he doing?

"There be different types of Fire. Knowin' which one be needed is a gift not many experience. It takes a Called One to carry such a burden."

"What does that have to do with me?" I ask, swallowing hard. I don't like where this is going. Why is he stoking the fire inside me? How does he know it's there?

"Yous been called. Called by the Fire to carry its Flame."

"What does that mean? Why me?"

"It ain't a responsibility to be taken lightly. There be great power in ya, Kenna. If ya don't be learnin' to use it correctly, it'll consume not only yerself, but those 'round ya."

I stare at Kohnrad in disbelief. I didn't ask for this. Why have I been chosen? There's got to be some mistake—I'm nobody. No one has ever needed me or even wanted me. Yet, I can feel the fire inside. It burns in my chest, a deepening ache that longs for something I don't understand.

"Burning One," Zeke murmurs, nodding in agreement.

His words intensify the fire within and I stare at Kohnrad, paralyzed with fear. I don't know what he wants me to do.

"Kenna," Kohnrad says, his voice steady and reassuring. "Look inside."

I can't. I don't know how. What does he mean?

"Close yer eyes and look inside yer heart. Do ya see the Flame?"

I close my eyes, expecting darkness, but there's a soft glow of light in the distance. I can hear Kohnrad, but see inside myself at the same time.

"Can ya see the Fire?" Kohnrad asks again.

"Yes," I whisper, feeling strange. My body tingles in anticipation, while my mind races with anxiety.

"Good, now move yerself closer."

"I-I don't know how."

"It be the same as out here. Just take a step forward in yer mind."

I will myself forward and startle when I look down and see my body moving.

"Whoa."

My pulse pounds in my ears, matching the pace of my racing heart. Sucking in a shaky breath, I search around me, but there's nothing to see except myself and the light ahead. I continue to draw nearer and soon make out a flame of fire set on a chest-high pillar of white, polished stone. The flame burns with an unusual intensity, but somehow doesn't consume the pillar.

I hear Kohnrad's voice, soft and commanding. "Kenna, reach yer hand out to the Fire."

Is he crazy? Yet I reach out, scared to do what he says, but unable to ignore his command. I feel the heat as my hand nears the flame and hesitate.

"It won't burn ya unless you be misusin' it."

A halo of vibrant blue light encircles the base of the fire, pulsing up and down in slow motion. I stretch my fingers closer, mesmerized by the flame's raw beauty. The heat engulfs my hand as I slip it deeper into the flame, but doesn't burn me, just like Kohnrad said.

A force of energy pushes my arm up, and a small flame appears in the palm of my hand. I can feel it—a rhythm, like music, dancing across my hand and reverberating up my whole arm into my chest. It feels alive, like it's part of me. How that's possible I don't know. I step away and watch in amazement as the small flame stays with me, pulsing to the rhythm of my heart.

"Open yer eyes, Kenna."

It seems strange since I can already see, but I concentrate and open my eyes, the room coming back into focus. I search my hand for the fire, but nothing's there.

Disappointment floods through me, and I look up at Kohnrad. "Where did it go?"

"Take another look. It be there."

I look again, focusing harder this time, and a faint blue wave of light appears, pulsating around my entire hand. The sensation of heat hits while a faint vibration tingles along my palm. A rush of unexplainable joy races through me, as though the fire itself is the source.

Ethan leans forward in his chair, a faint smile tugging at his lips.

"Do you see it?" I say, noticing his expression.

"See what?" Ronnie asks, a frown creasing her forehead. She shoots Zeke a questioning look, but he doesn't notice. His attention is focused on my hand.

"You don't see the color, the blue around my hand?" I reply, lifting my arm to show them.

Nola shakes her head, confusion clear on her face, but Zeke, though he says nothing, appears mesmerized. Ronnie's scowl deepens, and she tightens her arms over her chest.

"What do I do with it?" I ask Kohnrad, trying not to let Ronnie's reaction get to me.

"Ya give it away."

"What? Why?"

"Cuz it ain't fer yerself. Yer a Fire Holder. A restin' place for the Flame. If ya choose to keep it to yerself, yous gonna lose control of it and it'll consume ya. If ya use it wisely, givin' it away where it be needed, then yous gonna grow with it. It'll teach ya if yous let it, but never be assumin' ya understand its power, for it can't always be understood."

"In the woods. I felt it, but I… it…"

"It be a weapon as well as a gift. Yous gotta learn the difference."

Kohnrad looks at Ronnie, his eyes searching, and her posture stiffens under his probing gaze. He doesn't press her further, but instead moves on, turning his attention to Nola.

"Nola, yous be ready to let go of some of the darkness perm'nently? Are ya willin' to fergive yerself and let the past go?"

"I want to, yes, but I don't think I'm strong enough," Nola says, hanging her head.

"If yer willin', that be a start. It'll take time for ever'thing to be revealed and worked through. Only an open heart can accept what will be given. Are ya willin'?

Nola lifts her head, hope filling her eyes. "I-I think so. Yes. Yes, I am."

"Well then," Kohnrad says, turning his attention to me. "Kenna, yous gotta give her the Fire."

Without warning, Ronnie shoves herself up from the bench, elbowing me hard in the shoulder. The force knocks me sideways, and I wince, caught off guard by her abrupt reaction. Her face is flushed with fury, and for a moment, I'm overcome by her hostility. Without turning her back on us, she makes her way across the room and plants herself by the fireplace. Her whole demeanor is rigid and unyielding, daring anyone to approach.

At a loss for words, I turn to Nola, unsure if I should continue. This is all so strange—the Fire, Ronnie's reaction, Nola's wide eyes darting between Kohnrad and me. I don't know what I'm supposed to do, how I'm supposed to proceed. Does she remember what happened in the woods? Does she remember the fire? She hasn't asked about Bert or Raoul, but she hasn't yelled at me either, so maybe…

"Go on," Konrad says, an earnestness in his gesture urging me down the bench.

I inch closer to Nola, giving her time to refuse if she wants, but the words don't come. Instead, she offers a timid smile, tears hovering in the corners of her eyes.

"Are you sure?" I ask.

"Yes," she whispers.

The Fire surges at her reply, and the heat around my hand deepens, while the burning in my chest intensifies. Time seems to slow, everything happening with a dreamlike weight as I reach out, the tips of my fingers brushing her forehead. A searing pain shoots up my arm, and I gasp, unable to hold back a cry of shock.

"Hold steady!" Kohnrad commands before I can pull away.

The sensation is similar to a jolt of static electricity, sharp and buzzing through my arm into my chest. I grit my teeth, fighting the urge to pull away, and lean in as Nola's head falls back. Anguish and joy cross her features—a contradiction that somehow makes sense deep inside my gut. The heat and pain lessen, then vanish as if they never existed, and I pull my hand away. The Flame, along with its power, has disappeared.

"It's gone!" Nola exclaims. "Oh, thank you! It's gone! I feel so… clean!" She looks around in astonishment. "I can't believe it. I felt it. Kenna, I felt the Fire. It burned away the darkness!"

Throwing herself against me, Nola squeezes me tight, laughing and crying at the same time. I try to return her embrace, but she has me pinned against her.

"So, does this mean you're not mad at me anymore?" I mumble into her shoulder.

"Why would I be mad at you?" she replies, pulling away.

"You don't remember?"

"Remember what?" Nola wrinkles her brows, her eyes shifting sideways as she tries to think.

"The Dark Forest," I say. "And… Raoul."

Nola tilts her head, eyes narrowing as she tries to work out what I'm saying. "Raoul." His name rolls off her tongue like a question, uncertain and searching. "His voice… he was…"

I hold my breath, waiting for her to finish.

"He wasn't… good."

"No, he wasn't," I reply with a sigh.

Nola looks over at Kohnrad. "It was Raoul. He was the one who hurt me, right?"

"He did," Kohnrad says, his eyes filled with compassion.

"And you helped me find my way back."

"I just led ya to the Light. Yous did the rest yerself."

"Thank you. Thank you for showing me the light."

"Yer welcome, Nola."

Nola straightens her posture, a fierceness shining in her eyes as she looks back at me. "You hurt him. You hurt Raoul."

"Yes." A flutter of nervousness swirls in my belly.

"You hurt him bad?"

"I think so. I… I blinded him."

"Good."

"Good?"

"Yeah," Nola says, her voice gaining strength. "Yeah. Good."

I cover my face with my hands, dragging them down to my mouth. Whatever all this was that just happened has changed things. A door has opened—one I didn't realize had been locked shut. What it released has been waiting for a long time and it soars around me now, rejoicing in its freedom.

This thing I can name. It's hope.

"Your Majesty?"

"Yes, Messenger, you have news?"

"Yes, Your Majesty. The Keeper has entered the city and found the Sojourners."

"What of the woman? Has she been told who she is?"

"Yes, Your Majesty."

"And the Regent. He has not returned?"

"No, Your Majesty. It is unknown what has become of him. There is a word going around, though, Your Majesty. I hesitate to say anything without confirmation, but…"

"You may tell me. I will decide what to do with the information."

"Yes, Your Majesty. The word is the Dark One is on the move. He seems to have stepped up since the Regent's disappearance."

"I see. I do believe he will prove much more troublesome than his predecessor."

"That, too, is the consensus of the Watchers, Your Majesty."

"We will need to be very careful. I do not want him knowing we have been in his city. Have the Watchers keep cover for a few more days. If the Dark One returns, they are to leave at once and report back to me. Make sure Keeper is made aware."

"Yes, Your Majesty.

Chapter 9

"You are self-sufficient from the rest of the city," Zeke says, admiring the surrounding community.

"We have to be. Like you, we're not very welcomed in the Marketplace," replies Marcus.

We've been walking around most of the day, meeting the people in this tight-knit little community. They're delighted to have us, showering us with gifts, supplies, and food, while the children run circles around Charlie, throwing sticks and balls, taking their turns petting him. He basks in all the attention, and I grin at his tolerance and gentleness with these little ones. Nola's a hit with the kids too. They vie for her attention just as much as Charlie's. She laughs, threatening them with tickles as they scream and let themselves get caught.

A few of the older folks share stories of those who came before us, reminiscing about the good old days when the city was a place to be proud of. Their kindness towards us is refreshing, and it's plain to see they admire and love Marcus. Despite the difficulties of life here, the people still carry a joy and resilience that permeates the atmosphere.

Kohnrad and Ethan leave together on an errand while the rest of us make our way back to the house. It's been nice to take time and enjoy ourselves today. Still, I'm curious about the rest of the city. It's an odd mixture of old and new.

"Are there other little communities like this throughout the city?" I ask Marcus.

"There sure are. Some are like ours, with the people working together and helping one another out. Most though, are run by gangs of thieves that steal from whoever they can and destroy what little they have. They're filthy and run down, lacking even the most basic of necessities."

"That's awful."

"Yes, it's very sad. We try to go in where we can, but most folks in those communities are so full of anger and bitterness, they refuse our help. You've noticed most homes here don't have any windows and the roofs are stone, not thatched?"

"I have noticed," Zeke says, his eyes taking in the buildings.

"Why don't you have windows?" I ask. Hannah never did say.

"Well, every once in a while, one of them hotshots over there gets too big for his britches and thinks he can come over here and take over. They've tried to break in and burn us out, so we've made our homes burglar proof and fireproof. They've tried to steal our animals, so we've trained dogs and set up guards. All told, they're pesky at best—not really smart enough to do much more than cause mischief." Marcus shrugs. "So far anyway."

"We saw windmills outside of the city. You have wells?" Zeke says, his admiration for Marcus clear.

"We do. They're mainly for the stock in the outer fields away from the river. Beats having to haul buckets, that's for sure. We got a mill and a small dairy too. Fuel is a problem, though. We depend on the Traders to bring in what we need. Of course, we don't actually trade in the Marketplace, but we have a few folks who are willing to come around and make a deal on the side. Keeps the lights on, so to speak. The other communities struggle for supplies. Most of them have nothing, or very little, anyways."

"And the ones from the Marketplace?"

"They have their communities too. They're a lot better off than the rest of us. I'm sure you saw their fine clothing and elaborate homes when you came through. They take the best for themselves and leave the leftovers for the rest to fight over. They got a hierarchy based on riches and status. It's a brutal system. Every day, they have to prove themselves worthy to hold their position. They strut around and show off like peacocks. Annoying birds, those peacocks. Beautiful, but have you ever heard their call? Just awful. Anyways, they'll stab you in the back so fast you won't know it happened 'til it's too late. They all report to Cole, and he don't tolerate anyone questioning his word. We keep to ourselves as we can and stay off his radar. We get some leeway, being family and all, but not much. Like I said earlier, no one's been down this way for years, so we're mostly left alone."

"I thought you said your older son runs the city," I say, turning to face Marcus and Zeke while Ronnie and Nola wander ahead of us.

"Bah, in name only. He's just a pretty puppet. That boy ain't gotta brain cell left in his head. Cole's the one that really runs the show, and he don't show much mercy, I'm afraid. His hatred for the king drives him to destroy everything and everyone he can. He's referred to as the Dark One around here cuz his soul is darkened more than any other. I can't believe what that boy's become."

"You will be in danger for helping us then," Zeke says, the conversation turning serious.

"There's a good chance he'll find out you came through here, and he won't be happy. We'll tell him you turned back, but I doubt he'll believe us. He knows we work against him when we can. Our purpose here isn't hidden. I'm surprised he's tolerated us as long as he has, actually. It won't last. I've no illusions about that. I'm not sure when he'll return, so it's best if you move on as soon as possible."

I pull Zeke aside and fill him in on the closing of the path. He frowns, working out how we'll get out of the city. Trying to move a whole group undetected is going to be tricky.

His thoughts work their way around and he looks at Marcus. "Is there a way for us to get out of the city without being seen?"

"Yes, of course. There's an entry into the Pathway that is known only by Hannah and myself," Marcus answers. "Tonight, after dinner, we'll go for a walk and I'll show you."

***

"Once we leave the community, we'll be heading into some sketchy areas. We're near the northern gate now and will work our way southeast. Stick to the shadows and don't engage with anyone, just keep moving. They've got security closer to the Marketplace, so whatever happens, don't go that way. It's not safe for you there. Also, the later we're out here, the more dangerous it is, so we're gonna get there and back as quick as possible. I'm sorry, I wish it were easier."

"We are grateful for your help," Zeke says, gesturing for Marcus to lead the way.

When Marcus turns, Zeke gets my attention and nods at my compass pouch. Nodding in return, I acknowledge his silent request and step behind Ethan, falling to the back of our little group.

It doesn't take long to move out of Marcus's community. He wasn't exaggerating; the difference is stark. There are very few street lights working, and the ones that are do little to fight back the darkness. The area is dirty and run-down, with sewage flowing in a ditch next to the street. The stench is awful. We cover our faces, breathing through our mouths to keep from gagging. Only a few people are out as we make our way along the streets. Most are in for the night, their candles or oil lamps casting an eerie glow through their windows.

I have a hard time keeping an eye on Ethan. He blends into the deeper shadows, disappearing for extended periods, then showing back up without a sound. It's uncanny, and if I didn't know he was real, I'd be tempted to think he was a ghost.

We continue weaving between streets and alleys, sticking close to the buildings. The compass has been matching our way so far, but I'm worried. I hope Zeke and Ethan have a good sense of direction, because there's no way I'm going to remember this route. And if we try to move the group through here with just the compass, I'm afraid it will take too long and someone will discover us.

The occupied homes soon disappear, and we come to a dark, deserted area with broken walls and burned-out buildings. It looks like a war zone with all the destruction. Dead, broken trees are scattered everywhere and there are more weeds than stone on the road before us. The wind blows garbage across the street, and a stray cat runs along a building, disappearing into an alleyway. Ethan disappears too, so I move in closer to Zeke, shuddering at the eeriness of this place.

A crude, uneven brick wall soon looms in front of us, its rough surface a sharp contrast to the beautiful stone we've seen throughout the city. Marcus slows, his gaze flickering over the shadows, assessing the stillness of the street before leading us on. We follow the wall for some distance before stopping next to a mound of dead trees and brush. Marcus motions for us to stay quiet while he once again peers into the darkness. Satisfied no one is watching, he leans over and pulls away a section of branches from the wall, revealing an opening just large enough for a person to pass through. Keeping an eye on the area behind us, he motions for Zeke to go ahead, and I dart after him, not wanting to be separated.

"Whoa!" I whisper, looking around in amazement.

We've entered an overgrown wonderland. Hannah's story from this morning runs through my mind as I take it all in. Without a caretaker, the plants and trees have spread over everything except a long, golden pathway. I step under a flowering tree, inhaling its sweet scent, and out onto the walkway. Amazing! The path has a soft, iridescent glow, just enough to light the way ahead, but subtle enough to be contained within the pathway itself and not the surrounding garden.

"This is incredible," I say, watching the compass align its golden arrow with the luminous path before me.

"You're a Compass Bearer," Marcus says next to me, staring at the compass. "I haven't seen one of those for a very long time, and never one like that."

"The pathway glows like the arrow," I say, forgetting to be discreet.

"Yes, it's a special rock from the king's quarry. Another thing that's been destroyed." Marcus shakes his head in sorrow and looks around. I'm sure he's remembering how things once were.

He remains lost in thought as I turn around, trying to take it all in. It's so beautiful and there's an innate sense of joy in this place. I can envision travelers and the excitement they must have felt making the journey down this path. What a blow it must have been to lose this.

"Goodness me!" Marcus clutches his chest, the words bursting from him. "Well, young man, you've just confirmed my suspicions."

My heart pounding, I follow his gaze to find Ethan just a couple of feet away. Zeke steps beside him, the two of them an imposing presence.

"Hold on now! No need to get all riled up," Marcus says, throwing his hands up as if surrendering. "It's just been a while since I've been around a Shadow Walker. It takes a bit of getting used to, having someone appear out of nowhere like that."

That's what Raoul called Ethan: Shadow Walker. I move closer, the need to shield him stirring inside me. I grimace at the absurdity of the thought—he doesn't need my protection—but I don't move away.

"There are others?" I ask, looking between him and Marcus.

Marcus lowers his hands and gives Ethan a respectful nod. "A few over the years. It's a strange calling, not one for the faint of heart. Takes a strong character and uncanny intuition. The only ones I've known had a direct commission from the king himself. There's a testing required that most people can't endure. Trial by Fire, I've heard it called. Torture is what is sounds like. Either way, those who walk the shadows are the strongest on the path. They're the only ones impervious to the call of the darkness. Them and Keeper."

I whip around and face Ethan, firing off questions. "Is this true? Is that why Raoul called you that? What he did to you, was that your test?"

Ethan looks down at me, his eyes dark and dilated. His voice is hoarse, raw with emotion, not just damage. "Trial by Fire... yes. Given a choice... I chose to walk."

He chose the Fire. He knew, and he still chose it.

"That does explain a few things," Zeke says with a faint smile. He nods at Ethan, similar to how Marcus did—a show of respect and honor.

Ethan says nothing, but a quiet understanding passes between him and the two men. Zeke's right; it does explain some things—like Ethan's ability to blend in no matter where we are, his quiet observance and attention to everything, his strength and quick thinking. I no longer see a young man with scars standing before me; I see a warrior with battle wounds.

I'm not ready to let him off the hook, though. He has some more questions to answer first.

"You know Kohnrad. Keeper. You've met him before today. Am I right?"

Ethan's eyes twinkle and his mouth tips up in a lopsided grin. "Yes. Captain."

"Captain? You've known him this whole time?" I glare at Ethan, my hands resting on my hips.

Not the least bit intimidated, he nods and waits for my response, that knowing grin still on his face. I wish I could be mad at him, but I can't. He's done nothing to betray us; he just hasn't offered information we didn't think to ask. Now that sounds familiar. And Kohnrad… he's turning out to be more than I first thought as well.

"I'm sorry, but we must head back," Marcus says, halting the conversation. "These are the hours of the troublemakers, and I don't want them finding us anywhere near the wall."

Throwing Ethan a look that says we'll talk more later, I follow Marcus through the hole in the wall. We wind our way back, taking a few detours to avoid the sounds of laughter and shouting from people nearby. When we return, Ronnie and Nola are deep in conversation with Hannah. Charlie lifts his head to look at us before lying back down, choosing the warmth of the fire over saying hello.

The men gather around the table to discuss plans, and Zeke calls Ronnie to join us. Nola stays by the fire with Hannah, the two huddled together, talking and holding hands, oblivious to the rest of us. Marcus unfolds a sheet of paper, laying it on the table, his rough hands smoothing out the wrinkles.

"Here's a list of items you'll need to get through the Great Mountains."

"I don't suppose there's a magic wand that can transport us over them?" I mutter under my breath, nervous now that we're getting closer to doing this. Zeke throws a disapproving look my way, not finding any humor in my comment.

"Sorry," I mumble, though I still wish there was some other way.

Marcus continues with his instructions, his demeanor as serious as Zeke's. "It's a tough trail over the mountain. You'll want your packs light—any extra weight will tire you out and slow you down. The air's thin up there, and you're gonna feel it, so stay hydrated. I'll have a mule for you tomorrow. You won't be able to take him through the wall, so I'll send a boy out across the fields and have him tie him to a tree just inside the woods. I can't take a chance of drawing attention, so he'll only be carrying water bags. You'll have to pack everything else out and then switch things over when you get to him. He's sure footed and been up the mountain many times, so he shouldn't give you much trouble."

Ronnie butts in. "Why are we going through the city when you just said you're going to take the mule across the fields? Wouldn't it be easier for us to go that way instead?"

"Easier, yes. Safer, no. There's no protection out there. Everyone has access to the fields and would report you long before you made it to the path. There's also guards stationed along the wall keeping things in order. If they recognize you, they'll shoot, no questions asked. Like I said earlier, they've got orders to not let any travelers through. Especially those on the King's Path."

"They'll shoot us, as in kill us?" Ronnie asks, an eyebrow raised.

"Everything opposed to this path is out to kill you — all of you. If you haven't figured that out yet, then you need to understand it right now. We're not playing games here. People have died protecting this path. I'm putting my community in danger by having you in my house. If you're not fixed on walking this path, no matter the consequences, then you need to head on out the way you came, right now."

No one breathes or moves a muscle, including Hannah and Nola. All eyes are on Ronnie. She looks shocked. No one's ever questioned her motives. Harold may have challenged her ability to lead, but never her devotion to the Path. There's always been an unspoken acceptance that she, and the others, are set on finishing this journey. I've never heard anyone say otherwise.

Ronnie's face is beet red, her lips pressed together in a thin line, her jaw twitching. The silence stretches on and she doesn't break it—doesn't apologize, doesn't explain.

"I mean no disrespect, Ronnie, but you're obviously struggling with something," Marcus says, his voice calm but firm. "For the safety of all of us here, you need to get things figured out—and soon. We'll help you if we can, but you can't lead this group if you're not sure of yourself or where you're going."

Ronnie's fury is undeniable now. We can all see it.

"Is that what you think?" she growls, her eyes sweeping over us. "You all think I'm unstable? Poor Ronnie, she's lost it, can't seem to get her act together. It's to be expected from someone like her. Is that what's going on here?"

We sit in stunned silence. Ronnie's eyes are wild and accusing. I've never seen this side of her—her wounds so open, so raw. My heart aches, and I sense a burning welling up in my chest. I remember Kohnrad's words from this morning: What darkness is Ronnie holding on to that she won't give up?

"Ronnie, maybe I can—"

"No!" she snarls, shoving herself away from the table. From me. "You *will not* touch me. I don't need your fire!" She jerks away, her voice hard. "I have every right to hold on to my anger. The things done to me, that I had no control over, no say in." Her breath hitches, a tremor in her voice. "No woman should *ever* be made to do those things. To *be* those things."

Her gaze sharpens, and her voice drops. "How could Keeper tell me to forgive? A man," she scoffs, "right, as if. No *man* has any right to tell *me* to forgive. I will never forgive. Never!"

Ronnie stands over us, gasping for breath, tears of anger stuck in the corners of her eyes. Her hands clench into tight fists, and she looks ready to attack anyone who dares confront her.

No one says a word or moves to comfort her. Who could after that outburst? The logs snap in the fireplace, and a chair creaks as someone rises. Hannah approaches and, without touching Ronnie, offers what we can't.

"Ronnie, dear, I am so sorry for your pain. I can't imagine what you've gone through. How unfair it seems. It's too much to ask. I know what that feels like. Why don't you come with me? We'll have a sit down, just the two of us, and talk. Woman to woman."

Hannah's voice is gentle and understanding. No condemnation. No pity. Just compassion and love. Ronnie looks at her, her face twisted with pain. She must see the sincerity in Hannah's expression because, without a word, she lowers her head and allows Hannah to lead her away.

"We'll just go next door and visit a neighbor," Hannah says, her arm wrapping around Ronnie's waist. "She's a widow and deaf as a doornail. She won't mind the hour and will give us some privacy to talk."

Hannah leads Ronnie outside, pulling the door shut behind her. The latch clicks into place, and the room falls into an uneasy silence.

"Well," Marcus says, clearing his throat. "I'm sorry that all erupted like that, but better here and now than later on the trail. If anyone can help her, it'll be my Hannah."

Zeke sits with his head bowed over his hands, his face etched with anguish. "She will let no one in to help her. She does not know how. Her wounds are deep and festering. I am afraid for her." Zeke's voice cracks as he struggles to contain his emotions.

Nola slides onto the bench next to him, placing a hand over his. He turns his head, acknowledging her with a tight smile, then looks away, removing his hand from hers. Hurt flashes across Nola's face as she slips her hands into her lap.

"I wish you had more time. I really do," Marcus says, leaning in towards Zeke. "But you need to leave soon. Tomorrow is packing day, and I'll send the mule. You'll need to head out very early the next morning, before dawn, when all the revelers have worn themselves out and drunk themselves into a stupor. That'll be the safest time, but you won't be able to use any light until you get out and up the path. The guards shouldn't follow you, but their arrows have a good range, so please, be careful until you reach the woods. They don't pay as much attention to the King's Trail these days, but it'll be better for us if you're not seen."

Ronnie's outburst has magnified the seriousness of the situation. If she isn't okay, are we going to leave her behind? I don't think Zeke will, but if she's a liability, will he have a choice? Or... will he choose to stay behind with her? Maybe I could stay with her instead. Then I wouldn't have to cross the mountains. Or—

"Oh, I almost forgot," Marcus says, interrupting my thoughts. "There's an iron gate across the archway to keep travelers from accessing the path. You'll need a key to open it. To the right of the gate, in the stone archway, along the bottom, there's a loose rock. Pull it out, and you'll find the key. You won't be able to lock up after you leave, so please put the key back where you found it. I'll return in a night or two and lock things up. Also, there's no path through the field anymore. It grew over years ago. But once you reach the trees, you'll find it right quick. That's where the mule will be."

Marcus works his way down the list, filling us in on what we'll need for supplies and gear. He advises us to ditch our small personal tents and take on two large, heavy-duty ones instead.

"You're better off grouping together at night for warmth, and having a spare could save your life. I've got coats and blankets and such for you. There's also a tunnel full of supplies, so anything you forgot or run short on, you can restock from there. You'll want to get up there as quick as you can. Keeper said it was open a few days ago, but storms can roll in without warning. Could be rain, hail, or snow—sometimes all at once—and all in a short amount of time. That tunnel will be the only shelter you'll have on the mountain top. Past it, the other side's the worst for weather. You'll hit snow there for sure."

The guys continue to work out the logistics while Nola and I move away to get the sleeping mats ready. I can't help the excitement in my voice as I lean in, keeping it low, and tell her about finding the Path behind the wall and my discovery regarding Ethan.

"That makes sense, I guess," she says, not showing as much interest as I thought she would.

"What does?"

"About Ethan. You know, how he moves between trails. I wondered how he managed that trick." She shrugs a shoulder and throws a mat down. "Now we know."

Trick? Her cavalier attitude irritates me. How can she be so dismissive? I think back over our journey so far and realize I've never seen her have a conversation with Ethan. In fact, she's been rather unfriendly towards him from the start.

"Don't you like Ethan?" I whisper, not wanting him to overhear.

She shrugs again. "He's kind of creepy, if you ask me. Like, he never says anything, he just watches everyone. It makes me uncomfortable."

"He saved you from the fire, Nola. And he talks. It's just difficult, because his voice is damaged."

"Well, I didn't any of know that, so you can't expect me to feel sorry for him like you do."

"I don't feel sorry for him! He's stronger because of what he's gone through. I have compassion and admiration for him."

"Sure, whatever. Call it what you want. He's so not my type, so if you're interested, by all means, knock yourself out."

I freeze, my hand gripping a blanket, unsure if Nola just said what I think she did.

"He's my friend," I say, trying to keep my voice low, but anger creeps in.

"Great. I'm sure that makes you feel good. I bet he needs friends."

"Nola, that's rude and uncalled for."

Nola looks up, surprised by the sharpness in my voice. "I didn't mean anything by it. If you want to be friends with the guy, go ahead. It's your choice."

"You could be friends with him too, if you got to know him."

"Yeah, so not interested," Nola says, straightening up from a mat. She looks over at the guys with an impish smile. "I've got my sights on someone better."

I glance behind me to make sure they're not looking at us. "You mean Zeke?"

"Of course," she answers, rolling her eyes.

"But he's with Ronnie."

Nola stops what she's doing and puts a hand on her hip. "Not necessarily," she says with a hint of attitude. "I mean, he cares for her and all, but I don't think it's romantic. Like, he's not in *love*-love with her. She's too old for him." Nola shakes her head, as if a relationship with Ronnie is some kind of joke.

"Age doesn't always matter with love," I reply. And Ronnie isn't *that* much older than Zeke.

"Right, but it's something else. Zeke told me a while back that Ronnie saved him. He'd been beaten and left for dead. She found him and took care of him, helped him heal—physically and emotionally." Nola frowns. "I guess when someone saves your life, there's a bond that's not so easily broken, you know?"

I did know, in fact. And doesn't she realize what she just said? Ethan saved her. Kohnrad saved her. Ronnie stayed by her side and kept her going when she would have given up. That should mean something. But I don't think it does because Nola has placed her bedding next to Zeke's, with Ethan's on his other side. Nothing like taking advantage of the situation, right?

Placing the folded blanket I've had a death grip on, along with Ronnie's mat, next to my own, I wonder if Ronnie has noticed Nola's infatuation. I'm pretty sure Zeke has. I poke at the fire and add a few logs before sitting in one of the rocking chairs. I thought Nola would join me, but instead, she heads over to the table and stands near Zeke. She throws me a mischievous look behind his back, giving an exaggerated wink before laughing at something and laying a light hand on his shoulder. Zeke turns his upper body so Nola's hand slides off, but I can't see his expression to know what he's thinking. Nola smiles, and I swear she bats her eyes.

Good grief. Is she serious?

A sharp pang of disappointment nicks at my heart, and I look away. I push the chair into a gentle rock, my gaze unfocused on the fire. Somehow the close relationship I had hoped to have with Nola isn't happening. After what we went through, I expected things to be different, but nothing's changed.

No. That's not right. Things *have* changed. For everyone except Nola. It's like she missed it. That's what it feels like. We all changed, and somehow, she didn't—even with the healing that took place. It's like the incident in the Dark Forest had no effect on her, which is strange, considering it almost destroyed her. She hasn't asked about Bert or how we got to Kirkos. She hasn't shown much interest in Kohnrad either, come to think of it. It doesn't make sense. It's the opposite of what should be happening.

There's a gentle pull at my thoughts, like someone's called my name, but there's no sound. I look away from the fire and find Ethan watching me. He dips his head, and I know he's asking if I'm alright. Funny how I can feel that from across the room. There is a distinct bond there; it's both reassuring and unsettling. I try to smile, but the sudden rush of butterflies in my stomach forces me to drop my eyes.

Yes, things have definitely changed.

Later, as everyone settles in for the night, Ronnie and Hannah still haven't returned. I try to stay awake, but I'm too tired, and my eyes close despite my best effort. Much later, when I roll over, I'm relieved to see Ronnie in her bed, though she's not sleeping; she's just lying there staring at the embers of the fire.

Chapter 10

Ronnie's gone when we wake the next morning. Her gear is still along the wall with ours, but that doesn't mean much, depending on her state of mind. Tension radiates off Zeke as he stands, contemplating what to do.

"Ah, I thought I heard you moving around," Hannah says, stepping out of her bedroom. She grabs an apron from a nearby hook and ties it around her waist. "I'll get breakfast started while we wait for Ronnie and Marcus to return. They went to tend the sheep." She pauses just long enough to catch Zeke's eye before continuing. "Coffee's already made. Help yourself."

Zeke's posture relaxes, and a sigh escapes before he catches himself.

"I hope it's okay that Charlie went with them, Nola," Hannah says over her shoulder as she shuffles around her kitchen.

"Of course it is," Nola replies, jumping up to help her.

The two of them move in sync around the tiny room, like grandmother and granddaughter. It's such a contrast to the persona Nola portrayed last night. Hannah draws out a different side of her, one I hope will have a lasting effect.

Zeke, Ethan, and I work in tandem, pulling apart all the packs and reorganizing them with necessary supplies while working out weight distribution for each person. We'll be carrying heavier loads than we're used to until we get to the mule, and it's not going to be easy. Hannah announces it's time to eat just as Marcus and Ronnie return with Charlie.

"That dog is something else," Marcus says as we sit down. "Smartest creature I've ever seen. It's like he was born to herd sheep. Never seen anything like it. Nola, would you consider leaving him here with us? I could use a good workin' dog."

Dropping her fork, Nola calls Charlie to her and wraps her arms around his neck, holding him so tight he squirms. She loosens her grip but keeps one hand resting on his fur.

"No, I couldn't ever leave him behind," she says, her voice shaking.

"Well, you may want to consider it. Those mountains are going to be rough on him. You're going to need something to cover his feet, especially as the temperature drops. The exposure up there's gonna be like nothing you've ever dealt with before."

Nola looks at me, fear visible in her eyes, then turns to Zeke, ready to plead her case, but he beats her to it.

"Charlie is part of our team," Zeke says with firmness. "He will not be left behind."

"Oh, thank you Zeke!" Nola gushes with relief, offering a huge smile. "Thank you! You're the best!"

If he was closer, I think she would fling herself into his arms.

"I have something we can use for Charlie's feet," Hannah says, patting Nola's arm. "No need to worry. Marcus is too practical at times. He forgets the emotional attachment we get with our pets."

"Sorry, I wasn't meaning to cause a ruckus," Marcus replies, looking embarrassed.

"It's alright, dear," Hannah says, her eyes twinkling with affection. "That's why you have me."

Marcus and Hannah banter back and forth throughout breakfast, telling stories of their younger years. They laugh at each other and poke fun at their mistakes without being demeaning. I've never seen a couple interact like they do.

"Have you two ever been mad at each other?" I ask as soon as there's a pause in the conversation.

"Oh honey," Hannan says, laughing again. "Of course we have. You don't live with someone as long as we have without having a few blowouts."

"But you're so nice to each other."

"Hah!" Marcus says, slapping the table. "There ain't nothing like a woman scorned. My hide got blistered enough in the first few years of our marriage, let me tell you. But we worked it out."

"I'll let you in on a secret," Hannah says, leaning forward. "You keep the lines of communication open and don't say something you can't take back. That'll keep you going during the rough times."

"Right," Marcus agrees. "Honesty is key. Most often, the other person doesn't mean to do what you think they did to hurt you. Assumptions cause a lot of heartache."

"And keep your man well-fed," Hannah says with a wink.

"Yep, that helps. But you better praise her cooking too, or she'll sneak something in there that'll have you choking and chugging your water."

"You learned that lesson after only one incident. I was mighty proud of you, dear."

The room erupts with laughter and Marcus feeds it with more tales of Hannah getting the best of him. It's obvious he's embellishing the stories, but his devotion to his wife is endearing.

The conversation mellows out as we finish our food and clean things up. Ronnie's been fidgeting for the last five minutes, her face a mix of emotions: fear, sorrow, nervousness—all unlike her.

"Um, I'd like to say something, please."

We gather back around the table and quiet down so she can talk. She waits by Marcus, and when he gives her a nod, she looks out at the rest of us, not quite meeting our eyes.

"I want to apologize for my behavior yesterday. I said some... cruel things, and I'm sorry. I've already talked to Marcus and now I need to... want to... tell you why I reacted so... poorly."

Ronnie takes a deep breath and blows it out hard. Her hands are shaking and she shoves them in her pants pockets to hide them. Fixing her gaze on something behind us, she clears her throat, trying to find her voice again.

"There was a man, when I was a teenager, who made promises to me. I struggled to fit in with others my age and home was… messed up. So, I left. With him. He wasn't a good man. He did awful things to me… made me… do… awful things. I… he kicked me out after a few years and brought another girl in. She was so young and I couldn't… I just… I couldn't let him do those things to another girl. I tried… I went to the authorities, but nothing happened. So I… I took care of him… myself. I stopped him. Permanently."

"Oh," Nola says, shock registering on her face.

Tears hover in my eyes and I try not to blink. "Ronnie, I am so sorry—"

Ronnie puts up a hand, cutting me off. "There's more." Ronnie shifts her weight and puts her hand back in her pocket. "The girl. Angela… her name was Angela. She was really messed up. I tried to help her, but she couldn't function without the man telling her what to do. She… she killed herself. Because of that man, because of me."

Ronnie chokes on her words and bites her lip. Hard. We're silent, waiting for her to continue.

"I couldn't cope. I was so angry. Angry at my family for being messed up, angry at the man… I still can't even say his name… I was so mad for what he did to me and to Angela. I was so angry at myself for not doing better, being better. The only thing that kept me sane, made me not feel, was drinking. I drank until I didn't feel, didn't care. I ended up on the street, living under bridges and overpasses, surviving off dumpsters and people's pity. It didn't matter, as long as I was numb."

Ronnie pauses, looking down at the table, tears streaking her face. She takes a minute to compose herself.

"That's where I was when I heard a voice calling me. I was in a gutter, black out drunk, no idea where I was, let alone who I was." She looks up, still not meeting anyone's eyes. "But that voice reached inside me, called my name—my real name—and beckoned me to follow him. I swore I would never follow another man. I would never allow someone to have power over me like that again. Yet, that voice didn't demand anything from me. It just encouraged me to come to the Light, to make my own decision."

"Keeper," I whisper.

"I'd been alone for so long, had so much done to my body, I don't know if I would've lasted another night. I can't explain why I went. I don't even know how I made it, how I got out of there. But I turned my life around after that. I got help, got clean, and started walking the Path."

"You have done a good job, Ronnie," Zeke says with passion.

"Thank you, Zeke, but I haven't, really. I know what you're going to say." Ronnie holds up a hand, stopping Zeke from adding anything else. "The truth is, I've been on this Path a long time—longer than any of you. I should be further along than I am. I know everything about surviving on this trail, but I don't seem to know how to get anywhere. So, I've made the choice to step down as leader."

"Ronnie—"

"Zeke, it makes more sense for you to lead. It comes naturally to you and everyone respects you. I'll be your second if you want me, but you were born for this. This is your calling, not mine."

Zeke says no more, but he's watching Ronnie, weighing her words. She takes another deep breath and runs her hands through her hair, sending it out in all directions.

"Keeper was right," Ronnie snorts, shaking her head. "It was so hard to let that truth sink in. But I realized he offended me in order to provoke the darkness hidden inside. And boy, did it roar! The rage almost sucked me under. I thought I'd gotten rid of it years ago, but it was just biding its time, waiting to reveal its ugly head and take me out. I can't believe it almost won. After all these years, I thought… Well, anyway, I've fought too hard for too long to be brought down now."

Ronnie searches Zeke's eyes, looking for understanding. He reaches for her hand and squeezes, letting her know he's there. She whispers, "Thank you," then turns her attention to me.

"Kenna, I'm sorry for what I said to you. Your heart was in the right place. If your offer still stands, I think it's time I purge this bitterness once and for all."

Unable to speak, I just nod at Ronnie, tears wetting my cheeks. I look at my hands and see nothing. Where's the burning I felt for her yesterday? I take a deep breath, trying to remember Kohnrad's words. I close my eyes and search for the Flame, but don't see it. What if I can't find it without Kohnrad?

Then, in the distance, a flicker catches my eye, and as I move closer, the Fire becomes clear. I reach out and touch the Flame, running my fingers back and forth. Just like last time, my skin warms but doesn't burn. I cup my hand around the Fire and pull back, bringing a small Flame with me.

I open my eyes and look at my hand, watching the blue wave of light spread over my palm, recognizing the energy coursing through my body. Ronnie approaches my side of the table, and I rise to meet her.

"Are you ready?" I ask.

She fixes me with a determined look and plants her feet, bracing herself for what's coming.

"Yes. Hit me with it, Kenna."

I reach out and gently lay my hand over her heart. There's no searing pain, no shocking jolt. Instead, the heat spreads like warm water flowing over my hand. It bubbles and ripples with a gentle rhythm, and Ronnie begins to laugh. Tears of happiness roll down her cheeks. She continues to laugh and cry, and it seems endless, this flowing, this euphoria. I watch in amazement as years fall away from her face. Her body relaxes, and it's as if I can see the bitterness and unforgiveness draining away from her body.

Finally, the warmth fades, and I take my hand away from Ronnie's chest. Her countenance has changed so much. The hardness is gone, replaced by a glow of youth that surrounds her. She throws her arms wide and spins around, still laughing. It's contagious, this joy she has. It expands and overwhelms, filling us to overflowing, and we laugh with her. Even Charlie jumps around, barking in excitement.

My sides ache, yet I can't stop, don't want to stop. This laughter is different from before. There's a cleansing in it. A release. A healing and restoring that's unexplainable, yet so right. It takes us to a realm of purity where darkness can't reside, where time and worry don't exist. It purges and strengthens, breaks and restores. I could stay here forever.

I don't know when or how we stop laughing; it just seems to happen. But the joy, the peace, they remain for a long time.

Marcus and Hannah spend a while talking with Ronnie, and then Zeke pulls her aside. His words are hushed, but whatever he says causes Ronnie to throw herself into his arms. Zeke holds her tight, his eyes closed, head bowed. The longer they stay like that, the more it reinforces my opinion that Nola's assessment of them is wrong. There are more feelings between those two than she thinks. And the age gap no longer seems so extreme.

Pulling away, Ronnie swipes at her swollen eyes, then laughs and tries to regain some composure. "Well. I don't know about you guys, but I feel fifty pounds lighter! I had no idea I was carrying so much heaviness. And everything seems so much brighter. Like I have new eyes. This is so crazy, but in a good way!"

"The Way of Light be also a path to wholeness," Kohnrad says from behind us.

We all turn in surprise. None of us heard him come in — except Ethan, I guess, who stands next to him, a smile tugging at the corner of his mouth.

"Yous gotta journey to get it, though," Kohnrad continues. "It be like a river. The current shifts and reforms as it moves, keepin' things fresh and clean. But if it stops and has no outlet, it becomes polluted and unusable."

"I think I get that," Ronnie says, stepping forward, her eyes locking on Kohnrad. "When I held on to my anger and unforgiveness, it polluted my mind and darkened my heart. I thought holding on to it made me stronger, but actually, it stopped me from moving forward. I pushed it down so others couldn't see it, but all it took was someone to give it a good poke, and all the ugliness came to the surface."

"In order to receive healin', yous gotta choose to embrace the Light. It don't be feelin' the same fer ever'one, so don't be expectin' it to look the same." Kohnrad shifts his gaze around the room and smiles. "Now, I needs be headin' out and so do yous all. The Dark One be on his way back. Get yer gear and get outta here tonight."

Kohnrad draws close to Marcus and Hannah. "He be in a rage, so yous best be havin' everyone lie low for 'while." Looking at Zeke, he continues, "I's be providin' yous a distraction in the Marketplace just 'fore dark. Move quick and get ever'one out and up into the woods. Yer gonna be needin' all the distance yous can get and the path ain't easy."

"You think he will come after us," Zeke says, understanding Kohnrad's meaning.

"Well now, that be dependin' on my story tellin'. Ever'one saw yous enter the Marketplace and head this way, but no one's seen ya since 'cept the trusted ones. So I's just gotta convince 'em that yous all left in the night, back that way yous came."

"Will they believe you?" I ask.

Kohnrad sighs and shakes his head. "Not likely."

***

"Keep to the shadows and watch your step," Zeke instructs. "Ethan, you will bring up the rear. Ronnie, Nola, if we are separated, find a safe spot and stay there until Ethan or I can come for you. Kenna, I want you and the compass with me. Is everyone in agreement?"

Nola shoots me an annoyed look as I step past her to join Zeke, but she doesn't argue. This is the first time since the Dark Forest that she's aware of what's going on as we travel. If she'd shown some interest earlier, I would've told her about working with Zeke—and reminded her it was her idea.

The streets are quiet as we head out, the people making provision for Cole's return. It doesn't take long to pass through Marcus's community and enter the more treacherous eastern segment. The stench hits, and once again causes us all to gag and retch into our sleeves.

It's cloudy tonight, the shadows deeper and more foreboding than before. Tension hangs in the air; it's thick here, as if the people sense something coming. A string of cursing sends us scurrying to the side of a building as two men stop nearby, arguing over a pack of cigarettes. Nola clamps a hand over Charlie's muzzle and wraps her other arm around his neck, hushing his growls. He quiets down as we wait, hearts pounding, for the men to move on.

Their voices fade as they drift away, still bickering. We wait a moment longer to make sure they're not coming back before moving on. Progress is slow and stilted as we navigate through the neighborhood, more near misses increasing the agitation of the entire group. But once we reach the deserted section, Zeke no longer needs the compass to guide us. He quickens our pace, directing us along the empty streets to the wall.

We stop when we reach it, letting Ethan and Zeke do a quick scan of the area. As we're waiting, Charlie whips his head around towards the town center. He stands alert, his ears pricked forward, listening to something we can't hear. I reach my hand out to calm him, but he bolts off at a full run, disappearing into the now dark night. Nola cries out and Ronnie clamps a hand over her mouth, shushing her. We freeze, holding our breath, listening for any sign that we've been heard.

"What has happened?" Zeke whispers, rushing back to us.

"Charlie took off," Ronnie replies, taking her hand away from Nola's mouth.

Nola whimpers, but doesn't cry out again.

"I am sorry, Nola," Zeke says. "We cannot go after him. Charlie will have to find us later."

Nola sniffles into her sleeve, trying to keep her grief muffled. Zeke's right; there's nothing we can do about Charlie. As much as it hurts to leave him behind, we have no choice but to keep moving.

We hurry along the wall to the brush pile where Ethan has already pulled away branches and stands guard, waiting. Zeke motions for him to go as we approach, and Ethan darts through the hole, nicking the sides as he disappears.

Zeke unhooks his straps and bends low to slide off his cumbersome pack. He's carrying the most equipment and there's no way he'll fit through the wall with it on.

"Kenna," he says, waving me forward. "Get to the gate and do whatever Ethan tells you to. Do not wait for me."

"Zeke, what are you doing?" Ronnie says. "We're not leaving you behind."

"It will take time for me to cover the entrance. If you keep going, you can get to the mule and switch over the gear before I catch up to you."

"What about Charlie?" Nola whispers. "How will he get to us?"

"He is a smart dog, Nola. He will find a way." Zeke grabs his oversized load and shoves it through the wall to the other side. "Now go. Ethan is waiting."

Nola lets out a soft cry, not wanting to go without Charlie. Zeke reaches for her arm, taking hold rougher than I think he realizes, and steers her to the hole. Ronnie pushes her through, and with a last look at Zeke, I follow after them.

"I can't believe this," Ronnie says in front of me, turning in a slow circle. "I had no idea it would be so beautiful. How sad that no one gets to see it anymore."

"Come on," I say, passing by and ducking under the flowering trees. "The gate's this way."

We plod along the semi-lucent path towards the archway, our bodies bent under the weight of our packs. The straps dig into my shoulders, and my neck is already aching. I can feel the sweat gathering on my back, and can't wait to get to the mule.

The wrought-iron gate blends into the night, and it's hard to gauge the distance in the dark, even with the soft light of the path. I don't see Ethan until we're right at the stone archway. The gate is unlocked, open just enough for us to squeeze through, and he signals for me to stay put while he slips out into the darkness. Nola huddles close while Ronnie watches for Zeke, muttering under her breath. The only other sound around us is the chirping of crickets and our heavy breathing.

I stare out beyond the gate, searching for any sign of Ethan, but all I see are tiny beacons of light blinking in a hypnotic rhythm. It's an otherworldly feeling, and at that moment, I envy the fireflies' simple existence—their freedom, their ignorance of the danger that hovers so close.

Ethan reappears without a sound, more an adjustment of light than substance. He gestures for us to follow and stay close to the outer wall. Ronnie insists on being last, so I squeeze through the gate and head north, trying to keep up with a shadow I can barely see. He stops us a few hundred yards ahead and points to the top of the wall.

Guards.

Using his hands, Ethan instructs us to head diagonally, one by one, through the field up to the tree line. Then, he vanishes into the tall prairie grass, leaving me to try and guess where he is. I watch for movement, but he's impossible to see.

Minutes tick by like hours before I'm brave enough to go myself. I crouch as low as I can and creep along, pushing the tall grass aside with care so as not to draw attention. I focus on the darker shadow of the woods ahead, not daring to look back. My body aches from the awkward position and I soon drop to my knees, unable to continue the way I was. The rough grass pokes my hands as I move forward on all fours, the ground rising at a sharper angle and slowing my progress even more.

At last, I reach the edge of the field, and towering pines appear before me. I've made it to the tree line, but Ethan is nowhere in sight. My heart flutters as Nola crawls out of the grass beside me and collapses just inside the woods. I scramble after her, relieved to find the path ahead, just like Marcus said we would.

Without a sound, Ethan materializes in front of me, and I gasp loud enough for the whole city to hear. With a few short motions, he relays he's found the mule and wants my pack of gear. Relieved, I unhook my clasps and hand everything over, then prod Nola to continue up the trail while I wait for Ronnie and, fingers crossed, Zeke.

Shadows atop the wall confirm the presence of guards, but not much else is visible. Time drags on, and a breeze picks up, carrying the occasional murmur and cough across the field. Uneasiness settles in, knotting my stomach. Ronnie should have come by now. I scan the empty space between the wall and woods, searching for the smallest motion, the slightest noise to indicate someone is coming.

A sudden flurry of movement arises from the guards, and two dark figures straighten up, their distorted shadows moving into position just north of where we crossed the open field. I strain to pick out where their focus is, but the distance and lack of light keep me from knowing what's going on. The grass shifts before me, and I jerk back as Ronnie creeps out of the field and into the trees.

"Zeke," she pants, bent over her knees. "Behind me."

A shout erupts from the wall, and out of nowhere, a dark shape darts across the field, passing right in front of the guards. It's low to the ground, tearing through the grass like a wild beast, aiming straight for me. A muted thwump rises from the wall, then a soft hiss cuts through the air and a yelp pierces the night as an arrow thunks into a solid mass.

I bite back a cry, slapping my hand over my mouth.

Charlie! No!

There's a thud as a second arrow burrows into the ground, followed by a muffled curse nearby. Two more arrows arc through the night like a sigh, their landings swallowed by a sudden gust of wind.

Ronnie stands motionless beside me, her breaths coming in quick gasps. The moment stretches on until, at last, the guards relax and wander back to their posts. A few more minutes pass before movement stirs in the field again, and Zeke's wide frame comes into view as he sprints to the trees. A shout from the wall signals the guards have seen him, but no arrows come our way.

"Where is Ethan?"

"Up ahead," I stammer as Zeke drops to his knees, laying a bundle on the ground.

"Oh, no!" Ronnie cries, sinking down beside him.

Zeke has brought Charlie.

"Hold still!" he growls.

Charlie whines and tries to get up.

"How bad is it?" Ronnie asks.

"He is okay. It is only a nick. He was not far from me when he was hit, so I was able to tackle him before the second arrow landed."

Zeke sits back on his heels, and Charlie scrambles to his feet, eager to escape. He limps away, stopping to lick his back leg, then looks at us as if waiting for instructions.

"Go find Nola, boy," I command, and he takes off up the trail.

Nola has her face buried in his neck when we get to her and Ethan. The mule stands ready to go, our gear strapped across his back. Ethan throws my much lighter pack at me, and I hurry to clip my buckles.

"Kenna, you will set the pace with the compass," Zeke says before asking Ethan for the lanterns.

"But I'm the slowest one. I shouldn't be in the lead," I say, terrified to steer us into another dark forest.

"If you are unable to keep up, we will lose you in the dark. It is best to put you first, and we need the compass to guide us. Ethan will stay in the back with the mule."

"If we lose our gear…" Ronnie says.

"I have a tent; we will have shelter. Ethan has the best chance of disappearing if those guards follow us. We will sacrifice the mule if it is necessary. Now, we must get moving. Kenna, push as hard as you can. We need as much distance between us and the city as possible."

Struggling through the dread that wants to paralyze me, I step into the lead. The compass warms my hand, its vibration a small comfort in this ongoing madness. Somehow, its glow is just enough to see where I need to go, while the others light lanterns.

The trail takes us deep into the trees, winding back and forth at a constant incline. It's dark, and the wind has picked up. The treetops sway, and leaves rustle together, the sound unnerving in its resemblance to murmuring. I walk as fast as I can, stumbling often, but at least not embarrassing myself by falling on my face. It feels like we've been here for hours, and my legs burn beyond anything I've ever experienced before, but the fear of failure drives my determination to keep moving. If I slow down or stop at all, I'm done.

The trail narrows at the next turn, becoming more like a deer track wandering through the forest than a groomed path for travelers. Branches tug at my clothes and slap my face, scraping my cheeks. A spirited conversation with Kohnrad circles in my head regarding his negligence of duty. Some path keeper he is, sending us up here knowing the trail was like this. Totally uncalled for. His lack of competence really should be addressed. The only good coming out of this one-sided "discussion" is that it keeps my adrenaline flowing and my mind distracted. But of course, I won't tell him that.

I'm to the point where I don't think I can go any further when the trees disappear, and I think we've come to a small clearing. The ground drops out before me, and I pull back, my body quivering. What I thought was a clearing, is actually the edge of a cliff. The trail turns at a sharp angle to my left and continues uphill, with a steep embankment on one side and dark nothing on the other.

Straight out over the nothingness, I can see Kirkos. The city center is lit up, as are the inner rings. The outer area containing Marcus's community is as dark as the night, and there are no lights in the field or along the northeastern wall by the gate.

My pounding pulse strikes my temples, and my vision blurs. Nausea churns in my stomach, and I feel like I'm going to be sick. Everything tilts, and I feel weightless, unable to stop myself from falling. Someone yanks me back, lowering me to the ground, their hands firm against my shoulders. I sag against them, struggling to stay conscious.

"Drink," Zeke demands, shoving a bottle in my face.

I don't know how I can. I can't lift my arms or my head. My body is going numb.

"Kenna, drink. Come on. Swallow the water."

Zeke props my head up and pours water into my mouth. I sputter and choke, but he keeps telling me to swallow. At last, I manage to take a drink and my brain registers how thirsty I am. I gulp down as much as I can before Zeke pulls the bottle away.

"Let that settle first. It will help with the nausea."

I'm still lightheaded, but at least I can hold my head up on my own again. I lean forward over my shaky legs and take a series of slow, deep breaths, willing my heart rate to slow down and my body to realize it's okay.

"You did a good job Kenna. You are stronger than you think. And," Zeke says with a chuckle, "Kohnrad would be thoroughly chastised if he heard even half of what you said to him."

I squeeze my eyes shut and groan. So much for keeping the conversion in my head. Charlie's nose nudges my arm, squeezing his head into my lap, and I lay a limp arm across his neck, grateful for his presence.

"It does not appear that we are being followed," Zeke says, gazing out over Kirkos. "The guards must not have realized what they were shooting at. Still, they may try to track us in the morning. We will push on further, then make camp for a few hours. Ethan and I will take turns with watch and have everyone up at dawn."

Zeke helps me to my feet, keeping a grip on my pack to steady me as we walk another mile or so before finding a level spot to set up camp. Ronnie and Ethan work together to set up Zeke's tent, and I crawl inside without bothering to remove my pack. The last thing I remember is the feel of Charlie's fur alongside my face.

"I would like to know how this 'situation' has come to pass and whom I may hold responsible. I will have someone's head over this."

"My apologies, Master, but the Messenger cannot be found."

"Well, someone had better find him or you will all yourselves be suffering the consequences, and I will enjoy every drawn-out moment."

"Yes, Master, I understand. I have dispatched the searchers. This betrayal will not go unpunished. They will find this wretched creature and bring him to you."

"So then… tell me, Dark One. What is Keeper doing in my city? How does such a worthless brute come to be there, at the same time as the others, who, by the way, were supposed to have died but instead, have now vanished. It seems your superior has lost his touch, and is in desperate need of *discipline*. How unfortunate for him."

"Master, with your permission, I will set out at once to assess the situation. I assure you, anyone involved in this matter will be dealt with to the extreme."

"Will they now? If my memory serves well—which, of course, it does—you have family amongst the Resisters. A father and mother. Highly influential individuals who have been allowed to interfere without consequence. I do wonder if your… *relationship* will hinder your ability to properly execute my justice."

"They are of no concern to me, Master. I assure you, favor will not be an issue."

"And the brute?"

"My superior has been mistaken in assuming the man harmless. He presents himself as uneducated, but I do not trust him. He has a disturbing habit of showing up in places where he should not. If he is still around, he will be detained and interrogated—with the appropriate force, of course."

"Ahhh, yes. I do believe a nice public whipping will be just the thing to set the mood."

"That has always been my perspective, Master."

"Good. Serve me well, Dark One, and you may find yourself… elevated. Fail me, and your punishment will forever strike terror into all who hear of it."

"I will not fail you, Master. I will see to it that all of your orders are carried out to the utmost degree."

Chapter 11

I wake the next morning to the jangling of metal. Opening my eyes, I see horses standing all around us. They stomp and snort, steam curling from their nostrils. Heavily armed soldiers sit atop them, eyes fixed on us, weapons drawn and glinting in the pale light. A harsh-looking man dressed all in black steps forward, his movements slow, deliberate, as if time bends around him. He squats in front of me and smiles, but the smile does not reach his eyes—black eyes devoid of light.

"Well, it appears I have found you at last, Fire Holder. I look forward to breaking you."

The man rises to his feet and motions for soldiers to grab me. They're rough and crude, making jokes and squeezing me harder than necessary. I try to wrench my arms free, but they just tighten their hold and laugh. I thrash about, screaming for them to let go. The man steps forward and slaps my face, hard. I'm stunned and lose my breath. He laughs and tells me the more I struggle, the more thrilling I am to him.

"Kill the others. They are of no use to me."

Rage fills me and the Fire bursts into flames, igniting my chest.

"Oh yes," the man says. "That is what I want, dear one. Bring me your rage—all of your beautiful rage. Feed me with it. Be consumed and burn for me, Kenna. Do you still not realize what I am?"

He blinks, and his eyes turn reptilian. His features shift, twisting into something unnatural. A split tongue flicks from his mouth, tasting, smelling. His body uncurls, and it is then that I realize he's a serpent—the same one I saw in the fire. He grins, fangs dripping with venom and his black body rises, coiling as he prepares to strike. He lunges, and—

"Kenna, Kenna! Please wake up! Kenna!"

I'm jerked out of the suffocating darkness, disoriented and struggling to catch my breath. As things come into focus, I find Nola leaning over me, her eyes as big as saucers.

"Oh, thank goodness! Kenna, are you alright? You were thrashing and yelling in your sleep. I think you attacked Charlie!"

"Sorry," I mumble as I try to push myself up, only to fall onto my back with a painful moan.

"What's wrong? Are you hurt?"

"No, I'm not hurt. I just need a moment. My legs are killing me."

"You need to get up and move around. Warm up your muscles," Ronnie says, entering the tent and offering me a hand.

I grab hold, letting her and Nola help me to my feet.

"Was it the same dream as before?" Ronnie asks, concern knitting her brow.

I shake my head. "No, it was different. More... personal." Stepping outside, I take slow, aching steps, trying to clear my mind.

"Do you want to talk about it?"

"No, I'm fine," I lie. "I don't really remember it now anyway."

Ronnie and Nola watch me, unsure whether to press, but I wave them off, saying I need to walk a bit and stretch my muscles. Dawn isn't far off, and the lightening sky allows me to make my way without trouble. I walk far enough for some privacy, not wanting anyone to see how shaken I actually am.

I have found you… Fire Holder…

I rub my face, trying to erase visions of the dream and silence the voice.

Burn for me Kenna… burn for me… burn for me…

My chest hurts, the burning hurts, the Fire. I don't want it. Please, please just stop.

Do you still not realize what I am?

"I don't know who or what you are!" I whisper into the morning, wondering if I'm losing my mind—or maybe I already did back in the cave.

"Wake up, Kenna, wake up!" I hiss, pinching my arm. "Ouch!"

Ugh, this is stupid! Who in their right mind would choose me for anything? I'm no one important, and by far the most out of shape and unprepared person on this journey. I start to cry, too overwhelmed to stop the tears. I don't understand why I'm here. Why was I chosen? And why is it so hard? I can't do this. What if this dream comes true like the last one?

"Oh no. No, no, no, no. This can't be… I can't… what if they all…"

Unable to get enough air, I bend over, sucking in deep breaths, trying to keep from passing out. Mentally, I feel myself shutting down. I can't do this again—the dreams, the fear. I have to make myself numb, lock it all down. Darkness swirls around me, whispering relief, inviting me to let go.

A pair of boots steps into my line of vision and I glance up to find Ethan in front of me. I'm starting to not be surprised when he shows up like this. Almost.

Crouching next to me and points at my chest. "Keep Fire… burning."

I squeeze my eyes shut and shake my head. "I don't think I can. It's too much. I'm not strong enough."

"Yes… you are. Keep burning."

"Why Ethan? Why does it matter? What is the point of all this?"

"Not easy… to be chosen."

"No kidding," I reply, straightening back up. "I think someone chose the wrong person. I'm not made for this."

"Like a butterfly. Struggle makes you… stronger."

"Huh, now you sound like Konrad."

Ethan smiles. "Good."

"Yeah, I guess that's good." I say, feeling the darkness slip away. Wrapping my arms around myself, I stare down the trail, the weight in my chest easing. "Do you think he's okay?"

"He can take care… of himself," Ethan says, coming alongside me.

"I'm sure he can, but I'd hate for something to happen to him because of us."

"He'll call… if he needs help."

"How?"

"Through the Path."

"Okay, I don't understand that either, but you'll know if he needs us?"

Ethan nods yes.

"Alright. Well, thank you for the pep talk. I'm gonna hobble on back now."

Ethan lets out a raspy chuckle and rubs his legs to suggest they're sore too.

I roll my eyes, holding back a sarcastic smile. "Yeah, right. A warrior like you doesn't get tired."

He gives me his lopsided grin and shrugs his shoulders.

"That's what I thought," I mutter and shuffle back to camp.

Everything is packed and ready to go by the time Ethan and I return. Zeke hands me a biscuit and asks me if I'm okay walking with the mule for a while. We can back off on the pace this morning since there's still no sign of anyone following us.

The wind picks up, becoming stronger the higher we climb, and as the increasing daylight reveals our surroundings, I realize we're hiking up the side of a mountain. The trail is rugged and steep, and the mule I'm leading is much better at navigating the rough terrain than I am. He's big like a horse, but more surefooted, and doesn't seem to mind the conditions or the weight on his back.

"You look familiar," I say, squinting into the mule's face. He stares back at me with uninterested eyes. "Yeah, you probably all look alike, right? Get mixed up with someone else, called the wrong name. It's a rough life, huh?" The mule snorts and plods along, unconcerned. I loosen the rope, giving him more lead, and let him do his thing.

Around mid-morning, Charlie starts limping, so we stop to check his paws. Nola cleans them off and wraps them with the leather strips that Hannah gave her. The curious dog sniffs at the wrappings, but lets her finish. When she's done, he lifts his legs high in the air one at a time, trying to shake off the bindings as he walks. I laugh as Nola sweet-talks him into following her so he can get used to them. Poor guy, he looks ridiculous, but they will give him the protection he needs.

As we continue to gain elevation, the terrain undergoes a drastic transformation, and so does the weather. The trees disappear, replaced by short moss-like grass covering what looks like granite. Dark clouds fill the sky, and the temperature, which has been dropping all day, now feels sharp and brittle. Our breaths come out in short, ragged bursts, forming white puffs that hang in the air only moments before dissipating. The mule must feel it too, because he's snorting and blowing his nose all over me.

A short distance later, a thin layer of crunchy snow covers the ground and an icy wind bites at our cheeks, cutting right through our clothing. We stop to pull on the heavier layers Marcus gave us, wrapping our faces the best we can. There's no protection from the wind up here, so we push on without resting.

The weather continues to deteriorate as the day progresses. A mixture of rain and ice turns the snow into a treacherous mess. The mule, now irritated, tosses his head about, pulling the rope from my hands. Unable to keep him in line, I hand him over to Zeke, which puts me back up front, leading the way.

The freezing rain makes everyone miserable, icing over our clothes and melting down the back of our necks. I shield the side of my face with my wet mitten while trying to keep an eye on the compass and the path. It soon becomes apparent that we're headed straight into a dead end, as the mountain range wraps around us, leaving no way out. The path is visible only for a short distance before disappearing into the thick mist settling in. From what I can tell, we're in for a steep climb, so I stop the group for a short break, letting everyone catch their breath.

"Has anyone seen Ethan?" Zeke asks, looking around.

A quick consensus reveals that no one has seen him since we stopped to put on warmer clothing. How is that possible? It's been hours.

"Zeke, what if something's happened to him? It's not like he can yell for help," I ask, a tremor of alarm tightening in my chest.

Zeke braces himself against the wind, staring down the trail as if sheer willpower will bring Ethan back to us. We wait as long as we dare, but the temperature continues to plummet, and the rain shifts into solid ice pellets, increasing the need to keep moving.

"We don't have many options," Ronnie says to Zeke. He looks down at her and she nods towards the mountain wall. "Probably safe to assume the tunnel is up there."

"It will take time to get there."

"Staying here's not safe. Even with a tent, we'll freeze."

After a brief pause, Zeke comes to a decision and starts telling Ronnie what to do. "I need you to take the mule and get the girls to the tunnel. Do not stop until you reach it. Get inside and stay there."

"You're going to look for him?"

"I cannot leave a man behind."

"I know," she says, nodding with approval. "It's the right thing to do."

"If something were to happen and I do not return…"

"That's not going to happen, but if it does, we're capable women. We'll continue on. Now go."

Zeke hesitates, looking us over one last time, then hustles down the trail to find Ethan. Ronnie turns away, refusing to watch him go, and grabs the rope for the mule, instructing Nola and me to lead the way.

The trail rapidly becomes hazardous, a slick layer of ice covering everything. We've hit steep switchbacks and are struggling to stay upright. I've already gone down a few times, and Nola just slid down behind me. Ronnie is struggling too, but so far, the mule is managing okay.

The cold metal of the compass sticks to the fabric of my mitten, the soft glow of the arrow distorted by a layer of ice. I have to keep my head down to protect my eyes from the pelting ice and can only see a few feet in front of me. The trail is grueling, and I'm once again not feeling well, but there's no option to stop. If we do, we won't make it.

"There better be a tunnel or something up there soon," Ronnie yells over the storm. "We can't take much more of this."

"I know," I yell back, pushing ahead and leading us higher.

The hail switches to snow—small flakes at first, then larger, thicker ones begin to fall. The change feels like a blessing until the snow covers the trail, creating a whiteout, and I'm unsure where to step.

I slide to a stop as a rock wall appears in front of me, so close I almost walked right into it. Reaching out, I run my hand along the cold stone, searching for a hole or way through. My mitten catches on a handle, and looking closer, I make out the frame of a large metal door set into the side of the mountain.

We made it. We made it!

"We're at the tunnel!" I yell, squinting down the trail. Nola and Charlie emerge from the swirling whiteness, both of them covered in snow and ice.

"Is Ronnie behind you?" I ask, unable to see beyond a few feet.

"I-I don't know," Nola stammers, her teeth chattering.

My mind races, torn between backtracking to find her and opening the door to get us into shelter. Before I have to make the difficult decision, a form begins to take shape and Ronnie steps into view, the mule trailing behind her.

"Thank goodness," I sigh, and rush to tell her what I've found.

Ronnie hands me the frozen rope and moves closer to inspect the door. With a grunt, she forces the bar up and struggles to push the door open, revealing a pitch-black hole.

"Kenna, we're going to need a lantern," she says, stepping into the tunnel.

Brushing snow away, I search through our gear for the lanterns and the pouch of matches. My wet, frozen mittens make it nearly impossible to grab anything, so I yank them off, the cold air biting at my skin as soon as my fingers are exposed. The mule shifts in agitation, clearly unhappy to be left standing outside in the storm.

"I'm trying, boy," I mumble, yanking a lantern free. I huddle as close as I can around the match and struggle to get it lit, each failed strike leaving my hands more numb and clumsier.

At last, the flame holds, and I shove it under the glass. The wick lights and the lantern blazes to life. I stumble towards the doorway, the mule pushing at my shoulder, and call out for Ronnie. A hand takes the lantern from me just before the mule shoves his way into the tunnel, forcing me up against the rock.

Snow swirls around the entrance, blowing its way in after the mule. Nola struggles with the door, finally slamming it shut and sealing us inside. It's cool inside, but still warmer than outside. The light reveals a row of supplies along one wall, all covered with large tarps, and a cord of wood disappearing down the tunnel.

"Get the mule unloaded and rubbed down," Ronnie says, taking off her pack and wet jacket. "Put him at the far end for now." She picks up a nearby ax and heads to the woodpile.

Nola and I unhook our packs and begin the arduous task of unloading the mule. He's back to his indifferent self now that we're inside. I lead him to the other end of the tunnel and give him a good rubdown while Nola finds hay, along with a bucket of water. The bucket shakes as she sets it down, and when I look over, I find her shivering like crazy.

"Nola, get over by the fire and warm up. I'll be there in a minute."

"I'm w-worried," she says, her lips gray with cold. "How can we just sit here and w-wait?"

"Zeke and Ethan are both strong hikers. They'll be back soon. Now get yourself warm so you don't get sick."

I watch as she shuffles over to the fire. Ronnie notices her shivering and takes over, fussing as she does. I turn back to the mule, running a hand along his neck. He doesn't need anything more, but I stay a little longer anyways. In all honesty, I'm worried about the guys too. Ethan should never have disappeared. If he's gone, then something bad has happened, and Zeke might be walking right into it. I can't even begin to imagine what we'll do if they don't return.

The mule snorts and throws his head, sending drops of water flying and shaking me out of my haze. I give him a final pat on his shoulder and head over to the fire, stripping off my wet clothes as I go. Ronnie hands me a wool blanket for warmth, and I settle down near the fire to dry out.

"You're the ultimate pioneer woman," I say, watching her prepare food and boil water for coffee.

"A benefit of being on the trail so long."

"Well, I am grateful for your skills. It's amazing what you can do with so little."

Ronnie's movements are precise and calculated. She doesn't hesitate or second-guess; she just seems to know what's necessary and does it well.

"You know, I've never been part of a group before," I say, keeping my focus on the fire instead of making eye contact. "Not like this, I mean, where everyone has a skill that helps the group as a whole. I've never had anything meaningful to contribute. Not that I've done a lot here either, but no one's made me feel like I don't belong. It's just that… I've always been on the outside looking in, I guess. I couldn't relate to—or didn't care about—the same things others did. It always seemed so pointless. I… I didn't fit in because I'm too… different." I glance at Nola, but she appears disconnected, her eyes glazed over.

"I was too embarrassed to let anyone in," Ronnie says, her voice rising just above the crackle of the fire. "I couldn't have friends over because of my father's drinking and unpredictable temper. The kids at school called me stuck-up, but actually, I was terrified someone would find out and tell everyone. The loneliness was easier to deal with than the fear."

"I guess we've both come a ways in our thinking then, haven't we?" I say with a half smile.

"I told you a while back, us girls gotta stick together. I knew you were something special the moment you walked into camp."

"Really?"

"Yep. Zeke saw your light, but I saw your potential. Don't underestimate yourself, Kenna. There's more to you than you think."

Ronnie's words resonate deep inside, and I desperately want to believe them, even if part of me isn't sure it's possible.

Nola snaps out of her stupor with a jerk and asks Ronnie for something to dry Charlie off. She rubs his fur, breaking off the melting ice, then unwinds his feet to check his paws. The cut from earlier has scabbed over and looks fine. Charlie, happy to have his feet free, lies down to give them a thorough washing.

"If we keep the fire going, we should be warm enough through the night," Ronnie says, passing me a steaming bowl of food.

"How is Zeke going to see the trail in the dark?" Nola whispers, clutching her bowl to her chest.

My thoughts exactly. It was hard enough when it was daylight, but now?

Ronnie avoids Nola's question and continues to rearrange and sort our gear, split more wood to feed the fire, and check the mule. She opens the door once, but slams it shut when she gets a face full of snow. I can't fault her busyness. We're each worried and trying to cope in our own way.

More time passes, and Ronnie finally stops, just sitting and staring at the door. Nola has fallen asleep, her arm around

Charlie, a soft snore rising and falling. I pull my knees into my chest and lay my head down, letting the tears fall without Ronnie hearing me. Zeke's been gone a long time. Too long. Something's wrong.

Exhaustion pulls at me, and I feel myself drifting off to sleep. I don't have the willpower to fight it. Things seem so hopeless at the moment. Sleep is a sweet escape.

***

Cold air and shouting jolt me awake. Wind and snow whip into the tunnel as large shadows push their way past the door. Ronnie is already on her feet, running towards the commotion while I struggle to put together what's going on.

"Get him to the fire!" Zeke's voice breaks through the howling wind. "We need to remove his clothes. Someone shut the door!"

I scramble to my feet, bracing against the blizzard, and slide the heavy door shut. Slipping on the wet stone, I hurry back to where Zeke and Ethan have a large figure laid out on a mat. As they work to remove his boots and clothes, I realize it's Kohnrad and let out a cry.

"What happened? Where did you find him?"

"Ethan found him collapsed on the trail. We were too far ahead for him to get our attention. There was not a place for shelter, so he carried him the best he could until I came upon him."

Ethan is hardly recognizable, covered from head to toe in ice and snow, his eyes almost frozen shut. His whole body shivers violently as he struggles to help Zeke with Kohnrad.

I pull on his arm, wedging myself between him and Kohnrad. "Ethan, stop. Ronnie and Nola can help. I need you to come with me." I push him away from the others and begin pulling at his frozen clothes. "You have to get these off. We need to get you dry and warm."

Ethan grasps my wrists and stops me, his expression dark. His cheeks are raw from the wind, his lips cracked. How he has any strength left to fight is beyond me, and it takes a bit before I realize he's worried about his scars.

"I know," I say, lowering my voice. "But we don't have a choice. Please, get your wet clothes off. I'll get a blanket. No one's looking, okay? We have to do this. Now."

He holds my wrists a moment longer before letting go. Cold from his icy hands, I shiver and rub my skin warm, waiting to see what he'll do. I relax a notch when he raises a shaky hand to his coat and begins to work it open.

Grabbing a blanket from the pile Ronnie had the foresight to prepare earlier, I hold it out in front of him for privacy. He shifts, losing his balance before straightening up, revealing well-defined shoulders riddled with an array of markings. I look away, my cheeks warm as I wait for him to finish. When he reaches for the blanket, I duck my head and wrap it around him before guiding him to a mat by the fire.

There's a pot of coffee simmering by the flames, so I pour him a cup, instructing him to drink while I rummage through the packs for dry socks, pants, and a flannel. He lets me help him with the socks before waving me off to check on Kohnrad.

I join the others, who've gotten Kohnrad stripped and wrapped in layers of blankets. He's lying on his back with his head in Nola's lap, her hands tucked up on her chest as if afraid to touch him. When she looks up, I catch the fear in her eyes and gasp when I see why. Kohnrad's face is a mess. Dark bruising discolors his skin, both eyes are swollen shut, and his lips are split open and bloody.

Zeke rubs Kohnrad's legs and feet, working down one side then the other, while Ronnie focuses on his left arm and hand. Their movements are quick and aggressive, a sense of urgency defined by the blue tinge to Kohnrad's fingers and lips.

"Is he conscious?" I ask, my heart hammering in my chest.

"Not at the moment," Ronnie says, switching to Kohnrad's other side.

"What happened to him?"

"It appears he has been beaten," Zeke says. "Severely. It amazes me he made it up the path as far as he did. He had to have had help."

"Do you think it was because of us? Was he beaten because of us?" I ask, horrified at the thought.

"I think that is highly probable."

"Oh, Kohnrad, what have you done?" I whisper, kneeling by his side.

"It doesn't look like he fought back," Ronnie says, holding up his unbruised hands. "Or he couldn't. He's got rope burns around his wrists."

I put my hands over my mouth to keep from crying out further.

"He also has bruised ribs, possibly broken, and there may be internal bleeding," Zeke says. "We need to stabilize his body temperature without overheating him. Once that is under control, we can ice his ribs and face. We will take shifts and watch for fever or difficulty breathing. And he must drink if he awakens."

"Zeke, you need to rest now and get yourself warm. You've done what you can. We can take over," Ronnie says, nodding to Nola and me.

Zeke hesitates, then shrugs out of his coat and unlaces his boots as I hurry to get a blanket and pour another cup of coffee. He eases himself down beside the fire, taking the offered cup with a weary smile, his hands trembling.

Ronnie demonstrates how to rub Kohnrad's feet so I can take over while she continues with his hands. His skin is so cold I have to blow on my hands every once in a while to warm them up.

Nola continues to sit with Kohnrad's head in her lap but still doesn't touch him. Ronnie tries to encourage her to help us, but she jerks her head back, her eyes darting around the room as if searching for help.

"Easy, Nola. It's okay," Ronnie says in a low, soothing tone. "What you're doing is helpful. Just stay still and keep his head supported." She shoots me a questioning look, but I have no answer for Nola's odd behavior and can only shrug.

I keep a close eye on Ethan while working on Kohnrad, watching for any signs of distress. His body convulses once in a while as it adjusts to the heat of the fire, and his eyelids droop with exhaustion. I can see him fighting it, his gaze fixed on Kohnrad, worry etched into creases around his mouth and eyes.

Kohnrad is more than just Keeper of the Path; his wisdom and insight have brought healing and restoration. His words have prodded, offended, and challenged us to greater things. I never expected this strange talking man to become a friend and mentor. We owe him so much.

Ronnie and I rub Kohnrad's limbs until they start to redden, the heat from our hands blending with the warmth of the fire. We put a makeshift pillow under his head so Nola can slide out, and take turns keeping watch while the guys rest. Nola lies down on the other side of the fire, away from everyone, curling into herself. She hasn't said a word in hours.

Zeke and Ethan have both fallen asleep, and I encourage Ronnie to get a couple of hours herself while I stay with Kohnrad. He's so still, his breathing shallow and quiet. Moving closer, I stare at his bruised face, torn between crying and wanting to tell him so many things—things I didn't know I needed to say because, until now, I didn't realize how much I care.

I think of all he's taught me. How he's pushed me past my own limits, to do things I never thought possible. He's forced me to look at things differently, to see people differently. I never expected this journey to challenge and change me so much. All because of this man.

"You got me on this crazy journey. You better be here to see me finish it," I murmur in his ear, hoping he can hear me. Kohnrad doesn't respond, of course, and I wipe at the tears running down my cheeks. What did he do to deserve this? Why would he put himself in harm's way for us?

I must have dozed off at some point, because a hand on my shoulder pulls me awake. It's Ethan. He looks more like himself, but his cheeks are still red and his lips cracked. Using the wall for support, he lowers himself down beside me.

"Are you hurt?" I whisper, looking him over.

He shakes his head. "Sore," he rasps, running a hand over his bloodshot eyes.

I can only imagine how hard it must have been carrying Kohnrad up the trail. His height alone would be a struggle, but he has to outweigh Ethan by almost a hundred pounds.

"He hasn't moved," I say, keeping my voice low so we don't disturb the others. "I'm worried. Isn't there something more we can do?"

"Wait."

"Patience isn't exactly my strongest quality, you know." I cross my legs and lean forward, trying to ease a cramp in my back. "It's just… I don't know. I didn't expect to… *feel* so much on this journey. To meet all of you and become so attached. I thought it would be more… straightforward, I guess. Just stay on the path and get to the end. Easy enough, right? Ha, except that's not this path at all. It's so much more. So much more than

I expected. There's a… a depth, a fullness, an expanding of who I am. I'm not explaining it well, I know. I just feel so much… larger inside. Like I have more space to move and think and feel. It's no longer all crammed together, pressing down and suffocating me. Does that make any sense at all?"

"The Path opens doors… to walk out into wide… open… spaces."

"Yeah. It's wild and beautiful and terrifying all at the same time."

We sit in comfortable silence until I feel myself drifting off again. Unwilling to leave Kohnrad's side, I lie down where I am. A gentle weight drapes over my shoulders, a blanket settling over me.

"Thank you," I murmur, stifling a yawn.

I wake a few hours later, disoriented. We're so completely shut off from the outside, it's hard to tell what time of day it is. Kohnrad seems the same, which is both a relief and a concern. Scooting closer to the fire, I accept the cup of coffee Ronnie offers me, trying not to grimace at its bitterness. Cream and sugar are luxuries not often found on this trip.

Nola stirs, adjusting her blanket around her shoulders. She refuses coffee and stays on her mat, her gaze fixed on the fire. Her withdrawal from the group is troubling, and I'm worried she'll slip back into her stupor from the Dark Forest. She shouldn't though, right? She said she was healed. When things calm down with Kohnrad, I know I should talk to her.

After our meal, Zeke, Ronnie and I reposition Kohnrad and check his wounds. His bruising is darker than it was last night, and his eyes remain swollen shut. His lips are dry and cracked, so I use a wet rag to moisten them, wiping away the dried blood with gentle strokes. Zeke prods at his ribs, checking to see if they're broken. Kohnrad's right side is worse than his left, with a mottling of red and purple spreading from his side almost to the center of his chest.

"I do not think anything is broken, but I cannot be sure." An odd expression crosses Zeke's face. "What is this? Let me see his back." Ronnie loosens the blanket, and Zeke adjusts Kohnrad onto his side. Moving around to get a better look, he mutters under his breath and looks at Ethan. "He has been whipped."

Ethan's face blanches.

"I cannot believe I missed this," Zeke continues. "We must get his wounds cleaned and position him off his back. The skin is broken, but the cuts are not as deep as they could have been. It appears his clothing has protected him."

We set to work heating water and wash Kohnrad's back, checking him over more thoroughly to make sure we haven't missed any other wounds. Now that we're looking, we discover scars all over his body. He's been whipped before, possibly stabbed, definitely cut and burned. This man is not all he appears to be.

Ronnie makes a salve from items in the supply pile and applies it to the open wounds. Thankfully, there are only a few. The rest are just raised welts. We fill rags with snow to use as ice packs, placing them on his face and ribs now that his body temp has risen. We get him as comfortable as we can, but with all his injuries, I don't know if we're helping or hurting. Only time will tell.

"Your Majesty."

"You may enter, Messenger."

"Your Majesty, the Sojourners have reached the tunnel of the Highlands."

"And Keeper?"

"He has reached the tunnel. That is all we know. I'm sorry."

"Thank you. You may go."

"Yes, Your Majesty."

"Dark One, er... Captain. We've rounded up the ones you requested."

"All of them?"

"All but two, Captain."

"And which two did you let escape?"

"That's not what... Right, right, um, the leader and his wife have disappeared. Sir."

"These are the two responsible for the chaos in the Marketplace?"

"It seems that way, Captain."

"And your men did not think it prudent to send searchers out to get the situation under control?"

"Well, Sir, it's just that no one really thought much of it, you know. I mean, the man—he's just an ignorant wanderer. No one takes him seriously. My men had some fun with him and taught him a lesson, to be sure. He didn't walk away on his own, if you catch my drift. I don't know where that dog came from, though. Vicious thing. But those folks that helped him, there's only so many places they can hide. We'll find them soon enough and bring them in. You have my word, Captain."

"Your word is of no interest to me, and I find your ineptitude appalling. It appears you have grown slothful while I was away, which is truly unfortunate—for you, that is. But the situation has the potential to create a wonderful illustration the entire town will never forget. So, I will require your services one final time."

"Yes, Dark One. I mean, Captain, Sir. Whatever I can do to be of help."

"Guards, take this man and the others to the Marketplace. Strip them and ready my whips. I want the entire city present within the hour. No exceptions. I have a show to put on. One that will greatly please my Master."

Chapter 12

The storm rages outside for two long days. We take turns shoveling snow away from the door and mucking out the mule's corner. We're all a bit cabin-crazy, but at least the weather has made it impossible for anyone to come after us.

We tend to Kohnrad's wounds, turning him often to keep him from developing pressure sores. He lets out a few groans when we move him, which I take as a good sign. We're also able to get him to swallow small amounts of water—it's all we can do to prevent dehydration, although I suspect he's already suffering from that.

I have the last watch on our third night, early morning now, and to keep myself awake, I've been practicing finding the Pillar of Fire. I haven't yet figured out why it's always moving, but I am getting quicker at finding it.

An interesting feature, which I haven't completely proven yet, is that my time with the Fire isn't the same as time out here. Meaning, I can spend what seems like an hour messing around with the Flame, only to find a few minutes have passed in the tunnel. I've tested this theory while listening to conversations around me, and it seems accurate, but I've yet to confide in anyone to confirm it.

Back in Kirkos, Kohnrad said something about the Fire that keeps running through my thoughts. *"It be a weapon as well as a gift. Yous gotta learn the difference."*

I understand the gift part. When I gave the Flame away to Nola and Ronnie, they were healed. But in the Dark Forest, when I was scared and trying to protect Ethan, the Flame injured Raoul and consumed the woods. I don't know how much of it is me controlling the Fire versus the Fire using me as a conduit. Do my emotions affect the Fire, or is it my intent? Or is it both? Or… neither.

I've been itching to see if I can throw the Fire intentionally, but it's not exactly safe to be messing around like that while in the tunnel. And I probably can't do it anyways. Besides, I don't want anyone laughing if they see me trying.

So. Here I am, staring at the Pillar and wondering all of these things. I reach out, running my fingers through its flames. It pulses and flickers, beckoning, pulling.

"You seem like you want to do something," I say.

The Flame flickers higher.

I lift my brows in surprise. "Did you really just do that?"

It shoots up again.

"Okay, let's assume I'm not crazy, and you are actually communicating with me. How am I supposed to know what to do?"

The Flame lowers, the blue wave around it pulsing higher and higher. It begins to change, forming an image. I see Kohnrad lying on the floor of the tunnel, a rainbow of light surrounding him. As I watch, the colors rotate as if in a prism until the purest blue I've ever seen, ripples over his body. The color fades, and a brilliant yellow bursts forth, flowing like liquid gold, soaking into Kohnrad's skin until he glistens like a polished statue. Once more, the prism turns, and the yellow disappears, only to be replaced by a blinding white light. I close my eyes and turn away, unable to handle its glare. When I turn back, the light has faded, and the image is gone. Only the flame remains.

"Woah," I whisper. Now what am I supposed to do?

Closing my hand around the Flame, I pull away from the pillar and bring my focus back to the tunnel with Kohnrad lying before me. He hasn't moved, at least not that I can see. I open my hand and the pulsing blue Flame surrounds it. Its warmth heats my palm, and I wonder if it wants me to touch Kohnrad. I didn't think the Fire was for physical healing, but after what I just saw, I think it does more than burn away the darkness.

Uncertain, I reach my hand towards Kohnrad. What if I'm wrong? Will the Fire hurt him? The warmth in my palm pulses, refusing to be ignored, so, taking a deep breath, I place my hand on Kohnrad's side. The heat is instant, growing until my hand feels like it's burning. Kohnrad moans loudly, and his body stiffens, causing me to jerk back, thinking I've just hurt him.

A hand darts out, grabbing mine, and places it back on Kohnrad. Ethan. His body shakes as he covers my hand, holding it in place. The muscles in his forearm strain with exertion and a bead of sweat drips down his face.

The heat continues to build, becoming unbearable. There's a rushing sound in my ears, like a roaring wind. Everything swirls like I'm caught in a vortex. Fire erupts all around, flames dancing and pulsing higher and higher. I see a man standing in the Fire, burning but not consumed. Light surrounds him, illuminating him, while flames blaze brighter and hotter until I can no longer stand the heat. I feel like I'm burning from the inside out.

I cry out in anguish, and everything disappears as if sucked into a black hole. A flood of sound hits my ears—Zeke and Ronnie yelling, Nola screaming, Charlie barking. Putting my hands over my ears, I begin rocking back and forth. What did I do? What did I do?

Someone grabs me and holds me tight, stroking my hair, telling me everything's okay. I'm crying; I know I'm hysterical, but I can't stop. What did I do? What did I do?

"Kenna, it's okay. Everything's okay… Kenna, are you listening to me? It's alright. Everything's alright."

The words confuse me. How can things be okay? Don't they know what I did?

"Are they dead?" I blurt out.

"What? No! No one's dead. No one's hurt. Everyone's fine."

Someone's lying to me. Why would they lie to me? Are they trying to protect me? What have I done?

"Kenna, open your eyes. Look at me," a different voice says. A deep voice. One I've longed to hear speak for days.

My eyes fly open, and I see Kohnrad's bruised face looking back at me.

"There now," he says, offering a weak smile. "What's all the fussin' about? How's a man supposed to rest with all this noise?"

With a cry of disbelief, I throw myself at Kohnrad. He lets out a grunt of pain, but I don't care. He's alive! He's alive!

Ronnie pulls me back to her. "Careful Kenna, he's still sore."

I laugh, then cry, overwhelmed with relief. I can't believe Kohnrad's okay. But where's Ethan? Is he okay? I look around, terror seizing my chest. He was just here. Right here. Where did he go?

"I'm over here," comes his voice.

I find him sitting a distance away, leaning up against the tunnel wall.

"I'm fine, Kenna."

Needing to see for myself, I crawl towards him, looking for injuries.

"What happened? I don't understand. How are you okay?"

"Not my first time in the Fire," he says, his voice low and gritty, not the usual breathy strain.

"Your voice!"

"Yeah," he says with his lopsided smile. "I must've got some leftover Fire."

"But the heat. I thought…"

"It's been awhile. I'm a little rusty. And you were throwing some pretty big flames," he replies with a wink.

My face flushes. That's a compliment, right?

"So, you're okay? Really?"

"Better than okay. Now go harass Keeper for a while. I need to rest."

I give Ethan a big grin and turn back to Kohnrad. He's propped up on his side so he can drink and try to eat. Nola and Charlie sit close by, while Zeke and Ronnie have moved to the other side of the fire.

"You've been practicing," Kohnrad says when I settled down near him.

I'm not sure if he means in general, or on him.

"I… you said… you said it would teach me. I think it did."

"Tell me, what did it show you?"

"I asked what it wanted to do, and it showed me you."

"Really, did it now? That's a pretty smart Fire." Kohnrad chuckles, then winces as it hurts his side.

"So, did the Fire help you?" I ask.

"Did you think it wouldn't?"

"I wasn't sure. What if I was imagining things?"

"Yet, you still went ahead and used the Flame."

Dread fills my stomach. What he said is true. I wasn't sure what would happen, yet I still went ahead and used it.

"I'm sorry, I shouldn't have done that. I—"

"Stop, Kenna. Don't apologize. You did the right thing. You trusted the Flame. You're learning its power. Let it keep teaching you. If you grasp at it and try to use it for your own desires, it will burn you. But if you follow it, move with it, you'll grow as one, and its power will flow through you."

"Why does it move? When I look for it, it's always in a different spot. Why is that?"

"Well now, the Fire's alive and it does what it wants. If it could be tamed and made to stay in one spot, what would be the fun in that?"

"Ha, you're definitely feeling better. You're back to talking in riddles."

"Actually," Nola says, leaning in. "I think you did something to his voice. Not like Ethan's. I mean, how he talks." She turns to Kohnrad. "You've lost most of your accent. Like, you talk better."

I stare at Nola in shock. She's right! I hadn't noticed until she pointed it out, but now it's so obvious.

Kohnrad sighs and lays his head back. He starts to laugh again, but then catches himself. "I've gotta stop doing that."

My eyes narrow with suspicion. Why would the Fire change how he talks? That doesn't make any sense. I've got a funny feeling…

Laughter breaks out behind me. "You're busted, Keep," Ethan says. "You better tell them."

I look at Ethan, then back at Kohnrad as things click into place. "Is there somethin' I's be needin' to know?" I say, mimicking Kohnrad.

Ethan lets out a hoot. "Oh, she's got you! You're in for it now."

"I think I liked you better when you kept quiet, Walker," Kohnrad says.

"Might've helped if you had too, sir," Ethan retorts with a grin.

"Would someone please tell us what is going on?" Zeke says, looking at us in confusion.

Kohnrad lets out a frustrated sigh and tips his head back before answering. "My accent is fake. I only use it when I'm in the Outerlands."

I burst out laughing—stomach-holding, breath-stealing, obnoxious laughter. I'm laughing so hard I'm crying and I can't stop. It's so absurd, I can't believe it. A fake accent! Who does that? I try to pull myself together, but every time I think I've got it under control, it bursts through again. My stomach hurts from laughing so hard, and I can't sit up straight. Finally, I manage to get it down to just giggles, desperate not to look at anyone and have their bewildered expressions set me off again.

"I don't think I have ever had someone laugh at me like that before," Kohnrad says with a huff.

"It's just… you had the *worst* accent *ever*!" I start laughing again, and this time, everyone joins in.

"Hey now, I worked hard on that persona."

"I told you you overdid it," Ethan says, leaning his head back against the wall.

"Well, it served its purpose, didn't it? And since the cat's out of the bag, so to speak, I won't offend your tender ears with it any longer."

"I think I liked you better when you were—"

"You sure you want to finish that sentence?" Kohnrad growls.

Ethan grins, not the least bit intimidated. "You might as well tell them the rest."

"Wait, there's more?" I ask.

"Oh, there's lots more."

***

Apparently, all this stimulation has drained Kohnrad, so we'll have to continue our conversation at a later date.

Coward.

"Come with me, Kenna," Zeke says. "We need to clear the door and scout the Path."

With a bit of an attitude, I get dressed and grab a shovel. I can't believe it's still snowing, though the wind has died down, leaving only a feathering of snowflakes drifting through the air. Zeke and I work in silence, clearing snow away from the back door and dealing with the mule's disgusting mess.

The snow is a good two feet deep, with drifts climbing higher than my waist. Without the wind, a stillness lingers—a peacefulness that follows a storm. It's beautiful up here, though we still can't see far. Just enough to know the trail follows a narrow ledge leading to another mountain canyon.

The work drains the last of the angst out of me, which was Zeke's intent, I'm sure. I follow behind him as he carves a trail through the snow. His stride is much longer than mine, and I struggle to keep up. We manage only a half mile or so before we're forced to turn around. The Path leads between two towering mountain walls, its route hidden beneath deep snow. Without the proper equipment, continuing would be foolish.

The snow finally stops, and the sun makes a weak attempt to peek through as we return to the tunnel. Inside, Ronnie has coffee and breakfast waiting for us. Kohnrad and Ethan are both sound asleep, so there's no chance of a conversation happening anytime soon. With little else to occupy my time, I lie down and soon drift off to sleep.

***

"—follows between for a good distance." Kohnrad's voice breaks through the fog of sleep, pulling me awake. I blink, momentarily disoriented, as his words sink in. "There are many drop-offs and false trails. The sun doesn't reach in there for more than an hour or so a day."

"Is there another option?" Zeke asks. "One that does not entail staying here for a week waiting for the snow to melt?"

"You're not going to like it," Kohnrad replies. "But no, there's no other way through." He finishes his drink and sets the cup aside before continuing. "The good news is no one's likely to follow us up here. The tunnel is the gateway to the king's land, and the canyon trail is deadly to those who don't know its ways. Only those who are familiar with it, or have a guide, dare to venture in.

"And you know the way?"

"I do, as does Ethan."

Of course he does. Nothing about Ethan should surprise me anymore. The man has so many layers, I'm constantly discovering something new. I am curious, though, why he's portrayed himself as a fellow traveler when it's becoming clear he's much more than that.

Zeke shows no surprise, but Ronnie and Nola exchange questioning looks. Ethan's expression stays neutral, although I think I detect a hint of red creeping up his neck. Oh yeah, things are definitely getting interesting around here.

"You will not be able to travel for several days with those ribs," Zeke points out.

"Bind me up, and I'll be fine. I've managed with worse."

"And the mule?"

"We load him down so we can travel light. He won't like it, but he won't cause any trouble. Ethan can break the trail. It'll be cold and slow going, but if we don't head out soon, another storm could hit and snow us in for weeks. The weather's unpredictable up here, no matter the season."

"How long do you anticipate it will take?"

"Normally, it takes two to three days from here to the outskirts of the king's land. Traveling with a group this size, one being injured, and a couple feet of snow on the trail, I figure two days just to pass the summit and get back down to the tree line. Then another two days or so to reach the city."

"So four or five days if all goes well?"

"That's under the best of circumstances." Kohnrad pauses, his eyes sweeping over us to make sure we're paying attention. His tone shifts, more serious now. "There'll be no fire until we reach the tree line on the other side. If things go sideways, or another storm comes through while we're still up top, we won't be able to travel. We'll have to hunker down and ride it out, and honestly, the odds of surviving aren't good if that happens."

He looks at Nola, his gaze softening. "Nola, Charlie's gonna need his feet wrapped, and we'll rig him a poncho to keep him dry. If he'll carry a couple of small bags, it'll make things easier for the rest of us."

Kohnrad glances down at Charlie, who's lying next to him, and scratches behind the dog's ears. The dog thumps his tail in approval. "Good boy," Kohnrad murmurs, then shifts his focus to Ethan. "There should be enough daylight left to trek out a bit. It'll help to know what we're walking into."

Ethan nods and shares a look with Zeke, a silent agreement passing between them before Zeke offers to go with.

"There's snowshoes and poles under that last tarp by the door. See if you can get to the Gulch. If it starts snowing again, turn around and head back. I don't want to have to come rescue you." His words carry both gratitude and a subtle warning. Ethan meets his gaze, his lips twitching into a smile, and acknowledges the unspoken meaning.

The guys bundle up and put on their snowshoes, each with a small pack of supplies and water for the trip. Sunshine enters the tunnel when the door opens, and I squint against the glare. I hope the good weather holds and things go well so Ethan and Zeke can get back soon.

With them gone, Nola and I help Ronnie change the dressings on Kohnrad's back. His ribs are still tender, and I can see it hurts him to move. The swelling around his eyes is going down, and the bruising on his face is a nice rainbow of color.

"You have a lot of scars," I say.

"Yep."

If he wasn't already hurt, I'd punch him. Obviously, not all of his "persona" was fake.

"Why did you pretend to be someone you weren't?" I ask.

"I wondered when you'd get around to that."

"Well, you're obviously more than you first let on. And what you did in Kirkos—why would you let them beat you like that? Why pretend to be nobody? Why not defend yourself?"

"Things in the Outerlands aren't always what they seem. Very few people or situations can be trusted. By appearing less than I am, I have the freedom to travel where and when I need to. No one worries about what I'm doing, and I stay off the radar of certain *unsavory* characters. Usually."

"And what've you been doing?"

"Gathering together the Remnant."

"Does he always talk like this?" Ronnie asks me, shaking her head.

"Yes," I reply. "Always."

"How annoying."

"Tell me about it," I say with an eye roll.

"Ladies, you know I can hear you, right?" Kohnrad says, raising a brow.

"Sorry, we're just having a bit of fun. But seriously, what does 'Remnant' mean? Are you talking about us?"

"Over the years, few have chosen to walk the Path to meet the king. An Enchanter has bewitched the people, seducing them into a blindness wrapped in riches and social standing. You saw this in Kirkos. No one's made it past that city for nearly fifteen years. Marcus and his community are all that remain of the king's people, and their time there is limited. The Dark One won't tolerate them much longer."

"Are you talking about Cole? Would he really hurt all those people? Even his own parents?" Nola says, her face betraying her concern for Hannah.

"I'm afraid so. Bitterness and rage consumed his heart at a young age, and the Enchanter used that to his advantage. Cole's darkness is very deep, and very cruel."

"This Enchanter," I say, glancing at Nola and Ronnie. "We met him… in the Dark Forest."

"You did."

"He tried to… He knew who we were. He said things. Things he shouldn't have known."

"His gifting allows him to see into people."

"You mean like Zeke?" Ronnie asks, joining the conversation.

"Similar, but not the same. The Enchanter's understanding is deeper, more personal. Where Zeke sees the overall condition, the Enchanter sees the little things that make a person vulnerable. What should've been used to build up and strengthen, has instead warped into a tool that destroys."

"So, he was trying to… to destroy us," Nola says, her voice quiet, almost as if saying the words pains her.

"Yes, that was his intent."

A flash of something flickers across Nola's face—an aching mixed with desire. She closes her eyes and holds very still, letting the moment pass before opening them again.

"But Kenna blinded him," she says. "So that means he can't see into people anymore, right?"

"Not exactly. The gift can't be taken back, for then it wouldn't be a gift. However, the way it's used… that can be altered. The Enchanter will find many things are no longer as they were."

"I don't understand," I say. "Why is all of this happening? What does it have to do with us?"

"It has everything to do with you. All of you. You are the last of the Sojourners to choose the King's Path before the War of Darkness."

"What—"

"Are you sure?" Nola asks, her voice rising in disbelief. "I mean, how do you know that?"

"Because Kenna has a king's compass."

"My compass belongs to a king?" I say, the words tumbling out before I can fully grasp their meaning.

"That particular compass belongs to a line of royalty. Only a Fire Holder can carry it. I admit, I was surprised when you showed up at the cabin with it. That compass hasn't been seen in nearly fifty years."

"How… How did you know I had it? I never showed it to you."

Kohnrad tips his head, focusing on my waist. "Look at the pouch you're carrying. See that emblem in the center?"

I untie the small bag from my belt and turn it over. In the middle is the faded outline of a compass surrounded by flames, similar to a shooting star. With all the times I've handled this pouch, I've never noticed the symbol before. I don't know how I missed it.

Slipping the compass into my hand, I run my fingers over the engraving on the lid. A king's crown. A king's compass. The gravity of what I'm holding hits me.

"Why…" I begin, but stop when I notice Kohnrad's expression. There's a faraway look in his eyes, like his mind has gone elsewhere. Only the twitching of his jaw betrays his calm exterior.

"Kohnrad?" I say, touching his arm. "Are you alright?"

Kohnrad visibly pulls himself back to the present, shrugging off whatever caught him away. "My apologies," he says, clearing his throat. "I, uh, wandered a bit."

"Okay, that's enough for now," Ronnie says, placing a hand on Kohnrad's shoulder. "Everyone needs to back off and let Keeper rest." She waves Nola and me away, murmuring to Kohnrad as he closes his eyes and lets her fuss over him.

Instead of joining Nola, I chose a spot further down the wall, needing space to myself. The compass vibrates in my palm, its warmth soothing despite the emotions warring inside me.

Part of me thrills at the symbol of power and history in my hand; the other shrinks in fear at the responsibility given with it.

A shudder overtakes me as the echo of an ancient voice whispers through my mind—one I hoped never to hear again.

"I know who you are now."

Chapter 13

I've taken the mule, who I've nicknamed Mac, outside for some fresh air as an excuse to get out of the dark tunnel. Mac snorts, bobbing his head as if he agrees with this decision, and stands, soaking in the warmth of the sun. Resting against his broad side, I fiddle with his mane, grounding myself in the simplicity of the moment.

A sudden chill sweeps over me, and an intense sense of dread—so strong, so absolute—doubles me over. I lurch forward, pushing past Mac, and stumble along the trail left by Zeke and Ethan. My mind is screaming "danger", but I don't know what I'm looking for. There's no movement ahead, and sunset is still a couple of hours away, so the guys won't be back yet.

I stop, frozen, unsure what to do. Is this real, or just my overactive imagination? Mac snorts and lets out a bray loud enough to snap me out of my stupor. With reluctance, I retrace my steps, trying to talk myself out of what I'm feeling, but it won't go away. In fact, it feels more certain than before.

The tunnel door creaks open just as I reach the mule, and Ronnie supports Kohnrad as he steps outside, his face drawn.

Charlie squirms by them, his paws kicking up snow as he darts down the path, nose to the ground.

"I'll be fine now for a bit. Thanks, Ronnie," Kohnrad says, waving her back inside.

Ronnie raises an eyebrow at me, casting a pointed look at Konrad before closing the door. Leaning back, Kohnrad gazes out over the mountains and I stop nearby, uncertain whether I should say anything.

"You feel it too, don't you?" he murmurs, his eyes distant, not meeting mine.

"Something's wrong." I wait for his reaction. Wait to see if he'll contradict me.

"Yes, something is very wrong."

My pulse quickens. "Do you think something's happened to Zeke and Ethan?"

"No. I think it's... Can you still see the Fire?"

I look at him in surprise. "What does the Fire have to do with it?"

Kohnrad looks at me then, his expression serious. "Just take a look, please."

I close my eyes, unsettled by his tone. I expect the pillar to be nearby, but it's nowhere in sight. With continuing unease, I move through the shadows, searching for the glow of the Flame.

There!

I tread slowly, the shadows deeper than I remember. My boot hits something hard, and I stumble forward, almost landing on my knees. Looking behind me, I find a low brick wall, only two layers high, forming a wide circle around the stone pillar.

That's weird. In all the times I've been here, I've never encountered anything except the Fire. Examining the wall, I wonder what its purpose could be. It's too low to keep anyone out, though I suppose it could contain the pillar. But why?

The Fire looks unchanged, burning the same as always, and leaps into my hand when I reach for it. "You look like you're doing okay," I say, smiling as its warmth spreads up my arm. "I hate to be one to say 'hi' and run, but I've gotta go."

The Fire hovers low, as if it's sad. Something has truly happened to my mind—I'm attaching emotions to a flame. Then again, I'm also talking as if it's a living being, so...

I return the Flame with reluctance and step away. "I'll be back later," I whisper.

Nearing the wall, I squint, trying to focus on what I think I'm seeing. I can't be sure, but it looks higher than it was a moment ago. The bricks seem wider, thicker. I stare without blinking, watching for any sign of movement, but nothing happens. Feeling ridiculous, I shake my head and step over, careful not to touch the brick. For some reason, I don't think this wall is a good thing.

Opening my eyes, I watch Charlie bounding through the snow in circles before he lopes over to us, tongue hanging out. I reach down and rub his ear as he leans into my leg.

"The Fire's still there," I say, answering Kohnrad's questioning gaze. "But it was further away than it's ever been."

Without a word, he continues to look at me, searching for more.

"There's a brick wall around the pillar. I thought it was only a foot tall, but when I went to leave, it seemed higher. I've never seen anything else there before. It's always been just the Fire."

Kohnrad frowns and runs a hand down his face.

"What do you think it means?" I ask, looking up into his troubled eyes.

"It means the Serpent of Darkness has found a way to contain the pillar. If it succeeds, it'll cut off access to the Fire and use the Flame for itself."

My heart skips a hard beat, stealing my breath. *Serpent?*

"What is this Serpent, and how can it do such a thing?" I ask, my voice trembling, afraid I already know.

"It is… the enemy of the… king… and…"

Kohnrad's face has gone ghostly white, and he's sweating profusely despite the cold. Afraid he's going to collapse, I try to help him move so I can open the door, but I'm only chest-high to his tall frame, and he doesn't budge. Then, in slow motion, like a toppling tree, he slips sideways.

I throw all my weight into holding him up, but I'm failing to keep him upright, and we're both going down. Shouts break out behind me, and over my shoulder, I see Ethan kicking off his snowshoes as he runs towards us. He slips in beside me and takes on Kohnrad's weight, allowing me to get out from under him. Zeke shows up on his other side, and between the two of them, they move Kohnrad's sagging body away from the entrance.

Fumbling with the lever, I push the door open so they can walk Kohnrad inside. I want to follow, but I need to grab Mac. He's not happy about going back inside and pulls against the rope until a sharp bark from Charlie jolts him forward. Yanking the stubborn mule inside, I holler for Nola to get Charlie and close the door.

Ethan and Zeke lower Kohnrad down onto his mat, while Ronnie lays a hand on his forehead. His breaths are ragged, and he's not opening his eyes. Beads of sweat glisten on his hairline.

"What happened? What's wrong with him?" The questions come all at once, bombarding me with noise.

I stand there, my eyes darting from person to person. "We were talking, and he just started not looking good."

"I'm fine," Kohnrad mumbles. "Stop fussing. I just need… to… rest."

"You're burning up, you stubborn man!" Ronnie says, tugging on his jacket. "Get his coat off. We need to get his fever down."

Nola twists her hand into my sleeve and pulls me aside. "Can't you do that fire thing on him again?" she whispers.

"I don't know," I whisper back. "I don't control it."

Nola's face blanches, then flushes red. "So you're not even going to try?"

"I didn't say that."

Nola leans in, forcing me back a step. "Then do something," she hisses.

"I… Just give me a minute." I back up another step, but Nola moves with me.

"You can't let him die."

I raise my hands up to keep her out of my face. "Nola, it's not my—"

"Yes, it is!"

Her accusation shocks me. "What are you talking about? I didn't—"

"He risked his life for us! You have to help him. You have to!" Nola's shoulders sag, and she covers her face with her hands. Sobs break through, and I realize she isn't blaming me like I thought.

"Hey, I'm sorry. Of course, I'll try." I reach out, placing a hand on her shoulder.

She lowers her hands but keeps her head down. "I've never had anyone do what he has done for me, you know?" Nola looks up, her eyes red and filled with tears. "I didn't realize how much it mattered until… until…"

"I get it." I nod. "Until he got hurt, I didn't realize how much he meant to me either."

Nola sniffles, wiping her face with her sleeve. "So, you'll ask the Fire to heal him?"

"Yeah, I'll ask. Just… let me have a moment alone, okay?"

"Sure, just hurry. Please."

I turn away into the shadows and take a deep breath. Okay, I can do this. Closing my eyes, I focus on where I last saw the pillar. It's still there, surrounded by the wall, but something is different. A second outer layer now lines the original row, making the wall wider than before.

It *is* changing.

I hesitate only a moment before stepping over the bricks. Kohnrad said the wall is meant to contain the Fire, but maybe I can move the pillar and get the Fire outside the circle. I wrap my arms around the smooth stone and try lifting the pillar. It doesn't budge. Not even a bit.

I wonder if the Fire will burn without the pillar? Maybe I can take it with me and make a new stand. I scoop up the Fire with both hands but only get a small portion. I try again, but the same thing happens. Only a small Flame comes away while the main Fire burns undisturbed.

"Okay, none of that worked," I say, studying the Flame. "Is there something else I should be doing to help you?"

A surge of energy courses through the Fire, and the flames shoot skyward, doubling in height. The blue wave on the outside pulses higher and higher, striving to catch up. Then, everything calms and the flame lowers, hovering just above the pillar until an image begins to appear. At first, it looks like mountains, but then a large plateau comes into focus, along with what appears to be a city.

The image continues to shift and refocus, sharpening until a beautiful stone building with balconies and pools and gardens appears. I lean in, trying to get a better look, when the Fire erupts in my face, shocking me back.

"Hey! That wasn't nice!" I say, as the Flame dances wildly in front of me. I stay a pace back, not wanting to get singed again. "Okay, I'll figure out the city thing later, but right now, I need your help. Kohnrad, Keeper, isn't doing well and I don't know why. I gave him the Fire from before, and he seemed better. But now he's not, and I don't know if I can even give him another dose or whatever, and I... I don't know what to do for him."

The Fire shoots up again, the blue waves pulsing along with it, before dying down and once more, showing the image of the city on the plateau.

"Yes, I get that. This city is important, and I will help you, but I need to help Kohnrad first."

The image flickers, then disappears as the Fire returns to a gentle, rhythmic burn.

"Are you going to help me or not?" I yell, frustrated.

Nothing changes.

"I'm sorry, I'm sorry! Please! Will you help me?"

The Flame continues as if it hasn't heard me and I hang my head in defeat.

"Ok. Well, goodbye then."

My feet move in slow motion, fighting to stay while my mind knows I need to return to the tunnel. I force myself to step over the wall, to walk away. A noise stops me, and I look back at the Fire, searching for the source. Everything looks the same, even the wall. I hold still, straining to catch what I thought I heard.

Nothing.

I release my breath and turn to leave. Then, I hear it again. The faint sound of… laughter, then… my name.

My eyes fly open in shock. That voice! I've heard it before.

"Kenna, did you get it?" Nola's words pull me back to the tunnel. "What's taking you so long?"

"What?" I croak, unable to manage more.

"You've been gone a long time. What's going on? Did you get the Flame or not?"

"I…" What does she mean? It shouldn't have been more than a minute or two out here. Has it really been that long? Has time changed too?

"Kenna?"

"No."

"No? You didn't get it? Why not? Isn't it working? Won't it let you heal him twice? Did you—"

"I don't know. I don't know why it won't let me, I just… I need to talk to Kohnrad," I say, pushing past her to get to where they've laid Kohnrad.

He's pale, his skin drawn and lips tight, as if he's fighting something. His chest rises and falls with shallow breaths, each one seeming harder than the last. He doesn't look well at all.

"How is he?" I ask, searching faces, hoping he's able to talk, if only for a moment.

"I am worried," Zeke replies, an edge to his voice. "His ribs are healing well. I do not think they are broken. His wounds are not infected, and I have not seen signs of internal bleeding. I can find no reason for his fever."

"Kenna says she can't use the Fire on him again," Nola says from behind me.

I cringe, irritation flashing through me.

"Can I talk to him?" I ask, pressing in closer, my voice tight with urgency. I know I'm being unreasonable, but a deep-seated fear is pushing at me, and I need Kohnrad to make it go away.

"Kenna, he's not coherent right now. I'm sorry, but he can't talk to you," Ronnie says, trying to lead me away, but I shrug her off and stay where I am.

The longer I stand there, the more frustrated I become. I need something—anything—to help make sense of this. Without a word, Ethan steps into my line of sight, blocking Kohnrad from view. I ignore him and shift to the side. He shifts with me. Still refusing to look at him, I move back over. He moves back with me, his movement deliberate and steady. He anticipates my next move, and once again, shifts with me.

"Stop it!" I yell, trying to shove him out of my way.

Ethan grabs my arms and pulls me close, forcing me to look up. "What did you see?"

For a moment, I'm disoriented, caught between the closeness of his body and the confusion of thinking he's talking about Kohnrad.

He asks again, his voice low and concerned. "Something's wrong with the Fire. What did you see?"

The confusion flees, and I search Ethan's eyes with surprise. "How do you know that?"

"We came back early because I felt something was wrong. There was a shift in the shadows."

I stare at Ethan's chest, trying to sort things out.

"Kenna, look at me. Tell me what's going on."

I glance back up, tears threatening to break loose. "The Fire wouldn't give me a Flame to heal Kohnrad."

Ethan remains still, waiting for me to continue.

I drop my head and look away, gathering my thoughts. "There's something going on with it. A wall has shown up. Kohnrad said… he said the Serpent of Darkness is building it to contain the Fire. I don't know what that means, but the Fire can't move now… and when I asked what it wanted me to do, it just showed me an image of a city on a high plateau."

Ethan's body tenses, his grip tightening, and I look up at him. The gravity of his expression sends a shiver down my spine.

"And?" he prompts.

"And…" I begin, unable to look away. "When I asked about healing Kohnrad, it just showed me the city again. I don't know if it can't heal him because of the wall or if it's saying to go to the city to get help. I don't know what it was trying to tell me."

"I do. It's Neriah, the king's city." Ethan lets go of my arms, putting distance back between us. Addressing the rest of the group, he says, "We need to leave as soon as possible."

"Keeper isn't well enough to travel," Ronnie says with concern.

"We don't have a choice. The Fire has shown Kenna the king's city. That's where we need to go."

"Do you think the mule will pull a sled?" Zeke asks. "There is a toboggan over on the wall."

"It may be our best option."

"Okay," Zeke says with a nod. "We will get everything ready now and leave at first light. You will break the path, I will be responsible for Keeper. We will get him to this city."

***

Plans are made and remade, things packed and repacked. A harness is made for Mac and another for Zeke, as he's the only one strong enough to pull Kohnrad when needed. Mac is hooked up and led around outside to test the sled and his cooperation. We work late into the night, checking and double-checking our gear and supplies. There'll be no turning back once we leave here.

Ronnie finds a box of dried herbs and makes a tea to help with Kohnrad's fever, while Zeke and Ethan bind his chest, preparing him as best they can. Either way, he's going to be uncomfortable.

We're all anxious and sleep doesn't come easily. I dream of darkness, and laughter, and a familiar mocking voice. I can't see who it is, but I know that voice. It haunts me and leaves me unsettled the next morning.

We eat a quick breakfast and load up the last of the supplies. Mac is antsy, no doubt as eager to get out of this tunnel as we are. So far, he's been okay with the harness and sled and everything else piled on him.

Charlie has picked up on the excitement too. As soon as Nola finishes wrapping his feet, he skips around the tunnel, giving us his goofy grin.

"Come here, Charlie," Nola says, grabbing at him. He leaps back, thinking she's playing a game. "Charlie, come!" The dog's tail droops, and he inches closer. Nola shakes her head, rubbing his ears. "Silly boy, I just need to finish getting you ready."

She hooks a small pack with a poncho around him, adjusting the straps so it stays in place without rubbing too tight. As soon as she lets go, Charlie shoots away, making a beeline for the open door.

"I think he's ready to go," I say, laughing.

"Yeah, he's tired of being cooped up and worried he's going to be left behind," she replies, shrugging into her backpack.

I help her adjust the weight and hand her a walking stick—Ethan's orders. With one last look around, I grab my stick and follow Nola out of the tunnel to join the others.

"Everything is ready," Zeke says, picking up Mac's lead rope. He and Ronnie will be in charge of the mule and Kohnrad. For this section at least.

Ethan adjusts the snowshoes strapped to his back and reaches for his poles, his expression stern. "No one steps anywhere but on the trail. There's no forgiveness through the canyon. One misstep could have deadly consequences."

With a solemn agreement and a final gear check, we close up the tunnel and head out. The trail is packed well from yesterday's scouting trip, providing an easy start, but the temperature drops several degrees as soon as we step between the high rock walls. Shadows plummet into deep crevices, their bottoms hidden in darkness. One quick glance down is all I can force myself to take before fixing my eyes on the trail before me. It's unsettling not knowing where things end or begin.

"The trail is unbroken ahead," Ethan says, bringing the group to a halt an hour later. "Everyone double-check your gear. It's going to be harder from here on out."

Zeke readjusts several items on the mule and switches spots with Ronnie so he can use the harness to guide the back end of the sled. So far, things have been smooth going. Mac hasn't had issues pulling the sled and Kohnrad hasn't complained at all.

"Let me break the trail and get a couple of feet in front of you before you follow," Ethan says, slipping into his snowshoes and tightening the bindings. "The path is wider here, but harder to navigate. Take your time, and if you lose your footing, try to fall forward so you can catch yourself."

He looks back at Zeke, waiting for him to signal he's ready. When he does, Ethan sets out, blazing a trail for us to follow. It soon becomes apparent why he told me to leave space between us. We need room to maneuver over the rocks and uneven ground, not to mention the blind corners and steep inclines. My boots sink a good six inches into the snow in spots, despite Ethan's attempts to pack it down.

Kohnrad groans as the sled tips from side to side, jerking over another mound of rocks. Zeke curses and yanks hard on the rope, bringing the sled back into alignment. We continue this way for hours, never moving out of the cold shadows, even though the angle of the sun shifts overhead. After a quick lunch,

I switch out with Ronnie and let Nola follow Ethan. I wish we could give Zeke a break, but he's the only one strong enough to do what he's doing.

We push on, and by early evening, make it to a shallow recess carved into the mountain wall with just enough of an overhang to provide shelter for the night. A giant gulch opens up before us, a wild river rushing along the bottom. The receding sun shines right into the space, warming the rock and our faces. It feels so good.

"Get the tents up first," Ethan says. "We have about an hour of sunlight left and it'll warm them up. I need to check the trail for tomorrow. I'll be back before dark."

"Ethan…" I want to say be careful, but it seems silly now.

His expression softens just a bit. "I'll be back soon."

I watch until he's out of sight, then go help set up the tents. We unload Mac, and Nola offers to rub him down and feed him. I help unstrap Kohnrad, and it takes three of us to move him into a tent, with Zeke doing most of the lifting. Ronnie has us sit Kohnrad up while she encourages him to drink the tea she brought along. He's still pale and barely conscious, but he doesn't seem as feverish as before. I hope it's because he's getting better.

The sun soon dips below the mountains, and a chill creeps in fast. Ronnie passes around a cold dinner that we eat standing up while watching for Ethan. Relief washes over me as he steps into camp a few minutes later and unhooks his snowshoes.

"Kohnrad's resting in the tent," Ronnie says, handing him a bowl of food. "He's not any worse."

Ethan nods and digs into his meal.

"How does it look for tomorrow?" Zeke asks.

Ethan finishes his last bite before answering. "Not good, but it could be worse. We'll climb most of the day. If we reach the summit by late afternoon, we can follow the ridge to the eastern slope. That'll lead us down to the treeline, which will give us shelter and fire."

"And if we do not make the summit in time?"

Ethan shakes his head and frowns. "The wind will shred our tents. If we don't make it over the top before dark, we'll freeze to death."

There isn't much to say after that, so we clean up and make sure Mac is secured so he won't wander off in the night. The guys join Kohnrad, and I climb into the other tent with Ronnie, Nola and Charlie. We sleep fully clothed, huddled together with heavy blankets, sharing body heat to keep warm. It's just enough.

Kohnrad is the same the next morning—still in and out of consciousness and unable to stand on his own. Ronnie gives him more tea, and we eat another cold meal for breakfast. My body seems to have adjusted to the high altitude of the mountains while in the tunnel. I'm breathing easier, and my legs feel stronger than before. I'm not as tired as I expected to be this morning, and I even had to tighten my belt up a notch.

Ethan and Zeke work on getting Kohnrad back onto the sled while the rest of us take down the tents. Mac snorts and shifts his weight around as we load him up, almost stepping on our feet more than once. It's the most agitation he's shown the entire trip, and I wonder if he knows what's ahead.

I can sense Ethan's worry about today's journey. There's a tightness in his jaw, a sharp edge to his movements that's hard to ignore. His focus is intense, calculations running through his mind—how much time we have, how hard we can push ourselves. The weight of it all would crush a lesser man.

The wind picks up as soon as we step out on the trail, buffeting us with a stinging cold that rips straight through our layers, burning our faces. Snow swirls around in small tornadoes, making it hard to see the path at times. We're spaced out more than yesterday, each of us struggling to stay upright and moving forward. I can't imagine fighting this all day. Whatever energy I had this morning is stripped away in a few short hours.

We climb wide, icy steps hewn into the rock, taking turns leading Mac so Zeke and another can lift Kohnrad. We slip and fall and have way too many near misses. I can't believe we're still alive. I'd cry, but the tears would just freeze my eyes shut. As it is, icicles hang off the men's mustaches and beards, and the cold has seeped into us all despite the layers of clothing and constant movement. My cheeks burn like they're on fire, and my toes have gone numb—definitely not a good sign.

We don't stop for lunch, and our breaks aren't really long enough to count as breaks. There's no point in arguing or complaining. If we don't keep moving, we won't make it in time and we all know it. I can no longer tell if time is passing in minutes or hours. It's a never-ending blur. My lungs burn and spasm with each breath, my body rejecting the freezing air.

Ethan shouts up ahead, his words carried away before I can catch them. I struggle to gain footing on the high step before me, but once I do, everything opens up. We've made it to the summit.

The wind up here is brutal and vicious, its force tearing at everything. I'm colder than I've ever been in my life, and it feels like there isn't enough air to breathe. Yet, I can't help but marvel at where I am. It's the most exhilarating experience I've ever had. We're smack dab in the middle of a vast mountain range, and the view is breathtaking.

"It is the most amazing feeling. To be here. In this moment," Zeke says, trying to catch his breath.

"I've never seen anything so beautiful," Ronnie yells over the howl of the wind. Her cheeks are windburned and chapped, but she has a huge smile on her face.

Words are inadequate to capture the true majesty before us. A sense of reverence settles, an awe for this wild place with its severity and beauty. Nothing in all of creation can compare to what lays before us in this moment.

Leaning into the fierce wind, we walk the windswept ridge, making our way to the eastern slope. Each step is a challenge in balance and coordination. The rough, rocky ground grinds against the sled, irritating Kohnrad enough to rouse him to consciousness.

"Get me off this blasted thing before it kills me!"

"Hold still! You are just making it worse." Zeke hollers, rushing forward to help.

Kohnrad thrashes against the bindings holding him in place, jerking hard on the harness. Mac throws his head up, lifting his front feet off the ground. The sled tilts sideways, nearly tipping over. I grab Mac's halter, trying to hold him still, but he keeps stomping and throwing his head. I'm afraid he's going to bolt with the sled still attached.

Ethan untangles the harness while Zeke and Ronnie help Kohnrad. Once Mac's free, I lead him away from the chaos so he can calm down. He nudges my shoulder with his nose, blowing air across my cheek.

"We've put you through a lot, haven't we, boy?" I say, rubbing his neck. He tips his head, angling a long ear my way. "Well, if all the payment you need is an ear rub, then I'm happy to comply."

I turn so I can see what the others are doing while continuing to rub Mac's ears. Zeke looks like he's arguing with Kohnrad, who is trying to push himself to his feet. Ethan shakes his head and braces himself under a shoulder to help him up. Zeke huffs and moves to Kohnrad's other side. They struggle to get their feet planted and support his unsteady weight.

It's a long moment before anyone moves again. Kohnrad can't stand straight and leans heavily on both men. They move in slow motion, each man focused on the step before them. I hold my breath as Kohnrad stumbles forward, throwing everyone off balance.

Somehow, the three men make it to where I'm standing, Kohnrad shaking under the strain. I don't know how far he's going to go, but the guys are giving him a chance. They let him set the pace and begin a very slow descent as the ridge slopes down, leading us off the peak.

Ronnie hovers around the men until Zeke tells her to back off. She continues to stay close behind them until I ask her to help me with the sled. Between the two of us, one on each end, we guide the toboggan down the slope while Nola follows with Mac and Charlie.

The harsh wind lets up as we make our way back into a thin layer of snow. We follow the switchback down the steep mountainside, slipping and sliding on loose gravel. Up ahead, a commotion erupts—shouts and fumbling as the guys struggle to stay upright. Zeke stumbles and goes down hard, taking Kohnrad and Ethan with him. They tumble downhill, landing in a heap on top of each other.

Ronnie abandons her end of the sled and rushes towards the pile of injured men. I wedge the sled against a boulder, then scurry down after her, hoping like crazy someone isn't seriously hurt. When I get there, Ethan's already on his feet, trying to pull Kohnrad off of Zeke, who's pinned beneath him.

"Are you alright?" I ask, quickly looking him over. Blood oozes from a scrape by his eyebrow, and his pants are scuffed.

"Yeah. Help me roll Keeper over."

Ronnie and I push with all we have while Ethan pulls, and we manage to roll Kohnrad onto the hard ground. Zeke grunts, and Ronnie crawls over to help him. Ethan's hands probe

Kohnrad's side, checking his ribs, as I remove pebbles from his scraped cheek. He's not bleeding much, but he's going to have a few more bruises to add to his collection.

Zeke, on the other hand, is bleeding all over, and it takes us a minute to realize it's his nose and not something worse. Ronnie yanks off her backpack, searching for a rag, and tells him to lean forward so he doesn't swallow any more blood.

"Is anything broken other than your nose?" Ronnie asks, shoving a cloth at his face.

"Just my pride," he wheezes, holding his side with one hand and the rag with the other.

"Well, I think that's tough enough to survive. I can't believe you guys made it as far as you did. Stubborn men."

She wipes blood and dirt off his cheek while he grumbles at her.

"Let me see your side."

"I am fine, Ronnie. I just got the wind knocked out of me."

"That better be true. We can't afford another man down."

"We need to move Keeper back onto the sled," Ethan says, bringing Mac around.

"You are not helping," Ronnie says, pointing a finger when Zeke attempts to stand. "Keep the pressure on your nose."

Ethan explains to Nola how he wants the toboggan situated, then the three of us shift Kohnrad onto his side while she lines it up. We ease his bulk onto the sled, but, of course, the man is too tall and too wide to fit properly. I help Ronnie rearrange the supplies under the front so we can prop Kohnrad up, then Ethan hauls him forward so his feet don't hang off the end. By the time we cover him up and tie him down so he doesn't slide off, I feel like we've hiked another mountain.

Ethan checks Mac over, paying careful attention to his hooves, then sets to work re-harnessing him to the sled. He's quiet now, his movements deliberate and thorough. It's like he's gone somewhere in his mind—some place that sets aside the pain and discomfort and focuses only on the task at hand.

Before we set out again, Ronnie catches Zeke limping, and after a long argument, he confesses he twisted his knee when he fell. He's refusing to take it seriously, though, insisting we're in desperate need of shelter and a fire.

"I will go on until I am absolutely unable. I will not hold us back." Zeke's voice is firm, but the tightness around his eyes betrays the pain he's trying to ignore.

Ethan picks up the harness for the sled and adjusts the straps around his shoulders. Brushing off Ronnie's offer to lead the mule, Zeke reaches for the rope, his movements slow and deliberate as he compensates for his injury.

Ethan calls for the rest of us to get going. "Kenna, I need you out front. Use the compass for direction. The trail is rocky but solid. You'll do fine. We have only a few hours till dark. If we push hard, we still have a chance of reaching the woods tonight."

His face is set, and there'll be no arguing with him. I can see the resolve in every fiber of his being. Like Zeke, he's not stopping. But how much longer can these guys push before their bodies give out and they're forced to quit?

Still, we push on despite injury and difficult terrain. Zeke ends up using Mac as a crutch while Ronnie takes over his lead. Nola is helping Ethan keep the sled steady on the trail while Charlie races ahead, then circles back, his endless energy urging us on. Zeke's injury is slowing us down despite his fortitude, and as I try to figure out how we'll survive another night without a fire, I see them.

"Trees!" I cry out. "There's trees up ahead!"

They're small and scattered, but we've finally come down enough that the terrain is changing back to grass and trees. I can see a forest further on, and a surge of adrenaline rushes through my body.

Ethan calls from behind, breathing hard, his voice strained. "There's a spot… a quarter mile in… for camp."

I wave to let him know I've heard, and quicken our pace. It still takes nearly an hour to reach the woods. The sun is down and it's getting too dark to see. I'm fighting panic, trying to keep memories locked down—I can't allow the fear in right now.

"We should be close," Ethan says, just as I spot the shelter.

A small lean-to made from pine branches sits between two trees, a fire pit in front. There's a spot off to the side for a tent, just far enough from the fire to avoid stray embers, but close enough to benefit from its heat.

We need little instruction to set up camp, slipping into autopilot as our roles have been long since set. We push the sled, with Kohnrad still on it, under the shelter and get him situated for the night. No one suggests moving him into the tent.

The fire roars, flames blazing high, as we huddle close, warming our cold, sore bodies. I've never pushed myself like I did today. I'm exhausted and sore, but there's also a sense of pride in knowing that I didn't quit. None of us did. I can't believe we made it. I look at each person sitting around me. Exhaustion lines their faces, but I can see the same sense of accomplishment in their eyes.

We're not at the end of our journey yet, but we have reached a major milestone. Together, through the toughest situation, physically and mentally, we persevered and accomplished what most others could not. The pressure has bonded and strengthened us instead of breaking us. It has melded us together, made us into a team capable of supporting and anticipating one other.

The love I feel for these individuals aches in my chest. It's something I've never experienced before, and I realize I would do anything for any one of them. Little do I know just how much that will require—or how soon.

Chapter 14

"We'll need to keep the fire going to warm the shelter all night," Ethan says. "I'll stay with Keeper and keep watch. The rest of you can take the tent."

"No. We will take turns," Zeke says. "You do not carry this burden alone."

Ethan's shoulders ease, relief spreading across his face. This trip is taking an immense toll on him, and not just physically. It's obvious the responsibility he carries for each of us weighs on him. There's only so much he can do, though. He needs to let us take some of the burden.

"The two of you have put your bodies through an incredible amount of strain today. I think the women are capable of taking watch tonight." I get confirmation from Ronnie and Nola before continuing. "Get some rest. We'll wake you if there's trouble."

The guys are done in, even if they won't admit it. They've pushed themselves beyond anything I've ever seen, so the least we can do is take turns and let them sleep. I know they want to argue, but exhaustion wins, and they collapse inside the tent.

Wrapping myself in a wool blanket, I pass out others to Nola and Ronnie. While it's still cold, the temperature is warmer here and there's no wind—the latter being the greater blessing.

We sit near Kohnrad, sipping hot tea, each of us lost in our own thoughts.

"I'm worried," I say, breaking the silence.

"Me too," Ronnie murmurs, so low I almost don't hear her. She watches the fire, but her hands rub hard against her tin cup.

Hugging Charlie close, Nola kneads the fur on his neck and looks between Ronnie and me, tears glistening in her eyes. "What if we don't make it in time?"

This is my greatest fear. What if, after all we've done, it's not enough? What if Kohnrad dies before we make it to the city? We're so close, yet still so far away.

I don't know how to answer Nola. I don't know what will happen to us if Kohnrad doesn't make it. He's our leader, the one who's brought us together and given us a purpose. What happens if we come before the king without him? Does our purpose end if he dies?

Ronnie clears her throat, worry and fatigue lining her face as she pushes to her feet. "We'll figure things out in the morning. I'm heading to bed. Wake me when it's my shift." She makes her way to the tent, her movements stiff and slow. I know I'll feel the same soon enough.

Nola stays with me until her yawns become so frequent I tell her to go to bed. I'll take first watch. I throw more wood on the fire and settle down next to Kohnrad, making sure he's warm enough. The shelter's design captures the heat and holds it well, keeping the chill out. Kohnrad hasn't woken since Zeke's collapse on the rocky slope. Ronnie managed to get him to swallow some water earlier, but it wasn't as much as she wanted—and he hasn't taken anything since.

The fire snaps and pops, reminding me I haven't checked on the pillar since we left the tunnel. My vision blurs as I turn inward and hurry to where I last saw it. I gasp when I see the wall has doubled in height. I can still step over it, but at this rate, I won't be able to for long.

The Fire jumps erratically as I approach, like a caged animal, angry and wanting free. I pause, wondering if it's safe to come near. I stretch my arm out slowly, nervous to touch it. Heat brushes against my fingers and... Woah, what's that? I jerk my arm back and examine the Fire. Something's different. It felt like electricity running up my arms and tingling throughout my entire body. It wasn't painful, but it was intense. I can still feel traces of it.

I reach forward again, and the Fire engulfs my hand. Power surges through me, wild and intoxicating. I can feel it building, filling, and overflowing. It's the most incredible thing I've ever felt and I don't want it to go away. I throw my head back and laugh, the sound bordering on hysteria. This could consume me and if it doesn't stop soon, I know it will destroy me.

The thought shocks me, and I jerk my hand back, cutting off the flow, but the electric feeling is still there. I look down and instead of the Flame, I see both arms, up to my shoulders, engulfed in fire. Reacting out of instinct, I shake my arms to get the flames off, and fire erupts around me as if shot out of a flamethrower. I spin around in alarm, my arms outstretched, flames flowing behind them. My mind races in panic, thinking I'm on fire, but then it dawns on me: I'm not burning. There's no pain, just heat.

I stop myself and stand still, breathing hard, staring at my arms and hands. The Fire is only up to my elbows now, as if some of it has left. An idea comes to me then—one I had earlier in the tunnel. I wonder…

Curling my arm up, I watch the flames pulse around my hand before flinging it as if I'm throwing something. A streak of fire slams into the wall, scorching the brick.

Huh! It worked!

I try my other hand with the same result.

Excited, I throw two more fireballs, turning the entire section of brick in front of me black. The energy inside fades and I'm surprised at how fast I miss it.

"Imagine how powerful you could be with this kind of weapon," says a voice. Its soothing tone wraps around me like a cloak. "The Fire can no longer run from you. It is right here for you to take all you want. And you do want it, do you not?"

The pull is magnetic—the thrill, the euphoria. Yes, I want it.

"You were created for this, you know. You can just help yourself, and no one will be able to stop you. Not even Keeper."

The name slams into me, and I stumble back in bewilderment. It almost had me. I could feel the heat of the Flame, my body tingling in anticipation. My head clears, and a massive black snake rises up in front of me. Its forked tongue flicks inches from my face, its enormous coils following the contour of the wall. Large, reptilian eyes reflect my image, and with horror, I realize it's the Fire Serpent from the Dark Forest.

"Ahh, I see you recognize me. That is good. Yes, I like that very much." The Serpent's unblinking eyes flicker with excitement. "We could be friends, you and I. Partners even. You have so much potential. It is such a waste for you to follow that Keeper. He does not appreciate you like I do. I can make you powerful beyond your imagination. That feeling you had with the Fire, I can give that to you, and more. So much, much more."

I can't believe I'm listening to this horrid creature. The Serpent's hypnotic gaze intensifies the yearning for the Fire, and it's all I can do to shove it down.

"It is so easy, you know. It is right at your fingertips. All you have to do is create a little accident. Let the fire die out and forget to wake the others. Maybe remove a blanket or two from the Keeper—you will need them yourself to stay warm, after all, and can always return them before anyone notices."

The Serpent winds its long neck around, forcing me to turn with it. "See, it is not much, and he will never awaken, so there is no suffering. It will be so much easier for everyone without his burden. He is holding you back and putting you all in such danger. It would be a blessing for all, would it not?"

Bile churns in my stomach, rising to burn my throat. "No! I can't do that. I could never hurt Kohnrad."

"Oh, Kohnrad, is it?" the Serpent hisses, his nose coming within inches of my face, forcing me to bend back. "So, you are on a first-name basis, are you? How interesting." The Serpent rears back, tilting his giant head at me. "Foolish girl, do you not realize that I win in the end? It would be wise to figure that out now. For you see, I will have your Keeper either way. Did he really think I would not find out what he has done? As soon as my tower is built, I will have complete control of the Fire and will snuff out your precious *Kohnrad*."

"No!" I scream, throwing my hands out at the Serpent, but nothing happens. There's no Fire left.

The Serpent's grin splits wide as it slides in front of the pillar, cutting off my access to the Fire. The Flame erupts behind the darkness, but there's no chance of me reaching it. My only hope is to escape.

I dive for the wall and throw myself over, my shins connecting with the brick. I land hard on the ground, scraping my hands and knees. My shins burn as I pull myself forward and scramble to my feet.

"Open your eyes, Kenna! Open your eyes!" I yell, and force my eyes open, the Serpent's laughter echoing after me.

Shadows come into focus, and I find myself doubled over on the ground in front of the shelter. The fire has burned down to embers, and my muscles are stiff from the cold. I've been gone way too long. Somehow, the Serpent is stealing time with his wall.

I stagger to my feet, and a sob bursts out as I grab pieces of wood and throw them at the firepit, not caring where they land. Sparks explode into the night and smoke billows up before the wood bursts into flames.

Blinded by tears, I stumble over to Kohnrad and run frantic hands over him, searching to make sure he's still warm, still breathing. I collapse beside him, choking back a whimper. He seems the same. He's still alive.

The soft flap of the tent is my only warning before strong arms wrap around and pull me in, holding me tight. No words, just his presence. We sit like that for a long time, the fire once again warming the shelter.

Peace—the first I've felt since starting this journey—envelopes me and calms my distraught mind. This man who holds me amazes me; he always seems to sense when I need help and quietly lifts me up. He has the heart and strength of a mighty warrior, walking in shadow and fire, giving all he has to those around him. This man is all that's holding me together right now.

"I saw it again," I say, my voice breaking. "The Fire Serpent. It was at the Pillar of Fire. It wanted me to… to kill Kohnrad. I said no, but it doesn't matter. It's going to control the Fire and… and kill him itself."

My body shakes, remembering the Serpent's words. Fear threatens to break through, but a whisper of reassurance calms me down. The night is quiet except for the cracking fire and the occasional hoot of an owl. My eyes grow heavy as my body relaxes, the adrenaline draining away.

"Kenna, I need you to do something. Something hard."

Curious, I turn and face Ethan. "What is it?"

"I need you to stay with the group while I go on ahead."

"What?" I pull away, searching his face. Is he serious?

"We aren't going to make it in time. Not with Zeke's injury." Ethan's voice strains with emotion, and I can hear the fear I know he's trying to hide. "I need to go and get help, and I need you to stay here and lead the team."

Dread fills my body. Ethan is the strongest one in our group. What will we do without him?

"I-I don't know… Ethan, I'm not a leader."

"Yes, you are. You're much stronger than you realize. I need you to do this for me, Kenna. Please.

Tears burn my eyes, and I duck my head to hide them, embarrassed to be crying once again. I know Ethan's right, but I'm terrified of him leaving and having everyone rely on me.

Ethan cups my face and lifts my chin, forcing me to meet his gaze. His eyes search mine, pleading with me to understand.

"I can get to the city in less than a day by myself. I'll return with help. Keep everyone moving if you can. You have the compass to guide you. I'll come back, I promise. It's going to be alright."

I'm overwhelmed with so many emotions right now, it's all I can do not to shut down. Ethan must sense it because he pulls me back and wraps a blanket around us. I tuck my head against his chest and wrap my arms around him. I don't want to let go.

"Give me two days and I'll be back. I'll bring help, okay?"

"Okay," I mumble against his shirt. I feel the tension ease from his body, and he hugs me tighter, his cheek resting on my head.

"Thank you."

Before the sun rises, he's gone.

***

"So, he just left?" Ronnie snaps, upset that Ethan left without talking to everyone, not that it would have changed anything. Zeke's knee is stiff and swollen, and he winces with each step. There's no way we would have made it to the king's city today, even if Ethan were still with us.

Zeke insists we get him a walking stick, and he'll make his way down the path, no matter how long it takes. We need to position ourselves closer to the city for when help arrives.

Everything takes longer without Ethan, and we don't leave the campsite until late morning. I'm anxious about the path—where we're headed, if we'll have enough food or water, what the weather will be like. On and on my worries go. Two days may not sound like much, but in the wilderness, trying to keep everyone alive, it feels endless.

We're only a few hours in, and it's already apparent Zeke won't make it much further. The problem is, we're not in a good spot to camp. There's just enough snow to make things slippery, and we're on a steep section with no flat areas. Ronnie and Nola have been working hard to keep the sled from running into the mule, and I know they're tired and sore. Zeke holds Mac's halter, his knuckles white and his jaw clenched. He's in some serious pain, though he hasn't complained even once. I honestly don't know how he's still standing.

"Alright, guys, hold up. We can't keep on like this. Pull the sled in between those trees and brace it. I'm going to hike ahead a bit and see if I can find a better place to stop for the day."

"We will just keep going," Zeke says, his voice tight with obvious effort.

"Zeke, seriously, take a break. If I don't find anything, then we'll just make do right here. You've pushed yourself as far as you can. It's okay. We're a few miles closer than we were."

"It is not enough. Ethan will bring wagons. We need to be closer."

Zeke's right. They won't be able to bring wagons up the trail. I don't know what Ethan's plan is for getting us out of here, but knowing him, he's already got it figured out. He knows we won't make it far, so we just have to do what we can.

"Ethan will have a plan. He'll get us out, so just let me look, okay?"

"Zeke, quit being so stubborn," Ronnie says. "Go Kenna. We'll wait."

Nola gives me a weak smile and I smile back before taking off downhill. About twenty minutes later, I come to a river cutting through a narrow gorge. A decent-sized bridge crosses the gap and there's a small area where we can set up camp. Further downstream, there's access to the water.

Perfect.

It takes longer going uphill, but I push hard, eager to get everyone moving. I reach the spot where I thought I'd left the group, but they're not there. I go a bit further, thinking I must have been mistaken. Still nothing, though I notice manure on the trail from Mac. We were definitely here earlier.

Backtracking to where I'm sure I had left them, I look around and see evidence they were here—there's the mark from the sled resting against the trees. But where could they have gone? They wouldn't have headed back up, not with Zeke's knee.

I hike back down the trail, searching for any signs to tell me what happened. Then I see it: a narrow, but well-traveled deer trail branching off a sharp turn. If a person wasn't paying attention, or using a special compass, they might step onto this path. Faint mule tracks, with grooves from the sled, confirm this is where the group went.

Why didn't they wait for me?

I follow the winding trail, thinking they must be around the next bend. They had to realize this isn't the path—it's hardly wide enough to fit the sled. The minutes stretch out and I begin to worry. It's too far. They should never have continued on this long.

After another turn, I finally spot them. Charlie barks a greeting and comes bounding over, happy as always to see me.

"Hey boy, you keeping everyone safe?" I say, reaching to rub his head. He licks my hand, then prances back to Nola, who sits near a large pine tree with her knees drawn up, rocking and crying. Zeke is on the ground next to her, leaning against the base of the tree.

"What happened? Why didn't you guys wait for me?" I ask, taking in the scene.

Ronnie stands rigid next to Mac, her face blotchy and red, shooting fiery glares at Nola and Zeke. I've never seen her so mad, not even at Kohnrad.

"We thought we could help cut some time off by meeting you," Zeke says with a groan, rubbing a hand down his face and leaning his head back against the tree.

Ronnie huffs and nods towards Nola. "I was outvoted."

Of course. Nola would do whatever Zeke suggested.

"It's all my fault," Nola sniffles, shrinking under Ronnie's animosity. "I thought I was still on the path. I didn't realize there were no footprints until it was too late and there was nowhere to turn around."

"Okay, well, I found a place by the river where we can set up camp. It's just a mile downhill. Well, more now, I guess, but we'll get Mac turned around and—"

"I am sorry, Kenna, but I cannot continue," Zeke says, hanging his head. His dreads fall loose, covering a portion of his face. "I have let everyone down."

Looking closer, I see the sweat lining his forehead, and his dark complexion is much paler than normal. It's obvious he's in a lot of pain, and I know he wouldn't stop if he could help it. At least he's thinking clearly enough to pack what little snow there is around his knee to ease the swelling.

I shift around, taking a better look at our surroundings. The fir tree is enormous and makes an ideal shelter. We can set up our tents on either side and build a fire in between. There's still plenty of daylight left to gather wood and make camp. We'll be fine. We can hike to the path in the morning and get down to the river, if nothing else. I figure Ethan won't be coming until the afternoon, so we have time to work things out.

I'm about to tell everyone the plan when I feel something cold and wet against my cheek. Looking up, I discover big, fat snowflakes floating down.

You've got to be kidding me.

"Alright, we should get the tents up right away," I say, forcing the worry from my voice. "Let's put one under each side of this tree. We'll have to break a few branches, but that's okay, a layer of pine boughs under each tent will add insulation. Nola, if you can do that, please? And grab some branches from those trees over there too." I point to a grouping of smaller pines with full branches. "We'll put our supplies inside and use the tarps over the tops of the tents. And then somehow, we're going to have to get Kohnrad out of the snow."

Ronnie unhooks Mac from the sled, and I help her unload the gear before leading him out of the way with a small ration of hay. There's not enough left for another full day, and if it snows too much, he won't have access to what little grass there is.

We set up the tents and tarps as quickly as we can while the snow continues to fall. I have Nola put another layer of pine branches along the sides of the tent, while Ronnie and I gather firewood. I don't know how long we'll be able to have a fire if the snow continues, but we have to try. We gather as much as we can, placing some in the supply tent to stay dry. Ronnie arranges what rocks she can find to make a firepit, and soon after, has a fire started.

I step back and assess our setup, feeling satisfied we've done all we can for protection. Mac has found shelter under a nearby tree, so I tie his rope around a low-hanging branch to keep him there. We can't afford to lose him if he decides to wander. I drape my last blanket over him to help shield him from the snow—it's all I can do.

When I return, Ronnie is melting snow for drinking water. I fill a container for Charlie, who slops noisily and finishes before I can fill one for Mac. With the animals taken care of, the three of us push and pull the sled up alongside the tent opening. Zeke can't help, so it's just going to be us girls getting Kohnrad inside.

Ronnie and I each grab a shoulder, while Nola tries to lift his feet. If it weren't for the slippery texture of the tent bottom, we'd never be able to move him. And it's a good thing he's unconscious because I'm pretty sure we knocked his head a few times. As clumsy as the process is, we still manage to get a mat under him and cover him with a few blankets.

Ronnie tends to Kohnrad, then puts together a concoction for Zeke to drink that should ease his pain. She's still a little huffy towards him. I don't think she's going to let him off easy for this one. His stubbornness got the better of him, and Ronnie's gonna remind him often, I'm sure. The thought of their bantering brings a small smile despite the current circumstances.

"We don't have any protein," Ronnie says, handing out cups of broth and hard biscuits, which we greedily swallow down.

We try to sit by the fire, but the snow continues to fall, growing heavier by the moment. I'm worried we're going to get snowed in, and Ethan won't be able to find us. We do have the other pair of snowshoes, so at least I can hike out to the trail tomorrow and keep watch if we're stuck.

We discuss sleeping options, deciding Zeke and Ronnie will sleep on either side of Kohnrad. For now, Nola and I will take the tent with the supplies, but if we get cold, we'll all squeeze together into one tent.

With the heavy snow and thick woods, it grows dark earlier than normal, but it doesn't matter. We're all tired and depressed, and it's going to be impossible to keep the fire going. Nola takes Charlie into our tent while I help Ronnie with Zeke. He can't bend his knee, so it takes some creative maneuvering to get him situated, but we manage better than we did with Kohnrad.

Settling into my spot in the supply tent, I ask, "Nola, are you alright?" Charlie's stretched out between us, and Nola is turned away from me. She hasn't said anything since I first found the group, and I'm worried about her.

"Nola?" I try again.

"I'm fine," she mumbles. Her voice cracks, and it sounds like she's crying but trying to hide it.

"I know things are hard right now, but we'll be fine. Ronnie won't stay mad either, you know. It's just the stress—it's making everyone act a bit off."

Silence stretches between us.

"Will you talk to me, please? I'm worried about you."

Nola lets out a loud sigh and rolls onto her back. In the dim light, I see her silhouette staring at the ceiling. I wait for her to say something.

"I just don't know if it's worth it anymore," she finally whispers.

"What's not worth it?"

"All of it. This. The path. Getting out of here."

I prop myself up on one elbow, stunned by her confession. "Are you serious? Why would you say that?"

"Isn't it obvious?" she huffs. "No one needs me—not since you started leading with the compass. And after my mess up today, well, I'm pretty sure no one will ask me to lead ever again."

Bitterness radiates off of Nola. The exuberance and self-assurance she had the first day I met her, so many weeks ago now, has vanished. I don't think she's been the same since the Dark Forest. She lost something there. The revelation and freedom she gained from Kohnrad didn't... grow. She returned to how she was before the incident with Raoul, but without the spark that set her apart. Where Ronnie's entire demeanor has improved after her healing, today's reaction notwithstanding, Nola's hasn't. And her comments now just reinforce these ideas, leaving me wondering what to say.

"Nola, mistakes happen," I venture. "We've all made them on this journey. You don't get disqualified because of them. We're all learning as we go."

"It just seems pointless now."

"I don't understand. We're so close. How can you want to give up now?"

"Keeper isn't going to make it. There's nothing for us in the city. It's all been a waste of time."

Nola's answer is a dagger to my heart. "No. That's not true," I whisper, certain she's wrong. "It is not true!" I say louder, with more conviction. "We will save Kohnrad. He's not going to die!"

"It's hopeless Kenna. The sooner you realize this, the easier it'll be. There's no point in dragging it out."

Nola turns away, shutting me out. Her words settle in the darkness, heavy like the snow outside. I remain awake despite my weariness, unable to shake the hopelessness that threatens to take over. It hovers, ready to take root the moment I let my defenses down. But I refuse to give up. I refuse to believe we won't get Kohnrad the help he needs. To think otherwise leads to a darkness I don't want to explore.

"Your Majesty!"

"Messenger, what is wrong?"

"Your Majesty, the Shadow Walker is here. Keeper and others are still on the Mountain. There are injuries, and they require immediate assistance."

"Tell me, Messenger, who is injured?"

"Your Majesty, I am afraid Keeper is one of them."

"I see. Have the Walker tended to. Tell him I will send men to retrieve the others."

"Your Majesty, the Walker insists on going back to the mountain. He made a promise to return for them."

"Very well. Find out what he needs and see that it is taken care of with the utmost haste. Use whatever resources you deem necessary. I want them brought back here as soon as possible."

"Yes, your Majesty."

"And Messenger, bring me word of Keeper as soon as you receive an update."

"I will deliver the news personally, Your Majesty."

Chapter 15

With only a few hours of sleep, I wake up early, anxious to check on the weather. Snow falls away as I push the tent flap open and step outside into a captivating winter wonderland with snow everywhere and more coming down. Well, the fire's definitely out and needs to be restarted—if possible.

Pushing my way through knee-high drifts, I check on Mac, though there's not much I can do for him besides clearing the snow off his back. Visibility is poor, and I can't see the trail from yesterday at all. There's no way we'll be able to leave until I can break it open. Nola and Ronnie will have to get the fire going, and we'll need to see if Zeke can walk. Otherwise, it's going to take a couple of trips to get everything, and everyone, out of here.

I head back to the tent to get my gear. "Nola. Nola, wake up." I shake her gently, pushing aside the worries of last night.

"What?" she moans, shrugging away from my hand.

"It's still snowing," I say, digging through my gear and pulling on an extra layer of clothing. "I'm going to take the snowshoes and break a trail so we can get out of here."

There's no response as I grab my gloves and readjust my wool cap.

"I'll wake Ronnie and check on the guys. You'll have to help get the fire going, okay? We need to melt snow for drinking water. Make sure Mac gets some, and Charlie. Nola?"

"Whatever."

"Nola! Wake up! This is important!"

"Yeah, I hear you."

"Okay, well, Charlie's going to need to be let out soon, so make sure you get up."

Nola doesn't move.

"Nola, you're awake, right?"

"Uh huh."

"We shouldn't stay here too long, so as soon as we have water and a quick meal, we can head out."

"Got it, boss," Nola replies, yawning with exaggeration and waving me off.

With frustration, I pick up the snowshoes and push through the door. Ronnie will have to check on her and get her going. I don't know if she's being difficult on purpose or what, but I don't have time to fight with her.

My boots sink deep into the snow as I make my way to the other tent. I flatten out a small area to stand and lean the snowshoes against the tree. Brushing snow off the entrance, I peek inside. It's dark and humid, and it takes a moment for my eyes to adjust.

"Ronnie," I whisper, looking around.

Everyone's still asleep, bundled under heavy blankets. I check on Kohnrad, and he doesn't seem well. His breathing sounds labored, and his forehead is cold and clammy. We really need to get out of here. Soon. I find Ronnie and shake her awake. She's groggy and having a hard time focusing.

"Ronnie, things aren't looking good. The fire's out, and there's a lot of snow on the ground. I'm going to break a trail so we can get out of here. Can you get a fire going? We need water and something warm to eat."

"There's probably no point," Ronnie says with a yawn. "It's just gonna keep snowing and bury us."

"What? No, Ronnie, you need to wake up. Please, Kohnrad's not doing well. We have to get out of here. Ethan will be back today."

Ronnie rolls away from me, pulling her blanket up over her shoulder.

"Ronnie, please, will you get up and get a fire going? Kohnrad needs some of your tea, and I'm sure Zeke will need something too. Come on!"

She doesn't answer. It looks like she's fallen back asleep. What is going on? I check Zeke and shake his shoulder to wake him. He doesn't respond at all, so I lean in close to make sure he's still breathing. He's alive, just sound asleep.

I sit back in frustration. What's going on with everyone? First Nola, now Ronnie and Zeke. Something isn't right. Why can't they wake up? It's like they've been drugged, but we all had the same thing last night, and I'm fine. Okay. So... I'll get the trail done, then work on getting everyone up.

Outside, I strap on the snowshoes and take a few awkward steps. They're made for a much larger person, and walking in them takes more effort than I thought it would. I pull out the compass and get my bearings. At least there's one thing working in our favor.

I follow the compass arrow through the transformed woods. It's disorienting, with everything looking the same in a heavy layer of white. The snow's so deep I have to lift my legs high to get on top of it. It's exhausting, and I sweat through my clothes almost instantly, but I can't take anything off or I'll freeze. The snow's coming down so thick and hard, it's filling in the path behind me a lot quicker than I expected.

I move as fast as I can, but it still takes nearly an hour to get to the main path. The snow is lighter out here—softer, and not as deep. It's peaceful, beautiful even. If the others can get here, then things will be easier. We should be able to make it down to the river. Anything to get us closer to the city. Closer to Ethan.

I pack down the area where the two paths meet and make a little snow wall blocking the trail up the hill. If Ethan comes by here before I return, I want to make it obvious we're down a different path.

"Oh my gosh. That's it!"

I spin around, my snowshoes banging together. We're on a different path. That's what's wrong with everyone and why they're acting so funny. It's the reason for the oppressive feeling of hopelessness back at the camp. Everything makes sense now. Other than the Dark Forest, this is the first time I've experienced the effects of another path. But then, I'm not affected like everyone else, and I wasn't before either. My mind races, questioning why, but I shut it down. I need to get back and get everyone going. We have to get off this trail as soon as possible.

I widen out the path for the sled as I return, running different scenarios through my mind. If I can get Ronnie and Nola up and moving, we have a chance of getting out of here — I can't move Zeke or Kohnrad without their help. We can use the mule with the sled and make multiple trips if needed. Once we're off this trail, we should be okay, and no one will have to be put at risk trying to get to us.

The snow gets heavier the closer I get to camp. Of course! This is all the path's doing. I should have realized this sooner, it explains so much. No one's outside when I reach the tents, and there's still no fire. I let Charlie out, and he leaps through the snow, trying to explore and mark his territory all at the same time. He turns around in frustration, struggling to make it back to me.

Bending down, I give his ears a good rub, feeling for the poor guy. "I know, buddy, but there's not a lot I can do about it."

Both Nola and the others are still asleep, not responding when I call out or shake them. This isn't good. I make sure everyone is warm enough, then check Kohnrad's temperature again. He's still feverish and pale, and I don't know what to do for him. Zeke and Ronnie have always been the ones to take care of things.

Alright. Then I just need to do what I can at the moment. This seems to be my mantra today.

My path to Mac this morning is no longer visible, and I have to guess where the fire was last night. The snowshoes provide good packing, so I set to work clearing another path and give Mac the last of the hay. He seems content enough, even in this weather, but I know he needs water. I work my way around the front of the tents and the fire pit, then make a wide area leading to the trail.

Unstrapping the snowshoes, I stand them up along the tree trunk before realizing I should have done that with the sled last night. I dig through the deep snow, mumbling at my stupidity, until my gloves brush against the wooden top. Snow clings to the sled as I tug it free and pull it closer to the tree. I clean off what I can and lean it next to the snowshoes. If Ethan has to come here for us, the least I can do is have everything ready.

I tug on a drooping branch hanging over the firepit and watch the snow break off. I bump a few more—small avalanches dropping into piles around me. Better now than after I've got a fire going.

The cold seeps through my wet gloves as I clear the area down to the ground and grab dry wood from the tent. It takes a few tries and a lot of coaxing, but flames spark to life, crackling and sizzling against the snow. This would have been impossible if we hadn't thought ahead last night. The tree blocks most of the snowfall with its heavy-laden branches, so there's a good chance I can keep the fire going as long as I have dry wood. Unfortunately, I didn't plan on staying here this long, so we didn't gather nearly enough, and there's no hope of finding more.

It doesn't take long to melt the snow and take care of the animals. I gulp warm water until my stomach is full and I can't swallow any more. I get Kohnrad to take a few sips, but that's all. I'm worried he's getting dehydrated, but without help, I can't force him to drink more.

Rummaging through our supplies in search of food, I discover how bad off we really are. There's only a little broth left from last night, a few biscuits and some dried fruit. I had no idea we were so low. With this weather, there's no way to hunt—not that I know how to anyway—and Ronnie is the only one who knows what plants we can eat. Except everything's buried, so that doesn't matter either.

I sit by the fire, wrapped in a blanket, eating my meager meal, trying to stay warm. Charlie stares at me with woeful eyes, so I offer him my biscuit, which he gobbles down in one bite. I know it's not enough, but there's nothing else to give him. Keeping the path open so Ethan can get to us is vital, but without decent food, my energy is going to drop fast. Going back into the tent for a nap is out of the question; I'm worried I won't wake up like the others. There's no choice but to stay awake and stay warm.

Charlie goes with me when I walk the trail throughout the morning. Each trip gets harder and harder, my legs becoming heavy and clumsy. Every time, I stare down the hill towards the river, hoping to see help coming, but it never does. The longer the day drags on, the more I worry about having to spend another night in the snow. How long can I keep clearing the trail if Ethan is delayed? I should've used Mac and the sled, and gotten at least a few of them out. But then there'd be no way to keep anyone warm once I moved them. I would have to leave the tents, and a fire wouldn't be enough—even if I could find enough dry wood to burn.

I think about leaving all this behind. Just heading out by myself. Just walking away and not looking back.

"No! No, no, no, no. Come on, Kenna, you cannot give up!" The darkness of this place is seeping in despite my best efforts. "Ethan will be here soon. You just have to make it till he comes. You can do this." I rock back and forth, repeating this over and over. I can't give up. I can't.

The fire has burned down, kept alive only by the few sticks I throw in now and then. I will them to last longer than they should, but they don't. The pile in the tent is almost gone, my hope not far behind. I grasp at what little there is, striving to keep my mind positive, to not let despair take over.

"You know you'll never amount to much," an old familiar voice whispers, pulling me towards the darkness.

I cringe at the accusation. I've kept most everything locked away until now—the things I couldn't remember at first and then chose to hide once I did. I'm afraid if I open that gate, everything will come rushing out, contaminating what I have here. No one knows who I was before. What a failure I was. Here, in this place, I get another chance. I can be someone new, someone who matters.

But the voice seeps back in, eating away at my resolve. Squeezing my eyes shut, I hum as loud as I can, trying to drown out the words that invade my mind against my will.

"Who in their right mind would want a girl like you? Look at you, you're pathetic," it sneers.

No! Please! Why now? I look around, desperate for relief, but there's no one here who can help me.

"Do you really think these people like you? Come on now, you know better. No one actually *cares* what happens to you. No one *needs* you."

A heart-wrenching wail rises out of me, driving the voice away. I'm not that person here. I'm not. People like me. They need me. I have a place and a purpose. Kohnrad said so. He doesn't lie.

Charlie inches closer, his big, soulful eyes fixed on me. I brush off a layer of snow and wrap my arms around him, burying my head in his soft, wet fur.

"You like me, Charlie. If nothing else, you like me."

The crackling fire pops, pulling me from my self pity. I wipe my eyes and take deep, calming breaths until I feel stable again. A small flame flickers, teasing the edges of my conscience, beckoning me to return. I shudder at the thought; the memory of the Serpent is still too raw. There's no way I'm going back there. That creature terrifies me, and without Kohnrad's counsel, I don't know how to handle it. I feel like a coward, but the pillar will have to wait.

It's hard to tell what time of day it is with all the snow, but I figure it's close to midafternoon. Sleep is relentless in its call, and it's getting harder to stay awake. I should make another trek out to the Path. Ethan has to be coming soon. He has to. I don't think I'll survive another night if he doesn't.

Summoning all my energy, I trudge along, the snowshoes heavy on my feet. Charlie runs ahead and then back, encouraging me to keep going, barking when I stop to rest. Like before, the snow lightens the further I travel from camp and at the trailhead, there's still no sign anyone has been there.

I scoop out a place to sit in the shallow snow, my back against a tree near the intersecting trails, facing down the Path so I can keep watch. I take off the snowshoes, setting them next to me, and settle in to wait.

Charlie runs around, sniffing the snow, making his way down the path before turning back up. He chases a few leads into the woods, but returns often to check on me. Every once in a while, he stops and cocks his head, like he's listening. I listen too, watching the trail for any sign of people, but no one comes.

It's getting more difficult to see; shadows swallow entire areas, casting them into a deepening darkness. My old fear tries to rise within me, but I clamp it down. I've got too much on my mind to let that slip in. I'll have to head back if Ethan doesn't come soon. I can't stay here in the dark or I'll freeze to death. That is, if I don't die of fright first…

Charlie explores a while longer before lying down next to me, his head in my lap. It's his favorite position, I decide, petting his head. It's mine too.

Stiffness seeps into my muscles, the ache from sitting too long. Bit by bit, a chill settles in, but I don't want to get up yet.

I'll wait just a few more minutes. I'm still okay; I've got time. I'll move soon. I will.

The shaking takes over soon after, my teeth chattering, each tooth rattling against the next with relentless force. I attempt to stand, but my legs buckle, and I fall back, collapsing against the tree. My strength is gone, stolen away by the cold, my exhaustion, my delay. I waited too long.

I curl into a ball, trying to retain the last of my body heat. My body jerks and spasms with each new wave of cold. I can't imagine it getting worse, but it does—a burning, deep and bitter, rages through my muscles, and I cry out in agony. On and on it goes, burning me alive, shredding my dignity, emptying my soul.

Then, nothing. Nothing but sweet, warm numbness washes over me like a wave, the magnitude of its relief melting my limbs into the ground. It's a false sense of security. My mind knows I'm not okay; my body is shutting down. I can't move, can't call for help. There's no one to hear, no one to answer. My eyes close, and I can't open again.

Charlie whimpers, then barks. I try to reach him, but I'm drifting. There's no anchor, nothing to hold me. Images flash through my mind: meeting Kohnrad and laughing with Nola, working with Ronnie and leading with Zeke. And Ethan. His bravery and strength. Always there for me.

I tried Ethan. I really did. I'm sorry. I'm sorry I wasn't strong enough.

Charlie barks and barks. There are shouts and metal clanking, but it's all so far away. Like a dream. A dream with horses and warm blankets and fire.

I startle as my body jerks upward, coming around just enough to wonder what's going on. Did Charlie do something? My head falls back, hanging down, too heavy to lift. My eyes refuse to open, and a dizzying sensation twists through me, as if the ground beneath me is shifting.

"Kenna! Kenna!"

My name. Someone is calling me. I'm here. Right here. Or I was. Am I still here? There's so much shouting. What happened to the peaceful quiet of the woods? I just need a moment to think. I can't remember. Can't remember…

A force presses against my chest, shaking me. Someone is speaking, their words flowing over me, distant and muffled. What are they saying? I don't understand what they want.

Something touches my lips, filling my mouth. Reflex causes me to swallow, and the burn of liquid hits my throat, sharp and searing. I choke, convulsing as warmth crawls through my chest, fighting against the chill deep inside.

My name breaks through again. Why do I keep hearing my name? Who is that? I can't stay. I have to go. It's too much. Where's the Path? There's so much snow. Too much, too much.

Rest, I need to rest. Just for a bit… let me go… let me…

***

There's so much noise. Why is everyone shouting? Who's dying? Ow, what's that? Oh, my hands—my hands are burning, and my feet. My body… It feels like it's on fire! Did I fall into the fire? Help me, please… Help! Oh, it hurts! Make it stop, make it stop! Ohhh…

***

There's movement beneath me. The jingling of metal. A snort. Am I dreaming? It's those horses again. Why would there be horses in my dream? I should wake up. This dream seems odd. I'm shaking; it's so cold. Did I lose my blanket? Where am I? Why are my eyes so heavy? I can't open them. I'm so tired. So cold, and so tired…

***

I'm moving again, that dizzying sensation. Something wraps around me, holding me tight. It's still so cold. Everything hurts. Am I broken? Why would I be broken? Uhhh… that's not right. I just… want to be warm again.

I should get up. Yes, I should get up. But it hurts, it hurts so much. Why does it hurt? Something's wrong.

Struggling against the darkness, I force open my heavy eyelids, blinking slowly to clear my vision. Flames flicker, moving around me, burning my eyes. Turning away, I frown, unable to make sense of what's in front of me. It looks like a coat. Why would I see a coat?

A warm breath caresses my face. "I've got you. I'm here."

It takes all of my concentration to lift my head.

Oh. "Are you… real?"

"Yes. Yes, I'm real."

"You… came back."

"I promised you I would." Ethan's voice breaks as he ducks his head against my shoulder, pulling me closer.

"Are you… okay?" I ask, wondering if he's hurt. Is that why he's upset?

"Kenna…"

His eyes are so full of pain. What has happened? Who hurt him?

"I'm-I'm okay. You will be too."

Then why is he crying? Something's definitely wrong. I search his face for answers, my eyelids drooping despite the struggle to keep them open. His beautiful, sorrow filled face. I try to smile, but it's too much—my lips won't cooperate.

My eyes close, and my head drops back against Ethan's arm. Sounds float in and out, landing briefly, then taking off again. Never settling, always shifting. I cling to the memory of Ethan's voice, but can already feel it slipping away.

All comfort is gone, replaced by a constant jolting, rocking me back and forth. Violent shivers course through my body, stealing my breath. I'm so cold. Where is the fire? Did I let it go out? Confusion swirls around me, and I feel myself drifting away. I want to stay, but the darkness pulls too hard. I have no strength to fight it. It beckons, and I drift further and further away. I try calling for help, but my voice has disappeared.

Nothing remains but the darkness and the sensation of my body falling into emptiness.

"Your Majesty? I am sorry to disturb you, but I bring news."

"Come in, Messenger. I am awake."

"Your Majesty, word has reached us. The men have the Sojourners and should arrive within the hour."

"Their condition?"

"I am sorry, Your Majesty. It is not good. They were found snowed in a mile off the Path. It was a Dark Trail, and the Shadow Walker would not allow anyone to help. He was able to get them all out, but it took longer than expected due to their location."

"Is Keeper alive?"

"Yes, Your Majesty, but he is in very grave condition."

"And the Fire Holder?"

"She was discovered half-frozen by the trail head. Apparently, she had been keeping it open for help but succumbed to the cold before our men arrived. It is not yet known if she was found in time."

"Notify the physicians immediately and instruct the staff. I want everything prepared for their return."

"Yes, Your Majesty."

"And Messenger, please keep this quiet until I have spoken with the king."

Chapter 16

I feel like I'm floating on clouds—soft, fluffy, warm clouds. It feels so good to be warm. Smiling to myself, I let out a yawn and wonder what time it is? Maybe I can lie here and enjoy a few more minutes before everyone gets up. I listen for the chirping of birds or the rustle of squirrels scurrying around to tell me the day is beginning. But something's wrong—things don't sound right.

My eyes flutter open, taking in the soft glow of light around me and the canopy over my head. I blink and look again, confused by what I'm seeing. This is not my tent, and these quilts covering me are definitely not mine. I'm in a bed—a big, fancy bed with ornate wooden posts and sheer golden fabric draped all around it. This is not at all what I was expecting.

A fire burns in the huge stone fireplace at the end of my magnificent bed, its mahogany mantel lined with burned-down candles. Soft light pours in from a large window covered in the same golden cloth as the bed and candlelight chandeliers hang low throughout the room. I turn my head to get a better view, wincing at the stiffness in my neck. Closing my eyes, I try to remember what has happened. Flashes of images and sounds run through my mind, but nothing comes together enough to make sense. It feels more like a fragmented dream than an actual memory. There's just enough to entice, but not enough to remember.

Opening my eyes again, I take in the luxurious beauty around me. I've never seen anything like it. Stone and wood merge together in a deep, inviting richness, with wide chairs designed for both beauty and comfort. Small tables hold vases full of flowers and candles are strategically placed around the room. It's a remarkable combination.

A figure in a chair next to me catches my attention. He's slumped forward on the edge of my bed, his head resting on folded arms. I recognize his dark, wavy hair, and a rush of joy courses through me. I try to reach out to him, but my hand feels stiff and clumsy. My muscles awaken all at once, sending jolts of pain racing throughout my body. I moan, clenching my jaw against the pain.

Ethan lifts his head and stares at me with haunted eyes, his complexion pale. He looks horrible, like he hasn't slept in days. My throat catches when I try to speak, and he quickly reaches for a cup on the stand beside the bed. He's gentle and careful as he helps me take a few sips, but the tremors in his hands are concerning.

"Where am I?" I whisper, my voice hoarse and low.

"The King's Palace," he answers, adjusting the pillows under my head. He pulls the chair closer, his eyes never leaving my face, his gaze deep and searching.

Crinkling my brow in concentration, I try to remember what came before this. How did I get here? There was so much snow, and I was… I was waiting… then… It was so cold. I wasn't…

"You found me?"

"Yes." He strokes my cheek, blinking back the tears threatening to fall. There's so much emotion on his face, in his bloodshot eyes—pain, joy, disbelief. It's overwhelming, and I feel a wrenching in my chest as more memories filter in.

"Are the others…?" I can't finish. What if…?

"They're here."

I sigh in relief and close my eyes, my own tears sneaking out from the corners. They're safe. Thank goodness they're safe.

"I'm sorry," I whisper after a moment, unable to meet his eyes.

"For what?" He tilts his head, trying to catch my gaze.

"For letting you down. For not being strong enough."

"Kenna, look at me." He nudges my chin with his fingers.

Reluctantly, I look over at him. It hurts to have disappointed him so much. I wanted to be strong and capable. To be more than I've been told I was my whole life. I wanted to make him proud. To prove I was something.

"Kenna." He says, holding my chin so I can't look away. "You were strong. You hear me? You were very strong."

I shake my head, "No."

He withdraws his hand and sits back in the chair, his expression wary.

"No, I wasn't," I say. "I let them wander the wrong way, and then I… I couldn't get them out."

"It wasn't your fault. What you did—it saved them. Don't you know that?" Ethan leans forward again, grabbing my hand. His thumb caresses my skin as his gaze holds me captive. "Kenna, you built shelters and kept everyone warm, including the mule. You made a trail and kept it open so I could find you. Don't you understand what you've done? You kept a Dark Trail open. I don't know another woman who could have done what you did."

I search his eyes for the truth, knowing he won't lie. He means what he says. Did I really help? Was it enough?

"I… I thought I failed you."

Ethan lets go of my hand and leans back into the chair, staring at the ceiling. His shoulders hunch as he runs his hands through his hair, holding his bowed head. He shudders, then looks up at me with the deepest anguish I've ever seen.

"You didn't…" He chokes on his words. "You didn't fail me. I… *I* almost failed *you*."

"No." I shake my head and reach out my hand. "Never. You could never fail me. You're the strongest person I know, Ethan."

Ethan lays his head down on my hand and quietly weeps, his whole body shaking.

Oh, this tender man. He carries such heavy burdens. Tears cloud my eyes again, threatening to spill over. How is he still whole after all that has been done to him? How can his heart still care for others? I feel his pain and long for a way to make it go away, to ease the heaviness he holds inside. My chest aches with a deep and fierce emotion that burns like fire, searing my heart. I can't name it, can't explain it, but it roars through my veins with an intensity that scares me.

There's a gentle knock at my door, and an elegant woman, clothed in the most exquisite gown I've ever seen, glides into my room. She closes the door without a sound and crosses the room to my bed, the fabric of her lavender dress swishing with each graceful movement. With silver-white hair and striking amethyst eyes, she exudes an unmistakable air of authority and power.

"Oh," she says in surprise. "You are awake."

Ethan lifts his head and wipes his reddened eyes, attempting to compose himself.

The woman draws near, placing a gentle hand on his shoulder. A concerned frown creases her regal features as she takes in the dark circles under his swollen eyes.

"He has been by your side ever since he brought you here. I could not persuade him otherwise," the woman says, looking me over. "Tell me, my dear, how are you feeling?"

"Sore. And hungry," I answer before thinking.

She releases a throaty laugh. "Yes, I imagine you are. Well, I can help with both of those things. I will have the cook make you something right away—something light, I think, to ease your stomach. As for the other, a nice hot bath will do wonders for those sore muscles. I will send the girls up right away."

"Thank you."

"Of course, my dear." The woman smiles, waving her hand as if this were an everyday occurrence and no bother at all.

"I will have everything arranged. You will receive fresh clothes and your bedding will be changed out as well. You have been through quite an ordeal. We will see to it that you are well taken care of."

Returning her hand to Ethan's shoulder, she gives a light squeeze. "As for you, young man, you are hereby ordered to get some rest. Your vigil is over. You have proven yourself beyond measure. It is now time to take care of your own needs. Do I make myself clear?"

"Yes, ma'am."

"Good. I highly recommend a dip in the pools. Your *fragrance* is less than desirable," the woman says with raised brows. Her nose twitches, but her eyes gleam with amusement.

Ethan's face turns red, and he mumbles an apology.

"No need to apologize," she says, her tone gentle but firm. "Your loyalty and bravery are admirable. There is no greater honor than to risk your life for those you love." Her hand grazes his shoulder as she turns, leaving the room with the same soft whisper of swirling fabric.

"Who was that?" I ask in wonder.

"That formidable force of nature is Queen Theora," Ethan says with a short laugh and apparent devotion.

"Oh."

"She has that effect."

"I think she likes you."

"The feeling is mutual. She's been very good to me. I owe her more than I could ever repay."

"You've known her for a while then?"

"I have."

"Are you being evasive on purpose?"

Ethan smiles and shakes his head. "No, it's just a long story. I've known her for many years, since I was sixteen."

"Wow, you need to tell me that story one day."

Ethan nods, the side of his mouth turning up. "One day."

There's another knock at the door, and two young ladies peek in.

"Miss, Her Majesty says to get you to the bathing room."

"That was quick," I say to Ethan.

"The Queen is not known for wasting time," he replies with a smirk.

"Well then, I should get myself up and out of this bed. Which feels glorious, by the way. I've never slept on anything so soft."

I try to swing my legs out but can barely move them—I'm so sore. With a loud groan, I grab the bed to keep from falling. That's when I notice I'm not wearing my own clothes, but a long cream-colored night shirt. Suddenly, I'm very self-conscious and not sure what to do.

Without a word, Ethan scoops me up and carries me from the room. Now I'm beyond embarrassed, and I can feel my cheeks flushing. I don't want to be so needy, but I can't deny the flutter in my heart as I rest a hand on his hard chest.

Ethan strides down the hallway, entering a bright, cozy room containing a huge porcelain tub set near an equally enormous brick hearth. Settling me onto a nearby bench in front of the blazing fire, he turns away and leaves the room without looking back.

I stare after him, my heart pounding against my chest.

The young ladies swarm around me, slipping off my gown and guide me into the tub of warm water. I'm uncomfortable with my nakedness and want to cover up, but lack the strength to resist. The taller of the girls grabs a large black pot from the fire and pours in steaming hot water, creating a layer of scented bubbles.

"Oh, this is wonderful," I murmur, sinking back against the smooth, curved surface. The combination of heat and fragrance is like magic, releasing the tension from my muscles and leaving me in pure bliss.

The young women move about the room, chatting quietly, while I close my eyes and savor the moment. I can't remember the last time I've had a hot bath—it was definitely before this whole crazy journey began.

Soon enough, the girls return to work on my thick hair: a knotted mess that reeks of sweat and smoke. They sort through the tangles, combing it smooth before pouring warm water over my head. I sit with my arms wrapped around my knees while they massage my scalp and rub scented soap into my hair. It's all I can do not to moan in pleasure. I've never been taken care of like this before—it's absolutely amazing.

After rinsing and repeating several times, the girls apply an oil to make my hair smooth and silky, then help me out of the tub. Wrapping me in a large, soft towel, they lead me to the bench in front of the fire. I take my time combing out my hair, letting it air dry while they empty and clean the tub.

"You warm enough, miss?" asks a girl.

"I am, thanks," I reply.

"They say you were near frozen to death up that mountain."

I don't answer. Everything's still hazy, but I do remember being cold. Very cold.

"They say the Shadow Walker brought the others out all by himself. No one could enter that trail for fear of being overcome by darkness. Took him hours, they say. He had to bring them out one at a time."

I close my eyes, picturing the time and effort it would've taken Ethan to rescue everyone. How exhausted he must be.

"The queen sent near a hundred men, she did. They brought you all down on sleds till the snow ended and the trail widened enough for the wagons to reach you. You've been sleeping for two days. Everyone was worried you wouldn't wake up."

Two days? I had no idea.

"Do you know anything about my friends? Are they okay?"

"Oh yes, the ladies are fine. They're just down the hall. And that dark, handsome one is recovering too." The girls giggle, their cheeks turning pink. I smile at their obvious infatuation with Zeke. I bet he's got all the women here fawning over him.

"What about Kohnrad, Keeper? Is he okay too?" My voice rises with worry. Ethan didn't mention him. I should've asked.

There's an immediate shift in the girls' demeanor. Without a word, they spring into action, fussing to get me into a fresh nightshirt. They guide me down the hall to my room, change out my sheets, and fluff my pillows with practiced efficiency. The crisp linen is cool against my warm skin as I slide beneath the covers. I try once more to find out about Kohnrad while they stoke the fire and replace the candles on the mantle.

"I'm sorry, miss, but it is not our place to say. You'll have to talk to the queen." They bow their heads, refusing to make eye contact. "It's been a pleasure, miss. We're glad you're okay."

Then they slip away before I can question them further, and I'm left staring at the open entryway. There's a huffing sound in the hall, and a moment later, an older woman enters, balancing a steaming tray of food on a small stand. She's a bit on the heavier side, her face flushed from climbing up the stairs just outside my door. Her gait is uneven, hinting at a limp, but her eyes crinkle when she sees me and a warm, welcoming smile spreads across her face.

"Glad to see you're up," she says, her voice lower and more coarse than I expected. She sets the tray—and the funny contraption under it—over my legs like a little table. "It's been hard on that young man of yours, seeing you like this."

Taken aback by her comment, I struggle to explain. "Oh, uh, if you mean Ethan, he's not mine. I mean he…"

Amused by my stuttering, the woman pats my arm and throws me a knowing wink. "He's a good one, he is, but not everyone can see it. His past scares them. He needs someone who's not afraid of all that. Someone who knows what's down deep in his heart. He's not one to give his affections lightly."

She looks right at me while arranging my pillows so I can sit straighter. I don't know what I'm supposed to say, so I keep my mouth shut. The woman pats my arm again with an approving nod.

"There's hot soup and fresh biscuits for you. It should be easy on your digestion. The tea will help too."

The woman continues to stare at me, her head tilted as if that will help her see what she's looking for. Her gaze is penetrating but not unkind. Embarrassed by her intense scrutiny, I turn away and fiddle with my spoon.

"You're different than most girls."

I look up in surprise, my heart quickening. Her words don't sound like an accusation, but more like a statement—one tinged with curiosity.

"Yes," she nods, more sure of herself now. "You are. That's good."

She taps my tray with her wide hand and says, "Enjoy your dinner," before turning and limping out of my room.

An unexpected warmth fills my belly at her words. She approves of me for some reason, and it's a distinct difference from how most people see me—or at least how I think they see me.

I spread butter on a soft biscuit and take a bite. It's delicious, but at this point, even shoe leather would probably taste good. The soup is an interesting mix of vegetables and barley with a mild, tangy flavor. As hungry as I am, my stomach fills up way too soon, and I can't finish. Sipping my tea, I mull over the situation with Kohnrad. It can't be good if no one is allowed to tell me how he's doing. They wouldn't hide it if he died, would they? Someone had better give me answers soon, or I'll have to find a way on my own despite my weakness.

A smile tugs at my lips as my thoughts drift to Ethan. There are so many questions there, more than I'm ready to face just now. Setting the tray on the far side of the bed, I curl into the soft, inviting blankets. A strange lightness fills my head and I wonder, belatedly, if there was something in my drink. A long yawn overtakes me, and I sink happily into a peaceful, relaxing stillness.

***

"Sire, the Sojourners have arrived as requested."

"You may bring them forward."

The king's man motions us towards the dais where the king and queen sit side by side on tall, intricately carved stone thrones. Our steps echo in the vast hall as we approach their majesties. My legs tremble beneath me, but I stand without assistance. The ordeal on the mountain has left me extremely weak and easily exhausted. Ethan stays close, giving me space to do things on my own, but ready to step in if needed.

I haven't seen the rest of the group until now. Their greetings are brief, strained with anxiety and nervousness.

The king takes a long, measured assessment of us, his mouth set in a deep frown. It's clear we're not what he expected. Though we've been given fresh clothes, the simple linen pants and light shirts do little to hide our haggard appearance. I hadn't realized how much weight I'd lost until I caught sight of myself in a mirror. The mountains took more from me than I thought.

"Which one of you is responsible for my son's condition?" the king demands, bitter anger lacing his words.

His son? What is he talking about?

Ethan steps forward, breaking from the group. "I am, Your Majesty."

The king's eyes narrow. "Explain yourself."

"Keeper instructed me to stay with the group while he provided cover," Ethan begins. "He was ambushed and sustained numerous injuries. Members of the Resistance were able to get him out of Kirkos and partway up the trail. At that time, Keeper was conscious and able to alert me that he needed help. I came as soon as I could and, with the assistance of those traveling with me, was able to bring Keeper to safety and treat his wounds. However, upon reaching the summit of the Great Mountains, Keeper's condition worsened, and he has not regained consciousness since then."

The king strokes his chin, taking in the young man before him. "Tell me, Shadow Walker, how is it you are able to speak? I have not heard more than a few words from you over the years, and they were strained at best. Yet now, you stand before me and deliver an entire explanation with ease. Have you been deceiving us this entire time?"

The king leans forward, his countenance confrontational. He's a handsome man, his features softened by age, but his eyes carry a hard, unyielding glint. His aggression is confusing. I was expecting someone… kinder.

Ethan stands rigid, his body tense, a dark swirling full of agitated shadows pulsing around him. I glance discreetly at the others to see if they notice, but Ronnie and Nola have their eyes fixed on the king. Only Zeke watches Ethan.

"The Fire Holder healed me, Your Majesty," Ethan says, his voice steady.

The king's gaze sweeps over our group, and a cold sense of dread creeps up my spine.

"And what is that supposed to mean?" the king spits out. "Which one of you is called *Fire Holder?*"

My throat tightens, and I swallow hard, trying to find my voice. "I… I am, Your Majesty."

"Speak up and step forward so I can see you."

I obey, my body shaking from exhaustion—and perhaps a touch of fear. The pulsing shadows around Ethan deepen as I step alongside him. I want to reach out, to offer assurance, but I get the distinct feeling that I should not show any affection in front of the king.

Despite my weakness, I feel something strong rising inside of me. Heat moves throughout my body, spreading like a shield, crackling the air around me.

"I am the Fire Holder, Your Majesty," I call out again, and this time, my voice is strong and clear.

Queen Theora's gaze lingers on Ethan and me, her expression a mixture of wonder and worry. Can she see Ethan's shadows?

The king glares at me, his hostility thick and suffocating. He sits back in his chair with an air of disdain.

"So, you heal this young man, but not my son?" he says, waving a hand towards Ethan.

The question throws me, my mind still processing the implication that Kohnrad is his son. If this is so, then shouldn't the king understand how the Fire works?

"With all due respect, Your Majesty, I don't heal anyone. The Fire does. I only do what it allows me to."

"I see," the king says, leaning forward onto the arm of his chair. "And this *Fire* has chosen to heal an *orphan*, but not the king's heir? Am I understanding this correctly?"

I glance at Ethan, unsure how to answer, but he stares straight ahead, his face set like stone. Things are not going how I thought they would. How do I answer a question like that?

The heat in my chest continues to build, but I'm not afraid of it this time. Instead, I pull at it, encouraging it to grow, letting its strength wrap around me and fill me with boldness.

"Is... Keeper your son, Sir?" I need to know for sure before I continue this conversation.

"Of course. Were you not aware of this fact?"

"No, Your Majesty."

"It was Keeper's desire to keep his identity hidden, Sire," Ethan says.

The king scowls at Ethan, and I jump in to explain, wanting to deflect the king's attention.

"Your Majesty, I asked the Fire to heal Keeper and was shown to come here. I thought you would know what to do."

The king's gaze flicks between Ethan and me, his expression revealing shock before his eyes narrow and bore into me. He is not at all what I expected. This whole situation feels off.

"My son's name is Kohnrad, not this absurd title of *Keeper* you continue to refer to."

Seriously? Who is this guy? Is he really the king? I look to Queen Theora, searching for answers, but her face gives nothing away. Whatever her feelings are, she has yet to say a word.

"If my son does not recover," the king bellows, pointing a finger at Ethan, "I am holding you responsible, *Shadow Walker*. Do you understand what that means?"

"Yes, Your Majesty, I understand."

"Wait, Your Majesty," I interject, stepping closer. "How can you blame Ethan? He saved us. We never would've made it here without him."

The king surges to his feet, his face flushing red with anger. A vein throbs at his temple, looking dangerously close to exploding.

"Young lady, if it weren't for *you* and all this Remnant nonsense, we would not be in this position. My son went against every one of my warnings, and look where it got him. I will hear no more excuses from any of you. Is that clear? This pointless escapade is over."

What does he mean it's over? I look back at Ethan, but he's locked stiff, staring straight ahead. Should we appeal to Queen Theora? This can't be how this ends.

Flames crackling around me, I turn back to the king, intending to get some answers one way or another. This is not how things were supposed to go. How dare this man speak to Ethan with such derision, I—

With a subtle shake of his head, Ethan shifts, effectively tucking me behind him without drawing the king's attention. His presence calms the wild Fire, and it sinks down to a low burn. The reality of what I almost did shocks me. If Ethan hadn't stopped me…

"Now," the king says, puffing out his chest. He looks ridiculous, like a preening peacock, completely ignorant of the danger hovering below the surface. Marcus mentioned peacocks once. Now I understand his analogy.

"Since I pride myself on my hospitality," the king continues, "you will be treated as honored guests until you have recovered. Then, I expect your group to be on its way out of my city. Whatever game you were playing with my son is now over. You are dismissed."

Chapter 17

"What an ass. I can't believe that man is the king," Ronnie says, outrage getting the better of her.

We're down the hall in a day room, sitting on light-colored couches in front of a fireplace that takes up half a wall. Sunlight pours in from multiple floor-to-ceiling windows, all draped with a white gauzy material. French doors lead outside to a stone balcony overlooking a series of aqua-colored pools, each one pouring into the next by a series of small waterfalls. Surrounding the pools is a stone wall covered in dark green ivy and lined with an immaculate garden full of blooming flowers. Beyond the wall, fleeting glimpses of the city are visible, and from what I can tell, everything appears to be made from the same white stone. It matches with what I saw in the Fire, but brings me no comfort, as nothing else is right.

Squinting against the brightness, I massage my temples, trying to relieve the throbbing behind my eyes. It's a struggle to focus on the conversation next to me.

"He does not seem to be what we were told. I admit it is confusing." Zeke says. He moves his hand to rest over Ronnie's, and she lets out a snort before shaking her head in disgust.

I agree with Ronnie. I don't like the king either, and that's putting it mildly. How could Kohnrad have led us to believe this king is good? And if we're called to serve him, which I no longer want to do, why is he sending us away? Kohnrad promised that wouldn't happen.

"So, what do we do now?" Nola asks, her thin frame swallowed up in the plush couch. She lost something on the trip over the mountain. The tough-girl act has disappeared, leaving her looking frail and confused. She glances around, desperate for an answer, but the king's reaction has left us all uncertain, and no one knows what to say.

Ethan has stayed separate from our group since we entered the room, choosing instead to stand by the French doors overlooking the city. He's the only one not reacting in confusion or anger. The king's tirade didn't throw him off at all. He seemed almost… resigned. Like the king reacted just how he expected him to. Obviously, the king knows him, so I guess it's reasonable to assume Ethan would also know the king and be able to anticipate his reaction. That means Kohnrad would know too. Which means… he lied. Or intentionally misled us.

For some reason, Ethan has put a barrier up and shut us all out. I don't know if he's protecting himself or gone somewhere to process things, but it's jarring to my senses. Until now, I didn't realize how strong our connection was, how much I rely on his presence. He has some things to answer for, though, so he isn't going to get away with blocking me for long.

Everyone has grown quiet, staring at the fire or the floor—anywhere but me. We haven't had a serious conversation since I woke up. I know we need to, but the adrenaline rush from the confrontation with the king is taking a nosedive, pulling me down with it. I have no strength to fight it; my energy was spent on the king. Every beat of my heart sends my pulse pounding in my head. I just want to fall asleep and have it be gone. My eyelids flutter, and I'm on the verge of not opening them again when the door opens, and Queen Theora glides into the room.

"Good, you are all here. We do not have long and we have much to discuss."

She positions herself in a wingback chair, facing us, while Ethan comes to stand by her side like a guardian. She adjusts her pale teal gown around her legs and folds her hands in her lap, her gaze sweeping over each of us. Her presence is commanding, and I unconsciously correct my posture to match hers before noticing the others do the same.

"First, let me apologize for my husband's rude behavior. I am very thankful for what all of you have done to ensure Kohnrad was brought back here. My son has a very strong will and is man enough to make his own decisions. My husband does not understand this, but Kohnrad has the welfare of the entire kingdom in mind, not just our city here. He does not make his decisions lightly. There is great purpose in what he does, and I am proud to say he *has* accomplished what he set out to do, which was to bring you all here."

"Your Majesty, is Kohnrad alright?" I interrupt. I have to know what's going on, and she's the first person to talk openly about him.

"I am afraid not. My physicians have checked him over and can find no reason for his fever or lack of consciousness. They have been unable to determine a physical cause for his condition."

"His ribs are not broken then?" Zeke asks.

"No, just bruised and healing well. None of his wounds are life-threatening, so there must be another explanation. I must say, it is a hard thing to send your only son to save others, knowing he may die and not return to you. It is even harder to see the scars on his body and know he has suffered because of them."

My heart pounds at her words. Her son has suffered. And yes, he chose to, but it doesn't change the outcome—or the fear it must put in a mother's heart.

Queen Theora takes a deep breath, nodding to herself before straightening her shoulders. "Now, as for your purpose here. You have been called to join my son in his quest to save the kingdom."

"I thought the king invited us here," I say.

"He did not."

The throbbing in my head has become painful, and I'm feeling sick to my stomach. None of this is making sense. Have we risked our lives for nothing?

"I don't understand," I say, rubbing my forehead. "Kohnrad said those who come here are to serve the king, to join his kingdom. Was he wrong?"

I look around at everyone. Are they as confused as I am? Nola shares my confused look, but Zeke and Ronnie have suspicious looks on their faces, like they're realizing we've been set up, because that's what it's feeling like.

"So, this has all just been a ruse to get us here?" Ronnie asks, indignation making her voice rise.

Queen Theora sits forward, opening her hands in apology. "I am sorry if things have not been as clear to you as they should have. I will try to explain as much as I can in our short time."

Zeke and Ronnie exchange a look but say no more.

"The king you met today is not what he seems. He is not a true king, as in, he was not born for the throne. He took the title when I married him after my first husband, Kohnrad's father, was killed. Kohnrad is the true king, not my husband. My son has not challenged his right to the throne because it would hinder his movements. Instead, it has provided a way for him to search for those he needs while keeping track of the enemy. My husband does not approve of Kohnrad's… escapades, as he calls them. He does not understand the workings of the Kingdom."

Surely we haven't been called here just to help a wayward son fight his stepfather for the right to his throne. This should make more sense to me than it does. Why does everything seem so… clouded? I'm having trouble fitting the pieces together to make sense of the situation. What am I missing?

"My family," she continues, "comes from a long line of Watchers. We are able to travel in the spirit, to places in the present. Over the ages, we have been able to influence and provide protection for those walking the Path to the Kingdom of

Light. Unfortunately, the darkness has continued to grow, and our position has been relegated to observation only. Very few travelers have been found worthy of protection. My Watchers have been reporting back to me as you have been journeying here. We would have done more, but that would only have alerted the enemy of our interest in you and increased the danger you were in. It is an arduous task to watch and not be seen. Yet, I am afraid our interest has been noticed despite our precautions."

Queen Theora stares out the windows, her brow creased in worry. She has been very frank with her emotions since she sat down, a stark contrast to earlier when the king was present.

"My late husband was a Fire Walker, one who is able to walk among the Flames and not be burned. His family has overseen the Kingdom of Light for generations, passing down the kingship from father to son. Kohnrad is the last of his father's known family. There are no other… living… children. He has walked the Fire since he was born, and his abilities exceed those of anyone before him. There has never been one like my son, and it scares or offends most who meet him."

The Queen focuses her attention directly on me. My heartbeat quickens in anticipation of her words.

"The Fire showed Kohnrad years ago one who would handle the Flame and wield its great power. He vowed to find this person before the enemy could discover him *or her*. He has been walking the Path since, searching for the Burning One."

"So the rest of us don't matter, then?" Nola asks, her voice almost a whine.

"You matter greatly," Queen Theora says with conviction. "Each of you has been specifically chosen. We have watched you and seen your worth. Do not think that because your call is different, you are any less important. Together, you will be a mighty force and overcome great evil in this world."

"The current king does not have these abilities you speak of?" Zeke asks, his mind already one step ahead of us.

"He does not, nor is he tolerant of those who say they do. He has forbidden many things, so you would be wise to keep your giftings among yourselves. Our city is not what it used to be. Bitterness and fear have been allowed to grow, causing great unrest amongst the people. They question Kohnrad's birthright, claiming Durmad, my husband, as the rightful king. Many have turned away from the Light and have allowed darkness to invade. King Durmad fears what he does not understand. He thinks he means well, but he undermines what is truly good, and has opened the door of betrayal against himself and Kohnrad. I have placed only those I highly trust around my son, for I fear for his life and will protect him at all costs. If he does not recover soon, I fear for your lives as well."

A light knock at the door interrupts the queen, and a young man steps in.

"Your Majesty, time is short. You must hurry."

Queen Theora rises, her gown floating around her.

"My influence in the palace is in jeopardy. I may not be able to help you for long. My husband's temper is appeased by drink, and I will see that he is encouraged to indulge more than usual. If not, I fear he may do something rash. You must be careful. Stay near your rooms and be ready to leave at a moment's notice."

The queen shares a look with Ethan, then heads to a door hidden in an alcove on the far side of the room. She clicks it open, then turns back, her eyes deepening in color as they pierce into me.

"Kenna, you need to return to the Pillar of Fire. Soon."

With that, the queen turns and disappears through the opening, the door closing silently behind her.

***

"Use the pitcher of water on the sideboard to wet a cloth for her forehead," commands Ethan.

"And grab a bowl! I think she's going to be sick!" Ronnie says.

"Did she pass out?" Nola asks.

"I'm not sure," Ronnie says. "Kenna, can you hear me?"

"Yes… my head… it hurts."

Nausea churns in my stomach, and I'm desperate to hold it in. The pain in my head is more than I can bear, making me wish I could just tear it off. Flashing images of the Fire and Serpent invade my mind, increasing the nausea. I can't go back—that thing will kill me. The Fire said to come here, and we did. Isn't it someone else's job now to do something? I whimper, the pain overloading all my senses. I can't take anymore; just let me be.

"Kenna, I'm taking you to your room," Ethan says, lifting me into his arms.

"I can walk…"

"No, you can't. Just relax. I've got you."

Ethan moves swiftly along the halls, cradling me in his strong arms. I rest my head against his warm chest, thankful to feel his concern, even if it doesn't ease the pain. He climbs the stairs with ease and gently lays me on my bed, tucking a blanket around me before sitting down by my side.

"Ronnie's getting something for the pain. It'll help you sleep too," he says, brushing aside a stray hair from my face.

"Thank you," I whisper, my eyes open just enough to see him.

He leans forward and places a soft kiss on my forehead. "Get some rest. We'll talk later."

I close my eyes, my heart bursting with joy despite my distress. I was right. Something has shifted between Ethan and me.

"I want someone with her. She doesn't get left alone."

There's whispering, followed by the soft click of the door closing.

"Kenna?" Ronnie says, her footsteps drawing near. "Nola and I will be here, okay? I've got some tea for you. It'll help with the headache."

Squinting against the light, I make out Ronnie hovering nearby. She helps me sit up and holds the cup for me to drink.

"Drink it all, that's it. Now lay down so I can put this cool rag on your forehead."

"Is she going to be okay?" Nola asks, her voice further away.

"Yes, it's just a migraine. Her body's been through too much and needs more rest."

I sink back into my pillows and lay an arm across my eyes to cut the light. Whatever was in the tea is strong. I can already feel the sedative taking effect, easing the pain.

I sleep for several hours without dreaming and when I awaken, the sun is going down, filling the room with shadows. The chandelier remains dark, the only light coming from flickering candles on the mantle and the fire crackling in the grate. Nola and Ronnie sit side by side in front of the fireplace, speaking with hushed voices.

I sit up slowly, easing my stiff body to the side of the bed. My legs are still so sore I have to use my hands to pull them into position. Leaning forward, I feel my back protest.

"Umph."

Ronnie hears the sound and hurries over to help. "What are you doing? You should stay in bed and rest."

"If I don't move, I might never get out of this bed again. Help me to a chair, please."

Ronnie lets me lean on her and set the pace, while Nola hovers nearby, unsure what to do. Once I'm seated by the fire with a blanket, they pull in their own chairs so we can talk without raising our voices.

"How's your head?" Ronnie asks, examining my eyes.

"Much better than it was," I say, rubbing the residual ache in my temples. I did not need a migraine on top of everything else going on.

"I'll have more tea for you tonight. It'll take the edge off what's left."

"Thanks, Ronnie, I really appreciate it."

"Kenna, I'm so sorry for everything that's happened to you," Nola says, twisting her hands together. "It's awful knowing you almost died because of what we did. What *I* did."

"Nola…" Ronnie begins.

"Nola," I say at the same time.

Ronnie purses her lips and nods for me to continue.

"I know you didn't mean to. It wasn't intentional. It could have happened to any one of us. The important thing is we stayed together and made it out."

"We could've…" Nola says. She sits back in her chair and drops her gaze, clearly upset by what almost happened.

"But we didn't. We're okay."

"Thank you, Kenna," Ronnie says, her voice gruff with emotion, "for what you did. I don't know how you were able, but thank you."

"You were all… if Ethan hadn't come…"

"Like you said, we didn't and we're okay."

"Yeah, we're okay. Or will be soon." I try to smile but shudder instead, realizing how close we were to not making it. If Ethan hadn't come when he did… "So, tell me what's been going on since we got here," I say, shifting the conversation away from our near miss. "Did either of you know anything about King Durmad before today?"

"No, we knew nothing," Ronnie says, as Nola shakes her head. "Queen Theora checked in on us a few times, but that's it. We've been outside to a small courtyard and the barns to see Charlie, but not anywhere else. We've had no contact with anyone from the city either—just the servants here."

"Yeah, it's been weird," Nola says. "Like, I thought the king would want to see us, but he never even requested us to come until today. And now, he doesn't even want us here."

"Nothing is what we expected," Ronnie says, frustration tinting her cheeks red.

"I know. I had a whole different scenario made up in my head. It was nothing like this. Can you believe Kohnrad is the queen's son? That he's actually a king, or will be one, anyway?"

"I think it's pretty cool, you know," Nola says with a shrug.

Ronnie nods in agreement. "As crazy as all this is, it suits him. He's wise beyond his years and has the demeanor of a great leader."

"Yeah, he's sure good at getting his way," I say, rolling my eyes. "But seriously, it surprised me. Although, maybe it shouldn't have."

"It's concerning that he hasn't recovered since we got him here," Ronnie says, looking at me, her brow furrowed in worry.

I agree. I don't know what it means either.

"Not to be a downer, but what are we going to do?" Nola asks. "I mean, are we just going to leave Keeper here? Like, are we really going to have to leave when you're well? Or sooner?"

"I don't know," I sigh and lean my head back against my chair. "I didn't expect to be unwelcomed, so I don't know what happens now. I thought this whole time we were coming to meet a great king, not a false one."

"But we have met a great king, haven't we?" Ronnie says, her eyes twinkling.

I look at her in surprise. She's right. We did. We met the true king, even if we didn't recognize him. He's the one who came for us, showed us the way, encouraged and healed us. He even protected us by sacrificing himself for us. Kohnrad is our king, not that ignorant man who yelled at us today.

"Then why would the Fire tell me to bring Kohnrad here if the king isn't able to help him?"

"I don't think it was the king we were bringing him to," Ronnie says, shaking her head. "It was the queen."

I take a moment to process this. It makes sense after what we learned earlier. But Queen Theora hasn't been able to heal him either. So now what?

A sharp rap at the door startles us, and we stare at each other with wide eyes. Ronnie stands up, going to see who it is. As she opens the door, a large animal bursts into the room, racing straight for Nola. Charlie leaps up onto her lap, covering her in dog kisses. Once he's made sure she's okay, he comes over to check me out. He licks my hand until I laugh and make him stop. Satisfied that his people are fine, he positions himself down on a rug between us.

"How did you get him inside undetected?" Nola asks as Ethan pulls up a seat beside us.

He shrugs. "I've got a few friends here. Besides, he was making the stable hands nervous. They're afraid to turn their backs on him."

"Aw, he wouldn't hurt them, would you, boy? He just needs some lovin', that's all."

Charlie looks between us, his tongue hanging out. He appears innocent now, but his size is intimidating to those who don't know him.

"You feeling better?" Ethan asks me, his voice tender.

"I am. Thanks." I blush and fiddle with my blanket.

Ronnie raises a brow, a smile teasing her lips.

"I'm sorry I'm causing so much trouble." I say, desperate to divert the attention away from Ethan and I.

Ronnie reaches out and puts a hand on my knee. "We're a team, remember? We help each other out when needed."

Her words warm my heart, and tears burn the backs of my eyes. I blink several times to wash them away and squeeze her hand in thanks. She nods, then takes her hand back.

Frowning, she says, "We may need to keep you in bed a little longer than you want. We need an excuse to stay in the palace."

Right, we may not have much time. That means we need some answers sooner rather than later. Ethan has some explaining to do.

"You didn't seem surprised by the king's words today," I say. "Did you know he would react as he did?"

"Hey, that's right," Nola says, crossing her arms. "What was all that stuff about anyway?"

"That was a bit of a show," Ronnie says with a raised brow. "You've been holding back on a few things."

"I'll explain as soon as—"

He's interrupted by a knock on the door and Zeke peeks his head inside, a shy smile on his face. Ronnie jumps up to help him across the room, grumbling about him not using his crutch. She forces him into her chair, then pulls a stool over for herself.

"Kenna," Zeke says once he settles in. "I am glad to see you doing better. Let me say how sorry I am to have contributed to your... infirmity." He winces at the last word.

"Thanks, Zeke, but I don't blame any of you for anything, so please, let's just put it behind us."

"You are very gracious." Zeke nods, his hand rubbing his sore leg.

"So, we're all here now. I think it's time we're told what's going on." Ronnie drills Ethan with a hard stare. "The king knows you quite well, apparently, and Queen Theora. That was quite a story she told."

"Did Keeper lie to us?" Nola asks, echoing my thoughts.

"Not exactly," Ethan says, his voice heavy with regret. "He couldn't reveal too much until we were safely out of Kirkos for fear of the wrong ears overhearing. He was going to speak with you all before entering Neriah, but things didn't go the way we planned. I'm sorry for my part in keeping you in the dark, but it wasn't my place to tell his story."

"So, he knew we would be unwelcome," I say. "Why would he tell us to come here, then?"

"In hopes of changing the king's mind. To save the city, if he could. Either way, he needed you to get beyond the Great Mountains. To get out of enemy territory."

"Who is his enemy? This Dark One he speaks of?" Zeke asks.

Ethan shakes his head. "His enemy is our enemy."

"The Serpent," I whisper.

Ethan agrees, and everyone looks at us, confused.

"I've seen it," I say, the memory still vivid. "The Serpent of Darkness. It was in the Dark Forest when the fire broke out and then later, around the Fire Kohnrad showed me. It has built a wall to contain the pillar the Fire rests on. Somehow, it's trapped the Fire and wants to use the Flame for itself."

"Can it do that? I thought only a Fire Holder could touch the Fire," Nola says.

"I don't know." I look at Ethan for an answer, but he just shrugs and shakes his head. It's disconcerting that he doesn't know. I've jumped ahead by assuming he knows everything Kohnrad does.

"This King Durmad. How much of a threat is he to us?" Zeke asks Ethan.

"The king is a bully. His fuse is short, and his pride won't let him back down, which makes him both unpredictable and dangerous. He doesn't understand the principles of the Fire, so he tries to convince Keeper to abandon the kingdom and focus solely on Neriah. The king has been brainwashing the people for years, eroding confidence in the Fire Walker legacy. He wants to control Keeper and rule through him if possible. The king doesn't see the darkness and believes the city is unbreachable. His faith is in his own ability to negotiate peace, but the forces at play will not be satisfied until the kingdom is completely destroyed. No city or person is immune. Keeper sees this and is working to stop the darkness for good."

"The king's mind is shadowed," Zeke states. "His heart is being overcome by the very thing he does not see. Others in the palace have already succumbed to the darkness."

"I thought the darkness would be gone when we reached Neriah," Nola says. "Why isn't everything wonderful like I was told? How can there still be bad things here? How can the king be such a… a tyrant?"

"I've been thinking about that," I say. Nola always thought things would be perfect once we got here, but there were too many signs along the way stating otherwise. "Do you remember what Kohnrad said after he brought you back from the darkness?"

Nola scrunches up her face as she tries to recall. "He said… the darkness is in our minds. And if we stay in the darkness, it will infect our hearts."

I'm impressed she remembered. "Right, so I don't think it matters where we are. There is no perfect place in this world. If we allow the darkness in and let it stay, it will blind our minds and eventually infect our hearts."

"And we become like those who walk in darkness," Zeke says.

"So, darkness is an enemy. The Dark Trails, the Dark Forest… they're all connected to the Serpent of Darkness," I say, things finally clicking into place. "The Fire Serpent is the Serpent of Darkness. It's after the Fire, and in order to control it, it needs Kohnrad out of the way. That's why it wants to kill him."

"Yes," Ethan says. "It desires control. That is its goal."

"How are we to fight this darkness without Keeper?" Zeke asks. "He is the one who has shown us its lies and has opened our eyes to the truth. He is our leader, our king. How are we to continue without him?"

We look to Ethan for an answer, but he's looking at me. He nods, encouraging me to figure it out. He's so like Kohnrad.

"What has Keeper always pointed you to?" he asks.

"The Fire," I say.

"And what is fire compared to darkness?"

"Light. Fire is light."

"Right. Fire consumes darkness and leaves only light."

"So, we follow the Fire because it's light?"

"Yes."

"Okay, but what about the compass? I thought its purpose was to point me to the king's city."

"No, it kept you on the Path of Light, and the city is on that Path. I think the real answer is, the compass leads you wherever the Fire tells it."

"Then the journey was never really about the city or the king. It's always been about the Fire."

"The True King is very important, but he only does what the Fire commands. His city is a promise for those who follow him. It's to be a place of rest and peace. The Light is for those who enter the Fire. It's the Fulfillment of all things."

I don't quite understand that last part. It's too much to take in.

"Keeper has this Light inside him," Zeke says with reverence.

"He does."

"You have this Light also?"

"I do."

Zeke studies Ethan. "You hide it well."

"My gifting requires it."

Zeke nods in understanding. "Yours is one of great inner strength. I have not seen its likeness."

"So, Keeper walks this Fire, like the queen said?" Ronnie asks when the men fall silent.

"He does."

"So then, back to Zeke's original question. What do we do if Keeper doesn't wake up? How do we continue without him?"

"Do we have to leave him behind?" Nola asks, her eyes wide with worry.

Ethan shakes his head and leans over in his chair, his elbows on his knees. "I don't know. I thought the queen would help, and Keeper would wake up. The longer he stays unconscious… the less chance…" Ethan can't finish. He's trying very hard to be strong. "I didn't expect… to have to take his place," he whispers.

I tuck my sore legs up to my chest and wrap my arms around them, resting my head on my knees. We're really talking about leaving Kohnrad behind. But to what end? To save ourselves? I can't do that. I won't do that. He's our king. We serve him now, whether or not he's awake to appreciate it.

I lift my head and look at the others. "I won't leave him. They can kick us out, but I'll find a way back. If he's not safe here, then I'm not leaving him behind."

"Me either," Nola says instantly.

Zeke nods, and I see Ronnie smile in agreement. We look to Ethan for approval. We need him, but I'm determined to try without him if it comes to that.

"I'll speak to the queen. Without her help, we face charges of treason. The king won't hesitate to make an example of us."

Treason. We just agreed to go against a king and take his son. There's no good ending for this. If we succeed, we'll be on the run and hunted. If we fail? I tremble, knowing it won't be good.

My heart skips a beat as a soft knock comes from the door. Ethan puts a finger to his lips, silencing us, and slips out of his seat to see who it is. A servant addresses him in low tones, keeping us from catching any words. Ethan closes the door and returns to the group. Instead of taking his seat, he stands by the fireplace, staring into the flames.

I watch his profile, noting the tension in his features. His hands flex and curl, but stay down by his side. No one questions him, so we wait in silence, unsure of what's coming. Terrified it's the worst.

"The king shut down the pass to the tunnel. No one will be allowed through."

Everyone relaxes a notch. It wasn't news about Kohnrad.

"He's also set extra security around the palace and guards at the city gates."

"This means something to you," Zeke says.

Ethan sighs heavily and kicks at the stone hearth. "He's preparing for Keeper's death." Ethan looks straight at me. "He's making sure we can't escape."

My breath catches in my throat.

"He will hold you responsible, as he said," Zeke says.

"Yes. And Kenna."

Ethan turns to face us. "The king's men can't stop me, and if I have enough time, I can get all of you out of the city."

"Two of us are injured. You will not be able to do this," Zeke says. "You and Kenna should leave."

"What? No way! I'm not leaving you guys behind. If anything, he should get the three of you out. No one will come after you if they have us."

"Ethan, if you can get the women out, I will stay."

"Zeke, no!" Ronnie cries.

"Stop!" Ethan says, stepping between us all. "This isn't helping. Just… give me a moment. I'll figure something out."

He growls an incomprehensible word and leaves the circle, striding over to the lone window. Resting his hands on the windowsill, he looks out into the night. Ronnie places a hand on Zeke's leg to keep him still and tilts her head at me, motioning for me to go after Ethan. I slip out of my chair, taking the blanket with me, and shuffle up next to him. He hasn't shut me out this time. I can feel his uncertainty and fear.

"I need to go to the Fire, don't I?" It's not really a question—I already know the answer.

Turning away from the window, Ethan steps closer. "It's your choice." The turmoil in his eyes reflects my own.

"I'm afraid."

"If you need me, I'll be there."

I search his eyes. He's serious.

"Ethan…" The words catch in my throat. I'm terrified of confronting the Serpent, but I can't make excuses any longer. We've come to a wall…

Ethan reaches for me. "What is it?"

"The wall. The one around the Fire. The Serpent said something about it. I think…I think that's what's hurting Kohnrad." I look out over the city, but my mind is seeing the Fire and wall that encircles it. "He got worse when the wall grew higher. It has to be connected somehow."

"It makes sense. Kohnrad has a deep connection with the Fire."

"So then, I have to go. I have to talk to Fire and find out what to do. There isn't another way."

I can see Ethan weighing our choices—the need to save Kohnrad competing with his concern for my well-being. But he has to let me go. There isn't another option.

"I'll check with the queen and see how Keeper's doing. Then we'll decide how urgent it is that you go. You're still recovering and need rest."

I blow out a breath of frustration. I've grown stronger on this journey, my body adapting to the miles of walking and climbing. But the Dark Trail took too much, and I'm back to feeling as weak and useless as I did at the beginning. Even now, my legs are shaking from the strain of holding me up.

"Okay," I concede, feeling both thankful and guilty at the delay.

Ethan helps me back to the bed while the others quietly make plans to return to their rooms and rest. We don't know if—or when—we'll be forced to leave, so we need to make use of the time we have.

"Nola, it would be best if Charlie stays here," Zeke says as she heads for the door.

She glances down at Charlie, who gazes up at her expectantly, his tail wagging. With a quick look my way, she tells Charlie to stay and walks away, her gait stiff. Charlie sits, watching her go, then returns to the rug by the fireplace.

"We're just a few doors down," Ronnie says, handing me a cup of tea. "It's cold, but it will help with the headache. I backed off on the sedative in case we need to leave during the night."

I sip the tea and thank Ronnie. She offers a kind smile, then joins Zeke by the door. They go out together, leaving Ethan to linger by my bed.

"Go," I say, feeling a sudden shyness. "I'll be fine."

He leans forward as if to say something, but hesitates, then pulls back. At the doorway, he glances back, his expression unreadable. His jaw tightens, and without a word, he pulls the door shut behind him.

Chapter 18

A sound wakes me in the night. Someone is calling my name. Kohnrad? Kohnrad needs my help! I run down a long hallway, searching for his room. I'm coming! Where is he? I open door after door, each room dark and empty, until I reach the last one. Light bursts through the doorway, blinding me. I duck my head, squeezing my eyes shut, and stumble into the room.

As my eyesight adjusts, I make out the still form of Kohnrad lying on an enormous stone slab. That's not right. Why isn't he in bed? This room isn't right either. Where is the furniture, and why is the Pillar of Fire here?

A wall, barely clearing the top of my head, surrounds me, and it dawns on me that I'm within it. I spin around in panic, searching for the Serpent, but he's not here. Heart still pounding, I step closer to Kohnrad. He's so pale I wonder if he's alive. I touch his hand and gasp at how cold he feels. No one can be that cold and still live. Kohnrad's body ripples beneath my touch as if made of water. I can see through him, his very substance fading away. A heart-wrenching sorrow sweeps over me as I realize he's dying. It squeezes my chest, stealing my breath before letting go.

My vision blurs as everything around me shifts and swirls, changing shape, changing color. I turn in circles, dizzy and confused.

The wall burns with a strange fire—dark and menacing, stealing the light instead of creating it. It mocks me, rejoicing in its capture of Keeper, and the containment of the pillar.

"Nothing you can do, nothing you can do!" it chants, dark flames dancing.

A gentle breeze brushes against my cheek. An ageless, timeless whisper floats past.

"Come into me."

I glance around, searching for the source of the melodic voice, but no one's there.

"Come into me, Kenna," it breathes again, drawing me with its caress.

The Fire blazes before me, its flames expanding around the pillar like a halo. It becomes so bright I have to turn my head and shade my eyes. Wide stone steps appear before me, leading straight into the light. All around me is nothing but shadows. There's only the Fire, its call beckoning me, inviting me to enter.

A roar explodes behind me as I lift my foot onto the first step. The darkness reaches for me, desperate to take hold. I take another step, feeling the heat of the Fire. Another step, then another. Everything else fades away as the Fire envelops me. It's so bright, the flames burning white with a swirling rainbow of colors. One more step and I can take no more. I fall to my knees, overcome by the pressure and heat.

I'm on fire, being consumed, yet not burning. The Flames search deep inside my being, ripping open every door, shining into every dark corner. There is no hiding here. Everything is laid bare before the Light. There's no denying who I am, what I have done. I cry out in anguish as every piece of my soul is exposed and set aflame.

Nothing escapes judgment—every deed, every thought, every word spoken or held back. It's all seen and known.

I collapse face down, weeping, laughing—full of sorrow, full of joy. It's a purging and a filling, both violent and gentle. The extremes intertwine, creating a sweet agony that I fear will never end, and desperately want to continue.

"Only those who come into Me and die can know My fullness," says the Fire. "The Refining Fire is All-Consuming."

And I am being consumed, to the very core of who I am. Soon, there will be nothing left.

"There is no darkness in Me; therefore, you must purge all darkness from your heart. Only the pure in heart can stand before Me, so you must let go of all that has held you back. For the purer the Flame, the stronger its power—and the stronger its carrier must be. You are a warrior, destined before time to wield My Fire. You will be My Burning One, marked with My Flame, walking the Fire and Shadow both. You will have no boundaries, for My Own will lead you and take back the Land passed down through his lineage. He will be your king, but I will be your LORD. Look for My Flame and listen for My voice… I am always with you, now and forevermore."

The Fire fades, but the heat remains—wave after wave flowing over my body. I'm unable to move, unable to speak. I can only receive what is pouring into me, replacing what has been emptied: a hum of peace and strength.

"It really is too bad you chose to enter the Fire," a serpentine voice whispers from behind me.

My eyes fly open, and I find the base of the stone pillar in front of me.

"I would have found much more pleasure in keeping you alive than I will now in killing you."

The Fire Serpent! It's here.

A lingering heat remains while visions of the Fire and Flame dissolve into memory. I struggle to push myself up from the ground, my strength still not returned. Dark cerulean flames shimmer in waves along my arms, and I know I carry a healing Fire. I can't explain how I know, but I'm very sure that's what it is, and I know who it's for.

I search the area for Kohnrad. Where is he?

"Looking for your precious Keeper, are you? You cannot even spare a glance for me? I am hurt, Kenna, truly hurt."

Black scales glow in the Fire's reflection as the Serpent coils around me, its massive head leaning in. Cruel, unblinking eyes bore into mine and the putrid smell of death emanates from its breath, wisps of smoke trailing upwards from its nostrils.

"What to do, what to do. So many choices." The Serpent sways before me, its eyes never leaving mine. It feels hypnotizing, soothing.

Evil creature. I force my eyes away, refusing to play its game.

The Serpent hisses, but I ignore it, knowing it will incite its wrath. Instead, I watch the shadows along the wall, following their patterns, their sudden shifts. The corner of my mouth twitches, and I bite my lip to hide my smile. The Serpent isn't as aware as it thinks.

"Perhaps I should let you see your beloved Keeper. Maybe I will kill him now and make you watch."

"He's not really here though, is he?" I reply, returning the Serpent's gaze. "That was a trick. An illusion."

The Serpent rears back in surprise, its eyes flaring.

Good. It wasn't expecting that.

"Very clever of you," it says, its voice dripping with irritation. "No matter. You have no way to reach him and use the Fire, so… why not hand it over to me? I will put it to good use, I promise."

Interesting choice of words. The Serpent sees my Fire, but has made no move to take it. Instead, it asked me to hand it over. It appears the creature has limitations.

The Flames undulate along my arms, stronger than I've ever felt before. Maybe strong enough to fight the Serpent. But no, that's not what this Fire is for. It's for Kohnrad only. Its purpose is to heal. If I use the Flame as a weapon, it'll be wasted—or worse, it could become distorted from misuse and feed the Serpent instead of harming it.

What does the Serpent know of my Fire? Does it understand its differences? There must be something it knows if it's pursuing it this hard. But what would darkness want with a healing Flame?

Wait.

Darkness is the opposite of light, so… what is the opposite of healing?

Death.

The Serpent wants to use the Fire to kill—to kill Kohnrad and anyone else that gets in its way. I am not going let that happen. This creature will not get the Fire. If I can't get to Kohnrad, then I'll waste it or die trying.

"I see you have come to some semblance of resolve. Do not delude yourself, girl. No mere human can endure the methods I employ. Rest assured, you will give me all that I ask for."

"I'll die before I give you anything!"

"Oh no, you poor ignorant soul. Rest assured, I will ensure you do *not* die until you have surrendered exactly what I desire. You see, I have perfected the art of prolonging life while inflicting the utmost torment imaginable. What can I say? It is a gift."

The Serpent fixes its yellow eyes on mine, the predatory gleam daring me to flinch. Its coils tighten and shift with an unnerving rhythm, swaying back and forth in a grotesque dance while its tongue flicks in and out—tasting, testing.

"Okay, okay," I say, throwing my hands up in front of my face. "I'll make a deal with you. If I give you what you want, will you promise to let Kohnrad live?"

The Serpent uncoils a fraction, eyeing me with suspicion.

I cringe, taking a step back. "I know I'm not strong enough to fight you, and… and the thought of being tortured to death is terrifying, so I… I'm willing to strike a bargain. All in your favor, of course. I'll give you the Fire… but you have to let Kohnrad go and kill me quickly. Please."

The Serpent relaxes, bringing its head low, its smile stretching wide with victory.

"Now!" I yell, throwing myself over the Serpent's back, aiming for the wall.

A dark figure leaps from the shadows, thrusting a small knife into the Serpent's eye, tearing open a jagged line down the side of its face. A terrible shriek pierces the air as the creature rears up, thrashing its head in pain.

With uncanny precision, Ethan twists in the air, his feet already in motion as he hits the ground. Before I can even process his approach, he launches me up and over the wall, sending me tumbling down the other side. Unable to get my legs under me, I collapse in a heap, falling into the arms of a startled Queen Theora.

"You must hurry," the queen says, her face strained with effort as she tries to help me up.

With no more than a soft thud, Ethan lands beside us and lifts me to my feet.

"Take me to Kohnrad!" I gasp as we move away from the wall.

Together, they half-walk, half-drag me through a series of winding hallways until we reach a large wooden door guarded by several armed men. The Queen nods, and the guards step aside, their expressions serious and alert.

The room beyond is dim, illuminated only by a few flickering candles and the fire burning low in the grate. Queen Theora directs us to Kohnrad, then hurries to stoke the fire and provide more light.

Kohnrad's bed is enormous—far too high for me to climb onto by myself. Ethan boosts me up, and I slide over to

Kohnrad's pale form. He looks so close to death, much like the Serpent's illusion earlier. Touching his smooth cheek, I'm surprised at how different he appears without his beard. Queen Theora must have had his hair trimmed too. The wild man persona has vanished, replaced by a regal warrior. There's no mistaking his heritage now.

Leaning close to Kohnrad, I murmur into his ear, hoping he can hear me. "Kohnrad, I went in. I went into the Fire. It was the most amazing and beautiful thing. It gave me a Flame for you—to heal you. I don't know how this will work, but what the Serpent has done can't overcome you because you belong to the Fire."

There's no change on Kohnrad's face, and I glance nervously at Queen Theora. Reaching for Ethan, she grips his arm, her fingers white with tension.

"Do whatever it takes to save my son," she says, a quiver in her voice despite the fierceness of her gaze.

I close my eyes and take a deep breath, holding it until I have to let it out. The heat intensifies along my arms, the pressure becoming intolerable. Opening my eyes, I stare down at my flaming blue hands; bolts of electricity crackle in anticipation.

The Fire is ready.

Shifting onto my knees, I stretch across Kohnrad's broad chest, placing both hands over his heart. A deep roll of thunder rumbles around me, and I cry out as I'm yanked from the now into a realm of drastic extremes: Light and Dark, Life and Death, Fire and Serpent.

The Fire and The Serpent

An immense fire roars before me, wild and untamed, consuming everything around it. A man walks between the flames, untouched by the fire, carrying an infant. He lays the baby on a stone pillar, where the child grows into a young man—a man of fire who also walks among the flames and is not destroyed. He continues to grow strong and mighty, becoming a man of great compassion and conviction.

The scene shifts, engulfing me in complete darkness, and I fall through the void, clutching at the emptiness. I land on a hard, gray wasteland—the impact knocking the wind out of me. There's nothing to see but miles and miles of dried, cracked earth, with no trees, no grass, and no life. The arid, scorching land sears my lungs with every breath. My lips crack, blood drying instantly, while my skin tightens as every drop of moisture is sucked from my body, leaving me parched and brittle. It's insufferable. Unlivable.

A silhouette emerges from a large crevice in the ground, winding and curling higher and higher. A massive black serpent appears, smoke swirling off its skin, its odor so strong and repulsive I want to gag. The Serpent burns with rage and defiance, driven by an insatiable hunger for war and destruction.

The air ripples, and I see the Fire and the Serpent locked in a great battle. The Fire blazes while the Serpent coils around its base, capturing and smothering, burning yet never consumed. Just when it appears the Serpent will triumph, a man steps forth, his broad shoulders framed by flames. He carries a massive, burning sword and drives it into the Serpent's thick skin. The Serpent roars in fury, releasing the Fire, and turns its full attention to the man. Circling each other, the two opponents search for weakness. The man strikes again, but this time his sword catches between the Serpent's metallic scales, wrenching it from his hands. Unable to defend himself, he is caught in the Serpent's constricting coils. Though the man is strong and brave, the Serpent has stolen his breath, and he now straddles the threshold of life and death.

The air ripples once more, warping and twisting around me. Suddenly, I find myself standing before the Serpent, Kohnrad trapped in its massive coils, slumped over, pale, and dying.

The Serpent's eyes light up when it sees me, and it lets out a triumphant laugh. "Well, well. You have returned, Fire Holder. How utterly delightful. Victory is nearly at hand, and now, my dear, you shall be the finishing touch."

A figure appears in my peripheral vision—a warrior armed only with a knife, its slender blade catching the light.

Ethan! What is he doing here?

The Serpent's eyes narrow as it snaps its long neck around, its fresh scar raw and bleeding.

"Shadow Walker!" it hisses with rage. "Have you come back to your true Master at last? Do not think I have forgotten your betrayal. No one walks away from me and lives. I have a special place reserved for you, and will take great pleasure in orchestrating your punishment."

"Go for Keeper," Ethan says, ignoring the Serpent, and takes off at a dead run.

The Serpent's head swivels between Ethan and me, deliberating which of us poses the greater threat. Ethan's racing figure demands its immediate attention, and the Serpent turns to confront him.

Ethan lunges, using his dagger to inflict small cuts between its scales. The Serpent twitches and pulls away, but never loosens its grip on Kohnrad. I watch, heart racing, searching for an opening to reach him.

On and on, Ethan attacks and retreats, always moving, never stopping. The Serpent's rage heightens with each cut, its mounting frustration making it more and more careless. Its body lurches, struggling to anticipate Ethan's next move, and the Fire Sword breaks free, clattering to the ground. I sprint forward, taking hold of its golden hilt. It's much heavier than I expected, requiring both hands to drag it away. Kohnrad's limp body continues to fling about with every lunge, the Serpent's constricting coils growing tighter and tighter. Then suddenly, everything shifts. Kohnrad slumps to the floor as the Serpent wraps its immense body around Ethan, blocking all avenues of escape.

"I shall make certain your death is as slow and painful as possible, Shadow Walker. Your treason has earned you nothing less."

The Serpent continues to threaten Ethan while I dash over to where Kohnrad lies slumped on his side, unmoving and not breathing. Straining against his large frame, I push him onto his back and place my hands over his heart, just like I did in his bedroom. The Fire races along my fingers like electricity, snapping and roaring. Kohnrad's chest heaves, and I'm thrown backward onto my butt. Hurrying back, I place my hands on his heart again. His chest heaves once more, but this time I wrap my arms around him and hang on. His body sags to the ground, and I release my grip. With my hands still flaming, I press on his chest one last time and whoop when Kohnrad sucks in a ragged breath. Then another, and another.

"Yes! Yes! Come on, Kohnrad! Keep breathing! Come on! Come back to us! Please! Please come back to us!"

The Fire eases from my hands until I've given him everything I had.

Kohnrad's eyes flutter open, and a slow grin spreads across his face. "Kenna, dear, would you mind getting off my chest so I can get up?" he says, his voice hoarse.

"Kohnrad!" I cry, throwing myself on top of him and holding him tight.

He laughs and hugs me back before pushing me away. "Now, seriously, Kenna, I do need you to get off of me."

I hurry out of his way, filled with wonder and relief, as he sits up and takes note of our surroundings. His eyes harden when he spies the Serpent, and I look around for Ethan, fearing what I might find.

Perched high on its coils, the Serpent has Ethan pinned, leaving him no room to run. Yet, Ethan stands defiant, weapon raised, prepared to fight to his last breath. It's only a matter of seconds before the Serpent makes its final killing move.

In a swift, choreographed motion, Kohnrad rolls sideways, grabs his sword, and launches to his feet. A low growl emanates from his throat, rising into a powerful roar as the tip of his sword scrapes against the dry ground, carving a long, thin groove.

"Apophis, you foul Serpent of Endless Darkness, your days are numbered!"

The Serpent whips its giant head around, astonishment rippling along its dark scales. Gleaming eyes take in Kohnrad and his Fire Sword, before shifting past him to settle on me. Surprise quickly dissolves into irritation.

"Hmmm. Had I realized earlier how vexing a Fire Holder could be, I would have dealt with you much sooner. Be assured, I will not make that mistake again. When I am finished here, I will come for you, my little pest, and put a permanent end to your meddling."

"Kenna," Kohnrad says, eyes fixed on his enemy. "I need you to get as far back as you can. Stay out of the Serpent's reach. It won't hesitate to take you hostage and use you against me. Now go!"

"This is all futile, you know," the Serpent scoffs. "I had you once, and I shall have you again. You are no match for me, Fire Walker, just as your father was not. My darkness is spreading, seeping into hearts and minds, blinding them to the Truth. Soon, it shall be I who governs the Worlds, not the Fire. It is my destiny to rule, and rule I shall. No man can stop me."

"Your arrogance blinds you, Fallen One. You are a created being, just like the rest of us. Immortality is not yours to claim."

"Oh, but I shall have immortality once I seize the Flame," the Serpent snarls.

Kohnrad's movements are so subtle, he seems almost stationary, yet he's drawing the evil creature away from me while inching closer to it. His voice drips with sarcasm and derision, keeping the Serpent's fury focused solely on him.

"There's just one flaw with that thinking," Kohnrad says. "See, the Fire burns away all impurity. Only those who chose death can withstand its judgment and, in return, receive life. But a creature such as yourself—steeped in absolute darkness and pure evil—you will never survive. You'll be utterly destroyed. So, by all means, enter in and help yourself."

The Serpent writhes in agitation, its tail flicking side to side. Ethan darts through a narrow space in the Serpent's coils, nearly getting crushed when they slam back together. He's on his feet and running before I can even scream, the Serpent oblivious to his escape.

Kohnrad adjusts his movements, drawing the Serpent further around so its back is to me. Ethan follows, staying out of the creature's peripheral vision but close enough to help Kohnrad if needed.

"Come now," Kohnrad says, goading the Serpent. "You were once with the Fire. Surely you remember all this."

With a subtle hand movement, Kohnrad signals Ethan and continues to circle the Serpent, his posture relaxed and nonthreatening. The Serpent, consumed with rage, follows, spewing threats and vile accusations.

Kohnrad, ignoring its barbs, shakes his head. "You don't really think you can come back once you've been kicked out, do you?"

Ethan backs away, positioning himself in front of me as Kohnrad and the Serpent continue their slow, methodical dance.

"You've been stripped of your position along with your wings, Serpent. Your power no longer aligns with the Fire; it will always be less. You are but a shadow of your former glory, forced to crawl on your belly in humiliation. How far you have fallen, that your true nature has been lost forever. Such a vile name you now claim, *Apophis*."

Releasing a hideous, deafening screech, the Serpent lunges at Kohnrad, only to find that its coils—and with them, its power—are gone. As it collapses in shock, Kohnrad strikes a heavy blow across the back of its neck. The clanging of metal rings out as sparks fly into the air. The Serpent gasps, attempting to pull away, but it's too slow. Kohnrad presses on, landing a powerful blow to the side of the Serpent's head. It screams in pain, baring its long fangs dripping with venom. Kohnrad's muscles strain with visible effort, but he continues to wield his burning sword over and over, carving deep gashes into the thick, scaled skin. Each wound inflicts more damage, leaving the Serpent unable to retaliate. Sweat glistens down Kohnrad's back, and his face is red with exertion, but still he battles on, not once retreating.

The Serpent has spilled over itself in its frantic attempt to get away from Kohnrad and now lies in a twisted heap before him. Kohnrad raises his sword high, ready to deliver the killing strike.

"Stay back," Ethan warns as I step forward to watch the Serpent's death. He raises his arm to block my path. "It's not over yet."

A violent tremor shakes the ground, sending Ethan and me crashing to our knees. Kohnrad stumbles but keeps his footing as a giant fissure breaks open between him and the Serpent. Heat distorts the air above the chasm, and thick, black smoke billows forth, curling into hundreds of writhing serpents before dissipating.

The ground heaves and shakes, driving Kohnrad back until a canyon separates him from his foe. The Serpent coils itself up to its full height, vying once again for intimidation and fear, its gaping wounds bleeding dark against the ground.

"This is not over Fire Walker," it screeches across the chasm. "I *will* take your kingdom and destroy everything you hold dear. In case you have not yet heard, your dear followers in Kirkos have been tortured and left to die. Quite the spectacle I hear—all because of you and your little collection of misfits. My Dark One has purged the city of all who claim allegiance to you and your Fire. His fury is great and most exhilarating. I have not seen such passion for darkness in a very long time. No doubt you will find him… disturbing."

The Serpent lets out a nasty laugh and uncoils itself, twitching in pain. With a final hiss, it slides into the smoky crevice, disappearing from sight.

Kohnrad rushes to the edge, peering down into the abyss.

"Stay here," Ethan says, sprinting to Kohnrad's side.

They stand together, two battle-weary warriors, staring into emptiness. My heart aches for the pain they must be feeling. Victory was so close, and the Serpent has dealt a devastating blow. Ethan touches Kohnrad's arm and draws him away from the crevice. The anguish on Kohnrad's face is unbearable, his heart torn by the Serpent's words. What has happened to Marcus' community? What awful suffering have they endured because of us? Their faces flash before my eyes: their kindness and joy in helping us. Recalling the laughter of the children and their games with Charlie, I cup my hand over my mouth in horror. The children! Bile rises in my throat, and I retch onto the ground. What have we done?

My body spasms with dry heaves as my mind struggles to comprehend what's happened. Grief and guilt crush my heart. Those people did nothing wrong except help us, and for that, they lost their lives. The injustice ignites the Flame within, and fury races through me, burning away the sorrow.

"It's okay to be angry," Kohnrad says, squatting down beside me. "But don't let it take root and consume you. Anger's a quick growing weed that produces many seeds of darkness. Its multiplication knows no end."

"How can you say that knowing that they... they were..." Tears pour down my face and I hiccup, trying to stop them. "All they did was help us and for that, they lost their lives. And for what purpose? We lost the Serpent. It was all for nothing."

Kohnrad lays a large hand on my shoulder. "They did not die for nothing, Kenna. They knew the cost and chose to walk the path of martyrdom so we might live."

"But I didn't ask them to die for me! I don't want that! I don't want people to die because of me. My life isn't worth their death!"

"That is not your decision to make. The Fire gave them the choice, and they chose sacrifice. That is the greatest gift anyone could give another, and you have no right to diminish their glory. It's not about you or your worth. It's about the Fire and obedience."

"It's a heavy burden to bear," I whisper.

"Yes, it is, and my heart grieves at their suffering, but their sacrifice will never be forgotten. The Fire will see to their reward and they will enter its kingdom with great honor."

I lift my head in surprise. "The Fire has a kingdom?"

"Of course. It is a great and mighty kingdom. One that can never be destroyed. Where sorrow and pain do not exist and joy is complete. There is none other like it."

"Is this the kingdom the Serpent seeks to destroy?"

Removing his hand from my shoulder, Kohnrad sits back on his heels. "The Serpent will never touch the Fire's kingdom. It's a Kingdom of Light and Goodness, and its fullness is eternal. The Serpent's influence is limited to this world and its dimensions. Because of this, it will seek to destroy everything associated with the Fire in order to set up its own Kingdom of Darkness."

"You called it a created being, like us. So that means it can die, right? You were trying to kill it, weren't you?"

"The Serpent has limitations on what it can do. It's not all-knowing or ever-present like the Fire. It must rely on others and use them to carry out its plans. As for death, it doesn't have life like we do and, therefore, cannot die by ordinary means. But it will be consumed by the Fire at its appointed time, and its judgment will be great."

"So you can't kill it?"

"I will take the Serpent's life and send it to its judgment. That is my promise. But the time for that has not yet come."

I stifle a sigh. "You and your riddles… So, what are we supposed to do until then?"

"We fight. The Serpent's End of Time is nearer now than it has ever been, and it knows it. Its attacks have grown bolder and more frequent, its darkness deeper and more pervasive. It will destroy all it can in the short time it has left, so it's up to us to counter its plans and restore what we can to its rightful place among the Light."

"What about the Fire? Should we go back and destroy the wall?"

"That won't be necessary. The Fire's quite capable of taking care of itself. I imagine the wall's already gone."

Straightening up, I stare at Kohnrad in shock. "Are you kidding me? Was it able to free itself this whole time? All of this could have been avoided! Why would it do that?"

Kohnrad rises to his feet, looking at me with the patience of a teacher. "I warned you not to underestimate the Fire. Its ways are not our ways. There is purpose in all it does. Your character has been refined, your weaknesses and strengths revealed. You have gained friendship and unity. Each of you has faced great trials, yet persevered and worked together to accomplish what no others could. You'll learn this is the Fire's way."

"But you almost died!" I cry, throwing my hands in the air.

"I was always in the Fire's will. No matter how it worked out, I was willing to follow what was set before me."

"Even death?"

"I can only lose my body. My spirit will live forever with the Fire and Light, as will yours and all who honor and obey its call."

As if hearing something, Kohnrad lifts his head and gazes into the distance. His body tenses, and he signals to Ethan.

"We must return. The Serpent has set something in motion, and our time in Neriah is short."

Ethan nods and disappears. My mouth drops open, and I'm about to ask how he did that when everything around me shifts. In an instant, we're back in Kohnrad's room, and I'm leaning over him, my hands on his heart. Only this time, his eyes are open and he's grinning at me.

"Seems like déjà vu, me asking you to kindly remove yourself from my chest," he drawls.

"Yeah, it does, doesn't it?" I say, returning a grin as he sits up.

"My son!" the queen cries, rushing over.

"Mother," Kohnrad says, accepting her hug. "I'm fine, as you can see."

Pulling back, Queen Theora frowns at her son. "You have not been fine, young man. I have been worried sick. Things are not well here."

"Yes, I know, Mother, and I'm truly sorry, but things are going to get much worse, I'm afraid. I believe the Dark One is on the move and headed our way."

Kohnrad throws the covers aside, intent on getting out of bed, only to jerk them back up to his waist. "Umm… I seem to be in need of more clothes," he says, looking around. His eyes land on my outfit, and a smirk crosses his face. "And I think Kenna could use some as well."

Confused, I glance down and see my nightshirt bunched up around my thighs. Flushing with embarrassment, I try to cover my legs but instead manage to twist my gown tighter around my waist.

"Come here, my dear," Queen Theora says, bypassing Ethan, who's trying to hide his laughter. She wraps a blanket around my shoulders and helps me out of the bed. "I'll have someone bring you your clothes. Ethan, please make yourself useful and fetch the others. Time is of the essence."

Chapter 19

"The Serpent has yet to gain possession of the lands east of the Great Mountains, so this will be his next conquest," Kohnrad says, his long strides covering the floor as he paces like a caged lion.

The others have joined us, expressing their joy and relief at seeing Kohnrad well, but after a quick update on our situation, the atmosphere has turned tense.

"The city has natural protection with the steep sides of the plateau, so any army choosing to attack will have to use the only road leading in. Unfortunately, the Royal Army hasn't been maintained. The king chose instead to focus on trade routes with the cities along the sea. When the Dark One and his soldiers come, the Royal Guard won't be enough to protect the king, much less the city. Those refusing to follow the Dark One's decrees will be dealt with ruthlessly."

"I will send word to those loyal to us," Queen Theora says from her seat by the fireplace. "They will alert the Followers in the city of the danger. There are hidden routes kept secret for such a time as this. Only a few know of their existence. They will be discreet and efficient."

"Good, get them moving now, while the guards are still watching the front gate and the mountain pass." Kohnrad stops pacing and turns to Ethan. "How long has it been since we left Kirkos?"

"Twelve days."

Kohnrad shakes his head. "Twelve days. That's longer than I thought. If the Dark One is coming, he'll need to move a large force along a very treacherous route with few stopping points. My guess is he'll break his men up into smaller companies and have them regroup in the forest. We won't have more than a few days then, depending on the weather."

"They will make it through that soon?" Zeke asks. He refuses to sit and stands with most of his weight balanced on his good leg.

Kohnrad's brow furrows as he resumes pacing. "They could on horseback. It depends on how soon they set out after us and how long it takes to get through the canyon." Stopping mid-stride, Kohnrad pivots to face the queen. "Mother, can you send out the Watchers? Tell them to be quick and not to linger. The Dark One may have his own Seers, and I don't want him to know we're expecting him."

"What about the king? Will he be on our side?" Zeke asks.

Kohnrad looks at his mother.

"I will speak with him," she says, her mouth set in a frown. "But he will not see the threat like we do. He will try to negotiate and keep peace."

"You do not wish to take the throne and fight?" Zeke asks Kohnrad.

"If we had months or years to prepare, that might be an option. As it stands now, no. We need to evacuate the city and leave as soon as possible. Time is not on our side."

Queen Theora rises and shakes out her gown, still the elegant lady despite the circumstances. Kohnrad ceases his endless pacing and joins her, drawing close for her embrace. She gives him a quick kiss and caresses his cheek before stepping away.

"He will not be happy with you. Leave as soon as you can."

"And you?"

"I will head to the coast. If you are in need, you know where to go. Take care, my son."

Kohnrad bows his head as his mother turns and makes her exit. Silence hangs in the room, heavy and somber, until Kohnrad clears his throat. His face, unguarded and full of emotion, reveals the weight of the hard decisions he must make. The strength of his character is not lost on us.

Stepping alongside Kohnrad, Ethan's quiet presence offers comfort and support. A nod acknowledges his position, and Kohnrad takes a deep breath before addressing our group.

"I understand your reluctance to desert the city and its people," he says. "We will get out who we can, but if we stay and try to fight, we will lose. None of you are ready. We must leave. Believe me, the battles will come soon enough."

"We will follow whatever you think is best, My King," Zeke says, kneeling before Kohnrad.

Springing from my chair, I bow down next to Zeke. "You are my king, Kohnrad. I will follow you no matter where you go.

Sliding to the floor, Nola and Ronnie pledge their loyalty as well.

"I am honored to be your king," Kohnrad says. "You will be warriors like none ever seen before. Together, you will be unstoppable. Now, please rise and let's get back to the way things were. I'm your friend, as well as your leader. You don't have to address me as king unless I require you to."

Reaching sideways, Kohnrad slaps Ethan on the back. "You did good, Walker. I'm very proud of you. All those years of trying to train you paid off."

Ethan grins in response. "Glad I was worth the trouble, Captain."

Kohnrad clasps Ethan's hand and gives him a nod. I swear, those two can read each other's minds.

"Alright, now we go before King Durmad and plead our case. No matter what happens, I want all of you to remain quiet. Whatever he says, hold your tongues." Kohnrad's gaze locks onto mine, intense and unyielding. "Kenna, I need your word you won't say anything."

I narrow my eyes at him. "It's going to be bad, isn't it?"

"I'm afraid so."

"Why won't you let us defend you?"

"I don't need your defense, though I appreciate your passion. I know who I am and what I'm called to do. Nothing he says can change that."

"Then why waste our time with him?"

"Because he will have to give an account to the Fire, whether he believes in it or not. I'll offer him the opportunity to follow its ways or choose his own. His decision will seal his destiny forever."

"I do not suppose you will allow me to punch the man when we are finished?" Zeke asks, cracking his knuckles.

Laughing, Kohnrad shakes his head. "No, my friend, I think it's better you walk away and save your hand for another time."

"Kohnrad," I say, drawing close, forcing him to look down at me. "Are you going to be okay? He's been your father. I know you care for him."

Tears of pain glisten in Kohnrad's eyes. "It won't be easy. He was a good man once. It's been painful watching him harden his heart over the years. But he's denied the Fire too many times. It won't tolerate his rebellion any longer. He will make his final choice today, and it will grieve my heart greatly."

"So he won't choose the Fire."

"No, I'm afraid not."

"I'm sorry. I wish you didn't have to hurt like this," I say, wrapping my arms around his waist, hugging him tight.

"Thank you," he replies, reaching around to hug me back.

"I'll do my best to keep all thoughts inside my head," I say, stepping back.

Kohnrad eyes me with mock seriousness, the corner of his mouth twitching. "Just make sure they stay in your head. I heard mention of some choice words that made their way out while climbing the mountain out of Kirkos."

My eyebrows shoot up, and I whirl around to glare at Zeke. "Traitor!"

He stumbles back, throwing his hands up in defense. "Hey, the man deserved to know how you felt. I was just keeping him informed." He's trying very hard not to smile.

"You did have a lot to say," Ronnie says, joining in.

"Geez, did everyone hear me?"

"Yep!" Nola says with a giggle. "I gotta say, it was quite entertaining."

"Good grief," I say, slapping my forehead. I turn and wag a finger at Kohnrad. "See what you've done to me?"

He throws his head back, roaring with laughter.

"You've come a long ways, Kenna," Ronnie says, giving me a side hug. "Just know for future reference, all secrets will be used against you whenever humor is needed."

Her words have their desired effect, and a laugh bursts from my chest. "Thanks, guys. It's good to know you've all got my back."

Ethan moves closer, smiling down at me and winks. "I'll stay close and see that she behaves, Keep." There's something different flowing from him—something I haven't felt from him before. It feels like... joy.

"Yeah, don't worry. We know how to keep her in line," Nola says with an exaggerated eye-roll.

"Hey now! I'm not that bad, am I?"

"You are easily provoked," Zeke says, crossing his arms.

"I'm just…"

"Fiery," Ethan finishes with a smirk.

Kohnrad looks over his ragtag group of warriors and smiles with pride. His eyes meet mine, and he nods. "Yes, she is."

***

"That is ridiculous," King Durmad says. "I refuse to believe this so-called army is coming to kill everyone."

"Not everyone, Father—just those who pay allegiance to the Fire. You will have to choose whom you will serve."

"Nonsense! I serve no one. I am the king!"

"Father, the Dark One will take your throne and your city. The Royal Guard isn't capable of defending us. We must leave at once."

"Dark One!" The king rolls his eyes and sighs. "Why can you not use names like a normal person, Kohnrad? You have given me no proof that those coming are hostile. I will not abandon my throne based on unsubstantiated rumors. Surely, they are reasonable people, and we can reach some form of negotiation. I have valuable access to the trade routes along the sea. As for the city, I will not have you inciting panic or rioting. Not a word of this discussion is to be spoken of outside of this room. Is that clear?"

Kohnrad doesn't respond. The queen's Watchers returned just prior to our audience with the king, reporting three companies of troops on the Mountain. We have only two, maybe three, days to clear the city. Messengers have already been sent, and the evacuation started.

King Durmad paces before his throne, mumbling to himself, while the queen stands off to the side. Kohnrad has given as much information as he can without compromising his mother or our group. Our time is running out and the king is not listening.

"This is why I am still king, you know" King Durmad says, swinging his arm wide. "All this drama and theatrics. I should have stopped all this nonsense years ago. These fairy tales you believe in, making everyone out to get you. How can I hand the throne over to you when you have no sense of reality? You would have us at war with everyone within days!"

"Darling, I think you are—"

"Theora, now is not the time to be pandering your son. Enough is enough! This latest ordeal has destroyed whatever sense he had left. Or was that just one of his latest ploys to gain attention? No matter, I will not jeopardize my city because of his paranoia. If he is unable to handle the kingship, then I think it is best he leaves.

Whoa! Did the king just disinherit Kohnrad?

"Durmad, you forget yourself! Your position as king is temporary and in name only. My son is the true heir to this throne."

"Woman, your son has proven himself incompetent and irresponsible on every account! He has abandoned his responsibilities to run around the lands on so-called holy missions. That is nothing more than an excuse to avoid doing his duty. I am prepared to challenge his right to the throne, and I can tell you, I have a majority in my favor."

"That is absurd! The Kingdom has always had a Fire Walker as its king. Your inability to understand this has jeopardized Neriah and all its inhabitants."

"Mother," Kohnrad says, his voice carrying across the dais without rising in volume. "Let him have the city if he chooses. It won't last. My kingdom is more than a place."

Queen Theora looks between her scowling husband and her son. Shaking her head, she steps down from the platform.

"You are a foolish man, Durmad. I will not support your decision to remain neutral. You must choose a side, and unfortunately, you have chosen death."

"And just what do you think you are going to do, Theora? Walk out of here with your son?"

"I will not stay and watch you die. I will do what is necessary to save my people, and whatever my son chooses to do, I will support him as the true king of this kingdom."

"You are as crazy as he is!" King Durmad spits out, his face turning purple. Sweat streams down his temples, and foam gathers at the corners of his mouth. He lurches forward, his movements resembling a puppet manipulated by a drunken master. "I can have you all thrown in the dungeon right now, you hear me? I am the king! Me! Not him. This is my throne!"

The king throws himself onto his throne, smacking its arm for emphasis. "You are a disgrace, Theora. You and your son. Such a waste, all these years I spent trying to prepare him to take over. All for nothing, that is what it has been. Well, no more, I say. Get out of my sight! All of you! Get out, get out, get out!"

Giving the king a look of utter disgust, Queen Theora turns on her heels and boldly marches away, her head held high. Kohnrad walks beside her, looking like the regal king he is destined to be. Knowing this will be the last time any of us lay eyes on King Durmad, we fall in line behind them.

Just before reaching the door, I glance back and see the king slumped in his seat, looking miserable. His hand clutches his heart as he watches the queen walk away. He notices me watching him and straightens up, hatred creeping into his expression. His mouth opens, no doubt ready to hurl another insult, but I turn and leave, not giving him the chance.

I kept my promise; I didn't say a word. But Kohnrad didn't say I couldn't throw a little Fire at him.

Chapter 20

"Your Majesty, the… guests have arrived."

"Ah, yes, yes, show them in, please. Welcome gentlemen, welcome to my city."

"Where is your queen and her son?"

"Oh, um, they are around here somewhere, I suppose. They do not trouble themselves with matters best left between men. The boy is a bit simple, if you get my meaning, and you know how women can be. Haha."

"Take some men and search the premises. If you find any of the others, bring them here as well."

"I say, what do you think you are doing? You cannot just come in here and do what you want."

"And why is that?"

"Well, because I am a king! There are protocols to follow, you know."

"Ahhh, but you are not actually a king, are you now? Not a *real* king, anyway. There is not a drop of royal blood in your veins. No *Fire*."

"B-b-but, how can you know such things…? They are of no matter. I sit on this throne. The people listen to me. In fact, they love me."

"Hmmm, you see, though, it does matter. It matters greatly. If I am to take a kingdom for my Master, I must have its king, and that most definitely is not you. So, I will ask you one last time: Where is the queen and her son?"

"I-I-I do not know! I swear upon my throne! They left days ago. They abandoned the city and… and took half the people with them. All who are left serve me. So, you see, that… that makes me king. They left the city to me. It is mine."

"That is unfortunate, but does make things easier if your words are true."

"They are, they are. I am the king! You will have to deal with me. I have the power here."

"Oh no, you most certainly do not. You have absolutely nothing to offer me but your blood. Your pathetic, *powerless* blood."

"But—"

"Keep him alive until you have verified the queen and the others are not here. Bring my whips. We shall see what this city has to say about their *king*."

"Hey! What do you think you are doing? Let go of me! I am a king! You cannot do this to me. Unhand me!"

"Unhand you… Why, that is an excellent idea. Forget the whips. Start instead with his hands. *Unhand* him as he has so requested."

"Oh, ohhh! What are you doing? No! No! Stop! Please, not my hands! No…"

"Dark One, Sir, the palace has been searched. Only a few servants and guards are present."

"Kill them. Send men into the city. I want anyone who is sympathetic to the queen brought in without delay. I want to know how she escaped and where her son has gone. Do whatever is necessary to get me what I want. Understood?"

"Yes, Sir!"

"And would someone please finish off this caterwauling fool? His kingship is over. This city now belongs to me."